UNDER A SICILIAN SKY

LISA HOBMAN

B
Boldwood

First published in Great Britain in 2021 by Boldwood Books Ltd.

Copyright © Lisa Hobman, 2021

Cover Design by Alice Moore Design

Cover Photography: Shutterstock

The moral right of Lisa Hobman to be identified as the author of this work has been asserted in accordance with the Copyright, Designs and Patents Act 1988.

A CIP catalogue record for this book is available from the British Library.

Paperback ISBN 978-1-80048-886-1

Large Print ISBN 978-1-80048-887-8

Hardback ISBN 978-1-80280-200-9

Ebook ISBN 978-1-80048-889-2

Kindle ISBN 978-1-80048-888-5

Audio CD ISBN 978-1-80048-881-6

MP3 CD ISBN 978-1-80048-882-3

Digital audio download ISBN 978-1-80048-885-4

Boldwood Books Ltd
23 Bowerdean Street
London SW6 3TN
www.boldwoodbooks.com

UNDER A SICILIAN SKY

LISA HOBMAN

B
Boldwood

First published in Great Britain in 2021 by Boldwood Books Ltd.

Copyright © Lisa Hobman, 2021

Cover Design by Alice Moore Design

Cover Photography: Shutterstock

A CIP catalogue record for this book is available from the British Library.

Paperback ISBN 978-1-80048-886-1

Large Print ISBN 978-1-80048-887-8

Hardback ISBN 978-1-80280-200-9

Ebook ISBN 978-1-80048-889-2

Kindle ISBN 978-1-80048-888-5

Audio CD ISBN 978-1-80048-881-6

MP3 CD ISBN 978-1-80048-882-3

Digital audio download ISBN 978-1-80048-885-4

Boldwood Books Ltd
23 Bowerdean Street
London SW6 3TN
www.boldwoodbooks.com

To Mum and Dad. I don't know how I got so lucky to have such amazing parents, but I'm grateful that I did. I love you.

To Mum and Dad. I don't know how I got so lucky to have such amazing parents, but I'm grateful that I did. I love you.

PROLOGUE

After taking off from JFK, actress Ruby Locke sat in her business-class plane seat, with her head almost in her lap and her hands knotted in her otherwise perfectly styled, once titian coloured hair. She had always loved her natural, fiery colour and this was the first time in her thirty years on earth that she'd had to dye it for something *other* than a part. But this new chocolate brown was all part of *the plan*. Doubled over, she knew she must resemble the inflight emergency crash-landing diagrams, but, in reality, the only thing crash landing was her life. Oh, and her career... not to mention her reputation... and absolutely *not* considering her pride, self-esteem and dignity. She'd gone from being adored to being hated in a shorter time than you could say *Jack Robinson*. Never had she experienced such venom, such malevolence and animosity, from people she hadn't even met. And how quickly, she had discovered, a porcelain, English rose could be knocked from its pedestal and shattered into a million pieces.

Perhaps if the plane did crash, she'd escape with the pity of some people, at least.

She sat upright and balled her hands in her lap, fighting the urge to slap herself for the ridiculous, macabre thoughts. She knew that none of this was her doing. She would *never* have *thought* those vile things, let alone posted them online for all to see. She clung onto her innocence like a life raft. Surely at some point in the next week or so this would all be over, the fact that she had been hacked would come out, and people would realise she was a victim in all this too?

At least the agency had splashed out on business class for the first leg of the journey. The space surrounding her had meant she didn't have to smile at other people; or worse still, have other people berate her to her *face*. Although she hadn't been separated completely from the other passengers, they had all seemed to be too busy sleeping or watching movies to bother her, so she had felt comfortable in her window-seat location, being brought delectable wine in proper glasses and served haute cuisine fit for royalty.

After a brief stopover at Leonardo da Vinci airport in Rome and a change of plane, Ruby sat in economy class for the second leg of her journey. Her skin was make-up-free and her hair was tucked up into an unflattering baseball cap with some American university logo on the front. She had slipped on an oversized hoodie and the largest sunglasses she could find that covered half her face. She got a few funny looks, but she put those down to the fact that she didn't remove any of her disguise items for the whole hour-long flight, regardless of the heat in the cabin.

The pilot announced the plane's descent into Falcone Borsellino Airport, Palermo, and her stomach flipped. She was about to step into her new normal. She was minutes away from the type of invisibility set aside for those in witness protection. Only, as a well-known, multi-award-winning actress, this would be the first time, since leaving performing arts school nine years earlier, that she'd be alone. All alone. And she had no idea how on earth she would cope.

1

NINE DAYS EARLIER – VALENTINE'S DAY

The colour drained from Ruby Locke's cheeks. 'Come on, Valerie, surely it's clear I was hacked!' She slumped into the plush leather armchair in the office of Montez and Spark, her New York agent. 'I am *not*, nor have I ever been, a vile bigot! Surely my fans will see that?' Exasperated, she waved her hands at Valerie's laptop as her heart pounded at her insides. 'Those posts were so obviously not things *I* would say!'

Valerie Montez sucked in air through her teeth. 'It's just not as simple as that, honey. Social Media can end the careers of stars that recommend the wrong toilet paper. But this... this is *so* much worse than that. The posts went viral in a matter of hours. People jumped right on it with their responses. It's out there now and there's nothing we can do but fight the consequences.' Her Brooklyn accent was strongest when she *wasn't* on the phone; at those times, she put on this pseudo-British inflection that made Ruby giggle uncontrollably. But she had a heart of gold and for a born-and-bred *East* Coaster, boy did she know the movie business and Hollywood.

Ruby stood and paced the floor, hands on hips, with a renewed determination firing in her belly. 'No, I won't accept this. I'll go on TV and do a press conference. I'll explain that I was hacked. Surely that will solve everything.'

Valerie gazed at her with a piteous expression, her eyes crinkling at the corners. 'I'm sorry, Ruby, but I already tried to arrange that. No one will touch you at the moment. It's only a matter of hours since this happened so let's just give it a while, huh? Let's allow the dust to settle and take it from there.'

Ruby flopped down once again. 'I just want it to be over with. It's like... like a bloody nightmare come true. There must be a way to find out who did this? There must be a way to clear my name. To... to trace the IP address or... or something!' Her voice increased in both volume and pitch.

'There is, and we will. Just go back to your apartment and wait it out. I'll arrange for some security to—'

'Wait, *what*?' Ruby gripped the arms of the chair, her fingers leaving indentations in the chocolate brown leather. 'Security? Why do I need security?'

Valerie sighed and leaned forward, resting her elbows on her glass desk and clasping her fingers. 'People take these things very seriously. You only have to remember when Jack Matthias said those things about gun laws, his home was spray-painted, his maid sold her story. All hell broke loose. And now he's back to minor commercials and it's been *three years*.'

Ruby's eyes widened and she covered her mouth with one shaking hand. 'Oh. My. God. Are you telling me my career is over? Is that what you're saying? My career is over for something I never even said? Jack Matthias was *filmed* saying those things. He couldn't deny them! My social media accounts were *hacked*. I didn't make those comments. You know that!'

'I do, honey, I do. And we will resolve this. We just need time. Look, I've been your agent for ten years, sweetie, I took you on when you were still a young dance student, you were still a kid, remember? Like *my* kid. I would never steer you wrong.' She wagged her finger. 'Don't forget you could've located yourself over in LA but you chose to live here in New York so I could look after you. And I will. Please, leave it with me and let me do my job, okay?'

What she said was true. Ruby tended to look to the woman in her mid-fifties, with her dyed, perfectly coiffed hair, as a mother figure. Valerie had been in the entertainment business since her late teens, first as an actress, in a couple of cult favourites, before realising, in her thirties, that she had a knack for spotting talent in others. She was well respected in the business. Surely she could deal with this kind of thing?

Ruby's eyes stung and her throat constricted. 'I've worked so hard, I've sacrificed everything. I can't lose it all now. What the hell would I do? Apart from dancing, acting is literally all I know. But I can't even fall back on dancing. Even the Broadway theatre casting people will know about this.' She lifted her chin and stared at her agent through a fog of tears.

Valerie stood and walked round her desk to crouch before her. 'Hey, hey now, come on, Ruby. There's talk of an Oscar nomination, don't forget, that's huge for a Brit. Huge! You're a BAFTA winner, for Pete's sake. You don't get this far by having a crappy agent who doesn't care. You know I'm behind you. The whole agency is here for you. We know this business and we *will* get through this. I promise. No one's acting career is over, okay?'

Ruby managed a nod.

Valerie stood and her knees creaked as she did. She smoothed down her dark green velvet skirt. 'Good. Now I've buzzed Philippe. He'll drive you home.'

Ruby scrunched her brow. 'You've called Philippe? Where's Shelby?' Valerie's new assistant had been absent more than present in the six months she had worked at the agency.

Valerie frowned. 'Oh, she had to go home and deal with a family emergency. So, go open a nice bottle of wine and take a bath. Call Tyler and have him come over to cheer you up. I know he's in town because he was in the news this morning.'

Ruby nodded again, dabbed at her eyes and considered calling her fiancé as Valerie had suggested. 'Yes, yes, that sounds like a good plan. He texted to say he had landed at JFK last night but was too tired to come over.'

Unlike Ruby, Tyler Harrison favoured the bright lights of Los Angeles and although in the past he had tried to convince her to relocate, she had yet to take the jump, so he had given up. Somehow being on the East Coast was comforting for Ruby; it was a little closer to the UK. Their relationship was predominantly long distance but seeing as they were both so busy it didn't seem to matter. They made it work.

When they *were* together, things were intense, meaning they hardly stepped outside. And even then, in between their passionate times, Tyler was out on the balcony or in another room tapping away on his phone, trying his best to be discreet, but she knew he was chatting with someone. Ruby told herself it was just flirting and knew that it should bother her, but she wouldn't let it. He was incredibly popular and in demand. It was the sacrifice she made for dating him.

* * *

The limo had blacked-out windows, so at least Ruby could stare out at the passing, snow-covered, urban landscape without the fear of being spotted. The stunning architecture of New York's Museum Mile never ceased to bring a smile – even under today's dark cloud, she found the corners of her mouth turning upwards. The Met rose from the pavement like a giant stone sculpture, glowing in the winter sun and despite the chill in the air, crowds gathered on the steps like pilgrims waiting to worship. She often visited there to gaze upon the artworks, but in more recent years her disguises had required more thinking.

She pulled out her phone and logged into her social media accounts. She didn't even need to search her name. There, right before her eyes, were screenshots of her supposed posts. The comments underneath were almost as vile as the ones made in her name. People were calling her all the names under the sun and saying things like, 'It doesn't surprise me at all, you can tell by looking at her that she's a bigot,' and, 'I won't be watching any more of her movies, if she even has a career left.' That was what hurt the most. They were playing judge, jury and executioner when they didn't know the truth. There was a hashtag being used that simply said, #cancelrubylocke, and memes of her face with offensive graffiti on. Did these people realise what hypocrites they were being?

Her stomach roiled.

When she spotted the comment that suggested she should end her own life, she promptly deactivated her accounts, feeling that it had to be done for her own mental health. Then she dialled Tyler's number, maybe he could reassure her? Tyler was an all-round action hero, both on screen and off. Well known for his starring role in the World War Two drama *Heroes of Rapido River*, her fiancé was a heart-throb and a philanthropist to boot. His off-screen charity work made him the man that every magazine wanted on their cover. He could've had any woman in Hollywood, but he chose New York-based, Yorkshire lass, Ruby, and she still had moments where she couldn't understand why.

'Hey, my gorgeous Valentine, I was gonna call you. How are you doing? Are you okay? Not the best Valentine's Day you could've wished for, huh?' Concern laced his voice and her eyes welled once more.

'Oh Ty, I honestly can't believe this is happening. Who would do something like this to me? And why?' she sobbed. Paranoia had taken root in her mind and she suspected everyone; well, not *quite* everyone.

'I can't even begin to imagine, baby. It's just so... cruel.'

'I know. But what makes it worse is people don't seem to be giving me a chance to speak. They just presume that what's on social media is fact. I would never make such horrible comments about anyone.'

He fell silent and she sniffed, hoping he'd say he was coming over. They hadn't formally made plans for Valentine's Day due to their busy schedules, but she had hoped he would sneak into town to see her, and now that he had she hoped that, in light of the day's events, he would have made lovely plans to help cheer her up.

When he didn't speak, she took a deep breath. 'Are you... are you free this evening?'

'I'm, um...' He sounded distracted. 'What? Sorry, I was just checking my other... Sure, sure, baby. Of course. Want to come by my hotel? I'm in suite 450 at the Plaza, just off Central Park.'

'Wow, a suite at the Plaza?'

'Only the best for the Hero of Rapido River.' He laughed but the noise lacked humour. In fact, he sounded disinterested.

'Okay. I'll be right there. I just need to call home to shower first. Freshen up. I look a sight just now.' She laughed as she imagined the black circles of mascara around her eyes, a residue of her tears. 'I could give Bei Bei the panda a run for her money.'

'Hey, you'll always be my beautiful *bay bay*.' Tyler chuckled. 'See you soon,' he said in a sexy whisper and then the line went dead.

Ruby glanced at the blank screen with a smile at his joke, before slipping the phone back into her designer bag.

As the limo drew closer to the Upper East Side apartment block that Ruby called home most of the year, she could see a crowd had gathered close to the entrance. People were jeering at police officers who were trying to clear the rowdy throng.

She pressed the button to bring down the privacy screen. 'Good grief, Philippe. I wonder what that's all about,' she said when the back of the driver's head came into view.' Philippe, with his greying hair, square jawline and traditional good looks, was the type you'd often see in front of the camera, and at one time he'd been a stunt double. A back injury had put paid to his career, however, and now he was a chauffeur to the stars.

He cleared his throat. 'Erm... I think perhaps I'll take you to another location, Mademoiselle. This is not feasible for you just at this moment,' Philippe replied as he made eye contact in the rear-view mirror. He had lived in the USA for many years, but his French accent remained quite strong.

She laughed. 'Why ever n—' The first placard came into view and her blood ran cold.

GO BACK TO BRITAIN! EVIL BITCH!

There was a badly scrawled drawing of a red-haired woman with a giant cross drawn through it; the type of cross you got on *Family Fortunes* when you gave a ridiculous answer. She, on this occasion, *was* the ridiculous answer. And the question was *Which English actress's career has been ruined today?*

She swallowed hard. 'Erm... yes... yes I see what you mean, Philippe. C-could you take me to the Plaza off Central Park? It's where my fiancé is staying. But... could you phone Valerie and make sure there's security there first please?' she asked in a small voice.

He nodded and his eyes took on an expression of sadness. 'Absolument, Mademoiselle. Je suis désolé.'

'Merci, Philippe,' she replied and hit the button for the privacy screen once again.

People had always been so wonderful. So warm and welcoming. She had never felt out of place in the vast ocean that was America... until now. Her thoroughly English accent had endeared her to people, and she'd made some incredible connections since her first US role as a nanny in a kid's movie. Since then, her career had blossomed, with many serious, acclaimed parts in the most amazing screen productions. There had never been an iota of bad press about her. Her relationship with Tyler had only helped to secure her place in the hearts of movie-watchers globally, and they were now known as one of the hottest celebrity couples out there. His proposal had come very early on in their relationship and had been a shock, to say the least. It was done publicly, on a TV chat show no less, and although she wasn't sure at the time that she actually *loved* him she seemed to be swept up in the glamour and drama of it all. And, of course, she wasn't going to turn him down, not when they were surrounded by a live studio audience. Since then, she'd just got used to being with him. It was easy, comfortable. She'd learned not to be jealous. He was incredibly popular and often came home smelling of perfume, or with smudges of lipstick on his cheek from fans. Par for the course, she'd always told herself.

Although regular, normal dates weren't always possible, they managed to attend plenty of red-carpet events, always instigated by Tyler of course, and he would always walk ahead of her, to protect her, he said. Cameras would flash and he would often shield her from the lenses, choosing to thrust himself forward to, '*guard you from unwanted publicity, baby*'. She had found it a little strange to begin with, but as time wore on, she accepted it as just being his chivalrous way. And she got plenty of publicity of her own, anyway.

Now though, it amazed her how quickly people could fall from favour; how fickle stardom was. She'd always known that it was never a *guaranteed for life* situation, but this whole debacle reiterated that fact. The events of the previous twenty-four hours had floored her. From going to bed with a smile on her face as fans online gushed over recent speculation that she should be nominated for an Oscar for her latest film, to waking up to find that she had *allegedly* spouted off on social media about opinions she had never once even thought, let alone mentioned out loud. The things that were said in those posts made her feel physically sick. It was no wonder people were angry.

She had a massive struggle ahead to prove her innocence. She'd been hacked and it had been done deliberately to damage her career.

But the big question was, by whom?

2

Security was waiting for Ruby when she arrived at the Plaza at five thirty that evening, and she was hurried up the service elevator before being deposited safely at Tyler's suite. The two muscular, brutish-looking men silently stood guard outside the door as it was opened, and she was whisked inside.

The suite was cavernous and decked out in sumptuous fabrics with touches of gold and brocade. She felt like she had stepped through a portal to the Edwardian era.

Tyler pulled her into his embrace. He smelled divine and, of course, looked catalogue-worthy in his pale blue Oxford shirt and jeans. He then held her at arm's length. 'My god, you're so pale, honey. Let me get you a drink.' He rushed off to the minibar and poured her a glass of amber-coloured liquid. 'I was going to get you roses or chocolates but...' He didn't finish his sentence, leaving the area blank for her to fill in her own choice of excuse.

She slipped off her thick coat and sat on the plush couch by the window, kicked off her snow boots and socks and gazed out at the New York skyline as the winter sun began its descent. The sky glowed tangerine with the hinted suggestion of melting the snow, however, Ruby knew the hue was deceptive; she'd felt the chill in the air on her arrival, although she somehow felt that wasn't all down to the weather.

He joined her and handed her the glass. 'So, what the hell is going on? Has Valerie uncovered anything yet?'

Ruby took a sip of the drink and grimaced as the heat hit her throat. 'No. Nothing. I just don't get it, Ty. I'm not the evil person I'm being made out to be. I would never say those vile things. You'd think those people who've followed me for long enough would see that. But no, they want to believe the negative. It's just... just awful.'

'Did you delete the posts?' he asked, his brow furrowed with concern.

She sighed and nodded. 'Of course! As soon as I saw them. But it was apparently a futile exercise. People screenshotted them and reposted every-where.' She placed her drink on the coffee table and covered her face with her hands. 'I'm ruined. No one will want to hire me after this.'

Tyler took one of her hands and squeezed it tight. 'Hey, come on, don't say that. And anyway, you're due to start filming *The Girl and The Rose* next month. People will have forgotten all about this by then. Trust me. People in Hollywood are so damn fickle. You'll travel to LA and it will be as if this never even happened.'

She lifted her chin and locked her gaze on his. Was he just paying lip service? Or did he really believe it to be the truth? After all, he had been in the movie business a lot longer than her, so he probably knew how this all worked. 'Thank you. I don't know what I'd do without you right now, Tyler Harrison.' She reached out and touched his cheek.

'Aww, shucks. And hey, my followers have increased by ten thousand this week, so that's good.'

She wasn't sure of the relevance but knew how much his social media presence meant to him. 'Oh... great.'

He sidled closer and slipped his free hand into her hair. 'Now, what do you say I take your mind off this whole mess?' His mouth curled up into that pin-up style, heart-throb smile he was famous for and her whole body stood to attention. 'I could run us a bath too.'

She climbed into his lap and rested her forehead on his. 'That sounds wonderful.'

He leaned closer and sucked her bottom lip into his mouth, running his tongue along the swollen flesh, and she shuddered. His delight at her reaction was evident beneath her, and before she could say anything further, he scooped her up, carried her into the luxurious bedroom and set her down beside the bed, letting her bare feet sink into the deep, plush rug. The bed was huge with an ornate carved headboard and the chandelier above it cast little shards of light that danced across the parquet flooring in the rest of the vast space. He really was treated like royalty.

Dragging her from her reverie, although with no reluctance on her part, Tyler began to unfasten her white linen blouse, placing gentle kisses across her shoulder and up her neck. Her eyes drifted closed as she relished the feeling of his lips on her skin. He pushed the shirt away and let it drift to the floor, before doing the same with her jeans.

'My god, you're a vision in white,' he said as he stood back to appraise her there in her plain lingerie.

Suddenly feeling self-conscious, she covered her curves with her arms as heat rose in her cheeks. 'I wanted to shower and change before I came to see you. I wanted to put on something special. This is just my boring, everyday underwear.'

He shook his head as he slowly unbuttoned his own shirt. 'I wouldn't want you any other way than how you look right now.' Once stripped down to his fitted boxers he stepped closer and slipped his arms around her back, one hand sliding down to her bottom and giving it a squeeze. 'Now kiss me, my little English rose.'

She closed her eyes as his lips met hers and he devoured her, slowly and sensuously. Before she knew she had moved, he had lifted her onto the bed and placed her on the billowing white fabric of the duvet.

3

The following morning, Ruby woke at seven. Tyler had taken his naked self off to shower, leaving Ruby munching on the breakfast feast that had been brought up by room service; croissants, pain au chocolat and fresh fruit were revealed to her from under shiny chrome cloches and, seeing as she was alone, she dived in, trying a little of everything. Sod the diet. Tyler's phone vibrated constantly but it was password-protected so she had no clue who was trying to contact him.

At eight, she held her phone in her hand as she waited for her best friend, Kitty, to pick up the call. Once again, Ruby had forgotten the time difference, but instead of hanging up, she prayed that her friend would take pity and answer, even though it was one in the afternoon in Yorkshire and Kitty was no doubt up to her eyes in toddlers' lunches or something. More than anything, she needed to hear a friendly voice.

Kitty Swinton had been in Ruby's life since primary school and she was the one real person, aside from her family, that Ruby knew she could trust. The bubbly and bouncy blonde was her best friend, before performing arts school, before university and before fame, when Ruby was simply the daughter of an engineer and a florist, with dreams of being a dancer on the West End stage. Now Kitty Watson, she was married with two gorgeous children, Nelly, aged two, and George, aged five, and she was heavily pregnant with a third. The kids simply knew Ruby as Aunty Roo.

'Ruby! Good grief, are you okay? I've been worried sick,' came the voice at the other end of the call.

A wave of relief hit her, and she felt her eyes begin to sting with that all too familiar feeling. 'Hey Kitty. I'm great. Great. I just realised it's lunchtime there. I'm sorry. Should I call back later?'

'No, you bloody should not. Nelly has been up since four anyway, so she had her lunch at breakfast time. She's always the same when it's the weekend and especially when it's snowing. Typical. Anyway, you're not fine. I know something has been going on. I've seen social media. What the hell happened?' Her familiar Yorkshire accent was soothing and homely.

There was no point trying to hide the truth from Kitty, not that she wanted to. She knew her so well; far better than anyone else in her life. Kitty had been with her through thick and thin and she was lucky to have such a wonderful friend. 'A shitstorm of epic proportions. My accounts were hacked, and someone has posted as me, saying all sorts of horrendous, bigoted and cruel things.' A tightness restricted her throat. 'No one wants to hear the truth.'

'Bloody hell! Can't your agent do a press conference or something? Surely there's a way to get the truth out there?'

'Valerie's looking into ways to fight the fire, but it's not looking great just now. I'm due to start filming soon, but I couldn't even go home last night. There was a protest going on outside my block. I don't even get how those people know where I live. Anyway, I had to come to Tyler's hotel suite.'

'Shit, Roo, that sounds terrifying. But at least you have Tyler, eh? I wish I could hug you.'

Hearing those words made emotion spill over and Ruby let out a sob. 'Oh God, I wish you could too. I miss you so much, Kitty.'

'Oh sweetie, please don't cry. This *will* get sorted, I promise you. It has to. People will realise you're not that person and that you're a victim here too. Don't give up and don't bloody roll over and play dead. That's just not who you are.'

'Mummeeeeeee!' a loud but very young voice shouted in the background. 'Nelly spilled her juice all over my book and it's ruined to bits!'

'Oh heck. Sounds like you're needed,' Ruby said with a laugh.

'Ugh, I'm so sorry, but I think you're right. They're fighting like cat and dog at the moment. If Nelly breathes in George's direction, he gets in a huff. I'll speak to you later, okay?'

'Mummeeeeeee!'

'I'm coming!' Kitty snapped. 'I'm so sorry, sweetie. I love you.'

Ruby smiled, but her heart ached. 'I love you too. Bye.' The line went dead, and she placed her phone on the table.

She contemplated calling her parents and knew she would have to at some point but decided that perhaps that was a call she would make later when she had a glass of wine in her hand. Her mum and dad were not on any kind of social media and she presumed that the news of all this hadn't reached the international papers and TV stations yet. They were both worriers. She'd had to be so careful what she told them in the years since she relocated from home. Although they were incredibly proud of her, and supported her in her career, they panicked about her getting caught up with the wrong crowd, about drugs, stalkers and anything else that might happen to their precious daughter. The last thing she wanted was for them to become frantic and worry themselves sick. So, for now at least, what they didn't know couldn't hurt them.

Kitty's words resonated within her. *Don't roll over and play dead... that's just not who you are.* She was right. In the past, Ruby had always been the one to stand up and fight for what she believed in. This should be no different. Her mind began whirring with plans.

'Hey my gorgeous girl. What are you up to?' Tyler asked as he plonked himself opposite her at the small table, phone in hand and his eyes fixed on the screen.

'I was just chatting to Kitty. I miss her so much.'

Without looking up, he said, 'I can imagine. You're all the way over here and she's back in that little village. It's a long distance to be apart from those you love. But you have me.' He looked up and leaned across the table to squeeze her arm. 'Although, I have to go out. I have a charity event at the junior baseball camp today. I'd invite you along but...' He cringed. 'Maybe it's best if—'

'If I don't come because of what's happened. I understand.' She did, but she couldn't help feeling a little disappointed. She'd hoped he would invite her anyway, so they could show a united front. His willingness to leave her behind stung.

'Why don't you have a nice long soak, grab some room service at lunchtime and watch some movies? I hear there's a great one just released on pay-per-view about the battle at Rapido River.' He grinned.

She rolled her eyes but smiled regardless. 'I think I've seen that one... several times. The lead actor is quite dreamy, you know.'

His smile widened and he smoothed his hand over his hair. 'Really? I hadn't heard. Look, I'd better go. My driver's waiting.' He stood and slipped his phone into his back pocket.

A thought struck her. 'Oh shit, I forgot to sort breakfast out for the security guys.'

Tyler scowled and clenched his teeth. 'Ruby, honey, please don't curse. You know I hate that. And I took care of it already.' He smiled again. 'The next shift is outside now. You'll be perfectly safe. Call Valerie and check on what she's doing to sort out this godawful mess, okay? I don't care that it's Saturday, she works for you, remember. Bye, honey.' He kissed her on the top of her head, grabbed his jacket from another chair and dashed out of the door.

'Bye,' she said to the empty room.

* * *

Ruby sat by the window on the phone with Valerie as Tyler had advised. People on the streets below were bustling around, going about their normal routines as Ruby watched from up above.

'I'm trying to deal with it, Ruby.' Valerie sounded exhausted and exasperated. 'Believe me, this is not something I would usually be doing on a Saturday. I should be at a house-warming lunch at my friend's new place, but clearing your name is important to me too. I have a tech guy onto it, Shelby recommended him, but he's talking about VPNs and IPs and all I can think about is how it's like he's speaking a foreign language. And isn't VPN what you get when your pants are too tight, and your underwear is visible?'

Ruby stifled a giggle. 'That's VP*L*, Valerie. So, is he any closer to resolving things? Is there anything I can do to move things along? Should I contact some people and try to get on TV?'

'No!' Her answer was immediate and loud. 'Please don't do anything right now. Just wait it out, okay? The last thing we need is you being shot down in flames by TV journalists. We have to consider your current contracts. We need to ensure that *nothing* breaches those. And we have to wait until we have definitive proof that you didn't have anything to do with those tasteless posts. We'll resolve it. We will. But you have to be patient.'

'It's just so hard. I know how awful this must look from the outside. If people think I have such vile opinions, then they'll continue to hate me, and we can forget them queuing up to see my films. This is why I'm so eager for this to be dealt with now. Surely in this day and age it should be easy enough?'

'And it most likely is, if you know what you're doing. Now, where are you going to stay?'

Ruby scowled and rubbed her forehead as she got up and paced the floor in the plush suite. 'Stay? What do you mean? I'm going to go home. Tyler is only in town a couple of days, so I'll be heading back to my apartment as soon—'

'I'm afraid you won't. Philippe checked in there again. There's been a graffiti attack overnight. The building manager wants you out of there, at least until the dust settles.'

'Oh, my word. But my clothes? My belongings?' Ruby slumped down onto one of the gold tapestry armchairs.

'It'll be fine. I'll get Shelby over there to collect your stuff after her audition. We can have her take it to another location.'

'Audition?' Ruby was surprised to hear that the dour-looking girl was auditioning for anything. She could've given April from *Parks and Recreation* a run for her money.

Valerie paused for a moment. 'Uh, yes.' She cleared her throat. 'Everyone's a budding actor. Look, I'll book you into the Four Seasons.'

Ruby's heart sank and took her stomach with it. The thought of needing to have her possessions collected by Valerie's assistant was just too painful. The fact that she couldn't simply walk up to the doorman, Cuthbert, and have her usual chat with the elderly gentleman, made her insides knot. He was such a sweet man; somewhat of a grandfather figure to her. Had he heard about these awful comments too? And worse still, had he been caught up in the foray? She presumed he must know now, considering the graffiti and protests. She only hoped he hadn't been hurt or verbally abused in any way. *What he must think of me.*

'Yes, okay,' she eventually replied, reluctantly. 'I'll write her a list.' She was surprised at how quiet her own voice sounded. 'I'll have her collect my mail too. I was waiting on a parcel from home. My mum's apparently been knitting again.'

'That's nice. Now go and relax. Enjoy your time with Tyler.'

Tyler was a former client of Valerie's but had been snatched up by a bigger agency since he hit the big time. Luckily, Valerie wasn't one to hold grudges and still took credit for his star status.

'I will. And, Valerie... thanks for sticking by me. I really do appreciate it.'

'Pfft. No thanks needed, Ruby, dear. We'll get through this, you'll see.'

Ruby ended the call, stood and stared out at the hustle and bustle of the New York street below. People wrapped up against the cold, dashing from work, hot coffee in takeout cups gripped in gloved hands. She wished she was out there too, going about her business without a care in the world, instead of being weighed down by the troubles on her shoulders.

She hated herself in that moment for being so passive. Kitty's words rattled around her head once more and she grabbed her phone. Valerie expected her to be happy to wait for things to just happen, but that wasn't Ruby's style. Perhaps it was time to use some of her own connections, save Valerie more hassle. She dialled the number of someone she knew would lap up the scoop of her first post-apocalypse interview.

'Ruby Locke? Not a call I was expecting to receive but one I hoped I would. How *are* you, darling? In hiding I presume?' Veronica Lucas's voice dripped with syrupy sweetness. She had been the editor at the New York Star for around the same length of time that Ruby had been a well-known actor. Unlike Ruby, Veronica was a spoiled brat who had allegedly had her mind set on Tyler Harrison before Ruby met him. Veronica's father, media tycoon Archibald Lucas, gave her anything her heart desired, including the editorial role at his top tabloid – nothing like a little nepotism for keeping things in the family. But even *he* couldn't make Tyler see past the plastic, surgically enhanced exterior of his beloved, spoiled daughter. And even though she wasn't exactly keen on Ms Lucas personally, Ruby was very much aware that she had great connections and was a sucker for a good, breaking story. In addition, out of the people Ruby knew in the media, Veronica was the best of a very sour bunch.

'Oh no, Veronica, I'm not in hiding. Far from it,' Ruby lied. 'But I did wonder if you fancied a shot at helping me clear my name? Being the first point of contact for anyone wanting news on the stars, I thought I would give you first dibs on my story.'

Veronica scoffed. 'Clear your name? After the posts you put out on social media? How would that work *exactly*?'

Ruby sighed and rubbed at her temples. 'Come on, Veronica. I think you know me well enough to be aware I would *never* say those things. I was hacked. Valerie has a team working on things just now and the truth will out, but I thought you might like to get my story before anyone else. Of course, if you're not interested I can always—'

'Darling, I'm so glad you came to me first. I knew you couldn't possibly have said those terrible things. You're more shrinking violet than bigoted exhibitionist.'

Ruby scrunched her brow; was that a veiled compliment? 'I wouldn't say I was a shrinking violet... Anyway, we're digressing; I want people to know *my* truth. I want people to see me for who I am. To know how I feel about the things that were put out there as me, and how this has hurt me as much as the people it appeared to be aimed at.'

'Well, I can understand that, darling. I mean this could completely ruin your career, your relationship with Tyler, you could lose *everything*.'

Ruby clenched her teeth when she thought she noticed a hint of pleasure in Veronica's voice and she questioned her sanity in contacting her. But she was the person with the most clout, the biggest influence and longest list of contacts. 'So, do you want the interview or not?'

'Darling, give me five minutes and I'll video-call you. We'll do it properly; I'll record it and I'll use my connections to get the interview aired everywhere as soon as possible.'

4

Ruby was jolted awake by the slamming of a door, finding herself shrouded in darkness. For a moment, she was disoriented but quickly remembered where she was, and more importantly, *why*.

Her video interview with Veronica had been emotional and mentally draining. Ruby had almost believed that Veronica cared about *her*, rather than the scoop. Deep down, she hoped she was right and that it did the trick. She just had to wait for Veronica to let her know when the video would go live on TV now, and maybe then things could go back to some kind of normality.

Her neck was stiff from falling asleep, fully clothed, on the small couch by the window. The daylight outside had evaporated, giving way to the bright multicoloured lights of billboards, club signs and traffic.

'H-hello?' she called nervously into the space around her.

'Hey.' Tyler's response was terse. 'I'm going to take a shower.'

She picked up her phone from the coffee table, hit the home button and glanced at the illuminated screen. It had been a daytime event, so why was he back way past midnight? She put the phone down again and stood to walk towards his voice, flicking on the lamps as she made her way through the rooms. 'Is everything okay? You're so late.'

He laughed drily. 'Is everything okay? Hmm... let me think.' He tapped his chin, sarcasm dripping from his tongue. 'So... I was at a charity event to promote *my* movies and to spread the word about the fundraiser. But guess what?' He glared at her.

She swallowed hard and wrapped her arms around her body. 'What?'

He grinned, but the expression was rage-filled. 'Did they want to talk about my movies? Hmm? Did they want to know the details of the fundraiser? Erm... nope! All they cared about was you!' He jabbed a finger in her direction, and she flinched. She'd never seen him like this before. 'Oh yes, questions like, was I shocked at your behaviour? Were you usually hideous and bigoted, or was this new? What caused you to rant on social media? Had you done it to sabotage your own career or mine too?' He sighed heavily, a whooshing sound from his mouth. 'God, I have never felt so humiliated. The way people were looking at me. Me! Tyler Harrison, philanthropist goddamit. The chairman of the charity asked if I wanted to step down! I was asked if I would still be featuring in the next Spielberg movie or had I been dropped in light of this incident? How do you think that made me feel? Huh?' She could smell alcohol on his breath and there was a distinct red mark on his collar that looked remarkably like a lip print.

She stepped back. 'Oh Tyler, I'm so sorry. I didn't think—'

'No! That's the issue here, isn't it? You *didn't think* to use passwords that were difficult to guess. You *didn't think* to not leave your goddam phone lying around where someone could glean your information. You. Didn't. Think.' He punctuated his words by hitting his head with his index finger as his wide, unblinking eyes focused on her. 'And now, you're dragging me down with you! Jesus, Ruby, I didn't work this hard for this long to have my career trawled through the shit by my so-called girlfriend,' he shouted and ran both hands through his tousled auburn hair before staring at the ceiling.

She glanced down at the ring on her engagement finger. It glinted in the artificial light as if mocking her. Not one to give in easily, she stood her ground. Keeping her tone firm, she said, 'I did have strong passwords, Tyler, and you know I never leave things lying around. It's unfair for you to say that. I'm not an idiot, so don't make me out to be some brainless bimbo. And I never wanted any of this to affect you; it's not as if I asked for any of it.

Oh, and for the record, last time I knew it, this ring meant I was your fiancée not your girlfriend.' She held up her hand.

His nostrils flared as he lowered his head to glare at her once more. 'Yeah? Well, whether you wanted it to affect me or not, it certainly damn well has. And I can't have that happening, Ruby.'

'What did you say to them? Did you tell them it wasn't me?'

He scowled in incredulity as if her suggestion was preposterous. 'What? No. No, I was too busy trying to salvage the event. I had more important things on my mind, Ruby. My career is way more important than...' He clenched his jaw as he pointed at her.

She widened her eyes. 'Way more important than *me*? Is that what you were going to say?'

He rolled his eyes. 'I can't have this conversation with you. I think...' He hadn't addressed the engagement issue and that, above everything else, really got to her. He closed his eyes and rested his hands on his hips but didn't look at her. 'I think maybe you should go and stay somewhere else. I've called Valerie's driver, the French guy.' He waved his hand. 'Francoise or Pierre, or whatever the hell his name is.'

Annoyed at his random calling out of French names when he knew the driver, she pointed out, '*Philippe*. His name is Philippe.'

'Whatever. Anyway, he's outside waiting for you. I tried Valerie, but she's not answering. So... just go to another hotel or whatever. But just... maybe don't contact me until things calm down, okay?'

Her lip trembled and she placed her hand over her hammering heart. 'Are you breaking up with me?'

He exhaled through his nose and shook his head. 'I'm not... It's not... Ugh! I can't answer that question just now. I care about you; of course I do, but this... It's just too much. It's... it's too damning.'

Heat rose in her cheeks and her blood pressure seemed to increase until there was a swooshing noise in her ears. He *cared* about her? But where was the mention of love? 'So much for the whole *for better or worse* crap. The first sign of trouble and you dump me. And it's not even something I perpetuated. I did nothing wrong.'

He gazed up at the ceiling once again but made no move towards her. 'I'm not dumping you... I'm just... I need some space, that's all.'

She nodded as her eyes blurred with tears. 'Just admit it, Tyler. We're over.' She shrugged. 'Let's face it, if you need space from the person you proposed marriage to, then it's pretty clear what your intentions are. Why bother skirting around it?' At this point, she knew she was pretty much pushing him to break up with her, but anger got the better of her. And she wanted some kind of reaction from him that would show his true feelings.

He snapped his head towards her. 'Okay. Fine. We're over. Is that what you want to hear?'

Tears spilled over, but on the inside, it wasn't sadness she was filled with, it was disappointment. The man she thought she could count on, the one she thought loved her, the one who said he wanted to grow old with her, had just betrayed her. She had done nothing wrong, yet he couldn't stand by her. And all because he was worried about *his* reputation. He hadn't defended her. He hadn't held up his hand and said, 'My fiancée is completely innocent, and we will fight this together because I love her, and I believe in her.' He hadn't given her any time to prove her innocence. Like everyone that had protested in ignorance outside her apartment and the people who had scrawled the graffiti, he had been judge, jury and executioner.

And she was done.

Without responding to his stupid question, she walked, calmly, back to the bedroom and gathered her bag and coat, picked her phone up from the coffee table and slipped her feet into her snow boots. She paused before him, where he still stood in the arched hallway of the suite.

'Thanks for showing me your true colours, Tyler Harrison. I wish you all the very best with your future endeavours.'

And with those harsh, emotionless words, she left, closing the door softly, her dignity hanging by a thread.

But at least there was a thread.

5

'Mademoiselle,' Philippe said with a sad smile as he held open the rear door of the car.

Shivering both from anger and the cold, she placed her hand on his arm. 'Thank you so much for rescuing me again. I'm so grateful and I'm sorry for the late hour.'

He shook his head. 'Please, no apology, it is my pleasure. Now, where can I take you?'

She frowned and glanced at the asphalt beneath her feet. 'I... I actually have no idea.'

Philippe's brow crumpled. 'He did not book you a hotel?'

'No... well, he didn't say he had. Just... just asked me to leave.' She cleared her throat, determined not to waste any further tears on the shallow man she thought she would be spending her life with. 'Valerie mentioned booking me into the Four Seasons, so maybe I can bring that forward. Failing that, I can phone around and find something else. Can you wait whilst I do?'

He shook his head. 'Non. Absolument pas.'

Her heart sank for what must have been the hundredth time in the last twenty-four hours. 'Oh... I see. I know it's late, please forgive me. Just drop me at a motel and—'

'Sorry, non, you misunderstand. You will come home with me. My wife is happy to meet you.'

She gasped. 'Oh, no, Philippe, I couldn't intrude.'

'C'est bon. No one will expect you to go there, so it's safe, yes?' He smiled and she wanted to hug him.

'Thank you so, so much. I'll find somewhere for tomorrow, I promise. I'll check what Valerie has arranged. I won't outstay my welcome,' she insisted as she climbed into the car.

'You will stay as long as you need. Ce n'est pas un problème... It is no problem to me. Excuse me, I have been speaking to my mother at home in Lyon today and I slip into French all the time.' He rolled his eyes and laughed before climbing into the driver's seat. She didn't mind the French at all; she could've listened to him all night. She settled back into her seat and as the car pulled away, she felt her muscles relax for the first time in twenty-four hours.

After around forty minutes, the car came to a halt on the driveway of an attractive suburban home, on a wide treelined street. The tree branches were weighed down with the recent snowfall, making the image look too festive for the month of February, but beautiful all the same.

Philippe came around and opened her door. 'It's quiet, everyone is sleeping, so you are safe. No one will see.' He held out his hand and she took it to climb out.

'You live in a lovely area, Philippe,' she whispered.

'Oui, Jericho is very pleasant. Not too close to the crazy city.' He laughed. 'Come on inside.'

She pulled her coat close around her body and followed him up a few steps to the front door. It was opened before he could insert his key in the lock. A beautiful brunette woman wearing pyjamas and a fluffy robe beamed at them from the hallway.

'I can't believe this is the first time I've met you, Miss Locke. Welcome to our home. Please, come on in.'

Ruby stepped inside and shook the woman's offered hand. 'Oh goodness, please call me Ruby. And thank you so much for having me to stay. It's all very... I don't really know what to call the situation I'm in without swearing.'

The woman leaned in conspiratorially. 'It's after midnight and the twins are in bed, so swear if you feel the need. Although they could probably teach you some new words. I'm Jessica by the way. Philippe has told me so much about you.'

Ruby smiled but felt a familiar flush rising from her chest. 'Oh heck, I won't ask what he's said. Especially not under the current circumstances.'

Philippe put an arm around his wife. 'I've told Jess that you are innocent, because you are.' He shrugged as if he was stating the obvious.

Jessica shook her head. 'How anyone could think otherwise is beyond me. Now, come on and let me get you a drink. Are you hungry? Can I cook something for you?'

Ruby held up her hand. 'You're so kind and I'm very grateful but... would you mind awfully if I just went to bed? I'm exhausted. And it's so late, you must be tired too.'

Jessica nodded. 'Of course, you must be wiped out. I'll show you to the guest room. But if you need anything at all just holler, okay?'

Ruby followed her hosts along a corridor, admiring family photos as she passed. She hadn't realised Philippe had teenage children. She felt guilty for not enquiring more about his personal life.

Jessica stopped at an open door and gestured inside. 'Well, here you are. There's a bathroom just through the door in the corner and fresh towels on the bed. Sleep as late as you want, after all, tomorrow is Sunday. Or should I say today. Sweet dreams.' She turned to walk away, but Ruby grabbed her hand.

'Thank you. I can't express how much this means to me. Your kindness... it's...' She swallowed, trying to dislodge the ball of emotion in her throat.

Jessica pulled her into a hug. 'Honey, you don't deserve any of this. And Tyler Harrison doesn't deserve you. I couldn't believe it when Philippe told me what he'd done. Just goes to show fame doesn't cultivate humility, even if the folks appear to do good.'

Ruby smiled. 'That's so true. Thank you again.'

In spite of the late hour, she fired a quick text to Valerie to let her know where she was staying. Almost immediately there was a reply.

Suite on hold at Four Seasons as soon as you need. Will be in touch later when I'm awake! Flowers delivered to my office for you today with the message, 'I still love you, H'. Who is H? Stay strong. Val.

Ruby wracked her brains trying to think who H could be but came up blank.

Sleep evaded her. This had felt like the longest Saturday she had ever known and when she did eventually nod off, she was promptly awoken by arguing teenagers.

'You have to ask before you raid my closet, Bay!' said one female in a high-pitched tone.

A door slammed and another girl yelled, 'Yeah, well maybe if you were nicer, I wouldn't have to steal things! You're supposed to share! Tu es si méchant!'

As an only child, Ruby had never had the issue of siblings. She'd always wondered what it would have been like to have brothers or sisters, but judging by the noise coming from along the hallway, she'd had a lucky escape.

There was a gentle knock on the door and Ruby sat up, smoothing down the bird's nest of natural red curls atop her head. 'Come in.'

The door opened and Jessica appeared with a tray. 'I thought you might prefer breakfast in bed. I have croissants from the local bakery and some fresh coffee. I hope that's okay.'

Ruby smiled. 'You really didn't have to do that, Jessica, but thank you.'

A dark-haired girl appeared behind Jessica. 'H-hi, hi, Ruby Locke. It's an honour to meet you, ma'am.' The girl, who was around fifteen, curtseyed. 'I'm Bayleigh Brodeur.'

Jessica sighed. 'Bayleigh, go and eat your breakfast. Miss Locke doesn't need to be bothered. And you don't need to curtsey.'

'It's fine, honestly,' Ruby insisted. 'Although your mum's right. You don't need to curtsey, and you can just call me Ruby.' She giggled as Bayleigh's skin glowed pink.

Another dark-haired girl, almost identical to the first, appeared in the doorway. 'Mom, I wanted to wear the blue sweater, tell her to take it off.' She spotted Ruby in the bed and gasped. 'Oh shiii-ooot. Shoot, I'm so sorry to interrupt you. Miss Locke, it's a pleasure to make your acquaintance.' She too blushed.

'Girls, we're not in a Victorian era movie, for Pete's sake.' Jessica laughed. 'This one is Brienne.'

Ruby grinned. 'Hi Brienne. Lovely to meet you.'

'Oh my god, your accent is so cool. You're so... *British*,' Brienne said.

'I know, right? So cool,' Bayleigh agreed. 'I've seen all your movies. You're awesome. I want to be an actor too. It looks like such an exciting career.' The smile dropped from her face. 'Although... I know it can be kinda hard and scary too.'

'Okay, girls, let's leave Ruby to eat.' Jessica ushered the twins from the room before turning back to Ruby. 'Please don't worry; the girls won't say anything about you being here. Their father has instilled into them that they should never gossip about the details of his job and they take that very seriously. I just wish they'd apply it to other areas of their lives.' She rolled her eyes and closed the door behind her as she left the room.

Once alone again, Ruby devoured the fresh, crumbly croissants with a groan of delight. She was more of a tea drinker but made an exception on this occasion, letting the earthy aroma of the coffee wrap in her in its warm, comforting blanket. She wondered to herself why life couldn't be this simple all the time.

She reached down to grab her phone from her bag and realised she had several missed calls and messages from Kitty. One of the messages contained a link and simply said:

I'm so, so sorry, sweetie. I love you and would happily smash his pretty face in.

With a combination of trepidation and inquisitiveness, Ruby clicked the link. There on the screen was Tyler at his charity event. A buxom, heavily made up, blonde reporter – wearing lipstick the colour she had seen on Tyler's shirt – held a microphone in his face.

Flicking her hair and pouting her artificially plump lips, she said, 'So, what do you think of the comments made by your fiancée this week?'

Tyler's nostrils flared infinitesimally, but he plastered a clearly forced smile on his face. 'I have to announce that Miss Locke and I have parted ways. I *cannot* and will not condone anyone saying such horrific things, especially no future wife of mine.'

Ruby stared at the screen as a mixture of rage, sadness and bile rose within her. So, he had announced to the world last night that he had dumped her before having the common decency to tell her first? Was he hoping she would be watching so his life would be made easy? Maybe he wasn't expecting her to be at the hotel when he returned? She glanced down at the glinting diamond on her ring finger and removed it. No point wearing it any more. She'd drop it off at Valerie's office and he could collect the wretched thing from there.

As if Valerie had sensed her name being thought about Ruby's phone rang. 'Hey, Valerie. If you're calling about Tyler, I've seen the footage.'

'What the hell was he thinking? Who is this guy? I feel like I don't know him at all.' Valerie's voice was filled with exasperation.

'Tell me about it. I feel like such an idiot.'

'Hey, honey, you weren't to know what an asshole he is. He's clearly a better actor than either of us knew. I'm just so disappointed in him.'

Ruby sighed. 'Me too. Why did I waste so much of my time on him?'

'Love'll do that to you. But at least you didn't relocate to LA, huh?'

'Very true.'

Valerie paused for a moment before asking, 'Have you heard from him at all? Directly, I mean?'

'Not a word. Can't say I'm bothered though.' The last thing Ruby wanted was to hear the dickhead's voice.

'Didn't you have any wedding stuff to cancel?

Ruby scoffed. 'We never actually set a date, so nothing was ever booked. That alone should've been a red flag, eh?'

'Hindsight and all that. Oh, and more flowers have arrived from H. Any idea who that is?'

'Not a clue. It's a bit strange but probably just a fan. I've received gifts before, and I suppose I should be grateful it's something nice like flowers. It could be so much worse under the circumstances.'

'Ah well, at least you know you have a supporter out there. Look, the suite at the Four Seasons is still on hold as soon as you need. But let me know if you decide not to take it, okay? And, Ruby, we're gonna get you through this.'

There was another knock at her door.

'Thank you, Valerie. Look, I have to go but I'll speak to you later. Bye.'

She sniffed and wiped at her eyes. 'Come in!' she said as brightly as she could manage.

Philippe cleared his throat. 'Miss Ruby, I'm afraid I have seen Monsieur Harrison on the news and—'

Her lip trembled. 'It's okay, Philippe, I've just seen it.'

He shrugged. 'Now you see what I knew all along. Il est un sac à merde.'

She nodded, figuring out, with what little French she could remember from school, what he'd said. 'Oh yes. He certainly is a gigantic *sac à merde*.' And if she got the opportunity any time soon, she would tell him that to his face.

* * *

Sunday was family day for the Brodeurs. They graciously invited her to stay another night so she could join in with their board games. Bayleigh had suggested Trivial Pursuit and Ruby had gone on to answer every single entertainment question correctly.

'I think we should ban Ruby from answering pink questions!' Bayleigh said with a giggle. 'I say we make her answer all the science ones instead.'

'If that's how it's gonna be, maybe you should be banned from answering the sports questions!' Brienne interjected with a wink at Ruby.

'Maybe we could go out to the garage and play pool?' Philippe suggested.

'Oh yeah, Dad, let's play a game you can actually win, huh?' Bayleigh said and Jessica and Brienne laughed along as Philippe feigned innocence.

The day was so much fun, and as Ruby watched the four family members playing around and laughing with each other she smiled. The love that Jessica and Philippe had for their daughters shone in their eyes, and every so often they would share a secret smile that spoke of their love for each other too.

Dinner was pizza which was to be followed by a movie. Brienne and

Bayleigh sat, one on either side of Ruby, as Philippe cleared away the dishes and Jessica made a bowl of popcorn.

'I think you should choose what we watch, Ruby,' Brienne told her. 'I mean, I'm guessing there are certain movies you really don't wanna watch,' she said with a cringe. 'So, if you choose, we know you'll be happy.' She shrugged.

Ruby smiled at the sweet gesture. 'Thank you, Brienne. That's very kind. What type of movies do you both like?'

Bayleigh chimed in, 'I like horror, but my sister's a wuss and has to hide behind a pillow if we watch anything scarier than *The Addams Family*.'

Brienne rolled her eyes. 'Oh yeah? And who had to sleep with the light on last year after she watched that old movie about the kids in the woods and the witch?'

Ruby interjected, 'The *Blair Witch Project*? That scared the pants off me!'

Bayleigh nodded vehemently. 'Right?' She shifted in her seat and waved her hands. 'Oh my god, the tree outside my window was tapping on the glass and I had to get my dad to go out at midnight and trim the branch!'

Ruby giggled. 'Oh no, poor Philippe. Anyway, weren't you a bit young to be watching *The Blair Witch Project*?'

Bayleigh chewed her lip and appeared sheepish. 'Hmm... I was at a friend's house for a slumber party and her brother dared us to watch it. Brie had stayed home.'

Brienne gave a hearty laugh. 'Mom and Dad went ape when they found out.'

Ruby grinned and shook her head. 'Honestly, you two are hilarious.'

6

After dinner the following evening, Ruby helped clear the dishes. Whilst alone with Jessica in the kitchen, she told her, 'Jessica, I've heard from Valerie and there's a booking for me at the Four Seasons as soon as I can get there, so I'll chat to Philippe about driving me, and be out of your hair.'

Jessica placed down the dishcloth and turned to face her. 'Phil and I were talking and we agreed that you're welcome to stay here until things are dealt with. We both feel that being surrounded by people who believe in you, and who care about you, would be better than you being alone. Obviously, you're free to do whatever you think is best, but we wanted to give you the opportunity to stay.' She smiled warmly.

'Really? I don't want to intrude on your family, you've been so generous having me here at all, and—'

Jessica placed a hand on Ruby's arm. 'We'd love you to stay longer.'

Ruby beamed. 'Thank you so much. I can't tell you how lovely it's been to be surrounded by family chatter again. I've really missed that. I'll drop Valerie a message and say she can cancel the booking. Hopefully the matter will be sorted out soon and I can go home. But I'd love to stay a little longer.' She hugged Jessica tight.

Once the dishes were done, Ruby retreated to the comfort of Philippe's guest room once more. There had been no word from Veronica, and she was now wondering if the editor had decided not to help her after all. They weren't exactly friends, but Ruby had certainly felt a little more solidarity coming from Veronica during the interview, compassion too. She was relieved because, in her humble opinion, women in such high-profile positions should stick together and raise each other up, not treat one another as competition.

She picked up her phone and noticed several missed calls from her parents' number. Her heart sank and she closed her eyes for a moment as the realisation hit. *They know*. She hit the return call symbol and held her breath. The sound of her dad's worry-filled voice made her heart ache. 'Ruby, love, are you okay? We've been worried sick. Can you come home?'

'Hi Dad. I'm afraid I can't really do that just now. But I'm fine. Honestly. I'm staying with friends who live outside the city. Things are under control, so please don't worry.' Going home would bring its own issues. The last thing she wanted was to bring her parents into the mess surrounding her, so the longer she stayed away until it was sorted, the better.

'Hey lass, we're your mum and dad, o' course we'll worry, it's our job, don't forget. We love you so much, you know.'

Tears escaped the corners of her eyes. 'I know, and I love you too.'

Her dad went on to try and cheer her up with local news from Pontefract and then her mum took the phone and they chatted about her upcoming weddings and a 'right old cock up' that a groom had made by ordering the wrong colour flowers for his buttonholes. By the end of the call, she felt as though a weight had been lifted.

* * *

There was a light knock on the door, and it cracked open slightly. 'Ruby, there's a piece on the news about you. An interview. I thought you might want to see it.'

Her heart skipped at Jessica's words and she quickly rose from the bed where she had been trying to read but failing to concentrate.

Once in the living room, she perched on the arm of the sofa and Jessica gripped her hand. 'This could be the end of it, Ruby. This could be the help you needed.'

Ruby squeezed Jessica's hand as her heart pounded in her chest. She hoped her new friend was right. She just wanted to get back to normal sooner rather than later.

The presenter on the news show began to speak and it seemed everyone in the room with Ruby held their breath.

'Now onto a scandal that has rocked the movie world. Actress Ruby Locke allegedly posted some rather bigoted and vile comments on social media, for which there has been no apology. We now have an exclusive video interview that New York Star editor Veronica Lucas fought to obtain with the actress. Unfortunately, we can't show the entire interview due to time constraints, but here are the salient points.'

Cut to a split video-call screen showing a beautifully made-up Veronica and a puffy-eyed Ruby.

'So, Ruby, this all must have taken a toll on your career, would it be safe to say that's true?'

'It most certainly has. And through no fault of my own. I just wanted people to know my feelings. What it's like to be me. Anyone who thinks differently is crazy.'

'And what do you say to those who feel you should apologise for what was put out there?'

'I won't apologise. People need to know the truth. That's all there is to it.'

'And what if this changes how people see you?'

'I want people to see the real me. Not some airhead who can't think for herself. My feelings count too. I'm important too.'

Cut to the TV presenter who understandably appeared shocked. *'Well, there you go, viewers, Ms Locke in her own, unapologetic words. Such a shame, we all thought she was a different person.'*

Philippe immediately turned off the TV. 'Merde!' he shouted as he threw the remote control onto the sofa.

Ruby sat, open-mouthed, staring at the blank screen. 'No... no, no, no, no!'

Jessica covered her mouth with her free hand. 'Oh Ruby, I don't understand what just happened.'

She felt the colour drain from her face and her head began to buzz. 'They... they cut my interview! That's not what I said! They changed it all.

They twisted my words. Why would Veronica do that?' She shook her head. 'How stupid am I? Why did I think she'd be on my side?' Her mobile vibrated in her pocket. 'Oh God, the phone's going to go crazy now, isn't it? What do I do?'

She lifted her phone out and stared at the screen, finding Veronica's name flashing before her eyes. She excused herself and headed for her bedroom. Anger bubbled up from deep inside her and she shook violently as she hit the screen to accept the call.

'How could you? Why would you do such a thing? If it's because of Tyler, he's yours, you're welcome to him. Don't ever call me again.'

Veronica shouted over her, 'I didn't do that! Ruby, you have to believe me! Please! I would *never* do that. I heard what Tyler did to you and I was horrified. Who wants to be associated with a coward like that? I swear to you, I sent the whole interview and they hacked it to pieces for their own sensationalist appetites. I'm as disgusted as you are. My lawyers are on the case as we speak. And heads will roll when my dad finds out. He may be living in Hong Kong, but word travels fast.' Her voice was strained and emotional. 'I've uploaded the original to the newspaper social media and my own, but people are commenting, saying we reshot it. No one will accept that my version is the original. It's crazy. People are angry with me too, they're saying I'm helping you to lie and play the victim. I'm so sorry. I thought I could help you, but I've made things so much worse. But, Ruby, I will help you to get your name cleared. People *will* see the truth.'

'Why should I believe you after what I've just witnessed?' Ruby growled.

'Look, I know I was a bitch to you before when I first met you. I admit I was jealous that Tyler chose you. But I'm over it. I've been over it for so long. I'm engaged to someone else. We haven't gone public about the engagement yet because they're... they've just gone through a divorce. But I swear to you, I would never do this to another human being. I could tell how torn apart you are when I interviewed you. I believe everything you told me, and I hate that they did they this to both of us. I promise you; we will get to the bottom of this.'

Veronica sounded sincere and Ruby wanted to believe her, but her heart had been stamped on so many times recently, she didn't know which way was up. 'Keep me posted on what your lawyers say,' was all she could muster.

'I will. And look, if you... if you want to get away for a while, I know a place. You could just take some time for yourself. It's the least I can do to help. All you have to do is say the word.'

'I'm not running away, Veronica. I—'

'I'm not suggesting you run away. Far from it. But you don't deserve this. I want to help. There's this villa in Sicily, near Palermo. A... *friend* of a friend owns it. You could escape from the madness for a while and work out a battle plan.'

'Thank you for the offer but... I really don't know what to do right now. I need to speak to Valerie.'

'I totally understand. You have my number. Please believe me when I say I *will* help you clear your name.'

Ruby's lip trembled at the sincerity and regret in the editor's voice. 'Thank you.'

'And, Ruby...'

'Yes?'

'You're better off without that douchebag.'

Ruby ended the call and silently walked to her bed, crawled into it and pulled the duvet over her head.

* * *

After rising early with a renewed determination, Ruby showered, dressed and while she waited for Valerie to arrive at Philippe's house, curiosity got the better of her and she searched Sicily and Palermo on the internet from her phone. She had to admit it was a stunning location, and if it came down to it there were certainly worse places she could escape to.

When Valerie arrived, she brought with her three large bouquets of flowers. The cards on each read, 'I still love you, H'. Ruby found it a little disconcerting, seeing as she still hadn't been able to think who H was but that they clearly knew where her agent was based, although at that precise moment it was the least of her worries.

After the usual pleasantries, Valerie launched into details of her plans.

Ruby stared at the woman in disbelief. Surely Valerie was kidding? What she had said was completely unexpected.

'I'm sorry, you want me to run away and hide? Innocent people don't do that, Valerie.'

'Sweetie, I know this isn't what you expected. And it's not what you want, but I've never seen anything blow up like this before. The interview with Veronica Lucas sent this thing into overdrive. It's a matter of time before people find you here and then all hell will break loose.'

'But the interview was doctored! Someone is out to get me, and I don't understand why. But I don't want to make things worse by running away.'

'I understand completely. But think about Philippe and his family. Do you want to put them through this?'

'Of course I don't. But I don't want to be forced into hiding either.'

Valerie sighed. 'I know, sweetie. I get it, but it's going to take a little longer to eradicate the lies than we first thought. We're working on it. The whole team.' She paused. 'Now, did Shelby bring everything you need this time?' Val's assistant had made her second visit to her current hideout after collecting more belongings and had even dropped off a bag of scarves, sunglasses, hats and a chocolate brown hair dye with no further explanation. Shelby only offered what was deemed to be essential information, making her feel like a fugitive.

'For now, yes. But she said it was still crazy at my apartment block and she thought she was being followed when she brought my things here. So you're right, I can't risk putting Philippe and his family in danger.' Ruby scrunched the fabric of her shirt in her fist. 'I feel like I'm being treated like the perpetrator here, instead of a victim.' She sighed deeply and thoughts immediately sprang to her parents. 'I'll just go home to England. At least I won't be alone there. And I'll be wanted for the right reasons. I could help my mum in the florists'.'

'No, you can't do that.' Valerie's tone was firm and decisive, brooking no argument.

Ruby scowled. 'Why? They're my family. *They* know I'm innocent.'

Valerie held out her hands. 'Because it's too obvious, Ruby. The press will find you, hound you, and as for your family... Up to now they've been able to stay out of the limelight. Do you want to push them forward? Have their names dragged through the mud too?'

Ruby huffed like a sulking teen. 'Obviously not.'

'Look, I have a location in Canada. It's a cabin in the mountains. I think you'll be fine there so—'

'Valerie, if I'm being forced to hide, can I at least choose my destination?'

'That depends on—'

'I've been offered a place in Sicily by Veronica Lucas. I've checked on the internet and it looks like a pretty island with good weather, even at this time of year. I've never been, so it's less likely anyone will know me there.'

'Veronica Lucas has offered to help again, huh? I suppose it's the least she can do under the circumstances. Although I hope it's not the same kind of help she served up last time. Okay, give me the details asap. This needs to be happening sooner rather than later.'

Ruby sighed in defeat. 'One second.' She grabbed her phone from her pocket and fired off a quick text to Veronica to confirm that she would like to take up her offer after all and included Valerie's contact information. 'There. Veronica has your details, so she'll be in touch to work it out with you.' Valerie was a control freak when it came to her clients and it was better that she dealt with the finer details. The less Ruby knew, the less chance there was of her accidentally putting her foot in it again.

* * *

Thirty minutes after Valerie left Ruby, she called her. 'It's done. You fly out on Friday. The flight is over eleven hours and there's a stopover in Rome. When you arrive in Sicily, there will be a car waiting for you. There will be security at the perimeter of the estate and the owner... well, he won't bother you. According to Veronica Lucas, he's Scottish and he lives between Edinburgh and the Isle of Skye. There are local builders working on the house for him, but they've all been vetted. I mean, this guy is a millionaire, so he likes to have tip-top security.' That was a relief for Ruby. 'But you need to stay out of sight, Ruby. This is no joke. We don't need more reasons for people to hate you right now. There have been threats sent for you here at my office, an unpleasant new addition to things, and there has been some rather vile hate mail sent to your apartment. You don't need to read it but we don't want that to escalate. And the mysterious *H* has sent more flowers, each bouquet larger than the last. Only now he's taken to telling you that Tyler never deserved you and he can make you happy. It's creepy.'

Ruby's stomach roiled at the thought of it all. 'Oh God, it's really that bad?'

Valerie sighed. 'I'm afraid so. This trip to Sicily isn't a holiday, it's a necessity, and you're extremely well known so even though the property is secure you're only safe when you're there, okay?'

Choosing to ignore Valerie's rather scary monologue, Ruby asked, 'What about rent? Who do we pay?'

'Don't worry about that. It's all in hand. Oh, and I'll be speaking to the producers of *The Girl and The Rose* to find out when you're needed, so depending on how long you're there, we may have to arrange for you to be collected from Sicily and taken to the set. As you know, it's filming in Greece, so not too far away. Take your script, learn your lines. Oh, and... Shelby says she gave you the hair dye.'

Feeling rather bombarded, Ruby scrunched her brow. 'Yes, I forgot to mention the dye when you were here, she left it by mistake. Do you want to send her back for it?'

There was a pregnant pause. 'Erm... not exactly. It's... it's for *you*.'

Ruby stood quickly. 'What! Nononononono! I am *not* dyeing my hair, Valerie. I draw the bloody line there. Absolutely not. It's my signature. It makes me who I am.'

Valerie sighed deeply. 'Exactly.'

* * *

Brienne and Bayleigh stood by as their mother finished blow-drying Ruby's hair.

'It looks really cool, Ruby. I swear,' Bayleigh insisted, her hands clasped in a prayer-like hold. After her initial encounter with the lively girls, Ruby had quickly grown incredibly fond of the twins and had enjoyed spending time with them. She had appreciated their discretion so much, considering she had been a gossipy fifteen-year-old once. Philippe had certainly done a great job of instilling in them the importance of his clients' privacy.

'She's right, honey. It gives you an air of mystery,' Jessica told her with a wave of her hand to exaggerate her point.

Ruby harrumphed. 'I can't see how it will help. If someone knows me, my hair won't make a difference.'

'You do look completely different, though. Like a whole other person. I wouldn't recognise you,' Brienne said as she nudged Bayleigh and nodded, wide-eyed, willing her to agree.

Dutifully, Bayleigh said, 'Yeah, totally. A whole *entire* other person.'

Ruby appreciated what they were trying to do but was still struggling to accept the changes she was having to go through when she had done absolutely nothing wrong. 'Doesn't it make me look pale and sickly?' she asked, smoothing down the sleek, unfamiliar locks.

Jessica smiled down at her. 'You look beautiful, Ruby.'

Looking beautiful was actually the last thing on her mind. What she wanted was to be able to look in a mirror and see *herself*, not some complete stranger. In all of her thirty years, the fiery, natural curls had been the epitome of her *true self*. It was one thing to don a wig for a part in a film, but to make something so permanent was anathema to her. She had never shied away from being who she truly was and wasn't happy to have this dramatic change thrust upon her.

As if reading her mind Jessica chimed in, 'Think of it as a character you're playing. A temporary part that, someday soon, will be something to look back on with relief that it's over.'

Ruby nodded. She could only hope it was a part that wouldn't have to last long.

* * *

Later that afternoon, in the privacy of the guest room again, Ruby checked the time difference, it would be nine at night in the UK. She dialled Kitty's number and held the phone in front of her face. The reflection staring back at her was somewhat alien.

When the video call connected, Kitty gasped. 'They're making you wear a wig?'

Ruby cringed. 'Nope. They're making me dye my hair, Kitty. That's what it's come to.'

Kitty pouted. 'But... your lovely red curls...'

'I know. I can't believe this is happening. And now... well, now they want to send me away.'

Kitty scrunched her brow. 'What did you say?'

'They want me to go into hiding. It's ridiculous. Apparently, people are even more irate with me after that interview, for what they *think* I said, that they're causing all sorts of problems. So now I have to get a flight to the middle of nowhere, to stay in some derelict old house that's being done up for a rich bloke. I honestly can't believe this is my life now, Kitty. If I had followed my true passion and pursued a career in dancing and theatre, instead of attending that stupid audition all those years ago, I wouldn't even be in this situation. I was never supposed to be an actor. I knew it was all too good to be true.'

From a young age Ruby's parents had taken her to the Theatre Royal in Wakefield, and sometimes the City Varieties in Leeds, to see musicals. Shows such as *West Side Story* and *The Sound of Music,* and ballets such as *Swan Lake* and *The Nutcracker.* The spectacle of it all had gripped her, made a place for itself in her heart. She had known from around the age of five that she wanted to be up there, on a stage, in the spotlight, dancing for enraptured audiences. She had watched the movie *Flashdance* over and over and had mastered all the choreography, pretending she was Alex Owens, dancing for her dream role in a ballet production. It was all she had ever wanted: the thrill of the live performances, the excitement at what could happen, and the energy created by the music pulsing through her veins. Thinking about it now made her yearn for that feeling again.

Kitty sighed. 'Oh honey, why can't you just come home to England? Why are they treating you like a fugitive?'

Ruby huffed. 'Thank you! Both questions I've asked. Neither of which have been answered sufficiently. Well, apart from the one about England. I can't come home because it would cause trouble for Mum and Dad and I won't do that to them.' Her voice broke.

'Oh, chick, I'm so sorry. I wish I could help. Where are they sending you exactly?'

Ruby glanced over her shoulder conspiratorially. 'I'm probably not meant to say. But... oh, what the hell. It's a villa in Palermo. Keep that to yourself, okay? Some guy who's a friend of a friend of Veronica from the *Star*. Apparently, it's a Scottish property tycoon who owns it and he's having it renovated by local builders.'

'Oof, that all sounds a bit posh.'

Ruby looked into the camera. 'Hmm. I mean, I don't speak Italian, let alone Sicilian. I don't even know if they're the same language. And I'm going to be all alone out there. Mind you, at least it will be warmer than New York. Valerie wanted to send me to a cabin in the woods. And I've seen The Blair Witch Project. Anyway, Philippe says it's likely the internet won't be great if the house is being renovated, so what the hell am I going to do? I should be out there, in the public domain, making people see that I'm innocent, for goodness' sake. Maybe I should just quit and go back to dancing.' Kitty's expression turned sympathetic and Ruby's throat tightened. 'Oh, Kitty, don't look at me like that. I'll cry.'

'I know lovely, I'm sorry. I just wish I could do something. *Anything*. Even if it's just to give you a hug. If I wasn't six months preggers, I'd fly over to Sicily to hug you.'

'I could do with one right now.'

'When are you going to your hideaway?'

'Friday at midnight is when I'm being taken to the airport and the flight is at three. It's all so cloak and dagger. No wonder people think I'm guilty.'

'Those of us who really know you, know you'd never say such vile things.'

'Thank you.' Ruby sniffed.

'Is there a pool at the house?'

Ruby pondered for a moment but couldn't recall what Veronica had said. 'I'm not sure, to be honest.'

'Well, if there is, make the most of it. Take a mountain of books, get them to order you in some cocktails and treat it as a well-deserved holiday. It'll be warm and you won't have anyone to bother you. It sounds like bliss to me.'

Ruby grinned. Her friend had a point.

Kitty glanced over her shoulder. 'Yes darling, I'm coming.' She turned her focus back to her phone. 'Listen, will you call me when you get settled there? I've got to go and get the kids back to bed. They're both too excited about the blooming snow.'

As she spoke, a little blonde mop of curls appeared in the bottom corner of the screen. 'Aunty Roo! Your hair is funny,' George said with a scrunch of his brow.

Ruby grinned. 'Hi Georgie Porgie. Don't you like my hair?'

He swiped a stray curl from his eye. 'No. I like it when it's orange. I miss you. Are you bringing me some chocolate soon?'

Ruby giggled but had to fight back tears. 'I'll definitely bring you some chocolate, sweetheart, but I don't know when. And I miss you too.'

'I builded a snowman, can you come and see it?'

'Aunty Roo is really busy just now, love,' Kitty told her son. 'But why don't we take a photo of the snowman tomorrow and send it?'

He nodded, then turned to the screen. 'We're going to take a photo of Mr Snowman and send it to you. But we can't send the snowman because he lives in our garden. Love you, bye!' He kissed his hand and waved it at the screen before running away.

'Bye, sweetheart!' Ruby called to the boy's retreating form.

'Back to bed now, Georgie!' Kitty called after him, then turned her attention to Ruby again. 'So, you'll let me know when you get there?'

Ruby smiled into the camera, feeling anything but happy. 'Sure. Of course. Give Nelly and George a big hug from Aunty Roo.' Her lip trembled as she spoke.

'I will. Stay strong. Remember to contact me. Love you.' Kitty blew a kiss at the screen.

'Love you too. Bye,' Ruby whispered as the screen went blank and she was thrust into that awful feeling of loneliness once again.

* * *

The day before she was due to leave for Sicily, Ruby was called in to see Valerie. The fact that her agent requested a meeting *in person* and at the office was worrisome. It sounded too official. Philippe was driving her in to the city in his official capacity, but she was relieved to have a friendly face along for the ride.

'I wish you well, Ruby,' he said as they ascended in the service elevator of the office block. 'I'll be right outside once you're done. Try not to worry.'

She smiled but couldn't help noticing the niggling feeling of doubt that weighed heavy in the pit of her stomach. She knocked on the door of her agent's office and entered.

'Ruby, darling. It's so good to see you. The hair looks wonderful. Dark really suits you,' Valerie said as she air-kissed her cheeks.

She returned to the large, black leather armchair behind her desk and gestured for Ruby to sit opposite. Already it felt like a very official meeting and the sweat on Ruby's palms did nothing to change that.

'Now... I have some news... It's not good, I'm afraid.' The long, drawn-out way in which she was speaking, and the lack of eye contact, solidified in Ruby's mind that things were amiss, even without the content of Valerie's words.

She inhaled a deep, shaking breath. 'Out with it, Valerie.'

Valerie's demeanour took on that all too familiar turn: crumpled brow, downturned mouth, dipped head. 'I'm afraid the team at *The Girl and The Rose* have been in touch—'

Ruby swallowed hard. 'I'm fired.'

Valerie huffed air through her nostrils. 'Not exactly *fired* as such. But... filming has been postponed. They still want you for the role. They just feel that at this present time your name carries a somewhat... *negative* connotation that they don't want to mar their production.'

Ruby closed her eyes and slowly shook her head as she spoke through clenched teeth. 'I can't believe this. I thought it would have been dealt with and my name would've been cleared by now. Instead, I've had to change my appearance and I have to go hide in some run-down shack in a foreign country until goodness knows when. It's crazy, Val. It feels like people don't care. Like it's not important to anyone else.'

Valerie held up her hands. 'Hey, come on now, calm down, you know that's not true.' She paused for a moment. 'Okay, it may be true in the case of Tyler Harrison. But the rest of us are working hard to clear your name.'

Ruby glared at her agent. 'Are you? Are you really? Because it feels like very little is being done. I'm still being hounded. I'm still being discussed as public enemy number one. Valerie, as my agent you should be employing PR or lawyers or... or *something*. You won't let me speak out; you won't let me try to clear my own name.'

'You spoke out anyway and look where that got you,' Valerie snapped.

'I had to do something. I feel utterly useless, scared and alone. Do you understand?' The volume of her voice increased exponentially with her anger. 'I've worked so damn hard for my career and the actions of one spiteful, evil bastard have brought my world crashing down around my ears and you say calm down?'

Valerie didn't speak. She had the common decency to look upset, at least.

'Who would want to do this to me? What have I ever done to cause someone to hate me so much? If I've hurt someone, why haven't they confronted me? Given me a chance to right the wrong?'

When Valerie treated her questions as rhetorical, Ruby stood.

'I'm leaving now. I have a plane to catch and I need to pack. Please keep me informed.' And with that she left the office, closed the door and burst into tears.

7

The brief time at Leonardo Da Vinci airport in Rome consisted of a little duty-free shopping, head down, large shades on, hair in a messy bun, so as not to be recognised. Ruby's clothes were deliberately plain and indistinct, like nothing she would normally wear. She wanted to blend in, and it worked... to a point. When people began to mumble and point around her, she dashed away with her few new items of clothing, more shades, and a large sun hat. The flight to Sicily was a regular one, no first class available, but thankfully Valerie had contacted the airport in advance and Ruby was allowed a little privacy.

The mid-afternoon temperature, as Ruby exited the airport in Palermo, was surprisingly warm and springlike, and after dozing on the one-hour flight, she was relieved that no one seemed to recognise her with her bird's nest hairdo. The shades that covered the majority of her puffy face probably helped too. She found it incredible the amount of anonymity she had discovered with the help of a few changes; not that fans had ever been an issue in the past. She'd enjoyed the selfies and the spontaneous autograph sessions; the adoration and compliments had been lovely too. Sadly, those situations all seemed like a distant memory now.

The airport was surrounded by rugged mountains on one side and the crystal blue Tyrrhenian Sea to the other. The salty breeze felt cool against her skin and she inhaled deeply, happy to once again be on terra firma. If anything good could come of the situation, at least she was going to have an adventure and visit a completely new place.

She was greeted by her driver, an older gentleman who introduced himself as Angelo. He was pleasant enough but didn't seem to speak much English. He opened the rear door of the black saloon car and dutifully carried her cases to the boot.

She climbed in and lowered the window. It was her first visit to the island, and she wanted to soak up the sights, sounds and smells.

Once back inside the car, the driver set off, heading away from the airport but keeping to the coastal road.

The hedgerows were filled with signs of spring. The purples of wild orchids and the vibrant yellow of fennel accompanied by its aromatic hint of anise. The sky overhead was a little dull and cloudy, quite a contrast to the cheeriness of the wildflowers.

The driver communicated in his own language, gesturing at the views as they passed, with the odd, 'isn't it?' dotted in for good measure. At least he tried. All Ruby did was nod and smile sweetly, avoiding the urge to reply 'Bella' to everything he uttered. Was it even a valid word? Her little phrasebook was packed away in her suitcase, stupidly.

As they travelled to the house, Valerie called to tell her that security was already in situ in a small gatehouse at the property and that she wouldn't even realise they were there. That disappointed her a little. A bit of company wouldn't be so bad.

Due to roadworks, they took a detour and passed through a small, yet built-up, coastal city called Cefalù that was nestled into an imposing rock. The narrow streets were buzzing with people on mopeds, winding in and out of pedestrians like some kind of choreographed dance. She half expected music to play and a flash mob to begin in the square where the cathedral sat peering down on the residents going about their daily routines. She had presumed the swarthy Italian men she had heard about were just a stereotype, but she spotted several, shirtsleeves rolled up to their elbows, dark, almost black hair, swept back from their olive-skinned faces.

The sun made a welcome appearance as the sound of Italian speaking voices drifted through the open car window, and the smell of fresh pasta and coffee made her stomach grumble. She knew from the research she had done that this was the closest suburban place to the villa that had shops, eateries and clubs; although she was under strict instructions to stay away from any such place. In fact, she was under strict instructions not to leave the house!

They travelled undulating roads, edged with the fragrant tang of citrus trees. Cypress trees reached skyward, with their furry fronds seeking out the sun, and umbrella pines gave shade to the road, intermittently causing an almost strobe-like effect.

Eventually they ascended up into what felt like the middle of nowhere, and a set of wrought-iron gates came into view with the words *Villa Vista Mare* twisted into a pretty font amongst the posts. As she'd been told, a small, single storey gatehouse was situated just inside the gates, which opened automatically as the car pulled up.

A man in a white shirt and suit jacket approached the driver's window and the two men chatted briefly in Sicilian... or was it Italian? She couldn't tell.

The security guard, a shaven-headed hulk of a man, complete with holstered firearm, raised a hand towards her window but she guessed he couldn't see her due to the tinted glass.

The property was incredibly isolated, with the closest neighbours a fair trek along the road. The long driveway that led to the front of the property was lined with twisted and gnarled-trunked olive trees that had clearly been there an age. The house itself was beautiful and sat in an elevated position with the front overlooking the azure blue Tyrrhenian Sea. Her first impressions of the exterior weren't at all what she had imagined, a run-down ramshackle hut. The pale stone structure was covered in lush green vines and appeared complete from the outside and she wondered if the problems would begin at the interior because so far it looked too good to be true.

Outside the entrance was a little bistro table with two chairs; it was shaded by the vines which extended over a wooden canopy and she imagined it would be a nice place to sit and have a cup of tea in the nice weather.

She had been informed that a key had been left inside but the main entrance door would be unlocked as security were checking things regularly and there was only one way in and out of the estate. Valerie had said the builders would be in on Monday so there would be no one to greet her or show her around. She was told the location of the main rooms she would need, and was looking forward, although with trepidation, to exploring; especially now she'd seen the view.

Angelo carried her suitcases inside and left them on the tiled floor of the entrance. Ruby could smell dust, plaster and paint; not the aromas she'd hoped to be greeted with in a Sicilian hideaway, but she couldn't complain. Someone she didn't know had been gracious enough to allow her to stay here. Apparently, the fridge was full and she was to help herself to whatever she wanted.

She knew little of the owner, all she had been given was a name, Mr Adair. Nosey internet searches had brought up little on the man himself, so he was clearly someone who avoided social media – she wondered what that was like. The only photo she had been able to find was a rather blurry one of him, as a long-haired, stubble-chinned, bespectacled young man. Ruby knew you should never judge a book by its cover, but he didn't look like a property mogul; more like the lead singer in some nineties grunge rock band. She presumed he had changed since then, but as his personal internet presence was pretty much non-existent he would no doubt remain a mystery.

She left her cases and wandered through the villa, opening each ornately carved door and poking her head into every room she passed. The kitchen was modern-looking in one sense with its plain white, shaker-style units and pewter handles, but the patterned tiles on the backsplash were more traditional and colourful, the floor was tiled in terracotta and a stone plinth skirted the top of the room with large brass plates balanced precariously on it. A huge oak dresser unit covered one wall where the crockery was displayed, along with other pots and pans in shiny copper. An old gnarled table sat in the middle of the room surrounded by odd chairs and with a huge bowl of lemons in the centre, their scent fresh and strong.

The thick stone walls were bare, except for in the main sitting room, where they were adorned with paintings of seascapes and the odd nude study. A huge, tiled fireplace dominated one wall of the room and the vaulted ceilings gave it a sense of grandeur and space. There was nothing personal, however, no photographs, certificates or trophies.

Many of the rooms had stacks of furniture in the centre covered with huge, white dust sheets, but each had large windows with spectacular views either onto the lemon trees at the rear or the sea and sky at the front.

Her footsteps echoed on the tiled floors as she travelled from room to room, finding her bearings and wishing Kitty was there to *ooh* and *ahh* over things with. The house was quirky with many different levels but still nothing that told her more of the owners. Her curiosity was piqued, and she made a mental note to ask Valerie about her gracious host next time she spoke with her.

Ruby had been instructed to use the third bedroom along the corridor on the second floor, so she returned to the hallway, collected her cases and made her way up the curved stone stairs in search of her room. Tiredness was beginning to outweigh her desire to explore and she decided she hadn't even enough energy to fill her grumbling stomach. She counted the doors and opened the one she hoped was hers.

Once inside, she put down her cases and took in her surroundings. The room was sparsely furnished and functional. The walls were whitewashed and, like much of the house, a terracotta tiled floor lay beneath her feet. A carved, oak bed was against one wall, with a tapestry throw blanket like that which you might find in a British stately home. A teal, chinoiserie-style blanket box on legs adorned another wall, its intricate details and bold colour a contrast to the plain backdrop. And a large oak wardrobe took centre spot on another, the carvings of which matched the headboard of the bed. It was minimalist but comfortable and had everything she needed.

A Juliet balcony provided light and more of those stunning vistas that surrounded the house. Perhaps there was no real need for artwork on the walls with views like that, she pondered, feeling any stress she'd been carrying ebbing away. She opened the doors and stood for a moment, breathing in the salty air and fresh scent of the lemon and olive trees below. If she was to be a prisoner, there could be worse places to be locked up, she surmised.

* * *

After a restful night – the first in a while – Ruby awoke on Sunday to sunlight flooding in through the voile drapes at the window. The temperature in the room was a little chilly and she wondered if it might actually be warmer outside. She opened the double balcony doors again and, sure enough, the sun reached her skin, warming her momentarily before ducking behind a cloud. The distant whoosh of the ocean brought a smile to her face and she sighed in the closest feeling to contentment she'd had in days.

She glanced sideways and could see the security guard pacing in front of the gates as he smoked a cigarette and talked on his phone. She couldn't make out words, not that she would've understood what he was saying anyway.

A small dog, possibly a Yorkshire Terrier, appeared from inside the gatehouse and followed the guard as he paced. Every so often, the man stopped and bent to scratch the creature behind its ears, and Ruby giggled at the contrast in size between the dog and his burly owner. Eventually, the dog seemed to tire of following his master and flopped down in the shade of one of the olive trees. She made a mental note to introduce herself as soon as possible – to the dog, not the guard. She'd always been a sucker for a wet nose and a pair of big brown eyes.

She picked up her mobile phone and stared at the screen. No notifications. But then she remembered she had deactivated all her accounts. The stress of the vibrations and pings every second had been too much, and anyway, it would mean no more hacking. Although she could see there was no Wi-Fi, and the phone signal was on minimal bars. Perhaps it wasn't a bad thing. She could always enquire with the guards as she was sure they would need internet access, but then thought better of it. The peace and quiet was welcome.

She made her way down to the kitchen and found bread, cheese, fruit juice and all manner of other foodstuffs to tantalise her taste buds. She broke off a chunk of fresh bread and poured a glass of orange juice, then made her way back upstairs to explore a little more. At the end of the corridor, she discovered a covered terrace. It was open to the elements at one end and overlooked a swimming pool in the centre of a courtyard at the rear corner of the property. There was hardly any water in the pool and what was there was dirty and full of leaves; the one sunlounger situated beside it had seen better days too. It was strangely derelict in appearance and Ruby wondered why. The balcony, however, was the perfect shady retreat to eat breakfast and enjoy the fresh air. The furniture was surprisingly modern and comfortable.

She tapped at the screen of her phone and confirmed that the signal was sketchy at best. There was absolutely no public Wi-Fi that she could access, meaning video calls were out of the question. She hit dial on Kitty's number and willed the call to connect.

'Hey! You didn't call me when you arrived, you bugger,' Kitty said as soon as the call connected.

'Yes, but it was a reeeally long flight, and I was absolutely knackered. Anyway, at least we're in a similar time zone now. You'll get sick of hearing from me.'

'Never. So... what's it like? Are you surrounded by hunky guards and shirtless builders?'

Ruby laughed. 'Erm... not exactly. The security guard looks like something from a Russian spy movie and the builders aren't here until tomorrow. I'm not too bad just now, but I can see the loneliness getting to me.'

'Aw, honey. It must all be very strange for you. I've been watching the news, but they've been on about the Royals visiting America, so you're old news for now, at least.'

'That's a relief. Anyway, I wish I could video-call you and give you a tour of the house, but the signal is awful. There's no Wi-Fi that's immediately obvious either, which is absolutely pants. The house isn't as bad as I expected so that's good, and the location is stunning but talk about isolated. It looks like some kind of millionaire's row along the road.'

'No pool?'

'Oh yes, there's a pool, but I won't be swimming in it. It's filthy. Goodness knows what creatures might be living in there.' She shivered at the thought.

'Have you heard anything from Tyler?' Kitty asked with a certain amount of hesitancy audible in her voice.

'Nope. Not a damn thing. I left his ring with Valerie. I'm surprised he didn't ask for it on the night we broke up, to be honest.'

Kitty sighed. 'I must say, I'm in awe at how well you're handling the break-up. Unless it hasn't hit you yet?'

Ruby thought about it for a moment. 'In all honesty, I think I was relieved in the end. Looking back, it never really felt like love. It was all about press photos and publicity. Even the proposal felt like a popularity stunt. Okay, the sex was good, but the affection was seriously lacking now I think back on it. I was genuinely fond of him, but he was more bothered with how many followers he had than spending quality time with me. I think I was kind of... blind to his real personality, you know?'

'I can understand that, honey, for sure.'

'And he didn't stand up for me. How can that be love? I want to be important enough to someone that they will stand up for me, put me first. Like Gerry does with you.' Kitty and Gerry had met at sixth form college and had started off as friends. They had the kind of complete compatibility in their relationship that people aspired to achieve. Ruby especially.

'And that's what you deserve, chick. There's someone out there for you, I just know there is. Maybe you'll fall in love with Vlad the security guy?' She giggled.

'I wish I'd never said that about him now. He's probably a very nice man. He's just rather large and scary-looking. All that bulk is intimidating. Although, in complete contrast to his demeanour, he appears to bring his dog to work. A little Yorkshire Terrier, of all things!'

Kitty gasped. 'Really? Not a bull mastiff or an Alsatian?'

Ruby grinned. 'Nope, a dog like the one my gran used to have. Hers was called Sprinkles... I wonder if he puts little bows in its hair like she used to?' She chuckled at the thought.

'Try to snap a pic and send it,' Kitty whispered.

Ruby frowned. 'Of the dog?'

Kitty guffawed. 'The *guard*, you daft sod.'

'I will not!' Ruby laughed.

'Spoilsport.' Kitty sighed deeply. 'Ugh, I wish I could fly out to visit you. Although, even if I was allowed to fly, I'm so fat at the moment I think they'd have to put me in the hold.'

'I wish you could visit too, honey. And you're not fat, you're *pregnant*. There's a massive difference. Right, I'm off to make some tea and wander around the rest of the house. Maybe I'll go for a cuddle with Sprinkles mark two. Speak tomorrow. Love you.'

'Love you too, daaahling,' Kitty replied in a ridiculously bad, mock Russian accent.

'Nutter,' Ruby said and ended the call, giggling uncontrollably.

8

After a quickly prepared lunch of salad with the freshest, ripest tomatoes she had ever tasted, the creamiest, melt-on-the-tongue mozzarella that made her think of sunshine, and succulent, juicy olives that she presumed had been harvested from the trees in the garden, Ruby decided to wander around the grounds of the property. The temperature was certainly milder than in New York, but it was in no way 'tropical'. She slathered on coconut-fragranced sunscreen as she naturally did every day because of her pale skin, and dressed in linen trousers, a white vest top and a denim shirt. Her sunglasses finished off the ensemble and she was ready to go.

The grounds were extensive. More twisted, gnarled olive trees stretched from the ground and reached towards the sunlight, their leaves casting dappled shadows on the dusty, stoney ground. She encountered different levels, hidden courtyards and marble steps leading to a little elevated patio with far-reaching views over the Tyrrhenian Sea towards the horizon. It really was a stunning, tranquil place. Although she guessed it wouldn't be from Monday when the builders were back. She hoped they all had well-fitting trousers and decent personal hygiene. The last thing she wanted was to be surrounded by stinky men exposing their bum cracks to all and sundry. It really would ruin the ambience.

Valerie had texted to check in and say that the security men were called

Jacopo and Luca. They would be alternating their duties for the duration of her stay. Jacopo was in situ when she'd arrived. Both men were Italian, from the mainland, and could speak very little English, but they came from a firm that was used to protecting politicians and Italian movie stars, so they were apparently the best for the job.

Ruby sighed, *Great, two more non-English speakers...* Things were going to be interesting. The whole situation was less than perfect. She resigned herself to the fact that in-depth conversation was something she'd have to save for her calls with Kitty and her parents, although recent calls with the latter had ended in tears. Her folks were so worried about her and her dad had had some choice words to say about Tyler. She rarely heard her father swear, but this was an exception. He was clearly angry about the situation his 'little girl' found herself in. Her dad had even hinted at the possibility that Tyler could be the one behind the internet posts, citing jealousy of her blossoming career as the motive. She was ashamed to admit that the thought had crossed her mind too, but she had no evidence and truthfully doubted he would be so vindictive.

As she passed the gatehouse, Jacopo was leaning against the white-washed wall of the building smoking, *again*. He raised his hand in a wave and smiled.

She racked her brain, trying to remember how to say hello. 'Bog jurno, signor. Bella cornetto... erm... I mean... gee... or... nata?' She cringed and felt her cheeks flaming.

Jacopo pursed his lips, clearly trying not to laugh. 'Ciao, signorina. It is a beauty day.' She felt a little less silly on hearing his English, but he had certainly done better than she had. The little dog she had spotted came trotting out of the gatehouse and Jacopo immediately stubbed out his cigarette. 'Merda, vieni qui, Nerone!' He lurched for the dog and scooped it up in his arms.

'Oh, it's okay! He's sweet. May I?' she gestured at the dog.

'Sì, naturalmente.'

Ruby reached out and scratched the dog under his chin. The dog closed his eyes and his little tail wagged frantically. 'You're so cute, yes, you are,' she told the little bundle of fur in a silly voice kept only for those of the four-legged variety.

'This is Nerone... erm... I think, Nero, in English?'

Ruby had to stifle a giggle on hearing that the fluffy, cute, black and tan canine was named after a Roman emperor known for tyrannical behaviour, debauchery and murder. 'Hello, Nero. You remind me of Granny Dot's dog, Sprinkles, yes, you do,' she cooed.

'I think he like you, Miss Locke,' Jacopo said with a grin.

'Well, I like him. He's lovely. He's bell... bell...' She frowned and shook her head, trying to remember the correct version of the word.

Jacopo nodded in encouragement. 'Bellisimo.'

She wagged her finger. 'Yes, that! He's definitely *all* kinds of bellisimo.' Too embarrassed to speak further, she waved and turned to dash off towards the main house again, but the little dog, who had been placed back on the ground, followed her.

'Nerone! Dai!' Jacopo called after him.

'Oh no, it's fine! He can keep me company if that's okay with you?' Ruby said to Jacopo, who shrugged and then nodded.

'Sì, grazie.'

Thankfully, she located a bottle of red wine in the kitchen and decided to drink it with dinner. She hadn't eaten steak in ages, but tonight was to change that. She couldn't wait, and she got the impression Nero was keen too, by the way he followed her around the room, his tiny nails clicking on the tiled floor.

'Guess what, Nero? There's gelato in the freezer too. I may be in prison, but I'm going to enjoy getting fat and drunk while I'm here, and no one can stop me.'

The little dog tilted his head as if hanging on her every word.

She was currently on hiatus from her career and although she had spotted a room set out as a gym on her tour, she had also found a library with English books in, so she figured, what the hell, she was staying skinny for no one.

Another tour of the house with her furry companion revealed many derelict rooms, one of which had a mattress on the floor complete with clean bedding. Her stomach sank at the thought of perhaps the builders staying over. Although she didn't relish the thought of being alone, she didn't like the idea of strange men being here either. Especially ones she couldn't really communicate with.

* * *

Later that night, after devouring a juicy steak and yet more salad, followed by a huge bowl of gelato and a whole bottle of red wine, she lit a fire in the living room and sat watching TV shows she couldn't understand, with Nero cuddled on her lap. The little cutie was snoring his head off and she smiled down at him, stroking his soft fur. He'd enjoyed his little sneaky bit of steak but hadn't liked the gelato; that had made him sneeze.

A knock on the door startled her and Nero woke, jumped from her lap and began barking and running around in circles. With trepidation, she made her way to the door.

'H-hello? Who's there?'

'Miss Locke, it is Jacopo. I come to get Nerone for bedtime.'

Relieved, she pulled open the door. 'Sorry about that, Nero and I were watching TV. I lost track of the time.'

Jacopo smiled and nodded, but she wasn't sure he had understood her. Her little friend jumped into his owner's arms and Jacopo grinned. 'Grazie. Until tomorrow.'

She raised her hand in a wave to them both and closed the door. She pulled her shawl around her shoulders and went back to the living room where she stoked the fire, then curled up on the couch, pulling a blanket over her, and dozed off as the TV talked to itself.

* * *

A door slam yanked her, rather rudely, from a dream where she was paddling in turquoise waters, hand in hand with a faceless man. She had been on the verge of seeing his face when the loud noise occurred, and it thrust her back to the memory of the night Tyler had dumped her.

'Bloody hell, do people not get how to close a door quietly?' she chuntered as she listened for further noise. She glanced at the screen on her phone and was shocked to realise she had slept through the whole night on the lumpy old couch. No wonder her neck was stiff. She presumed the noise to be the builders and realised she was in yesterday's clothes which were now crumpled. She decided to make a quick dash for her room.

She poked her head around the door and spotted the back of a man with cropped dark hair, wearing scruffy jeans and a dirty T-shirt. He was speaking rapidly, in Italian or Sicilian, into a mobile phone. It appeared he was the only one to have arrived and she made a run for it before he turned around. *At least his jeans seemed to fit nicely*, she thought to herself, then immediately rolled her eyes when she realised that observation meant she had looked at his bottom. *Get a grip, Ruby. You don't need a man, especially not now.*

Once she was dressed in capri pants and a baggy white shirt, she made her way back downstairs. There was no sign of the builder so she set about making a pot of fresh tea, thinking he may welcome a cup if he took a break.

The man returned, still speaking at a rate of knots into his phone. He placed down the metal toolkit he was carrying, chucked his chin at her in greeting and she smiled. His hair was almost black, short but floppy on the top, and his chin was graced with dark stubble. His arms were thickset, his chest broad and, in fact, he had a look of *Desperate Housewives* actor Jesse Metcalfe – a man she had never worked with but had met several times. And he had vivid blue eyes, the colour of the Tyrrhenian Sea.

She realised she was staring, and as her face warmed a little too much, she gestured to the teapot. He gave her a thumbs-up sign and smiled, revealing a set of perfect teeth. Although these were not veneers, like those of her former fiancé. These were just the natural teeth of someone with evidently brilliant dental hygiene.

Bloody hell, she thought, *why is he a builder and not an actor or a model?* He was far better looking than Tyler Harrison. And that accent certainly made her insides quiver a little.

She poured a cup of tea and quickly made a hasty retreat up to the covered terrace. She wasn't there to ogle the staff, she reminded herself sternly.

She dialled Kitty and waited impatiently for it to connect.

'Hey, gorgeous girl. How's it going?' Kitty asked eagerly.

'Okay, I suppose.' She huffed. 'One of the builders has arrived so I'm no longer alone, but I need to find out which rooms he's working on so I can avoid him.'

Kitty scoffed. 'Avoid him? You can't go avoiding everyone while you're there, you daft woman. I know you; you'll be starved of conversation before long. Does he seem friendly enough?'

'Erm... I haven't exactly spoken to him. He's been on his phone rattling on to someone in Italian since he got here. I'm not sure he's paid to do that, to be honest, but it's none of my business.'

'What does he look like?'

'He's... erm... you know, a builder.' She shrugged. Her voice sounded strained even to her own ears. She paused and waited for Kitty to cotton on.

'Ruby Locke... do I detect a hint of embarrassment in your voice? He's a hottie, isn't he? Is he a hottie? Come on, tell me everything.' Kitty was getting rather too excited.

Ruby glanced over her shoulder. 'Stop it, Kitty! No, he's not a *hottie*, for goodness' sake. I mean... he's not ugly but...'

'Come on, description please. Hair colour? Does he have hair? Does he have a beer belly? Come on! Let me live vicariously, you meanie!'

After another quick check over her shoulder, she whispered, 'Okay, okay. He's bloody gorgeous, Kitty. I mean, handsome, dark hair, tanned, but my guess is that he knows it. No one's that perfect. I mean look at Ty. Gorgeous exterior but, boy, did he know it.'

'Oooh, I need to see. Send pics, pleeeease?'

'With what signal? You're lucky I'm calling you. And what would Gerry think if I did that?'

Kitty's husband came on the line. 'You were on speaker and Gerry can appreciate a handsome bloke because Gerry is perfectly secure in his relationship *and* his sexuality, thank you very much,' he said, and Ruby could picture his goofy grin.

She rolled her eyes. 'Good grief, you two are as bad as each other.'

'My wife is the bad influence, I can assure you,' Gerry replied.

'Anyway, even if I *could* send them, I'm not taking photos of people without their permission.'

'You really need to live a little more dangerously, you know,' Gerry insisted.

'Bugger off. I called to speak to your wife. And tell her to take me off speaker!' She giggled with a shake of her head.

'Charming. I'm off to put the kettle on, but I won't be making *you* one, Miss Locke.'

There was a shuffle as he handed the phone back to Kitty, and Ruby laughed, secretly wishing she could meet someone with a sense of humour like him.

* * *

Once her call was finished, Ruby trotted down to the kitchen again. She decided it might be a good idea to introduce herself to the builder, seeing as he was going to be working on the house whilst she was there, *indefinitely*. Although, on arrival, she spotted that he had left his dirty teacup, complete with a wet ring of dark liquid, on the work surface, which annoyed her. He wasn't there, so she decided to have a look through the books in the library. He could clean up his own mess.

The shelves in the large, square room were floor to ceiling and surprisingly dust-free. The room was clearly loved. An old, leather-bound wing-back chair sat in one corner, with a floor lamp beside it, angled at just the right height for reading. She ran her fingertips along the spines of Italian volumes that had certainly been well-read. Her fingers landed upon a section full of British classic novels by Brontë, Orwell and Austen, to name but a few, and she selected an old favourite, *Rebecca* by Daphne du Maurier. The sun had made another appearance, so she returned to the secluded, covered terrace to read in peace and quiet.

9

Boredom and melancholy were already setting in.

She'd only been on the island a couple of days, but Ruby found she already had too much time to think about what had happened recently, and that was doing her no good whatsoever. Finding it hard to concentrate, she placed her book on the coffee table and walked over to lean on the railing that overlooked the grubby swimming pool with its tired old sunlounger. Ignoring the rather unpleasant sight below her, instead she peered off into the distance and longed to be on the beach, dipping her toes in that crystal-clear water.

If only she had lines to learn or even a contract to read through. She was so used to spending her time poring over her latest script, responding to online interviews, appearing on radio or TV chat shows or at press junkets. Instead, here she was standing in a half-empty house with no internet access – although she figured there were probably positives to that – no one to talk to, no one to give her a hug and tell her everything would be okay, and no one to make her laugh. It all exacerbated the loneliness she felt.

Her mind wandered back to Tyler. The way he'd always pushed himself forward in photo shoots. The way she'd always ended up walking behind him into events. The way he whispered secretively into his phone when he thought she wasn't watching, or sent texts under the table, a wry smile on his lips. Why the hell had she put up with their superficial relationship for so long? Because, in retrospect, that's exactly what it had been, like some kind of marriage of convenience but without the nuptials. And the stupid thing was, if she was completely honest with herself, she'd known that all along. Why had she convinced herself that he loved her? Why had she made excuses for him? Was she really that delusional and desperate? Was it simple naivety, or was it a case of feeling that she couldn't change things because he was the kind of man she *should* be with?

Everything else in her life was decided for her; what to wear, what size to be, which interviews to do, what products to endorse. Had she really fallen into the trap of letting circumstance dictate her love life too? She'd always been attracted to personality first. Until Tyler. But with him, she was so gobsmacked that he, in all his outward perfection, wanted *her.* It was as if she'd let it all happen *to* her, rather than being an active part of it; as if she was somehow grateful to him. *Ugh, pathetic!* She scoffed in disgust at herself. Was she really the kind of person to fall for a façade? She hadn't thought so until now. Self-analysis was a dangerous thing, she realised. Well, she wouldn't be bitten by *that* snake again. Looks were definitely *not* everything. In fact, all she had learned up to now was that good-looking men were not to be trusted.

But even with all that, she missed the feeling of being loved, of being wanted, of being held. Her stomach knotted and she was so overcome with emotion and loneliness that a sob escaped her throat. How the hell did she get here? How did she end up a fugitive, hiding from the people who put her on the pedestal she'd now fallen from? The very people who had once hailed her as the next Kate Winslet now considered her evil and unworthy of their adoration.

She missed the simpler times of childhood; her dad's hugs and her mum's soothing singing voice that used to lull her to sleep. Their inexpensive family holidays to Scarborough, their treat nights out at Pizza Hut – things that she would give anything to do now. When did things get so complicated?

Her face was wet with tears and her heart ached. Maybe it was exhaustion or the fact that things had been building since Valentine's Day, but she'd never experienced homesickness and regret like this before. It was all-consuming, physically painful, so hard to bear. Was this accidental life she had found herself a part of really worth it? She was beginning to think it wasn't and that terrified her. She had no clue what to do beyond Sicily. She had no clue if her name would ever be cleared. And if it wasn't, what then? But, worse still, if it was... what *then* too?

'Merda! Spiacente,' a gruff male voice said from the doorway.

She snapped up her head and, to her horror, saw the hunky builder standing there, staring at her, a distinct look of concern furrowing his brow.

She didn't want anyone to see her like this, defeated and broken, the antithesis of everything she'd worked so hard to become.

She waved her hands at him. 'Go away! Please! Leave me alone!' she shouted in anguish as she swiped at the wetness on her face. Her eyes were no doubt puffy and red, her cheeks swollen, and her hair was definitely a mess from the change in water – something that always spoiled her natural curls.

The builder didn't speak, instead he held up his hands, rapidly turned around and left.

She immediately felt guilty for shouting at the poor man. He had clearly been worried about her; his expression alone told her that. And now she had pretty much ruined any chance of striking up a friendship with him.

She went to her room and splashed her face with cold water. Her reflection was just as she had feared. She looked a mess. She *was* a mess. In fact, her whole *life* was a mess. She knew she must find the poor builder and apologise. Although there was a huge problem with her plan; she had no clue how to communicate with him to do so. She grabbed her phone and dialled Kitty.

'Hello?' Kitty sounded like she was standing in a wind tunnel and the line crackled.

'Kit? Kitty, I need a huge favour.'

'Hello? Ruby? It's a... line... tunnel... to the seaside...'

More crackling, more swooshing.

Ruby blocked her other ear. 'Can you hear me? I couldn't tell what you said,' she shouted.

'It's... bad... s'up?' It was like talking to Norman Collier doing his faulty microphone act. Her dad used to find him hilarious.

'Look, I need a favour. I need you to text me how to apologise in Italian to the builder. The things I want to say are a little more than my phrase book can handle. I need to know how to explain that I'm probably hormonal and... ugh... I don't know... Something about my endorphins being all over the place. I've just shouted at him and I feel terrible. I can't get online to look it up. Can you look for me and text me how to say it?'

'Say... sorry... Italian?' The line cracked and buzzed, but it seemed Kitty had got the gist of what she needed.

Relieved, Ruby replied, 'Yes, just something so the builder knows I'm sorry, hormonal, and it was probably tiredness or endorphins. Something like that.'

'And *what*?'

'En. Dor. Phins,' Ruby enunciated.

'Translate... builder... strange...'

'I can't hear you. You keep breaking up.'

''Kay... the... line... tunnel now...' The call went dead, and Ruby was left with a beeping tone.

She placed her phone on her bedside table and decided on fresh air.

When she arrived at the gatehouse this time, a man she didn't recognise sat just inside the door on his mobile phone. She presumed him to be Luca and raised her hand in greeting. He smiled and nodded. She was a little disappointed that Luca's presence meant Nero wouldn't be here.

She cringed, not wishing to interrupt his call but needing to ask a question, nonetheless. She pointed at the house. 'Excuse me. The man... l'uomo. Has he gone now? The builder?' She made some ridiculous hand gesture that she hoped looked like sawing and then made her fingers into legs walking. 'L'uomo, erm... gone?' Her final gesture was that of a magician who had made something disappear. All she was missing was the cloud of smoke.

Luca nodded. 'Ah, Miceli? Sì. Tornando più tardi oggi.'

She had no clue what he'd said but he appeared to understand what she had asked. She knew *sì* meant yes, so it seemed that the builder had, in fact, gone. She nodded, thanked him in what she was pretty sure was Spanish, and smiled, before turning to wander the grounds again.

Around ten minutes later, a text arrived from Kitty.

You're a weird fish, lol! And what kind of place is that you're staying in??? Anyway, here is what you asked for!

There followed some Italian phrases and she quickly fired back a reply.

You're a star. Thank you so much. Love you xx

Once back at the house, she riffled through the cupboards looking for the ingredients to make her favourite biscuits. Thankfully, the list consisted of only three items, all basic staples: sugar, butter and self-raising flour. The cookies were quick to make and, she decided, the easiest way to apologise to someone whose language she didn't speak. She set about baking and singing to herself as she did.

Around thirty minutes later, the biscuits were cooling on a wire rack and she had finished the washing up. Using the information she had received from Kitty, she scribbled a note for the builder and left the baking under a clean tea towel. She read her message aloud in her best attempt at an Italian accent and couldn't help a swell of pride. *This should certainly sort things out.*

Caro construttore,

 Mi dispiace per gridare. Era la puttane gemiti o galline delifini rendendomi triste.

 Ruby

Feeling quite pleased, she mentally patted herself on the back for a job well done.

* * *

The sky looked dark and ominous and there was a distinct heaviness to the air, but it was still warmer than it would've been back in New York. Ruby decided to grab a quick bite to eat and then have a long soak before an early night.

She'd been immersed in reading *Rebecca* and hadn't heard anyone enter the house, so the sight of the dark-haired builder made her jump when she spotted him through the kitchen door. She wasn't expecting him to return, although now wondered if he was the one sleeping on the mattress in the room she had found. It made sense. The house was out in the middle of nowhere and driving in every single day must eat into his working hours. She did wonder where the others were though. She was sure there had been mention of builders... plural.

He was freshly showered and wearing clean jeans this time and a white T-shirt that stretched taut over his biceps. Feeling a little voyeuristic, Ruby watched with a smile as he lifted the tea towel and shoved a cookie into his mouth. He groaned and let his head roll back as he chewed, clearly enjoying it; the guttural sound made her insides flip. Then he lifted up the note and read it. There was a pause where he scratched his chin and then a shower of crumbs spurted from his mouth as he howled with laughter, and her small inkling of lust rapidly turned to anger.

What a pig! An ungrateful, unkind pig. Clearly my thoughts on good-looking men aren't unfounded! How dare he poke fun at me after I went out of my way to apologise like that?

The man appeared to read the note again and once more found it hilarious. This time, he was almost doubled over, guffawing at her apology, shaking his head. To top it off, he took out his phone and dialled. Once his call connected, he proceeded to laugh as he read her heartfelt words to someone on the other end. He, and no doubt his friend too, mocked her in Italian and she wasn't sure whether to walk in there and slap him or just to take the plate away. He didn't deserve her baked goods. Although she could tell her cheeks were aflame now and she couldn't actually bring herself to move in his direction.

It was no wonder her hunger had suddenly abated and she decided to forego dinner and take her bath early. All the way up the stairs to her room, she chuntered about the ignorant pig of an Italian and his ungrateful behaviour. She was glad she couldn't speak his language because if she could, she'd be giving him a bitter piece of her mind to spit out like he had the crumbs.

10

The following day, the air was just as heavy and muggy, the way it was in Yorkshire when a storm was brewing. The dark clouds remained overhead and Ruby shivered, thankful she had dressed in a long-sleeved top and jeans today. She pulled her cardigan tighter around herself and wandered through the house aimlessly, considering what the hell to do to occupy her time. As she approached one of the rooms, she could hear the builder hammering away with the radio blaring out at full blast. *Ignorant swine.* He was singing along tunelessly to some Italian rock song she'd never heard and would happily never hear again.

She took a seat at the kitchen table and waited for the tea to mash. The builder walked in, shirtless and glistening with sweat, and before she had a chance to pour herself a cup, he helped himself. Annoyed, yet again, at his lack of consideration, she glared at his back but became a little distracted by his muscles rippling as he cut a chunk of bread from a fresh, what appeared to be home-made, loaf. *Ugh, put a shirt on, poser. And help yourself why don't you?* She vowed to contact Valerie or Veronica and ask one of them to contact the owner in Edinburgh about this ignorant oik. Surely he was taking liberties?

'Buongiorno,' he said as he lifted his cup and nodded at her.

She stood and poured her own cup, then turned and smiled sweetly at him, tilting her head coquettishly. 'Bon Jovi to you too. It's so good that you can't understand a word I'm saying, you ungrateful, tuneless wonder.' She kept her smile in place and he grinned in return, nodded and held up his mug. Clearly, he thought she was commenting on that. 'I hope you enjoyed my apology cookies, even though you're a shit who took the piss out of me for the note I left.' She held up her own mug as if to say cheers. 'Au revoir, or whatever,' she continued sarcastically, very much aware she'd said goodbye in French, before walking out of the room and towards the covered terrace.

Once she'd eaten, she decided to venture down to the gatehouse and admire the view of the countryside from down there, a contrast to the sea views at the front. She doubted the security guards would bother her as they seemed to spend most of their time patrolling the grounds or talking on their phones.

When she arrived at the gatehouse, there was no sign of Luca or Jacopo and her heart skipped a beat. Nero was sleeping by the door and he awoke as she approached.

'Hey, Nero, my little friend,' she said as the dog trotted towards her, tail wagging and tongue lolling out. He rolled on his back and she scratched his belly. 'I missed you yesterday, yes, I did.'

Sensing an opportunity to experience a little freedom, she stood and walked slowly towards the exit. She glanced at the road beyond the gate, but a shake of the posts told her it was locked. She poked her head inside the door of the gatehouse and was surprised to see a row of small TV screens showing images of the exterior of the property. She stepped inside and looked through another door, where she found two twin beds, both neatly made. Another door led to a shower room and another a kitchenette. It was like a little house in its own right.

Feeling a little like a burglar, she hurried back to the main room and spotted Jacopo on one of the screens, he was chatting on his phone and wandering around one of the smaller terraces. He was quite a distance from where she was, and in spite of Valerie's strict instructions to stay out of sight due to the possibility of lurking paparazzi, a fight-or-flight feeling tugged at her insides. She saw a brightly coloured dog lead curled up on the console and reached out to pick it up. A button on the wall, just below a mounted phone and video screen looked enticing. She crouched and attached the lead to Nero's collar, then hit the button and a loud buzz sounded from the gate before it slowly opened.

It was now or never. 'Come on, Nero, let's explore,' she told the York-shire Terrier, who jumped excitedly on the spot and yapped. 'Shhh, this has to be our secret,' she told him.

The pair made a dash for it through the gate and jogged along the road, Ruby looking over her shoulder like some escaped kidnap victim. No one followed and she continued to jog. Realising she hadn't picked up any cash, or her coat for that matter, she briefly considered going back to collect them but decided it was too much of a risk. She would simply take Nero for a walk and return in hour or so, what harm could it do? She knew she faced getting in trouble when she did go back, not only as she had kidnapped Jacopo's dog, but also as she'd have to buzz to be let in, but a little taste of freedom was worth it.

The sun hadn't yet made an appearance and the heavy feeling still shrouded the area. She sincerely hoped a storm didn't hit whilst they were out.

After around ten minutes, she appeared to have reached the boundary of the property and the next one. She could see a man just inside the grounds up a stepladder, trimming away the foliage.

She crouched to pet the dog again. 'Ooh, look, Nero, shall we say hello?'

The man glanced her way. 'Buongiorno,' he called down to her.

She smiled. 'Hello!' she called back. 'I mean... erm... *buongiorno* back.' She immediately wanted to slap her own forehead. She glanced down at Nero and whispered, 'I really need to study that phrase book.'

The dog wagged his tail eagerly as if agreeing.

'Ah, you're British,' the man said as he climbed down the ladder and addressed her through the metal gates that separated them. 'I'm American myself.'

'So you are.' She peered over his shoulder to the beautiful house that stood behind him. It was another whitewashed, multi-level palace of a house. 'Wow, you have a lovely home.'

He glanced behind to the building, then back to Ruby. 'Thanks. I'm Clark.' He stuck his hand through the gate, and she took it. She guessed he was around forty. He had mousy blonde hair and very smiley, kind eyes.

'Ruu...becca. I'm Rebecca,' she replied awkwardly.

'Good to meet you, Rebecca. I felt sure you were Italian with your colouring.'

'Nope. Yorkshire lass through and through.'

He frowned. 'Yorkshire? Is that anywhere near London?'

She giggled. 'Not really.'

He cringed. 'Ah. I don't really know the UK, can you tell?' He smiled broadly. He was quite handsome in an unconventional, non-obvious sort of way.

She held up her index finger and thumb. 'Just a little bit.'

'So, what brings you to Cefalù? On holiday with your husband?'

'No, no husband. I... erm...' She hadn't really thought this through. 'Just fancied a holiday and a friend recommended this place as somewhere peaceful.'

He rolled his eyes. 'Oh, it's peaceful all right. A little too peaceful for me, but my folks owned the house, and I can't bear to part with it even though they're gone.'

'Oh gosh, I'm so sorry.'

He held up a hand. 'No, don't be. It's been two years now. I try to come out for a few months a year. Been thinking about selling up again, but every time I arrive here, I change my mind.' He paused. 'Look... I know this is a little forward, but would you like to come in for a coffee? It's fresh and Italian.'

She tucked her hair behind her ears and glanced back towards her temporary home. A few spots of rain hit her shoulders and she shivered. 'Oh no, I shouldn't, thank you though.'

He nodded. 'That's okay. I totally understand.' He paused for a moment. 'Although, I could bring it out onto the covered terrace and leave the gate open if that would make you feel better?'

She glanced behind him to the terrace he'd mentioned and then back at Clark. If he knew who she was, he was doing a great impression of someone who had no clue. And she reasoned that, with the gate open, she could make a run for it if she felt uncomfortable.

She'd spent so long avoiding risks of any kind that a surge of courage led her to reply, 'Oh, go on then. That'd be lovely.'

'Really? Great. Come on in.' He hit a button on the wall and the gate opened wide.

With a little trepidation, she followed him to the terrace and took the seat closest to the gate and Nero promptly jumped into her lap.

'To be honest, you're the first English-speaking person I've encountered since I arrived a few days ago. I've been feeling quite lonely,' she admitted.

He smiled. 'Huh, and here I was thinking I'd hooked you with my charm and wit.'

She laughed. 'Nope. Just the English thing.' He was easy to talk to and she began to relax.

He reached out to pet Nero. 'And who's this cute little fella?'

Nero snarled and snapped, thankfully missing Clark's hands, and Ruby gasped.

'Nero! That's not nice. Gosh I'm really sorry about that. He's usually so sweet.'

Clark frowned and examined his fingers. 'No, it's fine. I should've known better than to try and pet him when he doesn't know me. And Nero, huh? That's a big name for a little dog.' He smiled awkwardly. 'I'll go make the coffee.' He disappeared into the house and Ruby turned Nero to face her.

She narrowed her eyes. 'You can't behave like that, you know. That's not how we make friends.' The dog licked her nose and wagged his tail, and she took it as an apology. 'Ugh, it's a good thing you're so flipping cute.' She placed him back in her lap and he curled up, nuzzled into her.

Clark returned a few moments later with a cafetière and two mugs. Nero grumbled and Clark chuckled. 'Let me have the first mouthful, and then you and your dog know you're safe.' He grinned and she wondered if he watched a lot of crime drama on TV.

'Deal,' she replied.

'So, what do you do back in England?' Clark asked after he'd taken a good long gulp of his coffee.

'Oh... I don't... I mean I'm... in administration.' Yep, she hadn't thought this through at all. 'For the government,' she added with a nod as if that would be more believable.

His eyes widened. 'Oh wow. I'm just in retail.'

'What kind of retail?'

'Records. I own a good old-fashioned vinyl shop in New Jersey.'

'Oh! Really? I might have...' She clamped her mouth shut. 'That is, my friends might have visited your shop. I have friends in New York.'

'Really? Small world, huh?'

'Sure is.' She took a sip of the coffee. It was incredibly strong, and she had to fight the urge to shudder. She was definitely more of a tea drinker.

'Has anyone ever told you, you bear a striking resemblance to that actress? Oh god, what's her name...' He clicked his fingers together and Ruby fidgeted in her seat, panic rising inside her.

Nero must have sensed her fear as he woke with a start and growled again. She stroked his fur in long, slow motions in the hope that it would calm both her and the dog. As soon as Clark said her name she would bolt, she decided. She stared at him and hoped the horror she was feeling wasn't obvious in her expression.

Clark drummed his fingers in frustration. 'You know, the one with the long blonde hair, very prim and proper. She's British too.' He tapped his forehead. 'Jeez, I'm sorry, movies really aren't my thing... Wait a minute! Got it! Kate Winslet! *Titanic*. Bingo.' He held his fists in the air as if he was going to shout 'eureka' and Nero let out a yip that made him jump. He side eyed the dog and added, 'You really do look like Kate Winslet, only as a brunette, obviously.'

Relief flooded Ruby's veins and she almost collapsed back into her chair. She scrunched her face and scratched her head. 'Really? Do you think? No one has ever said so before,' she lied.

'Meh, maybe it's just me.' He shrugged. 'Like I said, music is more my bag.'

Eager to change the subject, she asked, 'So are your wife and kids here with you?'

He shook his head and for a moment seemed a little sad. 'No, I have neither. You'd think at thirty-eight I'd have both, but I guess the store and caring for my folks has taken all my time.'

'Oh, come on, you have plenty of time if that's what you want from life.'

He smiled. 'Got to meet the right woman first.'

Oh god, this is getting a little too deep. She cleared her throat. 'So, who is your favourite band? And if you say Led Zeppelin, I may have to leave.'

He grinned and shook his head. 'You dare to dis Led Zep, huh? Wow. Brave woman.'

'Yeah, well, when you've grown up with a dad who's obsessed with Jimmy Page, their music gets a little old, if you know what I mean.'

He tilted his head, eyeing her with apparent intrigue. 'Okay then, who do *you* like?' he asked, folding his arms across his chest.

She raised her eyebrows. 'I asked first.' She giggled and took another sip of the dark liquid.

'Okay, so I love Motown. Stevie Wonder especially. In my opinion, he's the greatest singer songwriter to have ever lived. But I love most genres, to be honest. I just love music. Not too keen on jazz though.'

She was quite impressed. 'Yes! I love Stevie Wonder too. My favourite song has to be "Superstition". It's got such a good dance groove. And the lyrics are quite apt just now.'

There was that head tilt again. 'How so?'

Realising she'd said too much, she waved a dismissive hand. 'Ugh, long laborious story for another time maybe. Ooh, I also love "I Believe". It was on the soundtrack to my favourite John Cusack movie and I've adored it ever since.'

His smile widened and his eyes twinkled, even though the day was dull and drizzly. 'Wow, a woman after my own heart. I'm not much of a cinema buff, but *High Fidelity* is one of my all-time favourites too. Probably because it's mainly about music. I had to admit to having you pegged as more of a rock ballads type. You know, Whitesnake, Kiss, Bon Jovi. Maybe it's the hair.'

She laughed and flicked her hair over her shoulder. 'Yeah, Paul Stanley, eat your heart out. Seriously though, I love most music too. Although, actually, I'm not too keen on screechy heavy metal and the builder who's working on the house I'm staying in plays it way too loud. He sings too. Loudly.' She rolled her eyes.

'Jeez, that must drive you crazy. Can't you tell him to pipe down?'

She pursed her lips. 'Not really. He works for the owner.'

'Shame. Look, why don't I go and put on some Stevie? There are speakers mounted in the exterior walls.'

Ruby was impressed. 'Your parents must have been very modern.'

He cleared his throat. 'Nah, I only installed them when I inherited the place.' He disappeared inside and a few moments later the opening bars to 'Superstition' began to play. As Ruby sat back and listened to the song's lyrics, a particular line grabbed her. She sincerely hoped the *good things* weren't only in her past.

11

Ruby heard a commotion outside of Clark's gates and she glanced at her phone screen. What was supposed to have been a brief walk had turned into four hours of sitting under the covered terrace, drinking coffee as the rain poured down outside. They had talked about music, TV shows, books and whatever other subjects Ruby could mindfully address without fear of highlighting who she was.

She saw Jacopo run by, talking on his mobile phone. Nero jumped from her lap and began to bark excitedly and she gasped. 'Shit.'

Clark glanced over his shoulder. 'What? Is everything okay?'

'Oh... erm... yes, fine, sorry. I just realised what the time is. I should really be going.'

He nodded and she thought she saw a flash of disappointment. 'Look, Rebecca, I know we've only just met, but I've really enjoyed this afternoon and I'd love to do it again sometime. Like you, I'm here alone and if you're going to be here a while it'd be nice to have someone to talk to.' He shrugged and lowered his head as if he was expecting her to shoot him down.

'That would be lovely, Clark. Perhaps you could give me your number?'

He beamed at her. 'Absolutely.' He reeled off the digits and Ruby added the details into her phone.

She stood and gathered up Nero's lead. 'Right, I really must dash. Thanks for the coffee and chat. It's been lovely.' She jogged out of the garden and up the road towards the house in the pouring rain with Nero. By the time she reached the gate, she was soaked to the skin and freezing cold. Luca was pacing back and forth just inside the gate. *Shit, both of them are here.* He looked up and as soon as he set his eyes on her, they widened, and he dashed for the button to open the gate.

Luca placed a hand on each of her arms and examined her before leading her towards the house. 'Merda! Grazie a Dio. Eravamo così preoccupati. Pensavamo che fossi stato rapito! Gesù. Pazza pazza!' He bombarded her with words she couldn't understand, although from his tone and demeanour she could tell he was angry with her.

'I'm so sorry! I know you must be upset with me. I didn't mean to be out so long.' She pleaded with her eyes and hoped he understood her apology.

Jacopo appeared. He was red-faced from running and the furrow in his brow was so deep it could've easily been filled with concrete. Nero jumped up at his owner and Jacopo crouched to pick up the dog. 'Merda, Ruby! We are terrified! Where the hell have you gone all this time? Valerie is trying to call you. You should not leave without saying to us. Don't do this!' he shouted. 'And I think Nerone is stolen.'

She held up her hands, guilt niggling at her more for the dog than anything else. 'I'm sorry, okay? I just wanted to take him for a walk! I was stir-crazy and I've seen nothing of the island since I arrived. I just wanted to walk. I really am sorry. But Nero is fine, aren't you lad?'

Luca stepped forward and addressed Jacopo. 'Cosa ha detto?'

Jacopo's expression softened and he sighed. 'Dice che voleva vedere l'isola e fare una passeggiata.'

Luca shook his head. 'Fanculo.'

Jacopo took a deep breath. 'Please, Miss Ruby, stay in the place, okay? We are responsible. Out there,' he pointed towards the gate, 'you are not quite safe, okay?'

Reluctantly, Ruby nodded, feeling like a chastised child. 'I really am sorry.'

Jacopo smiled. 'Nerone says he like his walk with you.'

Ruby grinned and reached out to fuss the little dog. 'Aww, I liked it too, Nero.'

Luca stared at them with a crumpled brow and shook his head. 'Pazza donna inglese.'

Jacopo threw him an annoyed look and then addressed Ruby again. 'He says he is very sorry for shouting.'

She had a feeling that's not at all what Luca had said. 'Okay, thanks. Well, I'm going inside. Is the builder still here?'

Jacopo looked confused. 'Builder?'

Ruby rolled her eyes and thought back to the note she had left for the ungrateful oaf. 'Construttore? Working on the house?'

For a moment it didn't appear her words had done much to resolve his confusion. But then it was as if a light bulb had been switched on. 'Ah, Miceli. He is in the house.'

Jacopo, the dark horse, could apparently speak more English than he had first let on. And whilst it wasn't perfect, it was a damn sight better than her Italian. Although she had no clue what a Miceli was, but she certainly wasn't going to make herself look even sillier under the circumstances, by asking.

'Thank you. Goodbye.' She turned and walked into the house, closing the door behind her.

She didn't bother looking to see where the builder was; instead, she grabbed a chunk of bread, some grapes and some cheese from the kitchen and retreated to her room. Despite pissing off the guards, she'd enjoyed her little wander outside the grounds, but all it had done was make her want to see more of the island. She flicked through the songs she had downloaded to her phone before her trip and hit play on a Stevie Wonder playlist. A smile danced on her lips as she devoured her bedroom picnic and texted Valerie to apologise for going AWOL.

* * *

Ruby was awoken sharply from slumber by a bright flash that lit up the room like the midday sun. She sat bolt upright, and in her confused state, panic set in and her eyes darted around the room looking for the paparazzo that had infiltrated her safe space. She remembered where she was, flicked on her bedside lamp and picked up her phone to check the time. Three o'clock in the morning.

When the flash came again and was quickly followed by an earth-shaking rumble of thunder, she was relieved to realise she was in the midst of the storm that had been threatening for the past two days. She switched off the light, snuggled back down in her bed and lay there, listening to the squall outside, thankful that she was warm and toasty.

She was dozing off again when an even louder, closer-sounding crash accompanied an even more intense flash of dazzling light and she let out a scream.

'What the hell?' The whole house shook, and she felt sure it wasn't just the thunder that had caused it.

She clambered out of bed, grabbed a hoodie and tugged it on as she left the bedroom and ran down the hallway towards the noise. Someone had put the lights on, but they were flickering, rendering the scene something akin to a horror movie. She immediately regretted her decision to run *towards* the cacophony and was about to turn around.

'Ahh shit! Why now? You stupid, stupid arse, Mitch! Jesus wept; it was my next bloody job!' The shouting and swearing was in a distinct, strong Scottish accent and Ruby panicked that an intruder had broken in. Then she reasoned that perhaps the property owner had arrived when she'd been sleeping. Although she'd had no warning that he was coming.

She tiptoed slowly forwards and poked her head around the corner to the covered terrace and saw the hole in the roof. The chimney stack had been struck by lightning and it, along with lots of rubble and bricks, was scattered across the floor. In the midst of it all, staring up at the hole was the Italian builder with his back towards her. No sign of the Scottish owner. *Very confusing.*

'How the hell do I sort this out?' a Scottish voice said from somewhere as the builder ran his hands through his hair and then covered his face and shook his head. 'Talk about shitty bloody timing.' This time the Scottish voice was muffled when it spoke, and she glanced around to find out where this intruder or interloper was hiding.

Jacopo appeared out of nowhere and began to speak to the builder in

Italian. The security guard was given instructions and ran to another room, returning seconds later with buckets which he began to fill with rubble. Where the hell was the Scot hiding?

Just then the Italian builder turned and saw her. 'Oh great, just what I need. Mrs Bloody Bossy Britches actress coming to tell me how selfish I am for letting the damn roof fall in, no doubt,' he said... but not in Italian... in *English*... with a distinct and strong *Scottish* accent.

She was tired for sure, but confusion clouded her mind. *So, he's the Scot I heard?* Nothing was adding up.

Indignant, she stepped towards him and opened her mouth to speak but clamped it shut, unsure what the hell was going on. Perhaps she was dreaming, and in her mind she was getting the builder and the Scottish owner of the house mixed up? She pinched her arm. *Nope... I'm awake.*

He glared at her. 'Aye, you've figure it out, eh? I'm not Italian after all. Even though you just presumed I was. Now, are you going to just stand there or are you going to go back to your room where you're safe and out of ma way?' he asked, rather too snottily for Ruby's liking. His angry demeanour was exacerbated as another flash of lightning highlighted his scowl.

The thunder crashed again, and Ruby physically jumped forward with the shock, landing only an inch away from the builder. She felt utterly ridiculous, like some damsel in need of rescue by a big, strong man. But she was none of the above and never had been. She couldn't help watching him as he watched her. His breathing was ragged as he stared down at her, his hair glistening where the rain had ingressed and soaked him.

She felt a little breathless and unsettled to say the least. 'S-so, you're the *owner* not the *builder*,' she stuttered, then immediately felt stupid as she had stated what was evidently obvious to everyone else.

He angled his head to one side but was still a little too close for comfort. 'The penny's dropped finally. I thought maybe the whores and dolphins had addled your brain with all that moaning.' She saw the hint of a smirk grace his lips.

She scrunched her brow, not a clue what the hell he was waffling on about but put it down to the shock of the damage. She stepped back and wrapped her hoodie around her, suddenly very conscious of the effect the cold was having on certain parts of her body – at least she told herself it was the cold. Annoyance niggled where the confusion had once been. 'Hang on, why didn't you correct me when I thought you were Italian?'

He cringed. 'Look, I was just messing with you.' He shrugged. 'It was entertaining watching you trying to speak "my language". I'm sorry. Can we start over? Although maybe not right now, eh?'

She wasn't sure whether to be amused or even more peeved at the man, however, she realised there was a more pressing issue at hand. 'Okay... fine. Can I help at all?'

He shook his head and kicked at the rubble. 'Na. Nothing I can do till the storm passes. Me and Jaco will go up and put a tarp over the bloody hole,' he said through gritted teeth. 'Go back to bed, eh?' He looked so despondent and Ruby felt a pang of pity for him.

She tucked her hands inside the sleeves of her hoodie as the chill of the open air nibbled at her skin. 'Can I maybe make you a hot drink for when you come down? You'll be freezing.'

He turned to her again. 'Thanks, but I have no idea how long we'll be. Just go back to bed. No point us all freezing our bits off.'

She sloped off to bed and once again pulled the covers over her head. The storm raged on for hours and only when things went a little quiet did she tiptoe out of her room to find the hole had been covered and the men were gone.

12

Sleep evaded Ruby for the rest of the night, so the following morning she eventually gave up and clambered out of bed with a thumping headache – no doubt due to both the copious amounts of coffee she'd consumed with Clark the previous day *and* the realisation that the Italian builder was in fact the Scottish owner.

She fired off a text to Valerie to ask the name of the villa's owner, explaining that there was a Scottish man here that she wasn't expecting. Valerie replied quickly.

His name is Mitch Adair. I wasn't aware he would be there either. Sorry about that. Crossed wires. He's apparently a nice guy though and only 34, wink wink. So you should be fine. V x

Ruby chuntered that he was so nice he'd let her carry on thinking he was Italian when he wasn't and she'd made a fool of herself because of it.

She made her way down to the kitchen and found Mitch sitting at the table drinking fresh coffee. The smell of it turned her stomach.

'Bon Jovi,' he said, and she glanced over to see him smirking. 'There's still some coffee in the pot.'

'I'm good thanks. Water's fine. I think I have a coffee hangover.'

'Ah yes, from when you escaped.' He chuckled, but she didn't find his choice of words amusing.

Silence fell and Ruby tried to decide if she was hungry or if the queasiness she felt was simply a combination of yesterday's coffee overload and irritation.

'How's the roof?' she asked, thinking back to the events of last night.

Mitch huffed. 'A mess. I'll need to get some professionals in to sort it out. It's a bit much for one man, I'm afraid.' He sighed. 'Look, I'm sorry I snapped at you last night. I wasn't in the best frame of mind and you happened to step into the firing line. And I'm sorry for stringing you along with the whole Italian thing. I honestly thought you were kidding around at first but then... Anyway, I'm sorry. I'm Mitch by the way.' He held out his hand and she shook it.

'I know that now. Although I don't think that's what Jacopo called you.'

He nodded. 'Ah no, Jaco calls me by my given name, Miceli. It's Sicilian for Michael. He started off calling me Signor Adair, but that made me feel ancient. He wouldn't call me Mitch though. I think it's a respect thing.' He shrugged.

'Right. Well, I'm Ruby... it's English for Ruby,' she stated simply with a wry smile as she sipped on her water. 'And you should be sorry. It was totally uncalled for and a bit mean.'

He smirked again. 'Aye, I know. Well, I've apologised now, eh?' His stubble was thicker, and his hair was messy and stuck out at all angles. Annoyingly, he still looked like something off a magazine cover.

She tilted her head and eyed him. 'While you're feeling apologetic, you can say sorry for taking the piss out of me too for writing the note,' she insisted defiantly, willing to brook no dissent.

He scrunched his forehead. 'I wasn't intentionally taking the piss. Honestly. I actually thought, at first anyway, that you were *trying* to be funny.'

She huffed. 'By apologising in what I thought was *your* language? A language I don't even speak? I thought I was being nice and all you could do was laugh. I baked those cookies to show I was sorry for shouting at you when you caught me crying.'

'Aye, I got that. But *English* is my first language. I figured you must have been told that.' He shrugged.

That familiar heat, a tell-tale sign, rose in her cheeks. 'Well... I wasn't, obviously. I mean, you even look Italian with your dark hair and olive skin. How was I to know? And maybe you could have made it clear that you were actually Scottish instead of letting me make a fool of myself.'

'Aye, but you did it so well. The cookies were really good, by the way.' He smiled and her stomach betrayed her by flipping.

'Thank you.' She wasn't about to start giving in to that sexy smile.

He pursed his lips, evidently trying to hide his mirth again. 'But the note... man... that had me in stitches.'

Anger bubbled up inside her. 'How is me being sad, lonely and a sobbing wreck amusing to you?'

He stood from the table and grabbed the note from the countertop. 'Allow me to translate, eh?'

'You don't need to do that. I know what it says.'

He pulled his lips between his teeth for a second and shook his head. 'Oh, but I don't think you do. I think you know what you *wanted* it to say... different thing entirely.'

She felt the colour drain from her face. *Shit, what did Kitty send me?*

He proceeded to read aloud the note she had written with such care and consideration. '*Dear builder, I'm sorry for shouting—*'

She placed down her glass and folded her arms across her chest. 'What's wrong with that? That's exactly what I meant to say.'

He held up a hand and continued, '*It was the whore's moans or dolphin hens making me sad.*'

Colour returned to her face, with a vengeance, and she feared spontaneous human combustion. 'What? That's not what I... that's... my friend...'

He smiled again. 'Whore's moans? Dolphin hens? I mean... what the hell were you *trying* to say?'

Ruby covered her face with her hands. 'Oh bollocks. I'll throttle her.'

'So, you see, I wasn't intentionally taking the piss. But I am sorry if I offended you.' His voice had softened and he crouched to meet her gaze.

She sighed. 'Hormones and endorphins. It was supposed to be hormones and endorphins.'

He grinned. 'Ah. Well, it was a good try.' He was clearly trying not to laugh again but failing miserably. 'I mean... you were close.' At that point, he burst out laughing and she stormed out of the room. 'Oh, come on! Have a sense of humour!' he shouted after her, but she ignored him, so he added, 'I thought you were really sweet to write it!'

She could hear him chuckling as she ran up the stairs to hide.

Once back in the safety of her room, she grabbed her phone and dialled Kitty's number. As soon as it connected, she blurted, 'Did you do that on purpose, Kitty? I've never been so bloody embarrassed in all my life! It wasn't funny. Well, not to me, anyway. Mr bloody Italy thought it was hilarious of course. I can't face him again after that.'

There was a pause before Kitty replied. 'Whoa, whoa, hold your horses, missy. What are you on about?'

'The note! The translation I asked for. It made no bloody sense.'

Kitty laughed. 'Yeah, I know. How did you come up with it? And what the hell were you talking about? Are you near a brothel or something? A brothel on a farm by the sea? You had me and Gerry in hysterics.'

Her cheeks burned. 'It wasn't meant to be funny! When I called, I asked you to send me the translation as an apology because I had shouted at the builder.'

Kitty frowned. 'Well, why were you talking about whores? And what did dolphins and hens have to do with anything?'

'I wasn't talking about whores, Kitty! I asked you to translate that I was sorry but that my hormones and endorphins were all over the place. Good grief, didn't you hear any of what I asked for?'

'It was a really bad line. I did say so. It's kind of funny though.' Ruby could sense the amusement in her voice as Kitty relayed the story to Gerry. She heard coughing and spluttering and Kitty burst out laughing. 'Haha! Gerry almost choked. He's had to dash to the kitchen because he has coffee coming out of his nose.'

'Gee, thanks, you two. I won't be asking for your translation services again.'

Kitty giggled. 'Oh honey, I really am sorry.'

'No, you're not, you shithead.'

Kitty laughed harder. 'You love me though, eh?'

Ruby rolled her eyes. 'It's a bloody good thing that I do.'

* * *

For the rest of the day, Ruby stayed in her room as much as possible for fear of running into *Mr Italy* again. She wasn't sure she could take the embarrassment of having him laugh at her further. As a distraction from her predicament, she texted Clark, who seemed happy to hear from her and invited her over again. Knowing she would need to tell Jacopo and Luca this time, she said she would love to visit, but she just wasn't sure when it would be.

She called her mum and dad to check in with them, and her mum was on the verge of booking a flight to come and visit. But Ruby knew how much she hated flying – her dad refused to fly at all – so she managed to convince her that it wasn't necessary. She loved her for offering though.

She had almost finished *Rebecca* and was wondering what to read next when there was a tapping on her door. She walked over and opened it to find Mitch standing there. 'Oh, hi. What's up?'

He wore jeans again, but this time with a pale blue button-down shirt, sleeves rolled up to the elbows. She was mildly distracted by his forearms for some peculiar reason.

'I wanted to see if you were hungry. I've got pizza in the oven and a bottle of Chianti breathing in the kitchen if you fancy?'

She was a little surprised by the invite. 'Oh... erm...'

He held his hands out at his sides. 'Look, I'm sorry for how we got off on the wrong foot. I'm trying to make amends here.'

Guilt tugged at her and she caved. 'Okay, that would be nice, thank you.'

His smile was warm and genuine. 'Great. See you in the kitchen in five?'

'Sure.' She nodded and he turned and left.

She quickly changed into navy capri pants and a white shirt, not because she wanted to impress, obviously, but because her clothing was crumpled from lying on the bed reading all day.

Pushing through the kitchen door, she was greeted with a rather romantic sight. The farmhouse table was laid with two place settings, wine glasses, napkins and candles.

'Ooh… anyone would think we were on a date or something,' she said nervously as she took her seat.

His face crumpled. 'What? No! The bulb blew in the storm and I haven't been able to get a new one, that's all. Believe me, romance is the furthest thing from my mind.'

All right, you could sound less disgusted at the prospect. 'Good,' she replied.

Mitch poured wine into both glasses and put a huge, rustic-looking pizza on a board in between them. It was piled with colourful vegetables, meat and olives and her mouth watered as she inhaled the delicious, spicy aroma.

Her stomach rumbled. 'This looks amazing. Where did you get it from?'

He frowned and shook his head. 'The pizza oven in the garden.'

She raised her eyebrows. 'Oh. You made it?'

'Don't sound so surprised.'

She took a slice and bit the tip. The herby tomato sauce mixed with the flavours of the rest of the toppings in her mouth and she couldn't help groaning. She snapped her eyes open and found him staring at her with a grin on his face.

He licked his lips. 'Good, eh?'

She put a hand in front of her mouth and nodded. 'Really, *really* good,' she replied around the mouthful of food.

'You were brave to wear a white shirt though.' He laughed as sauce dripped down her front.

'Oh bugger! Dammit.'

Mitch grabbed a damp cloth from by the sink and passed it over. 'You'll have to wash it tonight or you'll have a stain.'

She nodded as she dabbed at the red splodge and inwardly cursed herself. How much more could she do to make herself look ridiculous?

They ate in silence for a while and Ruby sipped at the Chianti. She felt herself relaxing and the tension that had tightened her shoulders before she came downstairs began to ebb away.

'So, you're clearly Scottish but speak fluent Italian. How come?' she eventually asked.

'My dad is Scottish, and my mum is from Sicily. They met when my dad was on a business trip on the island. I grew up mainly in Scotland, but my mum made sure I knew Italian because we spent our summers over here.'

'Oh wow. You must've loved that. Has the house been in your family long?'

He nodded. 'Aye, although it wasn't always this big. It's been extended over the years.'

'Do you have brothers and sisters?'

'I did. I had a sister, but she... erm...' He cleared his throat. 'She passed away when I was a teenager.'

Ruby gasped and covered the damp patch of fabric over her heart. 'Oh no, I'm so sorry.'

He nodded and took a large gulp of his drink. 'Aye, thanks. It was a long time ago. When she passed away, the property was neglected. My folks couldn't bear to come over.'

Silence fell between them again and Ruby struggled to find something to say, anything that would lift the heavy cloud that had descended upon them.

Finally, Mitch spoke again. 'So, you're escaping the public just now, eh?'

She paused and placed her slice of pizza back on her plate. 'I'm guessing you know the whys and wherefores,' she said, without making eye contact.

He shrugged. 'I don't judge folk.'

'There's nothing to judge. I didn't do anything wrong. I was hacked.'

He widened his eyes. 'Shit, that's bad. You see that's why I avoid social media like the plague.'

She nodded. 'I can completely understand that after what I've been through recently.'

'Aye, no one needs to know what I've had for my breakfast, or that I've been shopping for new shoes.' He chuckled.

She smiled. 'No, true. But for me it was a lifeline. It can be quite a lonely life being famous. You're very limited to where you can go and with whom. Online I had so many friends. So many people who I thought had my back, others in the business. We didn't get to meet often, but just knowing there was someone there who I could chat to about things, and they'd under-stand, you know? People were so kind. It made me feel less lonely. Then it all went wrong, and I was dropped like a hot brick, regardless of whether I was innocent or not. It was all so fast I almost got whiplash.'

Mitch sucked air in through his teeth. 'Ouch. Sounds shitty.'

'It was. It still is.' She swallowed hard. 'It's difficult not knowing who I can trust any more.'

Silence fell again.

Nervously, she broached the subject that had been intriguing her. 'Have you had issues before? I mean, the security at the gate is pretty intense.'

His cheeks coloured. 'Erm... I'm afraid that's all for you. It was a guest house before. But I was told there had been threats to harm you physically, so it was necessary. They've assured me it will all be put back to normal once this is over for you.'

Ruby's heart sank; he had sacrificed so much for someone he didn't even know. 'Why on earth did you let me come here?' she asked with a deep sigh and a shake of her head.

He shrugged. 'I was told that a friend of a friend was in danger and needed a place to crash for a while.'

'Did you know who I was?'

He lifted his chin and focused his eyes on her directly. 'Do you mean did I know you were a famous Hollywood actress?'

She had begun to hate that phrase recently. It had gone from being something to be proud of to something that stirred up a hornet's nest of regret in her stomach. 'Yes.'

His mouth turned up into almost sardonic grin. 'How could I *not* know who you are, Ruby Locke?'

'Not everyone does. Your neighbour doesn't.'

Mitch scrunched his brow momentarily, appearing a little confused. He paused and shook his head. 'Neighbour?' Then he laughed with a look of incredulity in his eyes. 'And I'm guessing he's faking that.'

She shook her head. 'Absolutely not. He's just not a movie fan.'

He raised one eyebrow and tilted his head. 'I'm not an athletics fan, but I know who Mo Farah is.'

She narrowed her eyes. 'Are you always this obtuse to your house guests?' she asked with a tilt of her head and a smile.

He laughed. 'I don't usually host people.'

She scoffed but in good nature. 'Figures.'

His smile faltered. 'Seriously though, Ruby, if someone is saying they don't know who you are, I'd be careful. It sounds suss to me. I mean, I don't watch every single movie that comes out, but I know the most famous stars. And let's face it, you're on that list.'

She sighed. 'Thank you for your concern, but he seems genuine and kind. I'm sure I'll be fine.'

Mitch shook his head and sighed. 'Aye, I hope you're right.'

13

The days were passing painfully slowly and word from the US about the hacking wasn't forthcoming, despite her numerous calls to Valerie, who seemed to be fobbing her off with excuses. She didn't understand what the delay was, but it was driving her mad. Surely it should've been dealt with by now? And the more she thought about the changes Mitch had been willing to make to his home, the more guilty she felt. She wanted to be able to free him from it all. Despite their less than perfect initial interactions, he seemed like a nice man, and this was supposed to be a place filled with good memories for him. The death of his sister aside, he had spent so many happy times here with his family and she felt she was intruding and marring those wonderful recollections.

Early on, just after the hacking and subsequent break-up, Ruby had received a spate of calls from seemingly well-intentioned friends in the movie business, offering their condolences on her split with Tyler, or wanting to share gossip about him – in which she had no interest – everything had gone quiet. It was shocking how quickly she had become persona non grata.

Her days were being spent reading outside at the little bistro table, with Nero at her feet, or on her lap, enjoying the scent of the lemon trees as it wafted in the ever-warming air. Spring was on its way and she longed to be on the beach with Nero and her book instead. But as much as she loved books sometimes even reading became boring.

She was ten days into her period of hiding and Nero had become quite attached to her. Often, she would walk around the gardens with him or play fetch with his ball as Jacopo watched, laughing and shouting encouragingly to his dog in Italian. With Jacopo's permission, she had even taken to letting the Yorkie sleep at the foot of her bed, where he curled up into a tiny ball and snored. Even though she craved some kind of normality, she knew it would be hard saying goodbye to the little dog.

She chatted on the phone and had text conversations with Clark, and he had invited her for coffee over and over, but she hadn't plucked up the courage to visit him again after the drama of last time. More than anything, she wanted to leave the confines of the gardens and explore, and the more time passed, the more determined she became, regardless of Valerie's protestations.

Her boredom was made worse by the fact that Kitty had gone away for a few days' break. She'd told Ruby she should still contact her to chat, but Ruby was determined to let her best friend have the much-deserved, uninterrupted time with her family.

She watched the news on TV, but there were still stories about her, every so often, and even though she couldn't understand what was being said, she guessed from the tone that her name was still mud and she was discovering how well mud sticks. Sometimes she missed the constant buzzing of her phone, the speedy catch-up with what was going on in the world via social media, but then she remembered why she was avoiding it and why she had deactivated her accounts. Although it was difficult going 'cold turkey', it wasn't worth the stress to reactivate her accounts, even if she could access Wi-Fi. She knew there was probably Wi-Fi if she asked, but she didn't want to open that can of worms – her willpower to stay offline would crash and burn if it was easy to access.

Mitch was busy working on the house with a couple of older builders, and when he wasn't busy doing that he disappeared in his car. Thankfully, he asked if she needed anything and she had given him shopping lists of toiletries and magazines, even though she'd much rather be able to go by herself. Perhaps she was being incredibly conceited in thinking that she would be so well known over here? And perhaps Valerie was being over-cautious?

It was the beginning of March and the sun was high in the cloudless sky above, deceptive considering she could feel the chill of the temperature outside through the opening of the covered terrace. Clark had texted to invite her over but had suggested she leave Nero at home on this occasion. She hadn't answered, figuring she needed to speak to the security guards first.

Ruby wandered down to the gatehouse and found Jacopo leaning against the wall tossing the ball for his dog. Her little canine friend ran to her and jumped into her arms, giving excited yips.

She nuzzled his fur. 'Hello, boy, I've missed you. Yes, I have,' she told him.

Jacopo watched with a smile on his face. 'I can help you with something?' he asked.

Coyly, she nibbled her lip for a moment and placed Nero back on his four paws. 'I'd like to go for a walk. Outside the gardens, I mean.'

He held up his finger and shook his head as he opened his mouth to clearly dispute her request.

'Before you say no, I only want to walk to the next property. I... I made a friend there. I'd like to visit. To get out for a little while. You and Nero can escort me there if you wish.' She pleaded at him with her expression and clutched her hands to her chest. She imagined she looked like the cat from the *Puss in Boots* animation but hoped it tugged at his heartstrings sufficiently for him to acquiesce. 'I'm so bored, Jacopo, and I feel like a prisoner here. I promise I won't stay away long. You can even come and collect me.'

He rubbed the back of his neck and cringed. 'I don't think this is a good idea to do. I don't think—'

'Don't think about it! I'll take full responsibility... erm... mea culpa.' She grinned, feeling proud of herself for saying something that she knew the meaning of *and* something that sounded *kind* of Italian.

He smirked. 'This is *Latin*. I'm Italian.'

Her imaginary pride-filled balloon deflated. 'Oh...'

He sighed and stared at her for what felt like an age. The crease in his brow was deeper than usual and she was expecting him to tell her to go back into the house. Eventually he wagged his pointed finger at her, like a chastising parent. 'I go with you and I bring you back. Sì?'

Her smile widened. 'Yes! Yes, that's great!' Without thinking, she lurched at the burly man and hugged him. 'Thank you, Jacopo. Erm... grazie, grazie, grazie.'

He laughed. 'This is better Italian.'

He grabbed his gun and his jacket, collected his phone and Nero's lead from the desktop and, once Nero was secured, he opened the gate. She almost skipped through as he held it open for her, feeling like Nero wasn't the only puppy on a walk, and tried her best not to trot along the road, letting her small taste of freedom get the better of her.

They walked in silence and the shelter of the high walls shielded them from the brightness of the sun. When they arrived at the tall, wrought-iron gates to Clark's property, she stopped.

'We're here. I'll just buzz him.' She pressed the silver button on the panel by the gate.

'Hello?'

'Oh, hi Clark. It's Rebecca, your neighbour.'

He paused. 'Rebe— oh yeah, of course, come on in!'

A buzzer sounded and the gate slowly opened, fully revealing the beautiful gardens and the house beyond.

Jacopo watched her as she stepped inside and Nero whined, clearly unhappy to be left out of the visit. 'I will be back in two hours.'

She gave him a sweet smile. 'Thank you, Jacopo. See you later, Nero!'

Clark came walking out of the house rubbing his hair with a towel. 'Hey, hi. How are you?' he asked as he kissed her on both cheeks. He smelled of fresh pine and tea tree. 'Sorry I sounded so vague back there. You didn't reply to my message and I fell asleep on the patio so I showered to wake myself up.'

She cringed. 'Sorry, I should've replied. I can go if—'

He shook his head and frowned. 'No! No absolutely not. Can I get you a drink?'

She smiled, relieved that he didn't want her to leave. 'Just water, thanks.'

'Great. Take a seat on the patio and I'll be right out. It really is good to see you.' He gave her a handsome smile before retreating indoors.

She took a seat under the cover of the shade and admired the brightly coloured flora and fauna of his well-manicured garden. Even though it was only early spring, the plants were vibrant and cared for. He clearly loved his garden, just her like her mum. A pang of homesickness hit her again and she chewed the inside of her cheek to abate the tears that were stinging at her eyes.

He returned carrying two glasses of water complete with slices of lemon. 'I was thinking, maybe we should head out for a late lunch or early dinner. There's a great little place down in Cefalù. They do the best Pasta alla Norma you've ever tasted; I promise you. Aubergines, fresh basil and cilantro, parmesan. Bellisima. What do you say?'

Ruby cringed. 'Oh... I'm not so sure I can go to—'

'I have a small motorcycle and spare helmet. It's not a long drive.'

'It's not that... it's just...' She wondered how much she could divulge without getting into a tangled web of lies that would eventually string her up. 'I'm... I have to be careful about being seen.' Her mind was whirring so fast she wondered how there was no steam erupting from her ears.

He leaned closer and lowered his voice. 'Rebecca, you're a real mystery. Tell me, are you in witness protection or something?' Concern etched his features.

Her cheeks blazed, but he had given her a perfect excuse. One she wished she'd thought of herself. She nodded vehemently. 'Yes. Yes, that's right. Witness protection. I can't say any more than that, I'm afraid.'

He held up his hands. 'No need. I completely understand. But if it's any consolation, the restaurant in Cefalù is mainly where the locals eat, so you're not likely to run into anyone who would know you.'

The thought of eating out at a proper restaurant filled her with nervous excitement. It would be a real test of her disguise, but she was so tempted. 'My... erm friend is collecting me in a couple of hours, so we'd need to be quick.'

He beamed at her. 'I'll go grab the keys.'

He disappeared again and she sipped at her water, letting the icy liquid calm the raging fire of anxiety that had begun to fill her veins. Was this a gigantic mistake that she would soon regret? Could someone be watching her here or was it all a little far-fetched to the point of it being a movie plot? Oh, the irony.

Clark appeared once more from the back of the property with a black, 250cc bike and two silver helmets, one of which he handed to her.

A realisation struck her. 'Oh dammit, I only have my phone, not my purse.'

He grinned as he pulled his helmet down over his ears. 'My treat.'

He was so lovely, his texts had kept her going and she was grateful to have met such a friendly guy. Not to mention handsome – not drop-dead, panty-melting gorgeous, but nice-looking. Perhaps he could change her view of the male species after all. 'That's very kind of you.'

Once seated behind him on the bike, she wrapped her arms around his waist, and they set off for the small, coastal city she had been driven through on her arrival. The journey wasn't long and took them through small hamlets nestled into the slopes of what she guessed could've once been a volcano. The greens of the vegetation and the golden tones of the stone buildings they passed were incredibly vibrant and the sky overhead was cloudless and azure blue. The rush of air, as they travelled at speed, was chilly against her skin and on occasions took her breath away, but the ride was exhilarating. Freeing. She could feel the toned muscles of Clark's stomach beneath her hands and several thoughts entered her head that she dismissed immediately. *No romance*, she reminded herself.

Ever the gentleman, Clark checked several times that she was okay and when he eventually pulled to a stop down a narrow side street, he helped her off the bike. They walked along the cobbles until they opened out into a paved square where an imposing, stone, Norman-style cathedral stood guard at one end atop a flight of stone steps.

'This is the Piazza del Duomo,' Clark said with a flourish of his hands. 'It took over a hundred years to build the cathedral. Can you imagine starting to build something that wouldn't be finished in your own lifetime?' It was a rhetorical question, and he shook his head in awe. 'Talk about a labour of love.'

'It's such a beautiful place,' Ruby said with a sigh as she soaked up the buzz of the afternoon atmosphere, in awe of her stunning surroundings. The lilt of Italian speaking voices and music floated through the air, along with the clink of cutlery and wine glasses, and the sweet scent of the fresh flowers that adorned every table. It felt so wonderful to be out in the *real world* and exploring a brand-new place. She closed her eyes for a moment and inhaled, committing everything to memory.

'It sure is. Now there's a little market at the other side of the square, do you want to look there first?'

Excitement washed over her, and goosebumps rose on her skin. 'Ooh, yes please!'

The walls of the buildings created a little microclimate and the sun warmed Ruby's skin as they wandered over to the stalls. All at once, she was hit by myriad aromas and sights. People were filling wicker baskets with produce and chatting to the vendors, and the sound of laughter warmed her heart. Fresh fruit and vegetables filled one stall; the biggest oranges Ruby had ever seen. She picked one up and inhaled the aromatic, citrus fragrance which made her mouth water.

Clark took the fruit from her and picked up another. 'Due per favore,' he told the stallholder and handed over some cash. Once they were paid for, he told Ruby, 'These are for you. I'll put them in my backpack.'

'Thank you, that's so kind.'

They passed stalls selling fresh fish, bread, local artwork and clothing. Clark stopped at a stall selling brightly coloured summer scarves. He picked up a violet-coloured one with a vivid flower print and wrapped it around her neck. 'Perfect,' he told her as he handed the money over to the stallholder. Ruby gasped. 'Oh, no, no, honestly you don't need to—'

'I insist. Now, come on, I believe I promised you the best Pasta alla Norma you'd ever tasted.' He took her hand and led her towards a pretty restaurant with tables set outside. Red cloths wafted lightly under cream-coloured umbrellas and Clark pulled out a chair for her.

'Actually, I don't have anything to compare it to. I've never actually tried Pasta alla Norma,' she admitted with a giggle. A lightness had washed over her, a sense of freedom and serenity had replaced the anxiety she had been feeling.

'Well, I can assure you, you're in for a treat.' A waiter approached the table and Clark spoke. 'Ciao. Potrei ordinare due paste alla norma e una bottiglia di pinot grigiot, per favore?'

The waiter jotted the order on his pad and, with a smile and a nod, walked away.

Ruby was silently impressed with his accent and his knowledge of the language. What was it about a handsome man with language skills that attracted her so much?

She glanced around nervously but was relieved to find that no one was paying the slightest bit of attention to her; apart from Clark whose gaze was fixed on her. He opened his mouth but closed it and shook his head.

She eyed him inquisitively. 'What? You looked like you were going to say something.'

He smiled and rubbed at his chin. 'I was going to ask you about yourself, but in light of your recent admission, I don't suppose there's anything you can tell me.'

The waiter returned with a jug of water, two glasses, a pot of olives and a jar of breadsticks.

Guilt niggled at her insides and Ruby picked up a breadstick. 'I love flowers, my favourites are red roses, clichéd but true. I love music... ah, but I already told you that.' She tapped her chin, trying to filter out truths that she could set free without consequence. 'I love to dance. I studied it as a child and then when I was older too.' She refrained from mentioning her performing arts studies for fear of giving away too much. 'It was my first love, before... Anyway, it was all a long time ago now.' She giggled and her face warmed a little.

Clark folded his arms across his chest. He nodded a little too conspiratorially for Ruby's liking. 'Okay, noted.'

Clark imparted a little more about his life and his record store. When he talked about things he was passionate about his face lit up, his eyes crinkling at the corners, and Ruby felt a little sad that they hadn't met under different circumstances. What he knew of her was a mixture of truth and fabrication, and she knew that most people would shy away from someone who hadn't been truthful from the start.

The waiter delivered their food and, after Clark had tasted the wine, he poured two generous glasses. Clark beckoned the waiter and whispered something to him before he left.

'You must have built up some good friendships over here in the years you've been coming,' Ruby said as she took her first mouthful of food.

Clark blushed a little. 'Oh... no, not really. We're quite a private family... well, we were. And now I'm more concerned with relaxing when I come over.' He shrugged. 'Anyway, what do you think?' He gestured towards her plate.

'Absolutely delicious. And I'm sure if I had tried the dish before, this would be the best by far.' She smiled.

He nodded and grinned. 'Right? I knew you'd love it.'

'So, do you know Mitch who owns the property next door that I'm staying in? The house has been in his family a long while. His parents may have known yours.'

Clark chewed for what felt like a long time. 'To be honest, I don't really know anyone. Like I said, we've always been a very private family.' He swallowed and took a large gulp of his wine. It was evident he felt uncomfortable talking about his past, so she decided not to pursue the matter further. He continued, 'So, what do you do for hobbies?'

Great, a question I can answer. 'Oh, well... I love reading. I think I got the passion from my mum. She's an avid reader, although she can have several books on the go at once. I prefer to take my time with one book. I don't think I'd cope with the flitting around. I think I'd get the characters mixed up in my head.' She laughed.

'I love to read too. What are your favourite genres? For me it's crime novels. I love a good whodunnit.'

She felt her cheeks warming. 'I'm a romance reader. There's nothing nicer than a love story with a happy ever after. But my favourites are the classics. *Wuthering Heights. Rebecca*—'

'Ooh, your namesake! Is that where your mom got your name from?'

For a moment, confusion clouded her mind until she realised what he meant. Of course, he knew her as *Rebecca* not Ruby. 'Oh yes, maybe it was.' She took a large mouthful of wine.

They finished their meal and talked about lots of very general things – something they were both more comfortable with. Clark hardly touched his wine, preferring to drink the water instead.

Once their plates had been cleared, a man appeared beside their table playing a violin. Ruby immediately recognised the tune as 'Isn't She Lovely' by Stevie Wonder and she lifted her chin to find Clark grinning at her.

'May I have the pleasure of this dance, Rebecca?' he asked, holding out his hand.

She smiled widely and shook her head. 'Did you do this?'

He nodded.

'I can't believe it!' She laughed as she took his hand and he led her to the small space between the tables.

As the talented violinist played, Clark swayed her to the music, much to the delight of the other afternoon patrons. Clark spun her around and she couldn't help giggling. The combination of sunshine, wine and dancing had made her forget her troubles for a while.

Once the piece ended, the place erupted in applause.

As they went to retake their seats, Ruby glanced at her wristwatch and gasped. 'Oh no! I need to get back!'

Clark huffed, but she could see by his bright expression that it was in good nature. 'It's like dating Cinderella.' His use of the word *dating* took her a little by surprise but didn't exactly bother her. He took her hand. 'Come on, let's get you home before the search party descends.'

14

They had just dismounted the bike back in Clark's grounds when Jacopo and Nero arrived. Ruby quickly thrust the spare helmet into Clark's hands and he handed her the oranges.

She lifted the edge of the scarf. 'Thank you for a lovely time, Clark. I love my scarf and will have the oranges for breakfast tomorrow. See you soon!' she called over her shoulder as she headed for the exit.

He waved and dutifully pressed the button to open the gate.

She smiled widely. 'Hi Jacopo. Thank you for coming to collect me.'

He eyed her suspiciously but chose to say nothing other than, 'Sì.'

She crouched and gave Nero a scratch behind his ears. 'Hello, my little friend.' The dog wagged his tail and jumped up to lick her chin.

Once back at Villa Vista Mare, Ruby spotted Mitch in a grubby T-shirt, on the roof with another man she didn't recognise. They appeared to be working on further repairs. As she stared up at the men, Mitch raised his hand in a wave, and she returned the gesture with a smile.

She made her way inside, followed closely by Nero, and up to her room. Tiredness had descended rather suddenly and although she'd missed a call from her parents, she flopped onto the bed and promptly fell asleep with the little dog curled into her side.

She was awoken sometime later by a knocking on her bedroom door.

When she opened her eyes into a night-filled room, she was quite shocked. *How long have I been asleep?*

She walked across the room and opened the door.

'Evening. Are you okay?' Mitch asked.

She tried to stifle a yawn but failed. 'I'm fine, thank you, why?'

'You've been up here ages and I got concerned when I couldn't hear you talking on your phone or anything.'

'Ah, sorry, yes. I think the wine just got to me, that's all.'

He nodded and leaned against the door jamb. 'I see your bodyguard is looking after you,' he said with a nod towards the snoring dog.'

Ruby giggled. 'Oh yes, woe betide anyone who dares to try and get in.' As if he knew he was being talked about, Nero awoke and lifted his head. He sneezed and rolled over onto his back, sticking his legs in the air.

'There's not many bodyguards that behave like that,' Mitch said with a chuckle and Ruby laughed. 'Anyway, Jaco said he escorted you along to the next property.'

Wondering why he was being so inquisitive, she folded her arms across her chest. 'That's right. I've made friends with your neighbour, Clark. Lovely chap. Very friendly.' She cocked her head at him and awaited his reaction.

He scrunched his brow. 'Right... right. How long is he here for? Clark, I mean.'

She stared at him with a frown. 'I presume he'll be here a while. It's his house after all. Why?'

He shrugged. 'No reason. I just didn't know I had "neighbours", that's all.' His use of air quotes annoyed her.

'Well, of course you do. His parents have owned the place for years.'

His eyebrows raised. 'Is that right?' He rubbed at the stubble on his chin. 'Funny, it's been a holiday rental, or some kind of Airbnb, for as long as I can remember.'

She huffed, feeling a little tired of his silent insinuations. 'I think you'll find you're mistaken. Clark and his family used to come out here during the summer.' She lifted her chin. 'But they're quite a private family.'

He chewed the inside of his cheek for a moment. 'Right. Okay... well, I've made gnocchi alla Sorrentina if you fancy it. There's plenty. And the light bulb in the kitchen has been replaced, no need for candles.' She saw a flash of a smile when he said that.

She hadn't the heart to tell him she'd eaten a large lunch. 'Oh, lovely, thank you. I'll stick a black top on and be down in a sec.' She smiled in return and was happy to see his mouth fully turn up at the corners.

'Good plan. See you down there. I'll take your friend back to his owner, eh?'

Ruby nodded.

'Nerone, forza ragazzo!' Nero jumped from the bed and scuttled off after Mitch.

* * *

The food smelled amazing and even though she had eaten quite heartily only a few hours earlier, her stomach grumbled and gurgled in anticipation. She took her seat at the table as Mitch served the meal.

'So, what is gnocchi alla Sorrentina?'

He took his seat opposite her. 'It's potato gnocchi baked in a tomato sauce and topped with mozzarella and fresh basil. Really tasty. Vegetarian too.'

'That sounds lovely, and it smells incredible.' He had piled rather too much on her plate and she huffed. 'Although I probably won't be able to eat much. I had a big lunch with Clark.' She cringed.

Mitch nodded. 'So, what else do you know about Clark then?' he asked as they tucked in.

Ruby chewed her first mouthful as she pondered how much, if anything, to divulge, but once again her tastebuds were brought to life by the tantalising flavours of the fresh ingredients, and she forgot to answer. He could certainly cook. Remembering he had asked her a question, she rolled her eyes. 'Plenty. I know plenty about him.' She changed the subject. 'Sicily is beautiful. I can see why so many people fall in love with the place. I bet it's incredible in summer.' As if he took the hint, Mitch told her about the beaches and clear turquoise seas situated not so far away, and as she relished the delectable meal before her, delighting in the fragrance of the fresh basil and the crisp fruitiness of the wine, she relaxed into the pleasant conversation.

Before too long, however, Mitch managed to bring them back to her new friend. 'I take it you haven't revealed your true identity? To Clark, I mean. And he is still pleading ignorance?'

Ruby placed her fork down. 'Look, I know you don't really know me, so forgive me for my bluntness, but I'm not some stupid teenager who gives her personal information out to all and sundry, and he hasn't called the newspapers, so...'

Mitch chewed thoughtfully. 'I'll take that as a no then.'

She huffed.

He took a swig of wine and eyed her with apparent scepticism. 'I know you think I'm poking my nose in where it's not welcome—'

'Or needed.'

He sighed. 'Or needed. But I'm just a wee bit bothered by this guy who's acting like he doesn't know who you are and is claiming to have owned the property for so long.'

Anger rose up like a fire from her stomach. 'What do you mean *claiming*?'

Mitch placed his glass down and paused before speaking. 'This home has been in my family for ages, as you already know, and I think I would know if someone was in the same position next door.'

She shook her head and scowled at him. 'It's not like you live in a semi-detached on an estate in England... or Scotland. And you said yourself that you didn't come over often after your sister passed away, so who's to say they didn't purchase the house then? Look, I appreciate you hosting me, I really do, but this big brother act isn't necessary. Anyone would think you were jealous or something.'

He laughed out rather too loudly and harshly. 'Jealous? Of what? Your money? I have plenty, thank you very much. Your "star status"?' *There are those bloody air quotes again.* 'I wouldn't thank you for it. And your apparent friendship with someone who could be a total psychopath, who you don't know from Adam? Cheers, but I think I'll stick to my status quo.'

She rolled her eyes so dramatically she almost fell from her chair. 'I think someone has been watching too many episodes of *Criminal Minds*.

May I remind you that I don't know *you* from Adam either. And, in any case, I'm quite capable of reading people. Clark is a kind-hearted, friendly man who loves music and just doesn't go to the cinema.' Her voice rose in both pitch and volume. 'And you shouldn't judge him when you know nothing about him.'

'Aye, well, neither do you!' Mitch shouted his reply, his face reddening.

As Ruby stood from the table, her nostrils flared and her skin burned with rage. Mitch stood too and stepped closer to her. There was something in his eyes that told her he was about to devour her. He clenched his jaw and swallowed hard as he stared down at her. Her insides flipped and the urge to throw herself at him was scarily overwhelming. She'd never met such a passionate, fiery man before and it worried her a little that she was attracted to it.

Needing to put some space between his heaving chest and her internal quivering sensations, she stepped back. 'Thank you for dinner. It was delicious,' she bellowed. 'But I think I will go to my room and read. That way I'm not subjected to the bloody Spanish Inquisition!'

She turned on her heel and marched from the kitchen and up the stairs, slamming her bedroom door behind her.

* * *

Ruby lay awake most of the night, tossing and turning, and playing the events of the last month over and over in her mind. She questioned everything now, and that made her feel uneasy and doubt her own judgement. What if Mitch was right? What if there was something amiss with Clark? But what if Mitch was the dodgy one and he was pointing out issues with Clark to cover his own deceptiveness? She longed, more than anything, to go home and see her parents. She hadn't returned their most recent call yet simply because hearing their voices and knowing how worried they would sound was already breaking her heart. Her life wasn't supposed to be this fraught. She was supposed to be happy; she *deserved* to be happy, didn't she?

The following morning, she felt bleary-eyed and down. She went downstairs to the kitchen to make a cup of tea, fearing coffee would only add to her building anxieties. Much to her chagrin, Mitch was there.

He turned when he heard her enter the room. 'Oh, hey. Are you okay? You look...' She was grateful he chose not to finish his sentence.

'I didn't sleep too well.' She hoped he would leave it at that; she didn't have the energy to argue.

He cleared his throat. 'Look, can we talk?' His brow was furrowed, and he hung his head a little, not quite making eye contact.

'If you're going to lecture me about my friends please don't. I honestly can't—'

He held up his hands. 'No, no, I promise that's not what I had in mind. Please, sit?' He gestured at the table.

Feeling sapped of anything resembling fight, she sat. He placed a mug of coffee in front of her and she hadn't the heart to tell him she didn't want it.

'Thanks. So, what do you want to talk about?'

He pursed his lips, stared at the table and then lifted his chin to address her directly. 'I owe you an apology. It seems all my conversations with you start that way.' He gave a small laugh, which she didn't reciprocate. His smile disappeared and he cleared his throat. 'I shouldn't try to stick my nose in your business. You're an adult. And you're no relation of mine. I think... I think I have this urge to protect you because of how badly you've been treated recently. I have to say, I don't follow your career avidly, but from what I *have* seen, you don't seem the type of person who would insult people on social media, so I one hundred per cent believe you weren't involved in what was put out there. My comments about Clark were unjustified. You were right. I don't know him. And I don't know every single person who lives around here. So, I erm... I know it's a wee bit twee, but I bought you some flowers for your room by way of apology.' He stood and walked to the other side of the kitchen, returning seconds later with a glass vase filled with fresh, brightly coloured blooms. His cheeks coloured as he held them out. 'I have no clue about flowers, so I hope you like them. I just gave the florist a figure and told her to do what she thought best.' He placed the vase on the table before an open-mouthed Ruby.

She recognised gentians, alstroemeria and purple calla lilies. The heady, sweet fragrance whisked her back to the days when she used to help her mum in the flower shop on a Saturday and she smiled as her eyes filled with tears. 'I don't know what to say. They're beautiful, thank you, Mitch.'

'You're welcome. I'm relieved that you like them. I literally have no clue what any of them are called, but they look pretty.'

She laughed and dabbed at her eyes. 'They do. They're lovely, thank you. You did well and this means such a lot. And apology accepted.' She sniffed and stood to hug him.

He squeezed her tight and she closed her eyes, inhaling his masculine, clean scent before pulling away awkwardly.

He exhaled and grinned as he sat down again. 'Phew. That's a relief. I was going to bake cookies, but I figured you might think I was trying to get rid of you.' He laughed again and his eyes lit up. He was an incredibly handsome man, if a little irritating at times.

'I adore flowers, so these are perfect. My mum is a florist and I miss fresh blooms.'

'Wow really? I thought you'd be overrun with the things being as famous as you are.'

She shook her head. 'Nope. It's all fancy gift bags with high-end make-up and jewellery these days.'

His eyes widened. 'Bloody hell, flowers are a bit crap then, eh?'

She laughed. 'Not at all. I prefer them, if I'm completely honest. There are only so many gold bangles a person can wear without toppling over.'

He laughed. 'Aye, fair enough.'

Whilst they were on speaking terms for a while, she decided she'd try and get to know him a little more. After all, with the lack of updates from the USA, she was likely to be in his house for aeons at this rate. 'How are the renovations going? I think I expected there to be more of you working on it, but you seem to be getting lots done. And it's a beautiful building.'

He smiled as if her appreciation of the place meant something to him. 'Thank you. Things are slow. I usually have a few local tradesmen here, but I paid them off for a while, under the circumstances. I didn't want you to be surrounded by loads of blokes you didn't know.'

She was shocked and humbled by his admission. 'That's so thoughtful of you. Thank you for doing that, but I hope it doesn't put your deadline back.'

He shook his head. 'There isn't one really. I don't usually have much time to work on it, but I've taken a step back from my other ventures to focus on it for a while. I needed the break anyway.'

'Is the property world so stressful?' she asked with genuine interest.

He rubbed at his chin. 'Not really. But life was getting that way.'

'I'm sorry to hear that.'

He sighed deeply and shrugged. 'Divorce will do that to you, I suppose. One of the most stressful things you can do besides weddings and property, ironically.' He laughed this time.

She didn't quite know what to say in response. 'Indeed, so I've heard. Maybe it's a good thing I'm no longer getting married.'

'Aye, sorry to hear what happened to you there too. You've had a lot of shit to deal with.'

'As have you. I'm sorry things didn't work out for you and your wife.'

He smiled again, but this time it was tinged with sadness. 'Nah, it's all good. We're still on speaking terms. It just turned out I was lacking in the breast and vagina department, not a lot I could do about that.'

Ruby widened her eyes and made an O with her mouth. 'I... erm...'

He seemed amused by her reaction. 'Hey, it's fine. I'm over it. We're friends and the woman she's with is kind of okay too.' He scrunched his brow. 'In fact, I think you know her?'

Ruby crumpled her brow. 'I do?'

'Aye, she's a journo for the New York Star. She's actually the reason you're staying here.'

Ruby gasped. 'Not Veronica Lucas?'

He nodded. 'That's her. My wife, Genevieve, met her at some swanky event I couldn't be arsed to attend and... the rest...' He shrugged again.

'Bloody hell. I had no idea. In fact, I'm floored. Veronica and I really butted heads at the start of my career because she made advances to Tyler when he and I started dating. Well, so he said, anyway. I had no idea she was bisexual... but why would I?'

'I had no idea about Gen being gay either. Turns out she was cajoled into marrying me by her folks. They weren't very accepting of her sexuality, and I was a successful businessman, so I suppose I fit their ideal. I felt for the poor lass once I'd got past my own wounded pride.'

Ruby was dumbfounded but at the same time wondered if the rift between her and her supposed nemesis had been all in her head, or at least put there by her ex. Tyler often talked about Veronica if they had been at events together, and now she looked back on it he did seem to enjoy watching her squirm when he told her how they'd danced together and shared a cab home. *Bloody shithead. He was deliberately trying to make me jealous.*

Mitch clapped his hands together, making her jump. 'Right, that's enough about my crappy love life. Let's change the subject, eh?'

She nodded in vehement agreement. 'Absolutely, mine too. So, tell me more about your plans for the house? When are you going to reinstate the pool?'

His smile once again disappeared, and he glanced at his watch. 'Oh, dammit, I've just realised, I need to go. Got some supplies to pick up in Palermo. Need anything?'

'Erm... no, thank you... but...'

'Okay, great. See you later.' And with that he stood and dashed from the room and subsequently out of the house.

Ruby was once again confused and perturbed by him. 'Thanks again for the flowers!' she shouted and then mumbled, 'I thought this chatty version of you was too good to be true.'

15

Ruby sat on the covered terrace, where she had discovered the signal was better, holding her phone to her ear.

'Hi, love! It's good to hear from you. Me and your dad were so worried. How are you doing?'

The sound of her mum's voice made her chest tighten. 'I'm not too bad, Mum. Just trying to get on with things, you know?'

'It's all you can do. Have you heard anything from Valerie in New York? Surely she has sorted it all out by now?'

Ruby sighed deeply. 'Sadly not. But she says they're working on it.'

'I just can't believe people think so badly of you. Why can't they see through the lies?' Her mum sounded on the verge of tears.

'That's social media for you. You make one small mistake, or in my case someone makes it on your behalf, and it's out there forever. Nothing on the internet can be completely erased. And I suspect that even if they do clear my name, I may be seen differently by people who choose to still think the worst of me.'

'I just wish we could do something. Or you could come home.' Her mum's voice wavered.

Ruby's eyes stung and she fought to sound calmer than she felt. 'Me too, Mum.' She took a deep breath. 'But the house I'm staying in is beautiful. So, it could be worse. I'm surrounded by blue skies and trees... Oh, and I've made a new friend.'

'Oh? Who's that then?'

'My neighbour. Well, when I say neighbour, he lives around half a mile along the road. But he's really nice. His name is Clark. We've chatted a lot and he took me out for lunch into Cefalù. It's nice to have someone to talk to.'

There was a pregnant pause. 'Does he know who you are? I just worry, that's all. I don't want people taking advantage of you.'

Ruby forced a laugh. 'He hasn't a clue. I feel a bit mean, to be honest. He thinks I'm in witness protection, so he knows I can't really talk about certain things. He's more of a music buff than a movie fan so he doesn't keep up with red carpet things. It's been good to have a small sense of normality, even if it won't last forever.'

Her mother sighed. 'That's nice. You need friends just now. But be careful, sweetheart. I do worry so very much.'

Ruby smiled and imagined her mum's face crumpled with concern. 'I know you do. But there's nothing to worry about, honestly. Anyway, tell me what weddings you've got coming up. Anyone I know?'

* * *

Later on, Ruby decided it must be her turn to make dinner. Mitch was still out so she would need to make something that could be warmed up in case he didn't return until late. She riffled through the cupboards and the fridge, looking for ingredients. Finding everything she needed to make a vegetarian lasagna, she set about preparing the meal.

It was just after seven in the evening when Mitch arrived home and she met him at the door. 'Hey, I've cooked and it's ready if you're hungry.'

He inhaled and smiled. 'Mmm, it smells great. Thanks for doing that,' he said breezily as he kicked off his boots. 'I'll grab a bottle of wine from the cellar.'

She widened her eyes. 'You have a wine cellar?'

He frowned and held out his hands. 'What good Italian host doesn't? Come on, I'll show you.' He headed along the corridor and opened a door that she hadn't noticed before, probably because it blended into the panelling. He flicked a switch, and a set of steps came into view, descending into a stone basement. Cool air floated upwards and made goosebumps rise on her arms. Mitch walked down, and she followed until she was in a room surrounded by rack upon rack of dusty bottles.

She gazed around in wonder. 'Blimey, you weren't kidding. This is like something from one of my movie sets.'

He gave a small laugh. 'Aye, it's taken a while to build up the stock and it's nowhere near full. But I do like my wine.'

She ran her fingertips along a bottle, leaving a clean trail through the dust in her wake. 'So I see. There must be hundreds of pounds worth down here.'

He cringed. 'More like tens of thousands of euros.'

'Wow! Shouldn't you save it for special occasions then? Surely dinner on a Tuesday with me isn't that special?'

He grinned. 'Are you fishing for compliments? And by the way, it's Wednesday.'

She tilted her head and eyed him with annoyance. 'Really?'

He held out his hands. 'For sure. Yesterday was definitely Tuesday.'

She whacked him playfully. 'You know what I mean.'

He rubbed his arm, feigning injury. 'Hey! And in answer to your *non-compliment-fishing-question*, I think a good wine is a nice accompaniment to any meal. Doesn't matter what day it is. If someone has gone to the effort of cooking, why not drink something with it that's worth drinking?'

'Okay, I'll let you off. So... which one are we having?'

'Hmm... I think a nice, crisp Gavi. It's Italian, of course. From the north-west of the country. I think you'll like it. It's fresh and fruity.'

She giggled. 'Ooh, just like me.'

He chuckled and shook his head as he lifted a bottle from the rack and blew off the dust. 'I bet you didn't know that Gavi was one of the first Italian wines to become popular throughout the world, did you?'

Ruby cringed. 'Erm... I had never even heard of it before tonight.'

'Well, you're in for a treat. Come on.'

So, he was a handsome property mogul, a wealthy one at that, and he knew rather a lot about wine. Ruby felt rather embarrassed that she could probably fit her sommelier skills onto a grain of rice. She was more of a, 'Ooh, that's a pretty label' type – something she certainly wouldn't be imparting to her host.

Signor Miceli Adair was certainly full of surprises.

* * *

They ate the lasagna and made small talk for a while. The Gavi was delightful, and for the first time ever when drinking wine, she could taste the different flavours Mitch mentioned: lime, nectarine, apple. After being made aware of the origins of the wine, she savoured it, enjoying every crisp, delicate mouthful.

Eventually she said, 'Look, I'm sorry if I touched a nerve earlier when I was asking about the pool.'

Mitch swallowed hard. 'It's fine.'

'I know I can be nosey. I come from a long line of *nosey bints*, as my dad calls them.' She laughed as she remembered her dad's turn of phrase and imagined his playful grin as he said it. 'He used to say me, my mum and my Granny Dot were like the *Pontefract Gazette* when we got together. We knew all the weddings and all the ones that fell through as well as their reasons for doing so.' She smiled fondly. '"You're a right set of nosey bints", he'd say, laughing his head off at us. My granny used to tell him, "There's nothing wrong with keeping abreast of the local happenings, Roger. You never know when it might come in handy." Bless her. I could imagine her being a blogger or something if she was still alive. Or a gossip columnist. She'd give Veronica Lucas a run for her money, that's for sure.'

Mitch sat and listened, his chin resting on his hand and his elbow on the table. 'You speak so fondly of your family.'

She nodded and gave a small smile. 'I miss them. Being famous is mostly great, but it means separation from the people I love, and a lack of privacy. It can be hard.' A lump began to form in her throat. 'The worst thing for me was my granny's funeral. It was overrun with fans and that broke my heart, seeing as it was supposed to be about saying goodbye to one of the most important people in my family's life. But the movie I was in at the time had just been released and everyone knew who I was. Especially in my hometown, Pontefract. The funeral directors had suggested that I didn't attend due to the number of fans who had already descended. They feared people disrupting the sombre proceedings, which is fair enough, I suppose. But she was my granny. I couldn't not say goodbye.'

He shook his head, a look of solemnity on his face. 'I'm so sorry to hear that. It must have been awful. Losing someone you adored and then not getting to say goodbye privately.'

Ruby inhaled. 'It's fine. I can't really moan about fame. I chose the life... well, it kind of chose me, but I didn't refuse it. I was terrified my family would think I was selfish for attending, but they didn't at all.' She paused as she thought about the older woman who had helped to mould her as a child. 'Granny once told me, "By the time I pop my clogs, you'll be a famous dancer. And I'll be looking down from up there with your Grandad Ed, smiling and telling all the other dead folk, "That's my granddaughter and I'm so proud of her."' She laughed at her granny's choice of words. 'Turns out she was almost right. I'm famous, just not how she expected, I guess.'

Out of nowhere, Mitch blurted, 'I can't reinstate the pool because it's where my sister, Alessia, died.'

Ruby gasped and she felt the blood drain from her wine-warmed cheeks. She placed her hand over her heart. 'God, I'm so sorry,' she whispered.

He pulled his lips between his teeth. 'She was two years younger than me. Precocious wee thing.' He smiled fondly, but his eyes were filled with sorrow. 'The kind of girl that everyone just adored, me included. I was very protective and that's why it hurts so much. Why I blame myself, I suppose.' He inhaled a long shaking breath. 'I was sixteen and we were out here for the summer. Mum was making lunch and Dad was out in Cefalù buying milk. Lessi had asked me to play catch by the pool, but I was in a mood about...' He shook his head, 'Something stupid that I can't even remember, so I was in my room. Anyway, she tripped and fell, hit her head. My mum found her floating face down in the water. She'd already gone.' He swallowed hard and exhaled roughly.

Ruby covered her mouth. 'Oh, Mitch, I'm so, so sorry. That's... It's awful.' Her throat constricted and her lip trembled. 'But it wasn't your fault. You were just a kid. And you didn't cause it,' she insisted.

He nodded and swiped at moisture that had welled in his eyes. 'Aye, I know that now. But for such a long time I hated myself.' He paused and glanced around the room. 'Mum and Dad wanted to get rid of this place but... When I'm here, I can picture her running around. Giggling and dancing, you know? Even now. I can hear her voice, see her in the library, curled up in that old leather chair with her nose in a book. How could I let that go?' He sniffed. 'My folks hung onto it for as long as they could, but they eventually put the place up for sale a few years ago and I bought it. They weren't happy at first, but when we talked it through, they understood.' He shrugged as if it had been the most natural thing to do. 'I don't come here loads but when I do...'

Ruby reached across the table and placed her hand on his arm. 'I don't think I would want to let it go either.'

He cleared his throat and straightened his spine. 'So... now you know why I was so reluctant to talk about the pool.' He rubbed his hands over his face and huffed the air from his lungs once again. 'Jeez, I'm sorry to pile that on you. I've never told anyone about it. Not even my wife. There are so few people who know; just my folks and closest friends back home who knew her, so I don't really know why I mentioned it. I suppose I just heard you talking about your family and... it all just came out. It's not something I talk about. I don't tell people,' he repeated with a look of surprise. 'I'm so sorry. You must think I'm a muckle cry baby.'

She smiled. 'Well... I don't actually know what a *muckle* is, but I don't think you're a cry baby at all. Far from it, in fact. I feel... *honoured* that you shared something so personal. But I hope you didn't feel pressured into doing so.'

Mitch smiled that wide, heart-stoppingly handsome way he had and simply said with a shrug, 'Muckle just means huge.'

16

Three weeks into Ruby's stay and it was mid-March already. Mitch, just as he had promised, had stopped interfering in her budding friendship with Clark and things felt a little more relaxed. She was seeing a fun side to the serious property developer and being there with him was feeling less like a forced isolation.

Although she was enjoying her time at Villa Vista Mare, thanks in part to the rapidly improving weather and her little canine companion, Ruby was increasingly concerned at the lack of progress being made by Valerie. Phone calls with her agent had been turned around on Ruby, and she had been accused of being too impatient and told that she didn't understand the intricacies of finding the culprit whilst simultaneously trying to remove the sticking mud from her reputation. She felt thoroughly chastised and she mentioned this in conversation over a cup of tea with Mitch when he took a break from renovations.

He had listened with that clear expression of concern she had come to know. 'Look, I know someone who is... who could... Never mind.' He shook his head and continued to drink his tea.

Ruby tilted her head. 'What? What were you going to say?'

Mitch cringed. 'I know I tend to interfere, and we've been getting on so much better since I stopped all that so...' He shrugged.

Ruby placed her cup down and fixed him with a stern stare. 'Come on, Adair, out with it.'

He sat up straight and held up his hand. 'Okay, but there's no pressure. I have a good friend back on Skye who's a bit of a whizz with the old technology stuff. I could ask him to look into things for you, you know with Valerie not getting very far.'

She smiled. 'That's really kind of you. I appreciate it, really, I do. I just... I have to tread so carefully. I already made a mess of things once and I don't want to do that again. Valerie has my best interests at heart. And she's been in the business so long... I think I'll give her a little longer. I mean, I really have no clue about any of this stuff. I have to believe her experts do.'

Mitch nodded. 'Aye, no worries. But the offer's there, you know...'

She was incredibly grateful to him. 'Thank you.'

* * *

Ruby had visited Clark a couple more times with Nero, who continued to growl at her friend, and on the occasions when Nero was left at the villa, the pair had snuck into Cefalù for lunch and a dance again at one of the ristorantes in the square. They sat at the same secluded table each time, meaning Ruby could enjoy the ambience and relax. When she was with him, it almost felt like life was normal. Her deception preyed on her mind, however, and sometimes she drifted off into a melancholic trance, only to be tugged from it by the handsome American as he regaled her with funny stories from his record shop.

The last time she and Clark had gone for lunch, he had spun her around the makeshift dance floor like a professional and she was so swept up in the moment that when he pulled her close as the music ended, she didn't stop him when he lowered his face to hers and kissed her. She hadn't been kissed by anyone but Tyler for so long that the feeling of his lips against hers was alien. It wasn't unpleasant, but there was no spark of passion, no lust. Nothing. The fact made her sad. But she brushed the sadness aside, sure that perhaps she just wasn't ready *yet*.

He'd gazed into her eyes and rubbed his nose down the length of hers. 'I've wanted to do that since the first day we met.'

Unsure what to say, she'd mumbled, 'It was... it was lovely.' Inwardly, she'd berated herself for sounding so incredibly lame, but Clark had seemed delighted with her response.

Before they climbed onto the bike, she'd placed a hand on his arm. 'Clark, I don't want to rush things. Is that okay with you? I mean... I know it sounds so cliché, but I'm recovering from a break-up and I don't want to jump into another relationship without giving myself time to heal. I don't want to hurt you.'

He cupped her face in his palm and smiled. 'We go at your pace. You're worth the wait.'

His reply gave her some relief, but she couldn't help feeling guilty at her lack of desire for him. She hoped that it would build. After all, he was such a lovely man and it was rare to find someone who liked her for *her*, rather than her star status. Eventually, however, she would have to come clean and tell him the truth. She could only hope he wasn't angry when she did. But the time wasn't right. Not yet.

* * *

Ruby awoke early on a bright Thursday morning in the fourth week of March, showered and dressed in a long dress with a cosy wrap. Jacopo had promised to walk her down to Clark's again, but this time they were going to stay at his villa and sit in the garden for breakfast, then possibly lunch, so Nero was going to tag along.

Clark was dressed in board shorts and a loud shirt, with flip-flops on his feet. He looked like a character from a surfing movie but somehow it suited him.

When Jacopo left without taking the dog, Clark glanced down at Nero with a look of disappointment. 'Oh, you brought your little bodyguard,' he said with a small, forced laugh.

Ruby picked up Nero and waved a paw at Clark. 'I pwomis to behave, Mister Cwark,' she said in a silly voice that seemed to appease her friend.

He handed her a tall glass of freshly squeezed orange juice, complete with umbrella. 'You're looking mighty fine today, Rebecca.'

'Why thank you, Clark, you look rather handsome too. I like the surfer dude outfit,' she replied with a smile.

He did a three-sixty turn on the spot, his arms out wide. 'I had a feeling you'd like it.'

She sat at the outdoor dining table on the covered terrace and Clark went inside, returning moments later with a tray filled with pastries, fruit, juice and a bowl of scrambled eggs.

Nero sniffed the air and licked his lips and Ruby whispered, 'I'll sneak you something, shh!' before returning her attention to her host. 'Wow, you've gone to such a lot of effort, Clark. This looks amazing.'

'Thank you. And you're definitely worth the effort. Come on, eat.'

She selected a crumbly pastry and a handful of fresh grapes, placing them on her plate, and took a large mouthful of the juice. They chatted for a while about general things until Ruby eventually asked, 'So, you've never been married?'

'Sadly, no. I was in a long-term relationship but... she... erm... broke up with me. Apparently, I wasn't serious enough about us. I think the record store came between us.' He shrugged. 'I was heartbroken for a while but... well, you have to get on with living, don't you?'

'Absolutely.'

Much to her surprise, he continued. 'I had a few flings after that, but nothing stuck, you know? There was one girl I was really taken with. A musician. Incredible voice. Like melted chocolate. But she was used to dating rock stars – clearly something I'm *not*. We fooled around for a while, but this time it was *she* who wasn't serious enough.'

Ruby listened intently but couldn't help feeling she had heard this romance story before. It bore a distinct resemblance to the movie *High Fidelity* – Clark's *one* favourite film. She shrugged it off, deciding she was being utterly ridiculous. *After all, there are only so many ways people can fall in love and the fact that he owned a record store was bound to make me think that way.*

Ruby felt a little light-headed and presumed it must be the lack of sleep from the night before. She drank more juice in the hope it would perk her up. Once their meal was finished, Clark cleared the table and took the dishes into the house. 'You sit and relax; I won't be long. I'll make some fresh coffee.'

As he had suggested, she sat for a few minutes, but the feeling of wooziness seemed to worsen. Deciding that a splash of cold water would help, she stood and entered the house, closely followed by Nero, who stuck to her like a limpet. She wobbled a little as she walked.

'Clark? Can I use the bathroom?' It was the first time she had needed to do so in his house and hadn't a clue where it was.

He didn't reply but she figured he wouldn't mind. She walked barefoot, along the cool, marble tiled floor and opened a door.

'Broom closet. Best not pee in there,' she told Nero with a giggle. She walked further, passing photographs of people she didn't recognise. Quotes underneath each print said things like, '*Wonderful house, can't wait to return*' and '*Fabulous location, well equipped, just what we needed.*' Ruby found this a little odd but figured Clark probably had rented the house out in the past, as Mitch had suggested.

Another door led to a library devoid of books. Apart from the odd dog-eared novel, and a pile of generic DVDs, bare shelves lined the walls, which was something that saddened her. She found it strange seeing as Clark had professed a love for reading crime novels when there wasn't a single one of that genre on the shelves. The room appeared totally unloved, a little like an afterthought even, and that rattled her. Perhaps he only said he loved reading to find common ground with her?

Another door led to a room in total darkness; closed blinds blocked out almost every ray of daylight, so she fumbled around the wall for a light switch. It smelled clinical and she could make out a white shape on the opposite wall.

'This must be the bathroom,' she told Nero aloud, as she slipped her hand up the wall to her left, finally landing on a switch. 'You can stay out here though, eh?'

She flicked the switch and gasped, almost falling over in the process.

Before her stood the white object that she had mistaken for a bath. It was a desk, piled high with papers. Not only that, but the floor was stacked with magazines and newspapers too. But it was the noticeboard that caused the gasp and a cold chill to travel down her spine. Above the desk was a cork board completely filled with newspaper cuttings, magazine clippings, articles, photographs... all of *her*.

Against the will of the alarm bells ringing in her mind, she stepped closer, her hands shaking and her legs fighting to keep her upright. There was a laptop open on the desk with her face as the screensaver; a shot taken on a film shoot. She wiggled the mouse, and a document sprang to life, titled, '*My love affair with Ruby Locke*' by someone called Hamilton Harlow.

'Hamilton Harlow? What the f—'

Nero growled, alerting her to someone's presence.

'You're not supposed to be in here,' came a terse voice from directly behind her, causing her to almost jump out of her skin.

Nero continued to snarl as Ruby slowly turned to face Clark, her whole body juddering, sweat beading on her forehead.

'Clark, what the... What is all this?' Confusion clouded her mind and her words slurred. She watched his usually open expression darken substantially.

'Why did you go poking around, huh? Who said you could search my rooms?'

She held up her hands defensively. 'I... I just needed the loo. I wasn't being nosey. I didn't mean—'

Nero's growls became more aggressive.

'Oh, shut up, you dumbass dog,' he said with a stomp in the animal's direction before turning his attention back to Ruby. 'If you'd just asked me, I would've taken you to the bathroom. Why didn't you just ask?' he snapped through clenched teeth.

'I tried. I shouted you but... Clark, what is all this stuff?' She blinked in what felt like slow motion and the room began to spin. When he didn't speak, she continued, 'How long have you known who I am?'

He rolled his eyes. 'Come on, *Ruby*, how dumb do you think I am?'

Her nostrils flared and her stomach roiled. 'You've known all along. You've been lying to me,' she whispered.

He laughed. 'Oh, and you've been full of truths, huh, *Rebecca*?'

Her brow crumpled as nausea rose inside her and despite feeling weaker by the second, she fought to stay alert. 'You obviously know why I couldn't tell you who I was! You have all the bloody information in your stalker material!'

He closed in on her and tucked her hair behind her ear. 'Stalker? Me? I think you'll find I'm a professional journalist, sweetheart.'

She wobbled again and clutched his arm. 'You're a journalist? But... how...?'

He slipped his arm around her. 'Oh Ruby, you really are so very naïve, aren't you? Blindly putting trust in people you don't know. You're so desperate for attention, it's pathetic. But that's okay. I like pathetic.' He shrugged and smiled at her as if she was supposed to appreciate his comment. 'And thanks to my role, I have my sources. It didn't take long for me to find out where you were staying and then to find somewhere close by. I've always wanted to meet you, to interview you. But mostly to get close to you. I knew we could be good together once Tyler was out of the picture. And I didn't even need to do anything to make that happen. Bonus.'

She shook her head, but the room seemed to follow every movement. She shivered at the realisation he may have spiked her drink, but she tried to shrug off the thought. She was being paranoid... wasn't she? 'I should've realised with your stupid love story. You took the plot right out of *High Fidelity*.'

He laughed again. 'That's when you realised?' He reached out and brushed her hair aside and his smile disappeared. 'But we've had a good time together, haven't we? And I figured today was the day to take things to the next level. Announce to the world that we're a couple. Now that you're all nice and relaxed, I can do the interview properly and then I can put it out there and tell our story.' There was sincerity in his gaze, as if he genuinely didn't think he had done anything wrong and that they could actually be an item, and that terrified her. 'I can forgive the lies, Ruby. I've been watching you for years. I've *wanted* you for years, so when this opportunity arose, I grabbed it with both hands.'

Ignoring his words, she focused on not passing out, even more positive that the orange juice wasn't what it seemed. 'Do you even own a record store?'

Again, he laughed, and at that point she thought she might vomit. But perhaps that wouldn't be a bad thing. She needed to purge whatever he had spiked her drink with. She pushed him and tried to get past. She needed to get out of there. She felt foolish, angry, but most of all terrified.

He stopped her and gripped her arms, causing Nero to bark. He glanced down at the dog again and took a different tack. 'Hey, little fella, it's all good. Me and your mommy are just talking.'

Ruby's head was swimming, she was too warm, too weak, he was hurting her. 'I want to go. Please just let me go,' she slurred.

He shook his head slowly and fixed her with a rather sinister gaze. 'Come on, Ruby. Now we're both in possession of the facts, we can drop the act. Just be ourselves. I... I bought you a ring. You don't have to wear it right away but...'

She gasped. 'You're ill. You need help. You can't just drug people to get your own way,' she slurred.

'But I love you, Ruby. And I know you'll learn to love me. I... I didn't drug you, not really. It was just a little herbal thing to help you relax. You're always so uptight, watching over your shoulder, and I wanted to help. I can help you to get your career back on track. It doesn't matter to me what you said in those posts, I still love you, just like I told you when I sent the flowers.'

So he's H. H for Hamilton Harlow! Ruby shook involuntarily, but as if oblivious to her discomfort Clark, or rather *Hamilton*, continued.

'We can buy a house here in Sicily.' He pleaded at her with his eyes. 'Just kiss me and you'll remember how good we are together.'

He lowered his face to hers, but she wriggled in his hold. 'Get your hands off me! You need to let me go.'

He pushed her up against the door jamb, so the wood pressed into her back and she yelped. He didn't seem fazed by it. 'Come on, you need to give me a chance. I'm willing to do the same for you, even though you lied to me. You and I were getting to know each other, let's not spoil that. Why don't we pick up where we left off at the restaurant a few days ago? I'm sure your fans will be happy to see you moving on from Tyler Harrison. He didn't deserve you, I told you that in the flowers too.' He made to kiss her again.

Clearly sensing Ruby's distress, Nero lurched forward and clamped his mouth on Clark's leg, and he cried out. 'Get him off me!' But he still had a grip on Ruby's arms.

She summoned every ounce of strength she could muster, raised her knee sharply and connected with his groin. He dropped to his knees, holding his crotch, groaning in agony, his face beet red.

He made gurgling, pain-filled noises but managed to choke out, 'You bitch! I gave you a chance to be happy, but I'm going to ruin you!'

Nero released his hold on the man's leg and went scuttling for the door, barking as he ran.

Adrenaline kicked in and she followed the dog and yanked the door open. Her heart was pounding at her ribs and she almost tripped as she lurched for her shoes by the chair where she had been seated. Nero yapped as if telling her to hurry, but her head was filled with cotton wool and everything seemed to have slowed down. She gulped in fresh air, picked up her belongings and ran for the gate.

What happened next could only be described as incredible timing. Fate. Kismet. Things like it only happened in movies, but she was a movie star, after all.

'Ruby! You need to get out of there!' Mitch shouted as he appeared at the gate. 'He's been lying to you! He's a fecking stalker!' His face was bright red with rage, his eyes wide and menacing, and in his hand was a crumpled newspaper.

Clark, or whatever the hell his name was, appeared from behind, hobbling and holding his groin. 'I'm not a stalker,' he coughed out. 'I'm a journalist. I'm writing a story on Ruby, that's all. Tell him, Ruby. This has all been a misunderstanding. Tell him, Ruby!' He reached out to her, but she whacked his hand away and Nero snarled again, threatening more of the same punishment he had dished out before. Clark pointed to the dog. 'That thing is crazy! I'm going to report you for owning a dangerous animal.'

Mitch cocked his head to one side and narrowed his eyes at Clark. 'Really? That's convenient, because the polizia are on their way already. When you report the dog, don't forget to add the information about the kidnapping and false imprisonment. Although maybe you wouldn't want to ruin your sparkling media career?'

'He spiked my drink too,' Ruby said as she turned her head to see Clark, aka *Hamilton Harlow*, and watched as his skin paled.

'I... I didn't drug her,' he said, pointing at Ruby but addressing Mitch. 'That's a lie. And she hasn't been kidnapped. She's free to leave,' he insisted, stepping back and eyeing the little dog warily.

Jacopo and Luca appeared behind Mitch.

Jacopo cracked his knuckles and Luca stretched his neck. They were more than ready for a confrontation.

Jacopo sneered. 'Se hai fatto del male al mio cane te la farò pagare...' he growled.

Clark held up a hand. 'Mi ha morso! Guarda la mia gamba!' he exclaimed, pointing to the bite mark on his leg.

Mitch said, 'I think you had better stop whining and open the gate, pal.'

Clark's stare moved to Mitch and he snapped, 'I was going to. Gimme a damn chance to move.' He stepped towards the wall-mounted exterior panel and hit the button to open the gates.

When the gap was wide enough, Ruby lurched forward and Mitch grabbed her arm, tugging her through the space as Nero jumped into Jacopo's arms.

Mitch folded her in his embrace. 'You're safe now. I've got you. Let's get you out of here.'

Once she knew she was safe, she turned to face her captor. 'You'll be hearing from my lawyer. And I would suggest you delete that godawful excuse for journalism from your laptop. I felt nothing when you kissed me, so we were going nowhere regardless of what you thought was going to happen.'

Something akin to hurt crossed his face. 'You keep telling yourself that, Ruby. You might convince yourself it's true, but I know we had something. I could tell when we kissed. I know you feel something.'

Empowered, she straightened her spine. 'Oh, I feel lots of things for you right now. But, believe me, none of them are positive.' And with that she gave him no chance to respond further, turning to walk away with her three guardians.

Mitch kept his arm around her as she walked. The effects of whatever had been put in her drink were thankfully beginning to wear off and she was relieved she hadn't drunk more.

'I can't believe you kissed him,' Mitch said with a hint of disdain in his voice and a scowl on his features.

She peered up at him, his face was still a little blurry, but she found her feistiness again. 'Not that it's any of your business, but *he* kissed *me*. He took me by surprise. Anyway, what is that you're gripping?' She nodded towards the newspaper.

Mitch stopped in his tracks and handed it to her. 'I don't think you're going to like it.'

She took the paper from him and looked at the front page.

La star del cinema, Ruby Locke, bacia un altro uomo durante la sua vacanza in Sicilia. Non c'è fine allo scandalo!

The picture accompanying the article showed her and Clark, the man she now knew to be Hamilton, in what appeared to be a passionate embrace, as they danced at the ristorante.

Her stomach roiled. 'What does that mean?' she asked with a wavering voice.

Mitch sighed. 'It says you were kissing a new man and there's no end to the scandal around you. Then the article goes on to the say that the man pictured, journalist and blogger, Hamilton Harlow, confirmed that the two of you were in love and planning your future together.'

She gasped. 'Shitty, shitty shit! You were right. I'm so stupid.'

Mitch reached out and touched her cheek, it was a tender action that took her by surprise. 'Hey, I never said you were stupid.'

'No, but you thought it. And I am.' Her eyes welled with tears and her stomach knotted. 'People will read that and think I don't care about what's going on. They'll think I'm a cold-hearted bitch on the rebound. Do you think it will be in other tabloids too? In the US and the UK?' She sniffed as her vision blurred.

He pressed his lips together in a slight grimace. 'I'm afraid so. I've already spoken to Veronica and Valerie. They've both tried calling you.'

'Oh dammit! I haven't even looked at my phone. I had it on silent while

I was at Clark's... Hamilton's... whatever the hell the barstool was called.' She pulled her phone from the pocket in her dress and, sure enough, there were a gazillion missed calls and texts from pretty much everyone she knew.

Her stomach knotted yet again as she lowered her head and burst into tears.

Mitch pulled her into his arms and held her as she poured out all her anguish, fear and regret into his chest. The warmth of his body against hers was such a comfort, and for a moment she wished she could stay there forever. But this wasn't her reality, and she knew at some point she would have to face the music.

17

Once back at the Villa, Jacopo and Luca fussed around Ruby, checking her for injuries. Jacopo kept repeating, 'Sono cosi dispiaciuto,' and the expression on his usually hard features told her he felt entirely responsible. Mitch rattled off to him a lengthy reply that seemed to appease him and then both guards returned to their posts. Mitch informed Ruby that they had to report the incident, so they needed to go and file the paperwork. She worried about them getting into trouble, or, worse still, losing their jobs through no fault of their own and she felt physically sick with remorse.

The local polizia came to the villa to interview Ruby and, with the help of Mitch as her translator, she told them what had happened at 'Clark's' house. They made copious notes and chatted amongst themselves, whilst Mitch smiled at her in encouragement, making positive nods and winks. Eventually, the officers informed her that, by the time they had arrived to speak to Hamilton Harlow, he had fled, no doubt knowing he was going to be in trouble for false imprisonment and drugging, or whatever the equivalent law was in Italy. The place he had falsely called his *family home* was locked up and cleared. They had searched the area in case he hadn't gone far, but to no avail. There was a 'be on the lookout' instruction circulated to the police across the island and also the mainland. Clark, aka Hamilton, was being treated as, and considered to be, a stalker – something which had been illegal in Italy since 2009.

When they were finally alone, Mitch handed Ruby a glass of brandy as she was still shaking whenever she thought about her ordeal; reliving it all for the officers hadn't helped. The pair sat in the library on leather chairs either side of the fireplace, Nero curled up on Ruby's lap, unwilling to leave her after their shared experience. After noticing Ruby was shivering, Mitch wrapped a blanket around her that smelled of him and lit the fire, despite the mild temperature outside. For a while, Ruby held onto the glass and watched the flames dancing around the logs that had been piled up in the grate, as she absent-mindedly stroked Nero's soft fur. Mitch fielded calls that came in to her mobile and his own, telling people things had been 'handled' and that Ruby was fine but understandably upset.

'Did he... you know, *hurt* you?' Mitch asked through clenched teeth.

She shook her head but continued to focus on the flames. 'Not really. Well, not seriously. Thankfully, he didn't have time. I drank a glass of the juice that was spiked, but I stopped when I began to feel peculiar. He can't have put much in it because the effects have worn off now. But I have a headache, like a hangover. Apart from that, he bruised my arms and scared me, but that's all.'

Mitch balled his hands into fists. 'Bastardo!'

Ruby's phone rang again.

Mitch took a calming breath, answered it and paced the room as he spoke. 'Hi Valerie. Yes, she's okay now. Right... ahuh... I see, yeah. Look, I have contacts I could give you that may be able to speed up the process... Okay, well just let me know. I'll get her to call you when she's feeling up to it. Bye.' He placed the phone on the coffee table and sat again. 'Your agent's worried sick about you.'

Ruby smiled even though guilt niggled at her. 'Poor Val. I do nothing but cause trouble for her.'

'Nah, it sounds like she thinks of you like a daughter. She was so angry about Clark, or should I say *Hamilton*. She's got people looking into him. I expected her to give me a riot for letting you go out, but she must be saving that for another time. Lucky me, eh?'

Ruby shook her head. 'Nope. This one's all on me. I can't have anyone else taking responsibility for my actions.' Her stomach clenched when she thought of the stress and inconvenience she had caused everyone. She scoffed. 'It's me all over. *Little Miss Independent. Little Miss Sort it Out Herself...* More like *Little Miss Stupid Arse.*'

The phone rang again and Mitch sighed as he picked it up. 'Hi Veronica. Yeah, she's doing okay. Shocked and upset but she's a strong lassie.' There was a pause where Veronica must have been speaking. 'Aye, well, he deserves everything he gets if you ask me. The sad little man. And I hope the police catch up with him.' Another long pause. 'Some line about owning a record shop. Aye, I know. Bloody idiot.' Ruby flinched, hoping it wasn't she to whom he was referring so harshly. 'Look, I don't mean to be rude, but I'm sure she'll call you once she's feeling better. Thanks for your concern. And hey... say hi to Gen for me, eh?'

Ruby was surprised to hear him behaving so cordially towards the woman who was now with his wife.

When he hung up the call, he told Ruby, 'Veronica has been doing some digging and it turns out our *journalist* friend Hamilton is more of a wannabe. He writes a blog about the stars but seems to mainly focus on you. I think we can safely say he's obsessed with you. But as far as being a professional journalist, that's a load of bull. He's applied for positions at Veronica's paper several times in the past, but his writing was nowhere near good enough. His blog doesn't get much traffic either by the sound of things. I guess he's no more than an obsessed fan who saw an opportunity to meet his idol and took it to the extreme. But we need to know how he found out where you are when no one else has.'

Ruby sighed. 'I was so foolish.'

'No, you can't blame yourself here. He sought you out. This is all on him.'

Eventually, when it seemed the calls had stopped, Ruby told Mitch, 'I'm so grateful to you for turning up when you did. I honestly didn't know what he was going to do. He was quite forceful once he realised I'd found out he'd been lying. He kept insisting that we could be together regardless of the lies and that really scared me. He was so delusional. He even bought me a ring.' She shook her head in disbelief.

Mitch crouched before her and eyed her with pity. 'As soon as I saw the front page of the paper and read the article, my suspicions were confirmed. He made the mistake of using his real name when the journalist spoke to him. I mean, that's pretty daft when you think about it.' He reached out and squeezed her hand, keeping his gaze fixed on her. 'But you will be okay, you know. You will get through this. All of it,' he whispered.

She felt the urge to hug him. His arms around her had felt so soothing earlier. But instead, she kept her eyes on his. Something crackled in the air between them for a moment.

His lips parted and he briefly glanced down at hers before shaking his head. He cringed and stood, stepping away. 'Oh... erm... and I checked out the property. I'm afraid it *is* used as an Airbnb; has been for years. I don't understand how he thought you wouldn't find out. He must be extremely arrogant or incredibly stupid.'

Ruby huffed. 'I certainly wouldn't say he's stupid. Cruel and unpleasant, definitely arrogant, but in no way dumb.' She shrugged defeatedly. 'He played me. I know I was crazy to trust him so willingly but... I just wanted someone to be on my side, you know? I wanted someone to like me again. It feels that this past month or so has been filled with so much animosity, and I hate that. And I know I don't deserve it, which makes the whole thing worse.' Her lip trembled. 'I'm not a weak person. Not under normal circumstances. I mean, I left my home to become an actor in a strange country where I knew *no one*. I made it work *on my own*. But on this occasion, I was a complete and utter fool. Just like I was with Tyler.' She shook her head as tears spilled from her eyes once again, and Nero lifted up his chin to nuzzle her face.

Mitch sat on the opposite chair and leaned forward. 'Hey, stop beating yoursel' up.' His voice was soft and filled with concern. 'There's nothing wrong with wanting to be liked. And there's nothing wrong with trusting people. The right people won't let you down.'

She raised her chin and scoffed at his comment. 'You're saying that to the girl with the worst track record at choosing who to trust.'

He smiled kindly. 'Aye, well, not all men can be as super-duper as me.'

She couldn't help laughing. He certainly seemed to be someone she could rely on. Admittedly, on the most part to piss her off, but after today's shenanigans she was willing to give him a pass.

'Nor as modest,' she said with a smile.

He grinned. 'You're going to be okay, you know,' he said once again.

She thought back over the events of the last few hours and wondered how he could possibly know that. 'I'd like to believe you. But you're completely different to me. You seem to have your life sorted out. Your businesses are successful. You own multiple homes. People respect you.' She shrugged. 'Can't say the same for me at the moment. I can't even go home, everyone hates me, and my career is potentially ruined. And in trying to rectify it all, I've simply made it worse.'

'Hey, I don't hate you,' Mitch insisted with a scowl.

She tilted her head and fixed her gaze on him. 'You don't particularly like me either. And you've been stuck with me under duress.'

'I don't dislike you at all, Ruby.' There was something indiscernible in his expression and he cleared his throat. 'I mean, I don't know you well enough. Not really. But you're not entirely to blame there. I have a tendency to keep people at a distance. I even did that with my wife. Looking back, I think that's why we survived for so long though. Especially knowing what I do now.' He went quiet for a few moments. He rolled his eyes dramatically and stood. 'God, I'm at it again. Pouring my heart out on you. I think I'd better go and do something useful before I cry too.' He laughed, but Ruby could see a hint of pain in his eyes. 'You go get some rest. I'll come and get you if anyone calls with urgent news.'

* * *

Later, once ensconced in her room with her canine companion, and after returning all the missed calls, and explaining herself over and over, telling everyone she was fine, Ruby felt drained and exhausted.

Her last two calls were to her parents – she kept the call short as hearing how worried they were, almost broke her – and to Kitty.

'Bloody Norah! What an utter psychotic arsehole! My god, you must have been terrified.'

Ruby sighed, tired of repeating the story but knowing she had to. 'I was. But it's over now. I just want to forget all about it. I want to erase the past couple of months, to be honest. I seem to be a shithead magnet, Kitty. What the hell is wrong with me?'

'Hey, there's nothing wrong with you,' Kitty insisted. 'You're lovely. It's everyone else that are the wazzocks. I want this to be over for you, honey. I wish you could just come home.' Her voice wobbled.

Ruby's eyes stung. 'Don't you start. I had my mum sobbing on me earlier, begging me to come home. If only it was that easy. I have to say, though, this place, as pretty as is it, it's a bit tainted now. It's lost its shine.'

'No bloody wonder, Roo. Look, you must be knackered. I'll let you go. Just promise to keep me posted, eh? Especially if they catch Hamilton Horse's Arse.'

Ruby giggled. 'And that is how he shall from henceforth be known.'

Kitty laughed too, and Ruby was relieved that the tone was lighter.

'I'll let you know what happens. Love you.'

'Love you squillions, chick. Bye.'

When everything had calmed down, Ruby lay in bed wondering how the hell she could have made a complicated and shitty situation even worse. She stroked Nero and said, 'It's a definite talent I seem to have acquired, lad, eh? One I need to rid myself of as soon as bloody possible.' The little dog wagged his tail and pawed at her hand.

Despite the million and one thoughts buzzing around her head, she drifted off into a nightmare-filled sleep, where she was locked in a room, surrounded by photographs of herself kissing 'Clark'. The door to the room was bolted and she couldn't escape the images. Her stomach turned and her heart pounded as she found a bathroom and locked the door behind her. Clark banged on the door, demanding to be let in and shouting that he was going to ruin her if she didn't come out. She curled up in a corner crying and begging him to let her go, but no one came to her rescue this time.

She was startled awake and sprang to a sitting position when someone began hammering on her room door and calling her name. Nero let out a series of yips and jumped down to stand guard as Ruby grabbed her robe and wrapped it around herself. Her heart skipped and her breathing rate increased. 'H-hello?'

'Ruby! It's me, Mitch.'

She dashed to open the door and sure enough, Mitch stood there, one hand scrunched in his dark mop of hair, the other over his mouth. 'Thank feck for that. You were crying out and I was getting worried, but you'd locked the door. Pack your stuff. You're leaving,' he informed her before turning to walk away.

Her heart dropped and panic set in. 'Whoa! Hang on! Why are you making me leave? I thought we'd sorted everything and—'

'Look out of your window.' She crumpled her brow and went to the double doors that led to the balcony. Before she could open the curtains, Mitch interjected, 'No! Don't open the curtains or the door! Just peep out.'

Doing as he had suggested, she made a gap between the drapes and stared down towards the main gate. Jacopo and Luca were both pacing back and forth, weapons drawn, and beyond the gate a huge crowd had gathered. Once again, there were banners with slogans painted on, this time in Italian but no doubt insulting, she could just tell. A couple in particular stood out, in vivid, blood red; one saying, *Cagna maledetta!* and the other, *Vai a casa puttana!!* She didn't know what they meant, but, from the angry way in which they were cast onto the placards, she could easily guess.

In addition to the baying throng, paparazzi were interspersed among them, like ravenous vultures waiting for a feast, cameras poised at the ready. The polizia had arrived and were trying to disperse the crowd, but Ruby could hear the chants and catcalls from inside the house.

She covered her mouth with her hand. 'Oh, my word. How...' She knew the answer to the unfinished question, however. Hamilton Harlow, aka Clark, had released details of her whereabouts. And he had no doubt published his blog post, which, because of the front-page news piece, had probably gone viral. She thanked her lucky stars she couldn't get online. She knew there was a very good chance that Mitch's property did have access to the internet, but fear had stopped her from asking for confirmation, and at that moment, as she stared at the antagonists below, she was relieved about that fact. She turned to face her host. 'I see,' she whispered. 'I don't blame you for kicking me out. I'm just so sorry about all this.'

Shoulders hunched, she walked towards the wardrobe, intent on retrieving her bags.

Mitch stepped inside the room until he was only inches away from her and held up his hands, his eyes wide with concern. 'No, you've totally misunderstood me. I'm not kicking you out. We're just... relocating.'

Facing him once more, she shook her head, her brow furrowed in confusion. 'Relocating? What do you mean?'

'I mean, I've been speaking to both your agent and the security firm, and there have been death threats now. They're no doubt fake and just made by idiots jumping on the bandwagon, but we can't risk it. There's been a private plane chartered and it's ready to get us out of here. Jacopo and Luca are being replaced when we arrive at our destination, just in case crazy Clark makes a reappearance, and Valerie is sending Shelby over to assist you, so you have someone from your agency close by in case anything else happens. But, to be honest, it's not somewhere anyone will expect you to be.'

Her heart skipped as relief flooded her veins. 'And you're coming too?'

He nodded. 'Aye, it's another one of my properties we're going to. My favourite one in fact. The one I call my real home. I didn't want to desert you. You won't know anyone there, but the locals will be intrigued and full of questions, so I figured I would come along and be a buffer. And I was going to return to the island in April anyway to see my folks.'

This time she nodded. 'Oh... okay. And where is it?'

He smiled. 'A beautiful wee village on the Isle of Skye called Glentorrin.'

18

Ruby contacted Kitty and her parents to tell them she was UK-bound but that she had to be careful because of the whole stalker issue. She didn't mention the newly announced death threats for fear of scaring them half to death. Her dad's heart couldn't take it and Kitty was heavily pregnant and could do without the added stress. The police had been in touch that morning with an update. They had tracked Clark's phone to a rubbish bin on the outskirts of Palermo where it had been dumped, so he was potentially in the wind now. That was until he made another mistake. The worry of him, or any other vigilantes, locating her on Skye was real, but she had to trust that she would be fine, otherwise she'd become a paranoid recluse, afraid of everyone and everything.

Mitch and Ruby—with Nero on her lap—sat in the back of the black car as the gates of Villa Vista Mare opened, and Jacopo slowly pulled the vehicle forward. Cameras flashed, rather pointlessly, at the blacked-out rear windows and Luca chuntered under his breath in the front passenger seat; his Italian grumblings were something Ruby had become accustomed to during her stay. Angry faces loomed through the glass and Ruby closed her eyes, leaned her head back on the headrest, stroked Nero's soft fur and tried to block out the sound of the raging protests. It was a relief to be leaving, but only because of the horrible events that had taken place with Hamilton

Harlow. Other than that, she'd been grateful to have such a beautiful sanctuary, even if it was short-lived.

'Jeez, is this something you have to put up with regularly?' Mitch asked as they inched out of the safety of the enclosure.

She opened her eyes and turned her head slightly towards him. 'Occupational hazard. Although there are usually less angry faces and more professions of love.' She laughed lightly.

'I couldn't cope with the adulation, to be honest. Or the notoriety. It's my idea of hell, being thrust into the limelight. I'd hate to be in your shoes.'

For some reason his admission saddened her, but she chose to make light of it. 'Says Mister Millionaire with his private jet.'

He scrunched his brow. 'Hang on... you think the plane we're going on is mine?'

She felt heat rise in her cheeks. 'Well, isn't it?'

He laughed out loud. 'Bloody hell, how much money do you think I have?'

Embarrassed, she shrugged her shoulders. 'Lots?'

'Not enough to buy my own jet, I can assure you. I'm only a millionaire on paper. It's all invested.' He laughed again and shook his head. 'My own plane... I wish.'

Ruby remained silent for the rest of the journey for fear of saying something else that would garner ridicule. She hadn't a clue how much planes cost. In fact, she hadn't much of a clue how much anything cost these days. It wasn't as if she went shopping alone on a regular basis – the chance would be a fine thing. There was nothing she would enjoy more than a saunter down Madison, Fifth Avenue or 57th Street.

She remembered, fondly, her Saturday shopping trips on the train to Meadowhall in Sheffield with Kitty when they were teenagers. Such an adventure, especially at Christmas time when the Disney shop was decorated like Santa's grotto. They'd talk about boys and point out the good-looking ones to each other, then giggle like crazy if one of said boys smiled at them.

These days, Ruby had an almost unlimited budget, a personal shopper and a stylist who would shop for her. And even though her eyes had been opened to the most sumptuous boutiques and incredible designers New

York had to offer, it wasn't quite the same. In fact, nothing was quite the same. She missed the simplicity of life before fame and the freedom it entailed. Going back to the UK was an exciting prospect, even though she was heading to a completely new location; another island she had never visited, only this time she could speak the language, at least.

Once at the airport in Palermo it was time to say goodbye to Jacopo, Luca and, the worst parting of all, Nero.

Ruby crouched to fuss the little Yorkshire Terrier and her throat tightened. 'I'm going to miss you, little buddy. Thank you for keeping me company, and for biting that nasty man's leg. You're such a special little dog and I'm going to miss you so, so much.' She buried her nose in his fur and sadness washed over her. Nero licked at the tears on her cheek and she lifted him up to say goodbye properly, her heart breaking a little as she did. 'Be a good boy, won't you? And look after your daddy. I know he looks tough, but he adores you.' She handed the dog over to Jacopo and wiped at her eyes as he gave her a sad, understanding smile and patted her arm.

She was a little sad to say goodbye to her guards too, and despite protocol she hugged them both tightly, thanking them in what she *hoped* was Italian.

* * *

As they sat on the plane ready for take-off, Mitch chuckled to himself. 'I can't believe you thought this was my plane.'

'Yes, it's hilarious,' Ruby replied snidely.

He nudged her. 'Oh, come on, I'm only pulling your leg.'

She closed her eyes and feigned sleep. Thankfully it worked and she managed to actually sleep for almost all the journey. What is it they say? Fake it till you make it?

Once they disembarked at Inverness International Airport, they were greeted by Shelby, Valerie's not so talkative assistant, who directed them to a Range Rover, again with blacked-out windows, and it's waiting driver. They were introduced to Ruby's new security detail, a flat-nosed man called Dougie who looked like he would feel at home in a boxing ring and had been employed simply in case Hamilton Harlow came back for seconds.

Dougie climbed into the passenger seat and Mitch and Shelby climbed into the back of the vehicle, flanking Ruby in the middle.

'How have you been?' Shelby asked once they were inside the vehicle. It was the most the girl had ever spoken to her.

'Oh, you know, great until Hamilton Harlow happened,' Ruby said with a sneer.

Shelby's brow crumpled. 'Yeah, I heard about that. What a douche. You must be exhausted with everything that's going on. If I can help in any way, just say the word.'

Ruby was a little taken aback by this change in personality and shook her head. 'Thanks, and I don't mean to be rude... but why did Valerie send you, exactly? I'm a little confused, to be honest.'

Shelby smiled sweetly. 'I was too when she suggested it. She said she wanted to be here for you herself, but with her other clients... well, it just wasn't feasible, I guess. So here I am,' she said, holding her hands out to emphasise her point. 'The next best thing. At your service.'

'Well, thank you for sacrificing your time to be here. Although, I can't really think what I will need your help with.'

Shelby grinned enthusiastically. 'Val has hired us a car that will be delivered to Mr Adair's home tomorrow. So, I can shop for you, collect books for you, pick up your favourite snacks, and you don't have to leave the house. That way, we know you're safe.'

The thought of being a virtual prisoner again made Ruby shudder, but after the events in Sicily, she understood why her movements should remain at a minimum. She felt bad that the poor young woman had been sent all this way to be a general dogsbody. It didn't sit well at all with Ruby.

Shelby continued, 'Your safety and comfort is of paramount importance to the agency until this whole situation is dealt with, Miss Locke. I don't want you to want for anything. And besides, the busier I can be, the better I will feel. Like you, I'm a long way from home and don't know anyone.'

Ruby appreciated the effort the young woman was making and resolved that she would make use of Shelby to ensure she was kept busy. That way, the assistant wouldn't have had a wasted journey.

* * *

The drive from Inverness was rainy and dull, but the scenery was magnificent regardless. The road was flanked on either side by green hills dotted with purple heather that was, in turn, sprinkled with frost. The mountains in the distance looked ominous with their caps of snow and crowns of cloud circling their pinnacles despite the fact it was almost April.

The car passed through tiny villages with almost unpronounceable names and small, cute, white-painted houses that backed onto open countryside. Pine trees lined the road on either side, as if standing to attention like soldiers, their spiky boughs swaying in the wind.

A break in the cloud gave way to a patch of blue sky, and the sun shone down on the once inhospitable-looking mountains, painting them in a golden glow. Ruby was reminded a little of the Yorkshire Moors when her dad used to take her sledging and she imagined Cathy from *Wuthering Heights* running freely out there somewhere with Heathcliff. She smiled and decided if Glentorrin was half as pretty as this it wouldn't be so bad.

They passed a small lake – or loch, she supposed – the surface rippling along as the breeze played on it, and she observed a bird of prey hovering above, watching the ground, ready to dive to retrieve its dinner.

The sun descended rapidly and as they passed a wooded area, Shelby pointed. 'Look! A deer! I've never seen one in the wild. It's so beautiful.' Her eyes seemed to mist over, her youth and innocence shining through.

Ruby glanced in the direction of Shelby's outstretched finger and smiled. Sure enough, the brown hide of the animal was a stark contrast to the gleaming white of the snow. 'Oh yes! That's so exciting!'

As she watched Shelby sitting there in awe of the wild animal, she thought perhaps she should be the one to look after *her*, not the other way around. The young woman wasn't long out of college so can't have been more than twenty-two.

Shelby turned to face her, beaming. 'I think I'm going to love it here.'

Mitch laughed. 'Aye, you'll see all sorts on Skye. Otters, deer, maybe eagles too. And if you're really lucky, you might spot a pod of dolphins off the coast. Although it's better if you go on a boat trip and there's not many of those at this time of year, sadly.'

Shelby grinned. 'I'm so glad I brought my camera. It has a zoom lens.'

* * *

The Skye bridge loomed before them and a shiver of excitement travelled along Ruby's spine. The vast structure seemed to defy gravity and her stomach flip-flopped as if they were on the ascent of a rollercoaster ride. Thankfully, however, the descent wasn't steep and the views from the car windows were incredible, even in the fading light.

The journey through the village of Glentorrin wasn't long enough for Ruby to make out much by way of details, but what she did see was quaint and pretty. Lights were strung around what appeared to be an inlet of water, and a few dim street lights highlighted a mixture of houses and shops, some with the amber glow of lamplight just visible through the windows. Rain was now bouncing off the pavements, forming puddles that reflected the strung lights. She hoped she would get the opportunity to explore but wasn't yet sure of the plan for keeping her out of sight.

The moon was high in the sky but partially covered by rain clouds when the driver pulled the car through the wrought-iron gates with the sign showing the name Glentorrin House. The driveway curved slightly, and the white, double-fronted house stood on top of a hill overlooking the village green and church. The house itself was quite modest, although it was clear it had been extended a little. There was a high stone wall surrounding three sides of the property and a large front lawn encased by a lower wall; she presumed that was to make the most of the view. It wasn't as large as the one in Palermo, however, and Ruby was filled with a little anxiety over the security.

'Well, here we are, folks, home sweet home,' Mitch said as he opened the door to exit the vehicle. 'I had my friend, Archie, come and light the fires and turn on the heating, so it should be nice and toasty inside. And Morag from the shop sorted out some basics until I can head to the mainland to the big supermarket. There are five bedrooms, but they're kind of wee. Hopefully you'll be comfortable though.'

Dougie, the suited security man, came around to the open door closest to Ruby and held out his hand. 'Miss Locke,' he said with a serious expression.

She took his hand and stepped out into the chilly evening air, the rain now abating. 'Thank you, Dougie. Please call me Ruby though. Miss Locke feels way too formal.'

When she inhaled, she could smell the salt in the air and the pine of the trees at the back of the house.

Dougie nodded. 'As you wish, Ruby. You go on in and I'll bring your bags.'

'Thanks. Where are you staying? Close by?' she asked, hoping it was somewhere nice.

He cleared his throat. 'It was decided, that, in light of the recent issue with the crazed fan and other possible threats, I should be on hand. So, I'm staying here with you.'

'Oh? Goodness, I hope that's not a huge inconvenience for you,' Ruby replied, once again feeling guilty for the sacrifices people were making on her behalf.

He smiled warmly. 'Not in the slightest, Miss. I'm happy to be of service.'

'Well, I hope you know how appreciated you are,' she told him.

He simply nodded once.

Ruby followed Mitch into the house and Shelby brought up the rear, while Dougie unloaded the boot. The small addition to the front of the property was a pitched-roof porch, its woodwork painted sage green and highlighted by lanterns hanging at either side. It wasn't huge, so they walked through into a hallway.

Mitch gestured with his hand. 'Okay, so over to the left is the living room and to the right is the kitchen which leads through to a dining room. There's a conservatory beyond the dining room with underfloor heating where you can sit and chill.' He pointed to each room as he described it and Ruby had to stifle a giggle because he reminded her of a rather brawny, stubble-chinned flight attendant. 'Down the hallway, there's a utility room, or laundry for those of us who've spent most of their time in the USA.' He looked directly at Ruby and she thought she saw him wink. 'And at the back of the laundry room, there's a wee shower room and toilet. There's a garage at the back of the house, where you can park your rental car when it arrives. I have a Land Rover in there already, but it fits two.'

They all followed him up the stairs in the middle of the hallway. 'As I said, there are five bedrooms but only four of us, so I'm thinking Ruby, as guest of honour, can have the largest of the rooms as there's an en suite and it links to a room that counts as the fifth bedroom. I have it set up as an office-come-library. I know you like books, so help yourself to any in there that take your fancy. There's a comfy chair in there too.' He turned to Shelby. 'I'm giving you the second largest room with an en suite. You're across the hall from Ruby. Dougie, you can have bedroom three which is small, but if you're anything like me that'll be fine. You have a wee en suite too. Although if you find that too cramped, feel free to use the main bathroom at the top of the stairs. I'll have the other back bedroom. I'll let you all get settled in and I'll go put the kettle on. Shout if you need anything.' He nodded and smiled, then headed back down the stairs.

Dougie had brought all the bags and placed them outside the relevant rooms so Ruby took hers, opened the door to her room and flicked on the light. The room wasn't huge but was pleasant enough. The walls were a simple pale cream and the furniture was in a sage green similar to the porch and a little distressed at the corners. The bedding was pale green with a faint damask pattern in cream and above the bed was a painting of what she presumed to be the village, only bathed in summer sunlight. In the corner of the painting was a signature that read *Reid MacKinnon* and she wondered if he was a local artist. In the corner of the room was a small but comfy-looking armchair and beside that a dressing table. Considering this was probably Mitch's room, it was tastefully decorated and not as masculine as she might have expected. She had everything she needed. A vase of fresh flowers sat on the bedside table and she smiled at how thoughtful a touch that was. He had certainly gone out of his way to make her feel welcome.

There was a knock on her door, and she opened it to find Shelby standing there.

'Is your room as cute as mine?' Shelby asked giddily. 'Mine is decorated in pale blue and white and there's a gorgeous painting of a building called the Lifeboat House Museum by some guy called Reid Mac... something. I wonder if that's here in Glentorrin. If it is, I'll definitely need to go visit. I adore museums.' Shelby's level of excitement was almost at fever pitch and Ruby giggled.

'My room is lovely too. Come in and have a look.' She stepped aside to let Shelby in.

'Oh, you have fresh flowers too. I have fresh flowers. He's so thoughtful. And a little bit dreamy too, don't you think? His accent...' She rolled her eyes and clutched her shirt over her heart. 'Just... wow!'

Ruby shrugged. 'If you like that kind of accent.'

Shelby gasped. 'Oh, I do. I *so* do. I suppose with you being British, you're used to hearing Scottish, huh? For me, it turns my knees to jell-o.' She shivered. 'Anyways, come see my room.'

Ruby found her hand being grasped and her body being tugged along.

'Tadaaaa!' Shelby's room was smaller but still very pretty and once again Ruby was impressed with the tasteful décor.

'I think we'll be comfortable here, Shelby. But let's hope it's not for long, eh?'

Shelby frowned, but then widened her eyes. 'Oh yeah, for sure. Not long. In fact, I spoke to Valerie earlier. They have a new team on the case. Apparently, the hacker used a super-strong firewall and a foreign IP address. It's taking more time than she hoped to get to the bottom of it.'

Feeling a little deflated at the news, Ruby sighed. 'Well, I think I'll go down and see if Mitch has made that tea.'

19

Mitch was leaning against the work surface in the kitchen when Ruby arrived. It was a bright room with white, shaker-style units and butcher's block countertops; again, very traditional but with a fresh modern twist, and very homely.

He gestured to the teapot. 'Can I get you a cup?'

'That'd be great, thanks. I suppose the one thing about being holed up in a Scotsman's house is decent tea.'

He laughed as he handed her a mug. 'Aye, and you'll be even happier that it's from Yorkshire.' He pursed his lips. 'I've often wondered how they grow tea in Yorkshire. But then again, there are vineyards in England so...' He shrugged.

Ruby took a seat at the large, farmhouse-style table. 'You have such a lovely home. I don't know why, but I half expected your mum and dad to be living here,' she told him as she sipped on the nectar-like drink.

He smiled. 'Nah, this is all me. They used to live here, but they're getting on a bit so it's better for them to be in a more built-up area, so they stay up the road in Portree. One-storey house, more shops, doctors, you know? Stuff they need, especially in the bad winters we have up here.'

'Did you and your wife live here in Glentorrin?'

He shook his head. 'No. Gen is a city girl through and through. We had a place in Edinburgh. An apartment. She hated being so isolated, so this place would've been no good for her, but it's home to me. My folks lived here until a year ago and I've just freshened the place up to my taste, you know? Hey, I'll be going up to visit them in the next couple of days. If you can escape, you could come with me. Portree is really nice. It's kind of the island's capital.'

She was taken off guard by his invitation. 'That sounds lovely. I'll just need to wait and see what Valerie says about me being out in public.' She sighed and lowered her head.

He sat opposite her. 'You must be tired of all this. But then again, I'm guessing it's not that different when you're *not* a social pariah.' As soon as the words left his mouth, he slapped a hand over it and widened his eyes. 'Shit, that sounded really bloody awful out loud. I'm sorry, I didn't—'

She held up a hand. 'It's fine. It's what I am at the moment.' She shrugged. 'Although I think I prefer the term *falling star*. It's less harsh and a bit more romantic, I suppose.'

'Do you want the Wi-Fi code? I can imagine you still need to keep abreast of the goings-on in movie land.'

She shivered involuntarily. 'Thanks, it will be handy for video-calling Kitty and my parents, but I won't be checking social media. I deactivated my accounts when people started saying I should jump off a cliff.'

'Shit! Really? My god, don't people realise that saying things like that can send people into a downward spiral. I've heard people actually take their own lives because of online bullying.' He shook his head in disbelief.

She nodded. 'I know. It's quite scary how intimidating a place the internet can be sometimes.' Deciding on a change of subject, she asked, 'So what made you get into property?'

He raised his eyebrows. 'Well, therein lies a tale.' He huffed the air from his lungs and his brow crumpled.

She cringed, worrying she had overstepped the mark again with her questions. 'I'm sorry, I wasn't intending to be a *nosey bint* again.' She felt the warmth of embarrassment rise in her cheeks.

He laughed and shook his head. 'Nah, you're fine. I... erm... was supposed to be an Olympic swimmer. Trained pretty much all of my childhood and teen years for it. Swimming was my life but... I had a nasty accident and ripped my shoulder quite bad.'

She winced at the thought of his injury. 'Ouch! How did you do that?'

He stared at the table as he spoke. 'I was working on a fishing boat in the summer holidays when I was home from uni. I hadn't had much training on the job, and to make matters worse I was doing a two-man job on my own. To cut a long story short, my arm got caught up in a rope attached to a pulley. It could've ripped my arm clean off, but I was lucky, I guess. Loads of surgeries followed and my swimming career and dreams of the Olympics were shattered.' The sadness in his eyes made Ruby's stomach clench and her eyes sting. 'Anyway, I got some serious compensation, and after thinking on it long and hard, I decided I should invest it. So, I bought my first property at auction; a run-down apartment in Glasgow that no one else wanted. It was a beautiful old building, but, my god, the place was in a state. Every kind of rot you can imagine, vandalism, anything that could be ripped out and stolen had been. It was a lot of hard graft, especially with only one good working arm, but I did it. Sold it for a massive profit, and I suppose the bug got me. My shoulder healed and I've been doing it ever since.' He paused and fixed his gaze on her. 'I've offloaded on you again. What is it about you?' He smiled, clearly abashed by his own rhetorical question.

She felt a flutter in her stomach of something she didn't wish to acknowledge, and rushed on, 'So, you have lots of houses then?'

He gave a nod. 'A few, aye. I flip some, but I rent some out too.'

'And this is your main home?' she asked with a tilt of her head, enjoying getting to know him.

He lifted his chin, clearly more comfortable on the subject of his houses. 'This place is where I feel most like myself, I suppose. But I have an apartment in Edinburgh, so that's where I spend most of my time. My office is in the city too. I bloody love that place, Edinburgh, I mean. Such an incredible city.' He smiled as if drifting off in his mind before snapping back to the present. 'Although these days I'm more hands-off. It all runs smoothly without me. Hence my reason for working on the Sicily house.'

Ruby nodded. 'Do you spend much time here on Skye?'

'Not as much as I probably should. It's a base and somewhere with happy memories of growing up. My best mate, Reid, lives in the village too... well, he *used* to be my best mate.' Another look of melancholy washed over him.

The name caught her attention. 'Ooh, is that the artist who painted the picture that's on the wall in my room?'

He nodded. 'Aye, I have a few of his pieces. He's a bloody talented guy. A good guy too. We were at school together, sat beside each other. We were inseparable when we were kids, we used to play cricket and football on the field down by the church. His brother, Kendric, used to tag along too. And this lassie called Leanna who used to follow Reid around like a lost puppy. She was besotted.' He laughed lightly at the memories.

Unsure about prying further, Ruby chewed on her lip. 'Did you have a falling out? You and Reid?'

Mitch pondered for a moment. 'Not exactly. We just... lost touch. Drifted apart as folks do, you know? He ran off to England to marry a girl he'd met when she was here on holiday. I got really bad vibes about her and I made the mistake of telling him so. That didn't go down too well.' He shook his head. 'She kind of stepped in between him and his friends. By the time they split up and he returned here with his wee lad, Evin, I'd moved to Edinburgh. We still say hello, pass the time of day and stuff when I'm here, but we're not close like we used to be.'

Ruby felt bad for him. She knew she'd be lost without her rock. 'That's a shame. I don't know what I'd do without Kitty, my bestie. We went to school together too and I've known her practically all my life. She's more like a sister really.'

'It must be tough, not being able to go round for coffee or out shopping with her, eh?'

She fought back a wave of emotion as she pictured Kitty in her mind. 'It is. But we speak almost every day. And she's the one who keeps me grounded. She's a mum now, so woe betide me if I step out of line.' She wagged her finger and laughed. 'She's got that stern mum voice and she's not afraid to use it.' Mitch laughed along with her. 'Seriously though, it's good to have someone in my life who I can trust implicitly.'

Mitch opened his mouth to speak just as Shelby arrived in the room, and he closed it again.

'Hey guys. What's for dinner?' she asked in that bright sing-song voice she had apparently found.

Ruby glanced at the clock. 'Wow, I hadn't realised the time. It's almost ten thirty. No wonder my stomach is growling.'

Mitch stood. 'I'll rustle up a vat of pasta and sauce. Thirty minutes okay?'

Shelby and Ruby replied, 'Perfect!' in unison.

Shelby sat beside Ruby. 'Probably won't sleep due to carb overload, but it'll be so worth it,' she said with an exaggerated eye roll.

Ruby's stomach grumbled and she placed a hand over it. 'I think my body clock is all over the place at the moment.'

Shelby glanced at her belly. 'Look, I was going to suggest maybe you and I could exercise daily from tomorrow?' Her eyes widened and she held up her hands. 'Not that I think you're getting fat or anything. It's just... well, exercise is good for PMH.' She shrugged.

Ruby scowled. 'What's that?'

Shelby grinned. 'Positive mental health.' She stated it as if it should be obvious. 'I know tons of workouts we can do right there in the garden. No need to leave the grounds.'

The feeling of claustrophobia that had been niggling in the back of Ruby's mind jumped to the forefront, and the thought of not leaving the grounds made her stomach knot. 'Actually, I think I'm too exhausted to eat. I think I'll go to bed.' She stood from the table. 'Sorry, Mitch. I hope you don't mind.'

He turned and eyed her with concern. 'Not at all. How about a couple of biscuits to munch on? I've got chocolate ones.'

She glanced at Shelby, and in light of their conversation shook her head. 'It's okay, sleep is what I need I think.' And with that she left the room and the sound of Shelby and Mitch chatting behind her.

Once in the quiet serenity of her bedroom, she texted Kitty.

Hey honey, I know it's late, so I don't expect you to reply. Just wanted to let you know am in the new house on Skye. It's lovely. Very homely. But Valerie has sent her assistant here and I don't really get why. She hardly used to speak to me, but now she's all friendly and chatty. It's sweet, but is it wrong that I'm suspicious? She's even suggested we exercise together, like we're big buddies. I know I'm being oversensitive and paranoid. Ignore me. I could do with being whipped into shape! Love you. Roo xx

Kitty didn't reply and Ruby surmised she must be sleeping, so she changed into her pyjamas, brushed her teeth and climbed into the bed.

* * *

Ruby awoke and glanced at the bedside clock. The number ten flashed bright in green. 'Bloody hell!'

She scrambled out of bed and opened the curtains to peer out. From her room at the front of the house, she could see right down to the inlet where the late-March sun glinted on the surface of the water. The sky was cornflower blue and down on the field at the opposite end to the church was a newly constructed building, scaffolding still surrounded it and some men were standing there with clipboards, and wearing high-viz jackets. She wondered what the building was. It looked like it had been sympathetically built to fit in with the others in the village but appeared too large to be a house.

Movement caught her eye and when she moved her focus on to the garden, she saw Shelby jogging around in skintight leggings and a fitted fleece top. Her breath was forming little clouds as she exhaled rapidly from exertion. She looked up and made eye contact with her.

'Shit!' Ruby mumbled. 'Don't invite me down, don't invite me down, don't invite me down.'

Thankfully, Shelby just waved up at her, a wide grin on her pretty, glowing features, her sleek, almost black ponytail glinting in the sunshine.

'Ugh, she's almost perfect.' Ruby closed the curtains once again.

She picked up her phone and noticed she'd had a text from Kitty.

Hi gorgeous. To be honest, I'm fat and need to exercise, so send her here to kick my bum! Is she one of those uber-pretty girls with perfect skin? If so, spike her food with butter! Lol! Only kidding… or am I? Anyway, the kids are driving me mad today so a few days on Skye sounds like bliss! Swap you? Any news on the hacking?

Ruby hit the reply button and typed a quick reply.

She's skinny, pretty and sweet too. I wish I could dislike her, but she's really nice. And BTW you're pregnant not fat! No news on the hacking. I'm on the verge of taking my own action again! And can you believe I've JUST got up? Off to find food. Bloody starving! Speak soon. Love you xx

Ruby had a quick shower and dressed in yoga pants and a hoody. Thankfully, no one was in the kitchen when she arrived downstairs and she clicked the kettle on to boil. She found fresh bread on a board on the worktop and cut a slice before slotting in the toaster.

Mitch arrived in the room. 'Afternoon!' he said with a grin.

She glanced at the clock. 'Cheeky. It's only eleven o'clock. And I must have needed the sleep seeing as I never stay in bed this late.'

He gave her a friendly nudge. 'I'm pulling your leg. You can sleep as long as you want. Nothing spoiling.'

'What's going on down at the village green? I saw some men standing by that new building.'

Mitch smiled. 'Aye, I wondered that myself, so I asked Morag when I went to collect the newspaper. Apparently, it's the new village hall. The co-operative has been trying to raise funds for a while and find a plot of land that was reasonably priced enough to build one. I donated a while ago but totally forgot about it. Anyway, it turns out the land was under their noses all the time, and the lottery have funded the majority of it. There's going to be a music festival and grand opening a week on Saturday. It's a big deal. All our village meetings have always been in the pub or the church, so the new place will be much better. They're getting an alcohol licence too.' He grinned. 'They have the Highland Games on the same field in August, so they had to make sure there was still enough room to carry out the events. Anyway, Morag was telling me there's going to be some local bands playing at the opening and some from the mainland too, provided there's no freak snow. Should be good craic.'

She nodded but sneered at the same time. 'Great, another thing I can't get involved with.'

'I bet we can sneak you in.'

She huffed. 'Hmm, I tried sneaking before, remember? Look where that got me.'

He grinned. 'I like a challenge. And anyway, no one will approach you with *The Rock* by your side.'

Ruby burst out laughing. 'Is that what you're calling yourself now?'

He joined in her laughter. 'Not me, you numpty! Dougie! He's built like a brick outhouse, so no one will try to cross him.'

Ruby laughed harder. 'Oh right! Hilarious! I might start calling him The Rock.' It felt good to laugh. She hadn't done enough of it lately.

'Anyways, you cheeky wee mare, are you trying to say I'm scrawny or something? I'll have you know, this is a swimmer's physique. Well, it used to be anyway,' Mitch said with another playful nudge to her shoulder.

She eyed him up and down. He was toned and muscular for sure, but he was around half the size of her new bodyguard. 'Let's just say, if you were in the ring together, I wouldn't be betting on you.'

He rolled his eyes and feigned hurt. 'Charming. And who's to say I couldn't outwit him with my intellect or something?'

Dougie appeared in the doorway. He hit his fist into his opposite palm and glared. 'Are you trying to say I'm some kind of doaty bawbag, mate?'

Mitch stopped laughing and the colour drained from his face. 'Erm... no, I... It was just a... I mean, not at all.'

Silence fell on the room and Ruby swallowed hard, unsure what to do.

Dougie burst out laughing. 'Your faces! You wee dafties!' He guffawed and pointed at the stunned pair, who eventually joined him in his mirth, although on Ruby's part her laughter was fuelled by relief.

When they had all calmed down, Dougie asked, 'So why were Mitch and me having imaginary fisticuffs then?'

'I was telling her there's an opening event for the village hall a week on Saturday, the thirteenth. A kind of music festival and I said that I'd speak to you about figuring out a way for her to attend it, if we can?'

Dougie rubbed his clean-shaven chin. 'Oh aye, I love a good festival. Let's gie it laldy, eh? What's the worst that can happen?'

Ruby wasn't at all sure what 'gie it laldy' meant and she could think of many things that could go wrong but didn't answer for fear of making him change his mind. A flutter of excitement tickled at her insides and she managed to refrain from jumping up and down clapping her hands... but only just. She hadn't been to a music festival in years. In fact, she realised, the last one had been the Leeds festival in the year of her eighteenth birthday. She had drunk way too much and as a result had thrown up outside the tent she was sharing with Kitty. Kitty, in her drunken state, had, of course, found the whole thing hilarious and they had fallen out for around an hour; that was until Fall Out Boy played 'I Don't Care' and they had bounced around in the mosh pit like a pair of escaped lunatics, hugging each other and belting out the lyrics.

'Oh, I forgot to mention, your wee assistant, Shelby, signed for the hire car,' Dougie told Ruby. 'It's parked around the back by the garage. I'm sure she'll pop out and pick you up whatever you need. She seems like a lovely lass.' He smiled as he spoke. It appeared her charms hadn't been lost on him. 'Aye, reminds me of my niece. So bubbly, you know?'

Ruby smiled and nodded. 'Oh yes, she's a lovely girl.' But still couldn't help wondering why she was here.

20

Ruby was sitting in the conservatory reading *Wuthering Heights* when her phone rang. Valerie's name flashed on the screen and she grabbed it eagerly, hoping that there was good news.

'Ruby, sweetheart, it's Val.'

'Hi Val, how are you?' she asked with a small smile.

'I'm good, I'm good. You?'

Ruby inhaled and peered out of the window to the pines swaying in the breeze. 'I'm... okay, I suppose. Do you have news?'

Valerie sighed deeply. 'We got close. So close. But the...' More sighing. 'I don't know... servers weren't serving, or the PQ address was scrambled on the internets, or some such fakakta I don't understand. But to cut a long story short, the sneaky little rat has evaded us again. We froze your online accounts, but somehow people are still sharing the crap out of the original damn posts. Go figure. I've had *hate* mail, I mean actual, honest to goodness letters in envelopes, addressed to you at the office. It's crazy. If I were you, I'd stay away from any kind of newspaper or magazine. You'll only end up sad. Oh, a bit of good news though, the stalker guy, Hamilton Harlow?'

Hamilton Horse's Arse, Ruby thought to herself with a small smile.

'Yeah, he's been caught. And get this, his name isn't Clark *or* Hamilton, it's Bryan. Bryan Moore. He's been arrested and it turns out he was trying to track you down again and he's still got files on you, but they've all been confiscated. He was caught when he blogged about being bitten by a dog or something and that the owner, Ruby Locke, never took responsibility. Idiot. Anyway, the powers that be tracked him down from a photograph he posted of himself outside a motel with a bandaged leg, and he's in custody. And Veronica Lucas is putting together a piece for her newspaper about you and your charity work and how you've been suffering on account of being hacked and wrongfully accused, but whether people will believe her or not is another thing.'

Ruby sat, head in hands, listening to Valerie's anti-pep talk and her heart sank so low she feared she may step on it when she moved. 'Val, I don't understand why this isn't dealt with by now. What kind of lawyers are working on it? What kind of experts? My life and my career are in free fall. I'm literally a falling star in a sky full of targeted missiles. Each one that hits takes me down further and I don't think I'm going to come back from this. Ever.'

'To be honest, the lawyers are older than dinosaurs. I'm looking into getting the help of some who are experts in cybercrime.'

Ruby sighed deeply and clenched her teeth, doing her best not to shout. 'But, Val, you should have done that weeks ago. You said you had.'

Her agent fell silent for a few moments and Ruby worried she had over-stepped the mark until eventually Valerie spoke. 'I know. I'm so sorry. I understand if you fire me. I was totally out of my depth with this. I've never dealt with the like and I had *no clue* how to make things right.' She sniffed and it was clear she was upset. 'I thought I could just work it out without throwing money at it. I was wrong. But I want you to know I'm on the right track now. I am. We *will* get to the bottom of it all. I promise you that, Ruby. Even if you fire me as your agent, which you have every right to do.'

Ruby's jaw ached from clenching so hard and when she looked down, she realised her fist was balled, her nails digging into her palm. Tears blurred her eyes. 'So, does this mean you've actually done nothing up to now? Nothing of any consequence?'

Valerie sniffed again. 'I'm so sorry. I really am. I honestly thought this would blow over.'

'But *you* said to me right at the start that it wouldn't! *You* were the one who sent me away because of all the shit being said about me and the threats being made. *You!*'

'I know.' Valerie's voice wavered. 'I know I did. But I was trying to get you to take a break for a while so it *would* blow over, and I had to make it seem more serious than I believed it to be or you wouldn't go. I was shocked when it didn't just fizzle out.'

Ruby heaved a deep, frustrated sigh. 'And why on earth is Shelby here? You've sent that poor girl all this way for no reason. The money you paid for her plane tickets could have gone towards sorting this mess out.'

'I... I wanted you to have a familiar face with you. Someone who could help you if anything happened. I just figured having her there would be a comfort to you.'

Ruby huffed. 'But we've hardly even spoken before this, Val. She's a lovely girl but you've sent her on a wild goose chase with no goose to actually chase. It makes no sense at all.'

Valerie sighed deeply again. 'You're going to fire me, aren't you?'

Ruby took a deep breath. 'Honestly, I don't know what I'm going to do at this point. My career is in tatters and you said you were sorting it all out. I trusted you, Val. I believed you. But you lied to me. How do I get past that?'

'I... I don't know. I'm so sorry. I dropped the ball. I made a huge mistake, but I was out of my depth. Maybe I'm getting too old to do this job. I don't know enough about social media.' There was such despondency in her voice.

'Look, Val, I need some time to process this. I need some time to think.'

Valerie sniffed again. 'I understand. I really do. And, as I promised, things will move forward now. I *will* deal with it or, at least I will find people who can help me to do so.'

Ruby closed her eyes. 'Okay. Bye Val.' She hung up the call and burst into tears.

'Hey, hey, what's happened, Ruby?' Mitch asked from behind her.

Ruby swiped at her tears. He had seen her crying more than he had seen her smiling at this point. 'Oh... nothing, it's fine.' She shrugged.

He walked over and sat opposite her on one of the wicker chairs. 'Nah. Not buying it. Something major has happened. Hasn't it?'

She shook her head no, but more tears spilled over and she nodded her head yes. She sobbed and covered her face with her hands. 'Everything is completely ruined. I'm no longer a falling star. I've gone completely super-nova, and not in a good way.'

'Shit, that sounds bad. What's changed?'

Ruby sniffed and rubbed her hands over her face. 'Nothing. That's the problem. Valerie said she was dealing with the hacking. That things were going well. Today I've discovered that she's done nothing apart from put two ancient lawyers on it, who know even less about cybercrime than she does, and that's saying something. I feel betrayed and that this has gone on too long for me to ever recover from it. People are still sharing the original posts and my name is mud *everywhere*. She could have made a difference, but for some unknown reason she chose not to.'

Mitch huffed the air from his lungs through puffed cheeks. 'Bloody hell. I can't believe that. Are you going to fire her?'

Ruby shrugged. 'Maybe. I don't know what to do.'

Mitch chewed his lip for a moment. 'Look, I know I have a habit of sticking my nose where it's not wanted, and I know I've mentioned this before, but I know someone who is a computer whizz. A totally unas-suming guy but he studied IT at uni and knows a lot about this kind of stuff. He lives in the village. Runs a campsite and owns an outdoor gear shop. I can ask for his help if you like? What do you say?'

Ruby sighed and shrugged. 'I say I have the grand total of nothing to lose at this point. Go for it.'

Mitch stood and clapped his hands together. 'Get your coat.'

* * *

Feeling a bit awkward in a flat cap borrowed from Mitch, with her hair tucked inside by way of disguise, Ruby glanced around the neat but very masculine living room of Mitch's friend's cottage: tartan carpet, plain walls, black leather sofas and a huge inglenook fireplace complete with roaring fire. What was lacking was any sign of computer equipment, however.

'Archie, mate, this is the lassie I told you about. But you have to keep this totally between us. Okay?'

Archie was a tall, slim man, ruggedly handsome with longish dark brown hair that was peppered with grey, and a beard that was more grey than brown. He wore a checked shirt with an Aerosmith T-shirt underneath and cargo pants. He definitely fit the outdoorsy bill that Ruby had expected, but in no way resembled the IT whizz she hoped for. Although she was more aware than ever that she shouldn't judge a book by its cover.

He stared and held out his hand. 'You're R-Ruby Locke. I've seen you at the cinema. Well, I mean not you *personally* of course, but you on the screen. What I mean is... I saw your films... like, all of them. I mean, I'm not a stalker or anything but—'

Mitch patted his shoulder. 'Aye, Archie, she's famous, get over it, pal. Can you help?'

Archie shook his head as if trying to dislodge something loose from his brain. 'Aye, aye, of course I can. A hacking wasn't it? I saw it in the papers. I didn't believe it was you who said those awful things. You're not like that. What I mean is you don't come across like that.'

Ruby smiled and shook his hand. 'Thank you, Archie. You're right. I didn't do it, but I need to find out who did.' She handed him an envelope. 'I've written all my passwords and sites on a piece of paper. I deactivated them and my agent allegedly froze them so they can't be reactivated, but I'm guessing you can circumvent that. Mitch says I can trust you.'

Archie saluted. 'No problemo. And you absolutely *can* trust me, ma'am. One hundred and ninety-nine per cent.'

Ruby narrowed her eyes and tilted her head. 'What about the other one per cent of that two hundred?'

Archie widened his eyes. 'Oh, well, I mean—'

She giggled. He may not have the appearance of a computer genius but it was clear his heart was in the right place. 'I'm joking. I'm joking. If Mitch says I can trust you, then I trust you.'

Archie's cheeks were bright red by this point. 'Oh, right enough, aye.' He grinned. 'Leave it with me, eh?'

Mitch patted his shoulder and shook his hand. 'Cheers, mate. I really appreciate this.'

Archie nodded. 'Hey, have you seen Reid since you got here? I reckon he'd love to see you. He got engaged, you know. Jules is a top lassie. He's a lucky beggar, that one.'

Mitch gave a small, uncertain smile. 'Not yet. But I'll probably see him at some point.'

Archie gave him a solemn look. 'You really should.'

* * *

Ruby felt relieved at having made a positive step towards sorting out the mess of the hacking. She only wished she had done it sooner. She relaxed a little as some of the weight she had been carrying in her mind since the call with Valerie began to dissipate.

As they walked back around the corner to Mitch's house, she linked her arm in his. 'You're turning into my regular knight in shining armour, Mr Adair.'

He glanced down at her and smiled. 'Just trying to help.' His cheeks coloured pink and Ruby thought how cute it was when he got embarrassed.

She stopped, still holding his arm. 'Well, I appreciate it. I appreciate you,' she told him with sincerity that she hoped he understood.

He opened his mouth to speak, but a split second later he lifted his chin and a wide smile spread across his face. Ruby turned to look at what had caused the reaction and spotted a couple walking towards them with a rather large, ginger-coloured dog.

'Mitch? Bloody hell! How long has it been?' The tall, handsome, auburn-haired man exclaimed as his dog wagged its tail frantically. 'Morag said you were here.'

Mitch walked towards the couple; Ruby's arm still linked with his. 'Reid! Mate! It's been too long.' The men hugged while Ruby and the pretty, blonde woman smiled at each other awkwardly.

Ruby bent to fuss the dog and he seemed to enjoy the attention.

'Mitch, this is my fiancée, Jules. Jules, this is my best mate from school, Mitch Adair.'

Mitch shook hands with Jules. 'Good to meet you. Archie was telling me you guys had got engaged. Congratulations.'

'Cheers, mate.'

'How's wee Evin?' Mitch asked.

Reid grinned. 'Ah not so wee any more. He's twelve now. Great kid.'

Mitch nodded. 'Grand, grand.'

Reid nodded, but then his smile disappeared. 'Morag told us about you and Gen. I'm so sorry.'

Mitch shrugged. 'Aye, it was rough for a while there, but it's all good now. We're still friends.'

Reid smiled. 'That's great. And who is your friend?' he asked, holding his hand out to Ruby.

Ruby shook his hand and opened her mouth to speak, but Mitch beat her to it. 'This is Roo, an old friend from uni.'

'Aw, that's great, lovely to meet you, Roo. Love the name,' Reid said with a warm smile.

'Good to meet you both,' Ruby said as she moved on to shake Jules' hand. 'I've heard lots of lovely things about you. And I love your artwork.'

Reid blushed and chewed his lip. 'That's very kind. Thank you.'

'Look, the two of you must come to dinner tomorrow night,' Jules interjected. 'You menfolk must have a ton of catching up to do.'

Again, Ruby opened her mouth to speak, but Mitch stepped in. 'Oh, I don't know, we're quite busy the now and—'

'Nonsense!' Ruby said with a scowl at Mitch. 'We'd love to come. What time is best?'

Jules beamed. 'Great. Let's say seven, shall we?'

Ruby nodded as she continued to scratch the dog behind his ear. 'Perfect. And who's this handsome chappy?'

Jules laughed. 'This is Chewie, and you've a friend for life there now.'

'Chewie! After Chewbacca! I love it.' She crouched to get a better look at the huge dog. 'I met your namesake, you know, yes, I did. Although, he wasn't wearing his costume, so I suppose technically I met the actor who plays your namesake, but... anyway, you're so gorgeous. Yes, you are.'

The dog licked at her face and wagged his tail harder.

She looked up at Mitch who was glaring at her. He turned his attention back to Reid. 'Well, I suppose we'll see you tomorrow night at seven then.'

'Looking forward to it,' Reid said. 'Well, we'd better get going. Chewie needs lots of exercise.'

Ruby laughed. 'I can imagine!'

They said their goodbyes and when Reid, Jules and Chewie headed off to continue their walk, Ruby and Mitch headed back towards Glentorrin House.

'Don't you think that was a bit careless?' Mitch said, without looking at her.

'No. And quite frankly I would rather you didn't speak for me, thank you very much. I'm a grown woman with a tongue in my head.'

Mitch stopped and faced her. 'I was trying to protect you. But you've probably gone and blown your cover now.'

She shrugged, unsure why he was so pissed off. 'I didn't think it would be such an issue with them being your friends.'

'Aye, but it only takes them to mention something in passing to someone else. You received death threats for god's sake. And why did you have to confirm any suspicions they may have by talking about meeting Peter Mayhew?'

She growled in frustration and placed her hands on her hips. 'No one is going to kill me, Mitch. I'm just me. And people meet actors all the bloody time. Conventions, meet and greets, who's to say I met Peter on a bloody movie set?'

He tilted his head, 'But I bet you *did* meet him on a movie set, didn't you?'

'Well... I... Okay, yes, but that's not the point!' She huffed. 'You made it more obvious by trying to avoid dinner with them.'

He pursed his lips and glared at her again. 'It just feels weird, that's all. We're not a couple, and going for dinner at another couple's house is a very couply thing to do. They probably think we're an item now.' The look on his face told her he was none too happy about that fact.

She scowled at him. 'Thanks very much! You make it sound like it's bloody abhorrent to be seen with me!'

He glanced around and stepped closer. 'Keep your voice down, will you? You sound like a banshee.'

'Oh, I've had enough of you. I really have.' She turned and stomped off towards the house and when she arrived, she slammed the front door behind herself and stormed up to her room.

A moment later, there was a light tapping on her door. 'Ruby? Is everything okay?' Shelby asked from outside her room.

She turned and opened the door. 'Hi, Shelby, yes, I'm fine. It's okay. I've just had a really frustrating day.'

Shelby's mouth turned downwards, and she regarded her with a piteous expression. 'Anything I can do to help?'

Ruby opened her mouth and briefly contemplated telling Shelby what Valerie had done... or not done, what Mitch had organised with Archie, and what had happened when they bumped into Reid and Jules, but she stopped herself, deciding she didn't want Shelby reporting back to Val, and she didn't know her well enough to emotionally dump on her. 'No, really, I'll be fine. I think I'm going to have a long hot shower and read my book.'

Shelby smiled and reached out to stroke her arm. 'I'm here if I can help in any way. I know we don't know each other that well but... well, I want you to know I'm here for you.'

Ruby smiled. 'That's very sweet and kind. Thank you.'

21

The following morning, Ruby awoke feeling down. She missed her parents and Kitty and even the texts from Philippe made her sad. He was driving for another famous person, a sports personality, and he seemed to be enjoying it. He sent a photo of his family all waving at the screen and seeing their smiling faces only made her miss them too.

As she passed Shelby's room, she heard the young woman talking on her phone. 'Yes, that sounds great. I'm sure I can drive over without being missed. It's a dream come true to get the audition. I'm so glad Miss Locke contacted you about me. She's such a great support and a great friend. And I'm glad you've accepted her recommendation in spite of the posts she made. I'm grateful to her for suggesting me for the role now that she is staying out of the limelight.'

Ruby scrunched her brow. What role? What contact? She would certainly need to get the bottom of that matter.

She made her way down to the kitchen with trepidation. She wasn't sure if Mitch would be speaking to her, nor did she know if she wanted him to.

He was sitting at the table reading what appeared to be a local newspaper. He glanced up at her but didn't speak.

She helped herself to tea from the pot and sat opposite him. 'Do you want to cancel tonight?' she asked sheepishly.

He closed the newspaper and placed it down. 'No. It's fine. It will be good to catch up with Reid, and I suppose there's a chance they haven't figured out who you are. And we can explain that we're just friends.'

She nodded and sipped at the steaming drink in her mug, letting the citrusy fresh flavour trickle onto her tongue. 'Okay. I just thought I would check.'

He sighed and rubbed his hands over his face. 'Look, I'm only trying to protect your identity, you know. I had to explain things to Archie, but the fewer people who know, the better, or at least that's what I thought.'

She gave a brief smile. 'I know and I do appreciate that. But I can't live as a prisoner. Hiding out will only make me look guilty. Obviously, I don't want the word to spread that I'm here, the last thing I would want would be for hundreds of people turning up baying for my blood. This is a lovely, peaceful village and I don't want to do that to the people here. But I don't want to live like some kind of recluse either. This is hard on me. I'm not used to any of it. But If you would rather I left then—'

'No, don't be daft. I'm not asking you to leave. Just to be cautious, that's all. For your own sake.'

'I know. I'm sorry.' She cringed. 'I'm not very good at this hiding away lark.'

He laughed. 'No, I've noticed.' His eyes locked on hers for a brief moment and her stomach flipped. He broke the gaze and stood from the table. 'We'll have a good night.'

'Yes, I'm sure we will. They seem like lovely people.'

He nodded. 'Aye, they do. I mean... Reid's changed, but he seems so much more settled. And Jules seems great. She's obviously good for him.'

Ruby made a fresh pot of Earl Grey and sat down at the table again. 'So, Morag at the shop sounds like the fount of all knowledge for the village.'

Mitch laughed lightly. 'Aye, you could say that. She'd probably fit right in with your *Pontefract Gazette* crew.' He shook his head. 'Seriously though, she's a grand lady and she can be very discreet when necessary, so don't worry about... you know.'

Ruby sipped her tea. 'I'm not worried at all. I'm looking forward to meeting her.'

Mitch looked deep in thought and fell silent for a while. Eventually he narrowed his eyes at her with his head cocked to one side. 'I'm intrigued to know... if you don't mind sharing, that is... how did you get into acting? Has it been something you've always wanted to do since being a bairn?'

She placed her mug down on the table. 'Strangely enough, no, it wasn't what I wanted to do at all. I had every intention of being a dancer and singer in musical theatre. Preferably Broadway or the West End.'

'Wow, that's some difference. What changed?'

She inhaled deeply, ready to tell her story. 'I studied dance from a very young age and won lots of trophies and medals. I was obsessed. I went to performing arts school and then studied performing arts at Becket University in Leeds. There was this film crew who came to the uni to hold auditions for a short film they were making. Just something about a girl who wanted to be a dancer and all my friends auditioned. They encouraged me to go too, so I did. Only I got the part. The film was shown at loads of UK indie film festivals and that's when I caught the eye of my agent. She was over in the UK with one of her clients and attended a film festival. The next day, I was called into the office at uni and there she was, Valerie Montez, agent to the stars. She signed me up and the next thing I knew I was auditioning for a part in a movie to play a nanny. *Nanny Always Knows Best*. It was a huge hit. And the rest...' She held out her hands.

He wagged a finger at her. 'That was *you*? I've seen that film.' He held up his hands as if defending himself. 'Years ago, and I have to say not by choice. It was played on a long-haul flight.' He laughed and shook his head. 'Who'd have thought that all these years later the nanny who always knows best would be sitting at ma kitchen table.'

Ruby laughed and rolled her eyes. 'You lucky man.'

After a pause he asked, 'Do you miss dancing?'

She sighed and nodded her head. 'I really do. I've especially missed it while all this crap has been going on. Right at the start I said to Kitty that this would never have happened if I hadn't attended that stupid short film audition.'

'Aye. I've often wondered what life would've been like if I had taken the job at the pub that summer instead of the fishing boat. I went for the money. Stupid mistake.'

Ruby lowered her gaze to her cup. 'I went for the possibility of fame. Now I've got it, I feel sometimes that I'd happily swap it.'

He leaned across the table and touched her hand, an involuntary shiver travelled up her arm. 'You do know this mess will get sorted though, eh? This isn't forever. You'll be leaving this wee little village soon and you'll never look back.'

'Oh, I think I'll definitely look back. Hopefully with a smile.'

* * *

After looking through her clothes, Ruby realised she hadn't really got anything suitable for dinner at Reid and Jules' house. Shopping by herself was out of the question. She was aware she needed to address the conversation she had overheard Shelby having, but that would have to wait.

She knocked on Shelby's door. It was opened as if the young woman was waiting behind it. 'Hey, is everything okay?'

Ruby smiled and nodded. 'Oh yes, absolutely fine. But I need a favour.'

Shelby grinned. 'Absolutely. Shoot.'

Ruby felt a little silly for asking. 'Could you possibly head over to the mainland and find me something to wear please? I'm heading out for dinner with Mitch to his friends' house this evening, and I don't really have anything suitable. In fact, I could do with a few warmer items. It might be spring, but it's a lot colder here than in Palermo and I didn't really have time to prepare for that. I can give you my credit card.'

Shelby's eyes lit up. 'I'd *love* to do that for you. Let me grab my coat and purse. Jot down what you need, your sizes, fave colours and styles and I'll go see what I can find.'

Relief flooded Ruby at how amenable Shelby was, and she decided that perhaps she had got the wrong end of the stick when she had overheard her on the telephone. 'Thanks. You're a star.'

Shelby tapped her lightly on the arm. 'Oh no, that's *you*.'

Ruby scribbled all the necessary info on a piece of paper and handed it to Shelby.

Next, she found Dougie in the conservatory reading a James Patterson book.

She cleared her throat. 'Ahem, Dougie, sorry to disturb you.'

He looked up over the spectacles perched on the end of his nose. 'Nae problem, lassie. What can I do for you?'

She knotted her fingers in front of her. 'I was thinking I'd like to have a wander around the village, get some fresh air. I don't want to bother you, so if you're engrossed in—'

'Och, it's nae bother. I'll grab ma coat. But first, let's go over the plan, eh?'

Ruby inhaled and cringed. 'There has to be a plan?'

He smiled warmly. 'It's not a big deal. Basically, I will let you walk ahead alone, and I'll hang back. I don't want to overcrowd you. In such a small place, it would look tae obvious to dae that. But, I'm there if you need me. I suggest a hat, scarf and maybe sunglasses as it's quite sunny oot anyways. Tuck your hair away like you did when you went to the computer bloke's house.' He winked. 'Then the job's a good yin. Oh, and I got you this, you know, just in case.' He handed her a small black box that on closer inspection turned out to be a panic alarm.

It sounded reasonable and doable. She popped the alarm in her pocket and a wave of excitement fluttered over her. 'Thanks Dougie. Can we go now?'

He placed his book down. 'Aye, course we can, lassie. That's what I'm here fae.'

Moments later, with the same hat she wore before and a borrowed scarf, Ruby popped on her sunglasses and headed out into the crisp early April air. She walked down the driveway and onto the main road into the village. A quick glance over her shoulder showed her that Dougie was wrapped up too and looked like a man on a stroll rather than a man on the lookout for security issues. She smiled to herself.

There was a pub called the Coxswain on the corner and further along a grocery shop. She guessed that must be where Morag worked. An elderly man came out with a small shopping bag and she heard a voice from inside shout, 'Bye just now, Hamish!'

Ruby walked over to the inlet, which was surrounded by what appeared to be a newly constructed barrier with padlocks on the openings for access to the boats. She leaned there for a moment and gazed out at the water where a light breeze played on the surface, causing ripples to glint in the sunlight. The sky overhead was vivid blue again, but there was that nip to the air that made her breath appear in little white puffs when she exhaled. Across the other side was a café called Tea for Two with several people sitting inside and a bakery called Caitlin's Cakes & Bakes that she could smell from her vantage point. She decided she would call in and treat the people back at the house to something delicious. If it tasted as good as it smelled, then they were in for a real delight.

Further along, there was an outdoor gear shop. She surmised that perhaps she could've sent Shelby there for the warm coat on her list. Mitch had said something about Archie owning an outdoor wear shop and she guessed that must be the place. It was a shame he didn't sell smart clothing too; it would have saved Shelby a journey.

A bus pulled up outside the bakery and several children got off. One of them walked into the bakery, others wandered off in different directions, all shouting their goodbyes to each other. She smiled as she watched them playing around; a game of tag began after the bus had pulled away, and she thought to herself that this would be such a lovely place to bring up children.

She walked on and at the end of the slipway was an old building, strange in shape with a glass panelled door. An image of an old lifeboat was made from coloured glass and took pride of place in the centre. The sign said *The Lifeboat House Museum* and again she remembered Shelby saying something about this after seeing a painting in her room. She wandered down and read the noticeboard. The museum was closed today but there was a poster about the upcoming village hall opening event. The poster stated that a surprise local celebrity would be there to officially open the building and her interest piqued. *I wonder who that could be...*

She sauntered back over to the bakery and, after a deep breath for courage, she pushed through the door. She hadn't purchased anything for herself in so long and was glad that she still had some UK currency after her last visit home.

'Hi there. What can I get you?' a red-haired woman, whom she presumed to be Caitlin, asked from behind the counter.

'Ooh... I think I might have to buy one of everything. The cakes look amazing.'

The woman laughed. 'Aye, not so great for your waistline, sadly.' She patted her tummy.

'Yes, but there are worse ways to gain weight,' Ruby said with a grin.

'For sure.'

'Seriously though, I could eat one of everything, but I'd better not. So, I'll take four pieces of shortbread, four tray bakes, you can choose which, a chocolate cake. Ooh and a clootie dumpling, just because I love the name.' Ruby giggled.

'Coming right up,' the redhead said as she began to package up the sweet treats. 'So, are you passing through or are you here for a wee break?'

Ruby glanced outside to see Dougie standing by the inlet, watching the water. She turned back to the shopkeeper and replied, 'Just a break really. Not sure how long.'

'Well, you've chosen a grand wee spot. Glentorrin is a lovely place. Friendly folk and surrounded by stunning scenery. I'm sure you'll love it.'

Ruby smiled and glanced outside again. 'I think I already do.'

Once she had paid for her baked goods, she said goodbye to the shop-keeper and left. She contemplated going to chat to Dougie but felt she may blow the cover he had so carefully planned, so she headed back to the house instead.

Once inside, she wrote a note and left the cakes on the kitchen table telling everyone to help themselves. The chocolate cake, however, she kept to take to Reid and Jules' later.

22

Shelby had done really well on her shopping trip. She had visited both the mainland and Portree on Skye. She had returned with two pairs of jeans, a warm coat, a couple of pretty shirts, some long-sleeved tops, a pair of black boots, some undies and several sweaters, one of which was navy blue and printed with *DREAMING OF SKYE*. Ruby held it up and glanced at Shelby with a raised brow.

Shelby blushed. 'Okay, I admit it, I totally bought that with myself in mind. But after what I've seen today, I think it may be true. I'm not sure I ever want to leave here.'

Ruby held it towards her. 'I think you should have this one.'

Shelby's eyes widened and her mouth made an O shape. 'Are you kidding me?'

Ruby shook her head. 'Absolutely not. You've done such a great job here with these clothes, it's the least I can do.'

Shelby chewed her lip. 'You do know I'm being paid, right?'

Ruby laughed. 'Well, I hardly imagined you'd be here with me if you weren't. Just take the sweater. It'll really suit you.'

Shelby took the sweater and flung her arms around Ruby. 'You're the sweetest, kindest movie star I've ever met. And I've met a few.'

Ruby was unsure how to reply, so she mumbled, 'Well, you're the sweetest assistant I've ever had.'

Shelby giggled. 'Technically, I'm the *only* assistant you've ever had, but I'll take it.' She almost skipped to the door of Ruby's room clutching the sweater, and shouted, 'Toodles!' over her shoulder as she closed the door behind herself.

Once again, however, Ruby wondered about the conversation she had overheard. She hadn't recommended Shelby to anyone for auditions. In fact, she had only recently discovered that she was a budding actress, but the fact remained that Shelby had been more than helpful so far.

* * *

At six forty-five, Ruby descended the stairs in pair of black jeans, black boots and a teal shirt with silver thread running through the fine, pale grey stripes.

Mitch was staring in the mirror, his expression crumpled. He turned to watch her walk down the last few steps. 'You look... erm... You look really nice,' he said, clearing his throat. He wore dark blue jeans and a V-neck sweater in navy blue.

She smiled and nervously ran her hand through her hair. 'Thanks, so do you. Although I need to make a decision about my hair. My natural colour is showing through.'

'You could always ask Shelby to pick you up another colour,' he suggested. 'Right, well, I've grabbed a bottle of wine. The cellar here is more of a wine *rack*, but I chose a nice bottle to take with us.'

'I bought a chocolate cake from the little bakery. I thought I could take that for after dinner. What do you think?'

He grinned. 'I say heck yes! Caitlin's baking is incredible. She's Jules' best mate, so Morag says, so I'm guessing she'll be happy.'

'Great! Let's get going then.'

Mitch and Ruby said goodbye to Shelby and Dougie, then walked out of the house and towards the village. The sky was a mixture of purples and oranges above them as the sun made its descent. They took a left turning along the road, past a B&B and up a lane lined with trees that made it dark.

Mitch took out his phone and flicked on the torch. 'One of these days they'll get some street lighting down here.'

Ruby linked her arm through his and squinted in the dim light. 'Yes, it's not somewhere I'd want to be walking alone at night.'

'It's not too far, don't worry.'

Around five minutes later, a house came into view with a pretty porch lit by fairy lights. It was a whitewashed building like so many in the village and there was a large garden surrounding it. Mitch knocked at the door and they could hear Chewie barking inside. Almost immediately the door was opened.

Chewie bounced around excitedly, as a dark-haired boy said, 'Hi! You must be my dad's friends. I'm Evin.'

Ruby bent to say hello to the dog, who proceeded to lick her from chin to nose, making her giggle.

'Hi Evin, I'm Mitch, you won't remember me, the last time I saw you, you were a wee lad. And this is my friend Roo.'

Evin stared at Ruby with a confused expression for a moment until Reid appeared behind his son.

'Hi guys! Great to see you, come on in out of the cold,' he said, stepping aside for them to enter. 'Here, let me take your coats.'

They shrugged off their coats and handed over the gifts they had brought.

Evin eyed the white box and grinned. 'Is this from Caitlin's?'

Ruby nodded. 'I've heard she's good.'

Evin rolled his eyes and nodded. 'And then some. Make sure to save me a bit, Dad,' Evin instructed as he ran off down the corridor, followed by Chewie.

Reid called, 'Aye, I'll try, son, but I'll no' promise!' Then he turned his attention back to Ruby and Mitch. 'Come on through, Jules is stirring the whisky sauce.'

Mitch clapped his hands and rubbed them together. 'Something smells good. What are we having?'

'Jules has perfected Chicken Balmoral, so that's what we'll be tucking into tonight.'

Ruby smiled. 'I have no clue what it is, but Mitch is right: it smells amazing.'

'Chicken stuffed with haggis and drizzled in whisky sauce. Bloody lush,' Mitch informed her with a wide smile as they followed Reid into the kitchen.

'Hi there, so glad you could make it. We haven't had a dinner party for ages,' Jules said as she walked towards them. She hugged Mitch and then turned to Ruby. 'And it's so lovely to have you here,' she said as she embraced her too.

Ruby was warmed by the friendly welcome. 'Thank you so much for having us.'

'Hey, Mitch, I've got something that might interest you. A new canvas I've been working on. Shall we leave the ladies to chat a wee while?'

Mitch glanced at Ruby, but she nodded her confirmation that he should go.

Once they were alone, Jules leaned her back against the countertop and fixed her attention on Ruby. 'Before things go any further this evening, I have a confession.'

Ruby felt her cheeks warming as a million thoughts seemed to rush around her mind. What the heck was she going to say? She tucked her hair behind her ears and nodded. 'Okay, go ahead.'

Jules cringed. 'I know who you are. Reid and I both do. And there's a strong chance Evin does too.'

Ruby swallowed hard and widened her eyes. 'Oh. Right.'

Jules held up her hands. 'Can I just say, though, we haven't told a soul. And I know you're innocent of the awful things that have been put out there. If we can help in any way, just say the word. I don't know if I have done the right thing in telling you. But I didn't want you to feel that you had to make things up about yourself this evening. It must be awful having to pretend to be someone else just to feel safe. I don't want you to do that. I just want you to have a lovely relaxing time and be able to be who you really are.'

Ruby's eyes stung a little. 'Thank you. That's really lovely. I appreciate it.'

'Reid's brother is a bit of a TV star.'

Ruby raised her eyebrows. 'Really? Will I know him?'

Jules giggled. 'Probably not, Kendric Mackinnon is a TV show host on the mainland. Scottish television. In fact, I'm not sure why I brought that up, it's not exactly the same, is it?' She shook her head, chewed her lip and then smiled. 'Look, I'm not entirely sure where Mitch fits into things, but he seems really lovely, and the way he looks at you—'

Ruby gasped involuntarily. 'Oh my word, no! We're not a couple. Just friends. Not even that really. I'm a guest at his house, but that's as far as it goes.'

Jules covered her mouth with her hand. 'Oh heck. I hope I haven't made you uncomfortable. I just assumed – wrongly, I now see – that you were, you know, together. I feel daft now.'

Ruby liked Jules right away. An honest, clearly northern lass, with a heart of gold. 'It's fine, honestly. He's a nice guy. Although, between you and me,' she lowered her voice and glanced briefly over her shoulder, 'he can be really bossy and opinionated too.'

Jules giggled. 'Can't all men? I think we need wine.'

Ruby grinned. 'I agree!'

Mitch and Reid returned through a door at the back of the kitchen. Ruby was lifted when she realised they were chatting like they had never been apart. Jules glanced at her and they shared a knowing smile.

'Right, folks, let's eat.'

They took their places around the table and Jules served the food while Reid poured more wine.

'Is Evin not joining us?' Ruby asked as Chewie arrived at her feet.

Jules laughed. 'No, he's watching *Iron Man* in his room with mac and cheese.' She picked up her wine glass and announced, 'I think we should have a toast. Mitch, I've told Ruby that we know her real identity so you can both relax. To friends, old and new.'

Mitch glanced briefly at Ruby with a look of mild panic in his eyes, but Ruby shook her head and smiled, hoping he would take that to mean all was well. Then they all said in unison, 'To friends, old and new.'

'So, have you two set a date for the wedding yet?' Ruby asked as she tucked into the tender chicken and relished the spices that flavoured the haggis, and the heat of the sauce.

'Aye, we're aiming for December. Christmas Eve to be exact. You guys should come,' Reid said with enthusiasm.

Ruby placed a hand over her heart and tilted her head. 'A Christmas wedding. So romantic,' she said, imagining a church surrounded by falling snow, guests wrapped up in tartan scarves and Chewie wearing a bow tie.

'We got engaged at Christmas so we figured getting married at Christmas would be lovely too,' Jules said, reaching to squeeze Reid's hand.

'How's the wee lad about it all?' Mitch asked.

'Oh, he's dead excited. In fact, I've asked him to be my best man.' Reid's eyes shone with pride.

A lump formed in Ruby's throat. 'Oh my word, it just gets better.' She dabbed at her eyes.

Jules laughed. 'Don't! You'll set me off! He's such a sweet boy. And I should say I'm surprised he didn't say something to you when he opened the door. He's very astute usually. He was watching *Nanny Always Knows Best* at Christmas with Grace, Caitlin's daughter. They're best friends.'

Ruby chuckled. 'He did look at me a little funny.'

'So, what do you think of our wee village?' Reid asked.

Ruby placed down her knife and fork and took a sip of her wine. 'It's gorgeous. So peaceful. And the scenery on the way here was to die for. I'm hoping I get to explore a little while I'm here. We have a rental car too, so I might go for a drive and see the sights.' She hadn't driven in years but figured it must be like riding a bike.

Jules leaned towards her. 'You should definitely go see the Quiraing. Absolutely stunning views from up there. You can do a loop walk. Reid and I have done it a few times with Chewie. He loves it.' She leaned down and patted the dog who was sitting calmly between them. 'I hope you don't mind him being here. I can put him in the other room while we eat if you like.' She cringed.

Ruby glanced down and reached for the dog. 'Are you kidding? Remove my new best friend from the room? No chance. And maybe we could borrow him if we go do the walk?'

Reid laughed. 'You might regret asking. He's got way too much energy, that dog. But if you're serious, then absolutely.'

'Oh, I am. I had a little Yorkshire Terrier keeping me company in Sicily.

He was called Nero. Such a cutie. I do miss him.' Her eyes misted over a little, but she rallied and turned to Mitch. 'What do you think? Maybe Dougie will be up for it? He's fit.'

Mitch grinned and shook his head. 'Aye, he might be fit, but I'm not so sure about me these days.'

Reid gently punched his arm. 'Ah, you're talking pish, man! You've a set of swimmer's lungs.'

Mitch guffawed. 'Aye, but he's wanting them back!'

* * *

The evening was filled with laughter, friendship and warmth. As she walked home with Mitch, Ruby noticed a feeling of calm had settled over her, the like of which she hadn't felt in a very long time. As they reached the village, she stopped and inhaled the cold Scottish air, filling her lungs with its fresh chill.

'I can see why people love this place so much,' she said dreamily as she watched the moonlight glint on the water.

Mitch wrapped his coat close around him. 'Aye, it's a nice wee place. And it feels even more like home again. That's down to you.'

She turned to face him. 'How so?'

He gazed down at her, his eyes alive with happiness. 'You helped me to reconnect with one of the best friends I ever had. I didn't realise how much I missed him until tonight. So, thank you. I know I was reticent about the whole dinner thing, but it was really good.'

Ruby's warm glow intensified as she smiled up at him. 'Jules thought we were a couple, you know.'

Mitch rolled his eyes. 'Ugh, I knew that would happen.'

She was, yet again, disappointed with his response. 'Don't worry, I told her we're just acquaintances.'

He tilted his head and narrowed his eyes. 'I'd have said we're friends.'

She smiled. 'Are we?'

His eyes twinkled in the light from the overhead bulbs strung around the inlet. 'I'd like to think so. Wouldn't you? We've been through a lot in a short length of time. The least we can be is friends. Comrades in the battle. Partners in crime.' He grinned.

She whacked his arm. 'Let's stick with *friends*, eh?'

'Deal.'

The two friends walked back to Glentorrin House in companionable silence.

23

Ruby climbed into bed and lay there for a while thinking about the evening she had just spent with her new friends. She longed to have a relationship as trusting and pure as Reid and Jules'. They had told her how they had met when Jules came to check out the place where her mum had grown up, and how Reid had been fighting depression. Jules had helped him after she spotted the signs; she had gone through it too after the loss of her husband. It was refreshing to hear people talk so openly about their experiences and she admired both of them for coming out on the other side even stronger. She was grateful it was something she hadn't had to deal with, but after the low points since the hacking, she could definitely see how easy it would be to start on the slippery slope.

Mitch had been shocked about Reid's situation and apologised for not being there. He seemed genuinely upset that he had been too preoccupied with his own life to know his friend was suffering. Of course, Reid patted his shoulder warmly and dismissed his apology, insisting it wasn't needed, but Ruby saw the effect of the news in Mitch's eyes. She felt bad for him, and for the years the two friends had lost.

Chewie had lain at her feet most of the night as if he knew she had asked to borrow him for a walk, and she already knew the red furball had captured her heart. They had always had dogs at home when she was growing up and until she met Nero in Sicily she hadn't realised how much she had missed the calming serenity a dog's presence created. Tonight had confirmed it. Sadly, having a dog was a no-go with her current lifestyle, especially now she had no one to share the responsibility with while she was away on film sets. The fact made her quite sad. In fact, seeing the little family before her made her realise she was lonely, and that was a stark contrast to how her life appeared to others.

At the end of the evening as they were about to leave, Jules had said she should pop to the museum after closing and she would show her around. Ruby was excited about that and had been grateful for the offer. She looked forward to finding out more about the special place in which she was a guest. After hearing her hosts wax lyrical about Glentorrin, she figured it had a certain magic about it, just like she had thought when she arrived.

Once back in her room, she texted Kitty to tell her all about her evening, then quickly called her mum and dad to say goodnight. Finally, she replied to Philippe, asking him to hug his girls for her and saying how much she missed them all.

* * *

The next morning, Ruby awoke to tapping on her door. She glanced at the clock to see it was only eight thirty. She grabbed her dressing gown and walked to the door, rubbing her tired eyes as she did. She opened it to find Mitch standing there looking anxious.

'Morning. What's up?' she asked with a simultaneous yawn.

'Hi, sorry to bother you so early. Archie has just been on the phone,' he whispered.

Ruby's heart skipped. 'Oh? Is there news?'

'Not just yet, but he's getting close. The hacker used an IP address that was jumping around, or something – he used technical terms – so he's still tracing it, but at some point, he says the hacker was definitely in New York. Is there anyone you can think of that might have been close to you that could have done it? I mean, the location can't be a coincidence.'

A wave of nausea washed over her. 'I went through all this at the time. I couldn't think of anyone who would do such a thing.'

Mitch pursed his lips and paused as if contemplating his next words carefully. 'Look, I know this is a horrid thing to ask...' He sighed and rubbed at his chin.

'Go on.'

He glanced over his shoulder. 'You don't think Valerie could have something to do with it, do you?' He kept his voice in a hushed tone.

Ruby gasped. 'No! Why would she? She's my agent. She's suffering too because of all this. And like you said, she sees me as a daughter figure.'

'Aye, aye, I know. But think about it... she was supposed to be sorting it, wasn't she? Then it turned out she wasn't. If that doesn't mark her as a suspect, I don't know what does.' He shrugged but eyed her with pity.

Ruby felt the colour drain from her face. 'She wouldn't... And anyway, she's useless with computers. I had to show her how to set up her screen-saver, for goodness' sake. And why would she want to sabotage one of her clients?'

He glanced over his shoulder again. 'Anyone can pretend they're crap with computers. It's much easier to pretend you don't know stuff than to pretend you do. But as for your other question... I honestly don't know. Could she have been trying to get rid of you? Is there another actor that she might have wanted to push forward but needed to get you out of the way to do so?'

Ruby felt weak at the knees. The more she thought about it, the more it seemed possible. Valerie had signed Aurora Santos, a beautiful Portuguese American actor, just before the hacking. Ruby had only met her once at an evening soiree Valerie had held to introduce her to everyone. And she was very beautiful; long legs, olive skin, long, sun-kissed golden hair. She was the stuff of every man's dreams. Perhaps Valerie did want to push her forward? She was getting lots of attention from film companies. But no matter how much she thought about it, Ruby couldn't let herself believe it was her agent. 'I feel quite sick, Mitch. I hadn't imagined it could be Val.'

Mitch reached out and patted her arm awkwardly. 'Hey, it might not be. It might be that Tyler Harrison prick.'

Ruby glared at him. 'Because that would be better?'

He cringed. 'Aye, sorry that was insensitive. But, hey, look on the bright side, at least Archie's getting somewhere. I know it seems to be taking a while, but he's running a couple of businesses and does freelance computer stuff on the side, so...'

Ruby shook her head. 'No, it's fine. I appreciate that he is *doing* something, unlike other people I could mention.'

He scratched his head and stood there stepping from foot to foot. 'I asked Dougie about us maybe going for a drive up the island today. I thought you might want to get out. I said we could go in my Landy seeing as there'll be three of us, and the back windows are tinted.' He frowned briefly. 'Shelby was there when I asked him, and I expected her to want to come too, but she says she has somewhere to be today and she doesn't know what time she'll be back.'

Ruby wondered if her trip might have something to do with the phone call she overheard. 'Great. I'll go shower and be down soon.'

He gave a swift nod and left her to her thoughts.

She closed the door and leaned back against it with a deep disconcerted sigh. 'Bloody hell. Who can I really trust?'

* * *

Around an hour later, Ruby, Mitch and Dougie were in Mitch's Landy and heading north on Skye. The road followed the eastern coast of the island and overhead was a blue sky mottled with fluffy white clouds. The temperature outside was mild, but Mitch had said they shouldn't let that lull them into a false sense of security as it could change in a split second. They travelled through a small town called Broadford and then further north along the coast, following the A87.

Mitch pointed out of the window. 'Off in the distance to the left you can see the Cuillin mountain range. Incredible views from up there.'

The mountain range was almost a black silhouette against the sky, each rise sharp and angular like a blade. Ruby wanted to go there, to take photos, to breathe the rarefied air right at the summit. She had never longed for the outdoors before, so the feeling was alien to her, but looking up at the rocky striations she felt quite emotional. Like up there she would be free from everything making her life hard at the moment.

Around forty minutes later, Mitch pulled onto the driveway of a single-storey house. It was one of four in a cul-de-sac that all faced out over the sea. The houses were similar in structure but not exactly the same.

Mitch swivelled around in his seat. 'I hope yous don't mind, but I thought we could stop for a minute to see my folks. Then I'll take us on a scenic drive.'

'Not at all. That would be lovely,' Ruby eagerly replied; human contact was something she was also craving of late.

Dougie cleared his throat. 'I'll stay with the car. I have some calls to make. Business to attend to, if you will.' It sounded very cloak and dagger, but Ruby figured what she didn't know couldn't stress her out.

'No problem. See you soon.'

Mitch and Ruby climbed out of the car and walked up to the front door of the bungalow. Before he knocked, Mitch turned to face her. 'I hope you don't think this is weird. Meeting my folks, I mean. It feels a bit like something we'd do after we'd been dating.'

His brow crumpled and Ruby couldn't help the twinge of annoyance at his expression. Why was it that every time that subject was mentioned he looked decidedly unhappy about it? Wasn't she good enough for him? And, more to the point, why did she care?

She crossed her arms over her chest, a fairly defensive stance. 'People can introduce friends to their parents, you know. I don't see why you have to make such a big deal about things.' She huffed.

He opened his mouth to speak, but clearly thought better of it, sighed and knocked on the door.

Moments later, an elderly lady opened the door and beamed at Mitch. 'Mio figlio! Che bello vederti!'

He leaned down and hugged her and she kissed both his cheeks and his forehead.

'Ciao mamma! Questa è la mia amica, Ruby. Lei è inglese.'

'Ah, welcome, beautiful girl, to my home. Come in, come in.'

'Grazie, Signora Adair.' Ruby was quietly excited that she had remembered the greeting that she had looked up in her phrase book earlier.

Mrs Adair cupped her face and gave Mitch a look that he clearly understood because his cheeks coloured pink. She grabbed Ruby's hand and led her through to the kitchen.

Ruby glanced at Mitch and he mouthed the word, 'sorry,' with a cringe. But the fact was, Ruby was in love with the old lady already.

'So, you come to Skye from England?' Mitch's mum's English was impressive – definitely more so than Ruby's Italian.

'That's right, Mrs Adair. Yorkshire originally, but I've been living in New York.'

'Please, call me Rosa. And what is it you do in New York?'

Ruby glanced at Mitch for some kind of direction, but he was too busy raiding a tin of home-made cakes, so she chose honesty. 'I work in the movie business.' She glanced over to Mitch, but he was busy munching on something that looked like a roll of dough with cream inside. Whatever it was, it looked delicious.

'Movies? That must be stressful.' Mrs Adair frowned. 'Do you see your mamma? Papà?'

Ruby shook her head. 'Not as much as I would like. They still live in England.'

'This is so sad. But you speak on the phone, sì?'

Ruby nodded. 'As often as I can.'

Mrs Adair whacked her son's arm. 'See! Ruby, she calls her mamma.' She turned to look at Ruby and gave a small wink that made her giggle.

Mitch rubbed his arm. 'Mamma! Non è giusto!' For a moment, he looked like a sulking teenager.

A man walked into the room; a white-haired, older version of Mitch. 'Hi there, son! I thought I could hear your dulcet tones. How long are you home for?' he asked as he pulled Mitch into a bear hug.

'A few weeks maybe,' Mitch replied with a slap to his father's back. 'Dad, this is my friend, Ruby. Ruby, this is Cullen Adair.'

Ruby held out her hand. 'Nice to meet you, Mr Adair.'

'Och, come 'ere,' Mr Adair said as he grappled her into a hug. 'And it's Cullen. Mr Adair makes me sound old. So, how do you two know each other?'

Mrs Adair interjected, hands out in front of her to emphasise her words. 'Ruby works in the movie business in New York.'

'Fancy that,' Mr Adair said with raised eyebrows. 'But that can't be how you met. Mitch can't act his way out of a paper bag. I've seen his school plays.' He nudged his son playfully.

'Cheers, Papa,' Mitch said with an eye roll and a smirk. 'We met when she needed a holiday. A mutual friend put us in contact, and she stayed at the house in Palermo for a wee while.'

Mrs Adair smiled widely and raised her hands. 'But now she is here. What can I make you to drink? Tea? Coffee?'

'Tea would be lovely, thank you.'

'Have some cake. If my son hasn't eaten it already.'

Once the tea was made, they were invited through to the living room to sit. The large picture window looked out over the front elevation and to the water in the distance.

'Wow, what a view,' Ruby said, gazing out.

Cullen joined her by the window. 'Aye, it's not bad, is it? It's like a living painting that changes every day. Mitch found us the place. He had the changes made too, to make the house suit us oldies.' The pride for his son shone through in his words and the look in his eyes as he spoke.

'You have a beautiful home.' Ruby glanced around at the myriad framed photos adorning the walls. It was like a timeline of Mitch's life. His sister was there too; bright eyed and smiling. She felt a pang of sadness that Alessia's life had been snuffed out so young. There were photos of a young Mitch in swimming trunks, a towel flung over his shoulder, proudly holding up medals and trophies. There was a shot of Mitch and his sister with a black Labrador, photos of them in a garden on a swing set in a place that looked distinctly like Glentorrin House, and photos of them in the garden she recognised as the one in Palermo. They were clearly a very close family and seeing the photos made her miss her parents even more. It also gave her more insight into the protective nature of the man who was hosting her.

24

When they were ready to leave the Adairs' home, Rosa and Cullen were generous with hugs and repeats of, 'Please come back soon,' and, 'Visit us any time!' Ruby sincerely believed they meant it too.

All too soon they were ready to return to Glentorrin via the scenic route Mitch had promised. Mitch took a small detour to the centre of Portree where there was an array of shops and cafés and Ruby felt sad that she hadn't had a chance to wander around at her leisure. Although she made sure she didn't show it. There was nothing worse than a privileged person filled with envy for something simple.

At the centre of the town was a war memorial in a kind of town square, remnants of poppy wreaths still lay on the steps, defying the winter weather just passed. A stone-built hotel sat on the corner of the street opposite and several grand-looking houses surrounded the rest of the precinct. People wandered around with bags of shopping, stopping to chat with friends. Smiles lit up the faces of everyone she saw and in turn it made Ruby smile.

'I'll just take you down Quay Street,' Mitch announced as he indicated to take a left-hand turn. 'I think you'll like it.'

He was right. The houses, each painted a different, sunny pastel colour, looked out over the water. The sky overhead was heavy with rain clouds and the breeze had picked up, causing the small, moored boats to bob around on the swell, clanking and clinking as they did. In the distance, two hills bowed down towards the sea and beyond that another island was just visible.

'You're looking towards Raasay over Loch Portree. It's prettier on a sunny day but worth a look anyway.'

'Definitely. Thank you, Mitch,' Ruby replied as she gazed out at the view.

The journey home took them a different route that cut across the island, through dramatic mountains and patches of snow, proof that winter wasn't yet ready to leave the place completely either. Eventually the road opened up onto what Mitch told them was Loch Harport. Further along the road, they got a clearer view of the Black Cuillin. From this angle, Ruby thought the mountains appeared almost otherworldly. Perhaps like the surface of some uninhabited planet, or a filmset from an outer-space movie. She was mesmerised. Even when it started to rain heavily, it looked beautiful. The sky darkened to the grey of freshly poured concrete and the tops of the Cuillin became shrouded in an eerie hanging mist. She pitied anyone who may have been caught out up there.

The rest of journey home was made in silence, apart from the Proclaimers CD playing 'Letter from America' in the background as they admired the views through the glass.

* * *

The more she saw of the island, the more Ruby contemplated buying a small property there; a bolthole or pied-à-terre; somewhere where she could escape fame and all the stress and hassle it brought. Over the last few weeks, she had looked upon her status with less and less positivity. The pros she tried to think of were eluding her and seemed outweighed by cons. She missed dancing, she missed shopping, she missed her parents, she missed Kitty. She missed having a normal life. These factors had always bothered her, but lately they had even more so.

Once back at the house, she dressed in a pair of yoga pants and a baggy T-shirt she usually slept in. She tied it in a knot at the waist, closed her room door and hoped that the rest of the residents would realise she wanted to be alone. She linked up her phone to the iPod docking station in the room adjoining her bedroom and pushed the small coffee table towards the wall.

She flicked through her downloaded songs until she reached Cindy Lauper's album *A Night to Remember* and forwarded the tracks until she reached the song 'Heading West'. She hit play and swayed to the music for a moment, eyes closed. As the song played and the music took her, she raised her arms and twirled on the spot, letting the emotion of the song carry her. In seconds. she was utterly lost in movement and feeling. Her eyes remained closed as her breathing quickened and her heart rate picked up its pace. Sadness washed over her as she listened to the lyrics that sang of moving on without regret and hoped that one day, she would have that strength.

But she had many regrets.

As she danced, she remembered the good times with Tyler, laughing, making love, holding each other. It had all been a lie, a publicity stunt. She should have known really. She was too 'normal' to be in a relationship with someone who held himself in such high regard, above everything *and* everyone else. If only she had realised that before she'd wasted so much time on him.

It felt good to surrender to the music once again, to be filled with endorphins racing around her veins. A kind of muscle memory took over as she reached and stretched, bent and pirouetted. Tears trickled down her cheeks from the conflicting emotions she had been trying to hold in check for weeks, but no one was watching so she didn't care.

When the song came to an end, she was out of breath and sweat had beaded on her brow, but she felt a kind of euphoria that only dancing seemed to bring her. She reached to pause the playlist and as she did, someone behind her applauded, causing her to jump and turn around to face her unexpected audience.

'Wow. I have no words... just... wow,' Mitch said with eyes that seemed to be glistening with emotion.

She swiped her hand across her forehead. 'You weren't... I mean... the door was closed.' She panted as she spoke.

He slipped his hands into his pockets and cleared his throat. 'Aye, I know, I'm so sorry about that, but I knocked and when you didn't answer...'

She felt her face warming from something other than her exertion. 'Sorry, yes, I was a bit preoccupied.'

He stepped closer and removed his hands from his pockets. 'You looked...' He shook his head. 'Sorry I shouldn't have—'

She waved her hand. 'Oh, it's... it's fine. What's wrong? Has Archie been in touch again?'

He took a few more steps. 'Aye. He has. He has names.'

Ruby gasped. 'Oh my goodness! That's incredible! Names? Plural? There's more than one hacker? Fantastic! I can go to the police; this can all be—'

Mitch held up his hand. 'Not quite.'

She frowned and stepped towards him, confusion taking over again. 'But why? If we have names, we can—'

He closed his eyes for a moment. 'They're fake. The names are fake.'

Her heart sank and she slumped onto the small sofa. 'Oh. Right. So we're no further forward? And anyway, how do you know they're fake?'

'Did you ever watch *The Big Bang Theory*?' he asked with a tilt of his head.

She scrunched her brow. 'Yes. I used to love that show!' She wagged her finger as a memory came back to her. 'In fact, I met Jim Parsons on a set once. He was such a nice guy. Very funny in real life.' She stopped, realising this wasn't really the time for name dropping. 'Sorry... I digress, what has that got to do with the hacking?'

'The names were Howard Wolowitz and Sheldon Cooper.'

'Oh shit. They're character names from the show.' She sank into the seat and let her head rest back.

'Yup. But, again, the bright side is that Archie has made more headway in the last few days than anyone up to now. It's all good. He *will* get there. He said I had to tell you so.'

She sighed and nodded. The high she'd had while dancing had been dashed. 'Yes, he's doing a good job. He clearly knows what he's doing.'

Mitch nodded with a look of sympathy. 'Aye, he really, *really* does. Please have faith. Anyway, grubs up. I've made a risotto. It's amazing, even if

I do say so myself. Although I can't take all the credit, it's one of my mamma's recipes.'

Her mood lifted at the mention of Rosa. 'Ooh yum. I'm starving. I'll get changed and be down soon.'

He nodded and turned as if to walk away but paused and faced her again. 'When you said you loved to dance, I don't think I expected such talent, Ruby. But that...' He pointed at the floor where she had been moments before. 'That was so beautiful. It made me feel...' He shook his head and briefly glanced at the ceiling. 'I don't know what it made me feel, to be honest... I don't think I have the words. But it was...' He smiled warmly. 'Your face... You looked so serene. So happy.' He shrugged. 'I'm blethering on. I'll leave you to get sorted.' He quickly turned and left the room.

* * *

At the end of their meal, Dougie stood. 'I'm getting spoiled, you know. The food's not usually this good on security detail. Anyway, I'm away to watch telly in ma room. *Strictly Come Dancing* is on repeat and I missed the last show, so...' He lifted his hand in a wave before leaving and heading upstairs to his room.

Mitch and Ruby shared a look of surprise and they both grinned.

'Now I wasn't expecting that,' Mitch said with a chuckle.

Shelby burst in through the door and slammed it behind herself before storming up to her room without saying hello. Mitch and Ruby looked at one another.

'I wonder what that was all about,' Ruby said as she picked up her wine glass. Although she had an inkling it might be something to do with the call she'd overheard.

'I'm keeping well out of it,' Mitch said as he cleared the table.

A lilting song played quietly in the background and Ruby strained to listen to the lyrics. The lead vocalist was singing about someone feeling like home and grounding her and Ruby's breath caught as a sudden rush of emotion washed over her.

'Are you okay?' Mitch asked, topping up her glass. 'You look a little lost in thought.'

'What's this song?'

He smiled. 'It's called "Somersault", by a band called Zero 7. It's quite old. I think it came out in the early two thousands. This track has Sia singing on it and I love her voice. It's great background music, eh? Very chilled out.'

'Yes. But the lyrics are so beautiful.'

He paused for a moment and listened. 'Aye, I suppose they are. I think we all want someone to make us feel like that, eh?'

'Absolutely.'

He sat again and closed his eyes. She fixed her gaze on him as he nodded gently to the music's waltzing beat, carried away by violins and guitars. Her stomach did a little flip as she took in the contours of his angular jaw and the small smile that turned his lips up ever so slightly. He ran his hand through his hair and a strand flopped back over his forehead. She wondered what it would be like to touch his hair, run her thumb across his cheek, feel his lips on hers... She was lost for a brief time, just watching him as his lips parted. But when she looked up, she realised he was watching her now too. If she hadn't known better, from his hooded expression, she'd have presumed his thoughts mirrored hers. Her heart skipped, but then she remembered his comments about relationships, and how he had protested at the thought of people thinking they were an item. She shook her head, attempting to rid herself of the desire for him that was building inside her. What the hell was she thinking?

'That meal was delicious, Mitch. Thank you,' she said, breaking whatever spell she had imagined had been cast.

He frowned, an infinitesimal action that she might have missed had she not been paying attention, and he said, 'I'm glad you enjoyed it. I was taught to cook from a young age. Mamma always said she wanted me to be a good husband.' He laughed. 'So, she gave me all the skills. I'm good at ironing too.'

Ruby smiled. 'Wonders never cease.'

Mitch leaned his elbows on the table and fixed his gaze on her. 'Look, I'm sorry I barged in on you earlier. That was out of line.'

Ruby frowned and placed down her glass. 'Hey, it's okay. It's your house after all. And I am, yet again, squatting in your room.'

He sighed. 'Aye, it's weird having the house so full. I'm not used to it.'

The landline rang and Mitch stood to pick up the kitchen handset.

'Hello?' There was a pause as someone spoke. 'I see... Aye...' He closed his eyes and pinched the bridge of his nose as there was another long pause. 'Okay. Maybe we should meet now. At the pub? Aye, she's here. Only bring the people you've mentioned though, eh?' He hung up and sat down again with a long huff. He rubbed his hands over his face and then squinted at Ruby. 'I'm afraid your cover's kind of blown again.'

Ruby was surprised at how unaffected she felt by the news. 'Okay. What's the plan?'

He rolled his eyes. 'We're meeting at the pub with the equivalent of your *Pontefract Gazette* ladies. I'd better go tell Dougie and Shelby. Look... let's not mention the work Archie is doing for us, okay? Let's keep that between you, me and him.'

Confused as to why that mattered, Ruby pursed her lips and shrugged. 'If you say so.'

* * *

Half an hour later, the main bar at the Coxswain looked a little like a village meeting. Chairs were arranged facing the fireplace and Ruby looked around nervously at the faces, some familiar, some not.

Mitch introduced people to Ruby as they arrived. Dougie stood at the back of the room by the entrance, his arms folded over his chest like a nightclub bouncer, and Shelby had joined them, her eyes were red and puffy, clear signs that she had been crying. Ruby decided she must speak to her and make sure she was okay. Jules, Reid and Evin were there, so too were the red-haired lady from the bakery who Ruby now knew to be Caitlin, Caitlin's twelve-year-old daughter, Grace, and Morag with her husband, Kenneth, who helped her run the shop and the B&B. There were a few more faces she didn't recognise, but they all smiled at her warmly.

They were soon joined by Archie, but Mitch whispered in his ear before he entered the room; Ruby guessed he was being instructed to keep the hacking investigation under his hat.

A huge, bearded man served drinks from behind the bar. Mitch informed her his name was Joren and that he ran the pub with his wife, Stella, who also joined the meeting, smiling warmly at Ruby as Mitch introduced them.

Mitch stood and addressed the gathered villagers. 'Right, folks. Thanks for coming at short notice. It's been brought to my attention that most of you have recognised Ruby. I'm not really surprised, and I don't think we could've expected to keep things a secret for long. But... and this is so important...' He put his hands together as if praying. 'What I have to ask all of you is that you keep it to yourselves. Ruby is here to escape the press, so the last thing we need is the likes of the local paper sniffing around. And we don't want people coming here just to spot her. She's not an exhibit, so let's make sure she doesn't turn into one. She'd love to be able to move around the village like any of you, so I'm hoping by having yous all here to talk about it we can make that happen. If you see that huge hulk of a man following her around at any point, don't worry. He's Dougie, Ruby's security detail. He's here because of what's happened and just to keep an eye out. So, if you notice anything that worries you, you can always mention it to him. Does anyone have any problems with what I've said? And has anyone told someone who isn't in this room about our esteemed guest?'

Evin put up his hand.

Mitch tilted his head. 'Evin? What's up, kid?'

Evin's cheeks flushed bright red. 'Erm...' He cleared his throat and stood up. 'I just wanted to say to Miss Ruby, welcome to Glentorrin. It's my favourite place in the world because I know everyone, and the people are all really kind. And your secret is safe because my uncle is famous too and I don't go round bragging to people because I respect his privateness.' His dad whispered something to him, and he blushed again. 'His *privacy*. Anyway, my dad and Jules say I'm really mature for my age. I'm twelve by the way. Oh, and... I thought you were really good in *Nanny Always Knows Best*.' He smiled and sat down again, and Reid and Jules praised him for his attitude.

Ruby stood. 'Can I just say a few words?' She glanced around the room and was greeted with nods and smiles. 'Firstly, thank you so much, Evin, I really appreciate that. I heard about your uncle being on TV too, so it's good to know you're experienced in dealing with such matters.' Evin beamed. 'I just wanted to say that I've had such a warm welcome and I love your village. The last thing I want is to bring crowds of people here, not if they aren't here just to see the wonderful place for themselves.' She hadn't felt so nervous in a very long time and her hands were shaking so she clasped them together. 'I've had a horrible time of things since the hacking. I'm sure you all know about that from the TV and papers. I want you to know that what they reported on were lies. I would never say those things. I love people for who they are and would *never* disrespect or judge someone because of their skin colour, beliefs, preferences, or anything like that. I want you to believe that I'm decent, friendly and not how I was portrayed. I'm just a normal person who happens to be famous. But I love to dance, I love to read books, I love to go for walks, just like everyone. It's not always easy for me to do those things, but I hope while I'm here I will get to do them all. I have no idea how long I'll be here. I'm hoping it won't be too long, and I don't mean that because of the people or the place, I simply mean that once I can leave it will be because my name has been cleared. And I want that *so* much.' Her throat tightened. 'I don't want to be hated, especially for something I simply didn't do. Thank you for listening.'

She sat down again and chewed the inside of her cheek in the hope it would abate the threatening tears as a spontaneous applause travelled around the room. She glanced up to see everyone smiling at her and relief washed over her.

A lady stood and folded her hands in front of her. 'I'm Morag. I think Mitch might have mentioned me as I own the shop. I just wanted to say welcome to Glentorrin. We're a friendly bunch. And we don't believe everything we read, so please don't worry. I, for one, don't take any heed of what was put out there. You seem like a very sweet young woman. And all I can hope is that Joe Public will realise that soon enough. If me and my Kenneth can help in any way, all you need to do is say.' She sat and gave Ruby a warm smile.

Caitlin stood next. 'I have to admit, I recognised you when you came into the bakery, although as a fellow redhead the hair did fox me a little.

But, like Evin, I respected your privacy, so I didn't say anything to you. In fact, I didn't say anything to anyone, not even Jules, and I tell her everything.' A rumble of laughter travelled the room and a few people agreed with her. 'But you are welcome to be here as long as you need. We look after our own in Glentorrin.'

Grace put up her hand and Mitch encouraged her to stand. 'Ahem... I'm Grace and that's my mum,' she said, pointing to Caitlin. 'You... you said you like to dance. Well, I like to dance too and to make new friends, so I'm happy to meet you. And if you're going to the village hall opening, I could teach you some ceilidh dances, if you don't already know them.' She sat quickly and her cheeks turned cerise. Caitlin kissed the top of her head and a chorus of 'Awww' traversed the room.

Mitch stepped forward again. 'Wow, thank you all so much. I really appreciate how great you're being. And I'm sure Ruby appreciates it too.' Ruby nodded. 'Thank you all.'

A mumble of chatter travelled around as people turned to speak to each other.

Mitch turned to Ruby and placed his hand on her shoulder. He bent down and whispered, 'This is why I brought you here. These amazing people.'

Ruby looked around the room through blurry eyes at smiling, friendly faces and her heart ached for the kind of belonging the wonderful people around her had. The realisation sinking in more so now that she missed her normal life, her friends and family, having someone to love like Morag and Jules, being able to pop to the pub for a drink, or to a museum during opening hours. She had known all along that money and fame didn't buy happiness, but she had always tried to be grateful for the life she was leading. Now, though, it was getting harder and harder to imagine going back to her former life, especially since she'd had a taste of this one.

25

After the meeting, Shelby had been quiet and almost back to her pre-hacking self. Ruby was still aware she needed to check in with her to find out what had happened to make her so sad, and, of course, to find out what the overheard phone call had been about.

Ruby found Shelby in the conservatory the morning after the meeting, she was staring into space and clutching a mug of coffee.

'Hey, Shelby. Are you okay? You've been quiet,' Ruby asked as she sat on the opposite sofa.

Shelby glanced up at her as if coming out of a trance. She frowned, shook her head and then plastered on the smile that Ruby now guessed was fake. 'Oh yeah, I'm great. Why wouldn't I be?'

'Look, I need to ask you something. I was passing your room the other day, and I heard you on a call with someone. You mentioned my name and I just wondered who you were talking to?'

Shelby's eyes widened briefly, then she laughed lightly. 'Pfft, oh, I was just checking in with Valerie, you know, see if there had been any progress.' She shrugged.

Ruby narrowed her eyes and shook her head slowly. 'No... you said something about me recommending you for an audition.'

Shelby's face drained of colour and she straightened her spine. 'Why were you listening in? You shouldn't be spying on me. That was a private call.' She bristled.

Ruby sighed. 'Shelby, just tell me the truth, okay?'

Shelby sneered. 'Why? Because everything should be about you? God, you're so damned privileged and yet you still moan and whine about every little thing.'

The comment stung and Ruby sat up straight. 'Excuse me? I'm sorry but that is absolutely not true.'

Shelby sighed and rolled her eyes. 'Really? *Oh, woe is me, I'm a rich actress who gets all the best parts in movies and gets to vacation in Sicily and Scotland whenever I feel like it.*'

Ruby clenched her jaw. 'What is this really about, Shelby? What's going on?'

Shelby stood. 'You wanna know? Okay, but you won't like it and I'll end up out of a job and a home,' she said with a jab of her finger in Ruby's direction.

Ruby sighed. 'Is it really that bad?'

Shelby flopped back onto the sofa, lowered her gaze and closed her eyes. 'I've done something really stupid.'

Ruby immediately presumed she was about to admit to the hacking and her hackles rose. 'Go on.'

Shelby sighed and her eyes welled with tears. 'I only came here because I had a chance to audition for something that you should've auditioned for. A British sitcom. I opened the email at the office after you had told Valerie you were relocating again, and I responded as her. I told them you weren't accepting auditions, because I know you're not at the moment and I didn't think you'd be interested in a sitcom anyway. So, I told them I had someone who would be perfect for the part. Then I forged a letter from you saying you wholeheartedly recommended me for the role.' Tears escaped and trickled down her cheeks. 'I was so happy when they called me to say I got the audition, and I drove to Glasgow to attend it.' She let out a sob. 'Then they gave the part to someone else, even though I knew I was perfect for it. It was all for nothing. I deceived Valerie, convinced her to let me come here and assist you, lied to you too. But all the effort I put in to get the part, the risk I took, was all for nothing.'

Ruby sighed deeply. 'Oh, Shelby... That's so disappointing. You can't do things like that. You're employed as a PA. You have access to private and confidential information, but you clearly can't be trusted.'

Shelby burst into tears. 'Please, please don't tell Valerie. It was a dumb mistake and I regret it and I'm sorry. It will never happen again. I don't want Valerie to be angry with me. She's been good to me and I don't want her to know I let her down. I'll quit. I'll go back to the US and I'll quit, I promise. Please, Ruby, all I ever wanted was to be an actress and I figured working for Valerie would be a good inroad. I was wrong. All I get to do is babysit people and fetch coffee. I don't even want to be a damned assistant. Acting is my dream. It's all I think about. Being amongst the drama of a set, being the star. Surely you get that?' She pleaded with her eyes and clasped her hands together.

Ruby pondered for a moment. In all honesty, she didn't get it. It had never been her 'dream'. Shelby had a desperation for it that Ruby had never experienced, maybe for dancing but not for acting, and she suddenly felt guilty for falling into her career by accident, when Shelby was someone who would clearly risk everything for it. Her heart softened a little.

'I won't mention anything to Valerie at this point. So long as you promise to never do *anything* like this again. You've put me in a very awkward position, though, Shelby. I'll need to think things through, and I can't promise that I won't tell her. Not only did you lie to Valerie, but you impersonated me, which, under the circumstances, was a very silly and thoughtless thing to do.'

Shelby nodded while sobbing. 'I know. I never meant to hurt you. I just really wanted that part. And I figured if I got it, you'd be happy for me and so would Valerie.'

Ruby shook her head, knowing full well that it wouldn't have been as clear-cut as Shelby presumed. 'Well, now you know that it's not a matter of lying your way onto a set. You can't just use my name to get a part. It doesn't work like that.'

'I know. I see that now.' She sniffed. 'I'll go pack my stuff.'

Ruby shook her head. 'No, don't do that. Not yet. Valerie will want an explanation for sure if you quit. Just leave things for now. Let me think.'

Shelby's expression brightened. 'Really? Thank you, Ruby. Thank you so much.' She walked over and hugged Ruby hard.

Ruby stiffened. 'Don't thank me, Shelby. I'm hurt and disappointed. After everything I've been put through lately, I didn't need this. But I'm not a *woe is me* person, in spite of what you seem to think. And we're not friends. I'm not doing you a favour. I'm thinking things through. There may still be repercussions when the production company give feedback on your audition and then you'll have a lot of explaining to do.'

'I... I diverted their emails, so it'll be fine.'

Ruby sighed deeply and shook her head. 'It's never good to clamber over people to get to the top, Shelby. You'd do well to remember that.'

Shelby didn't speak. Her nostrils flared and she turned and left the room.

Ruby flopped back onto the sofa, exhaling roughly and rubbing her hands over her face. She knew she should report Shelby, but for some reason she didn't have the heart to ruin her career. She wondered what else could go wrong. But at least she knew why Shelby was really here. That was one mystery solved.

* * *

The following week, the village seemed to be buzzing with excitement. The scaffolding had been removed from the village hall and the last check had been carried out by the building inspectors. Rainbow-coloured bunting had been strung all around the shops and houses and coloured lights had been added to the outside of the hall.

It had felt strange around the house. The atmosphere was heavy, and Shelby was hiding out in her room most of the time. When Dougie and Mitch had enquired what was wrong, Ruby had said there had been some personal issues at home and Shelby was taking some time out to deal with them. She felt guilty for lying but knew that the truth would create even more questions, such as, why on earth hadn't Shelby been sent home and fired?

Ruby had been able to walk around the village alone a couple of times, under the strict instruction from Dougie to use her panic alarm if neces-

sary. She had, however, noticed her bodyguard skulking in the background
– he was rather too large to operate incognito – but she couldn't exactly
blame him; he was serious about his work and wouldn't trust anyone, just
in case the worst happened. The villagers always greeted her with a warm
smile and she never felt like a famous person trying to fit in; instead, she
felt comfortable and at home. People would stop and chat, ask how she
was, recommend places for her to visit and she would crouch and fuss their
dogs, making even more canine friends. There was certainly something
magical about Glentorrin.

She was taking Chewie for a walk while Evin was at school, Jules was
working in the museum and Reid was working in his studio, and loved
having a furry companion again.

The weather seemed to be getting warmer, but there had been lots of
rain showers and on her latest walk she had called in to Archie's shop and
purchased a compact umbrella. As he cut the tags off her purchase, they
talked about the weather.

'Aye, nothing surprises you when you've lived here long enough. You
can get all four seasons in a day on Skye.' Ruby was immediately reminded
of the Crowded House song. He leaned closer, rather conspiratorially. 'Just
to let you know, I'm getting much closer to tracking down the hackers. I'll
keep you posted,' he said with a tap to his nose.

Ruby was both lifted and saddened by the news. She secretly hoped it
might take just a little longer, so she had more time in Glentorrin. She left
the shop humming 'Four Seasons in One Day' as the sun did its best to
warm her up.

She hadn't spoken to Valerie for quite some time and when her phone
rang while she was out walking Chewie, she considered sending her to
voicemail.

'Hi, Val,' she reluctantly said as she answered.

'Hey, Ruby. How've you been? I hadn't heard from you for so long I... I
thought I should check in.'

Ruby sighed as she stopped to gaze out at the sea. 'I'm fine, thank you.
Do you have any news?'

Valerie cleared her throat. 'I do, but it's not about the hacking, I'm
afraid. I've decided not to take on any more clients for a while. After this

situation with the hacking, I kind of feel that I should be taking a step back, rethinking and re-evaluating everything.'

Ruby felt awash with guilt again. 'Oh no, that's such a shame, Val.'

Valerie sighed. 'Yeah, it is what it is. Oh, and I don't know how much TV you're seeing or if the tabloids have picked up the story but...'

Ruby closed her eyes and clenched her jaw. What could it be this time? 'Please. Just out with it, Val.'

'Tyler Harrison has gone public with his new lover.'

Ruby opened her eyes wide. 'Bloody Norah. That was quick.'

'Indeed it was. He doesn't hang around.'

Ruby was again surprised at how unaffected she was. 'So, who is she?'

There was a long pause and an audible intake of breath. 'Aurora Santos.' She imagined the pinched expression on Valerie's face as she imparted the news. Maybe she had crawled under her desk too for fear of the fallout.

Ruby snorted. 'It figures.'

'I wanted you to know because it sounds like they may be about to announce their engagement.'

Unsure of where the mirth came from, Ruby laughed out loud, a raucous, unladylike sound that shocked the man walking by her. 'Wow! We should rename him Speedy Gonzalez.'

'Are you okay?' Valerie's voice was laced with pity and it irked Ruby a little. 'I know it must be hard to hear. I know you loved him, honey.'

Ruby thought for a moment about whether she had or had not, in fact, loved Tyler Harrison. Things happened extremely fast between them too, but it now struck her that he was the kind of man who loved the *idea* of love, and the excitement and publicity it brought – maybe more the latter than the former – and that when it came down to real life, he had no intentions of taking himself off the market permanently and committing to one person; there would always be another new, rising star to catch his eye and boost his ego.

He had met Aurora on the same day Ruby had, and he had flirted with her, but, of course, she had brushed it aside and made excuses to herself, 'He's being friendly,' and 'He's being nice because she doesn't know anyone.' However, with the gift of hindsight, she could've kicked herself for being so gullible.

'Do you know what, Val? I'm absolutely fine about it. I'm over him. I really, genuinely am.'

Valerie paused again before saying, 'Oh, great! That's great!' She cleared her throat. 'And... the small matter about whether I'm to continue as your agent...? You may be my only client going forward.' She laughed lightly.

With the latest revelation from Shelby, she hadn't had time to form a decision. 'To be honest, Val, I haven't thought about it. My head is all over the place just now. We've known each other for such a long time, and I don't like the thought of losing you. But the fact is, at least for the short term, you won't be getting me any new contracts. Not until this whole mess is cleared up. So, let's leave things as they are for now. Okay?'

'Yes.' The relief in Valerie's voice was evident. 'Yes, let's do that. Well, I should go. I've been in the office since seven this morning catching up, seeing as my PA is currently on loan, and I haven't even had coffee and it's coming up to ten here. Bye for now, Ruby. Take care.'

Ruby closed her eyes at the mention of Shelby and forced a positive, 'You too. Bye.'

Ruby crouched down in front of Chewie, who was sitting patiently beside her. 'Come on, you gorgeous boy. I should take you home. Even though I'm so tempted to run away with you. Yesh I am... yesh I am.' She scratted behind his ears as she spoke, and his tongue lolled out before he licked her from her chin to her nose. 'Eeuw! Thanks Chewie.'

* * *

Ruby knocked on the door at Reid and Jules' house and Evin came bounding to answer it.

'Hi, Miss Locke.'

Reid arrived at the door, wiping his paint covered hands on a rag. 'Hey Ruby.'

'Hi, Reid, we're back.'

'Has he been good?' the young boy asked, his cheeks turning pink.

'The best. Thank you for letting me borrow him. And you can call me Ruby if you like.'

The colour of Evin's cheeks deepened and he looked to his dad for approval.

Reid smiled and ruffled his son's hair. 'You heard the lady.'

Evin turned back to her. 'Thank you, R-Ruby. I think you might be Chewie's next favourite after his family,' he said, crouching to fuss the dog.

'Well, I have to say he's my favourite too.'

Evin gazed up at her from beside his dog. 'Do you think you might get a dog one day?'

Ruby smiled but felt a twinge of sadness. 'I'd love to, Evin. But sadly, my job is so busy and takes me to so many places it wouldn't be fair of me to get one.'

Evin pursed his lips and frowned as if deep in thought. Then he stood and beamed at her. 'I wouldn't mind looking after him for you if you got one! You could bring him here when you had to go off to do filming, and he and Chewie could be besties like me and Grace. What do you think?'

Ruby's heart squeezed in her chest at the sweet boy's suggestion. 'I think you're very kind. And if ever I do get a dog, I'll definitely bear that in mind. Thank you.'

'You should get a Vizsla like Chewie. They're the best dogs. Although they do tend to be a bit slobbery, so you have to not mind that.' He chuckled and then widened his eyes. 'Ooh, you could name him after that orangutan in that film with Clint Eastwood. I watched it with my dad. He was called Clyde, the orangutan I mean, I can't remember what Clint Eastwood's character was called.' He scrunched his face, trying to remember.

'He means *Every Which Way but Loose*. And Clint Eastwood played Philo Beddoe, son.'

'That's it!' Evin replied enthusiastically.

Ruby giggled. 'I think Clyde would be a superb name for a Vizsla. I'll make sure to remember that. Anyway, I'd best be off. I'll see you soon. Thanks again.'

'Chewie says thank you to you. And we'll see you soon, Miss... erm... I mean, Ruby!'

After dropping Chewie at home, Ruby made her way to the Lifeboat House Museum. It was almost closing time and she hoped she wasn't too late.

Jules greeted her with a hug. 'It's lovely to see you, Ruby.'

'You too. I've just dropped Chewie off with Evin and Reid. He's such a lovely boy.'

Jules narrowed her eyes. 'Which one?'

Ruby laughed. 'Well, all of them, but I meant Evin. He's so polite and sweet.'

Jules beamed with pride. 'He's very thoughtful. I adore him. If ever I have a child of my own, I think Evin will be the best big brother.'

'Oh, he will. I can definitely imagine that.'

'Anyway, come on, I'll show you around.'

As they wandered the display cases, Jules spoke passionately about each item, her knowledge and love for the place shone through. She pointed out the photo of her mum as a little girl, and a veil and photo of a couple on their wedding day. The story of the man who had donated them, Hamish, made Ruby's heart ache. *Oh, to have a love so strong*, she thought.

'I lived in the cottage next door when I first arrived up here, but my brother lives there now. Can't escape him.' Jules laughed. 'He's away on the mainland at our mum and dad's just now. It's a shame he won't get to meet you. He's a biiiig fan.' She rolled her eyes and shook her head, smiling. 'So how are things with you and Mitch? Still getting on okay?'

Ruby felt her cheeks warming and pulled off her hat. 'Is it warm in here or is it me?'

Jules nudged her. 'Methinks the lady hath a wee crush.'

Ruby dismissed the idea with a delightful snorting sound. 'Pfft! It's... no, it's nothing like that. He's lovely and obviously gorgeous-looking, but...'

Jules tilted her head. 'But?'

Ruby tugged at an invisible piece of thread on her sleeve. 'We're just friends. He's not interested in me. Quite the opposite in fact. When I told him that you thought we were a couple, he wasn't too happy.'

Jules frowned. 'Really? How strange. I got the feeling... Oh, anyway, it's nothing to do with me. I'm just a sucker for a romance. I'll stick to my novels. I should probably let you go. I bet he's rustled up something yummy for dinner. I heard from Shelby that he's an amazing cook.'

'Oh, I didn't realise she had been in. She never said.'

'Yes, she was on a shopping trip for you, she said. It was a flying visit, so she said she'd come back when she had more time.'

'Ah, right. Well, I should go, Thank you so much for the tour. You have a lovely place here.'

'You're welcome back any time. I promise I'll stop with the matchmaking.'

* * *

Ruby arrived back at Glentorrin house after her private tour of the Lifeboat House Museum. As she took off her coat and hung it on one of the hooks in the hallway, she heard Mitch on the phone. For once he was speaking in English.

'Aye, it's a shame. But maybe they don't need anyone to do it? Maybe that kind of thing isn't necessary these days.' There was a pause as the person replied. 'Aye, I get that, and he's right, but as you know we're supposed to be avoiding that kind of thing, Morag.' There was another pause. 'Thanks for understanding. I knew you would. I know I'm not her agent, but I kind of feel... I don't know... responsible, I suppose.' More silence. 'Aye, but to be honest I wouldn't have asked Shelby's opinion anyway. To tell you the truth, I don't even know why she's here.'

Ruby wondered what on earth they were talking about. She gathered that she was partly the subject but had no clue what Mitch was refusing on her behalf, so she was a little befuddled by that bit of the conversation. She hung around outside the kitchen door as he finished up the call.

'Hi,' she said as she stepped into the room.

He swung around and dropped the phone. 'Dannazione'

Ruby snickered. 'Sorry, I didn't mean to scare you.'

He placed a hand on his stomach and one on his forehead. 'Don't sneak up on me then!'

She tried to stifle a deeper laugh that was bubbling up. 'Sorry, it wasn't intentional. What was all that about? The call you were on? Sorry, I didn't mean to listen in.' She cringed.

He narrowed his eyes. 'What did you hear?'

She shrugged. 'That you're not sure why Shelby is here, and that you're not my agent, but you feel responsible.'

He closed his eyes and huffed as he pinched the bridge of his nose. 'Merda.'

'It's fine, Mitch. You can tell me what's going on. I'm a big girl.'

He opened his eyes and turned to face her. 'The village hall opening event on Saturday night. The TV star they had arranged to officially carry out the task, Reid's brother, Kendric, can't make it now. In all honesty, their relationship is still a little strained from what Morag said – I won't bore you with the intimate details – but she thinks he's chickening out because of that.'

'I'll do it,' Ruby blurted with a shrug, as if it was an obvious and easy decision.

Mitch gawked at her. 'You're not serious, are you? I've just spent ten minutes on the phone with Morag discussing the fact that you really shouldn't and couldn't do it.'

She walked towards him, wringing her hands together. 'Yes... I get that... but I'd like to help out. If it's just for the village.'

Mitch picked up the phone from the floor and the bit of plastic that had sheared off in its collision with the tiles. 'Crap,' he said as he looked at the bits. He lifted his head and scowled at Ruby. 'That's very noble of you. And it's a lovely thought, but the local press will be here. They're like vultures, that lot. You think Hamilton was bad?' He made a funny noise as he blew out through pursed lips. 'Your face will end up on the front of the newspaper, then that will get picked up by the national press, et cetera, et cetera. Snowball effect. Can you see the problem there?'

She stepped closer to him. 'Yes, of course I can. But after the kindness everyone has shown me, I feel like it's the least I can do.'

'The kindness they showed was to keep your presence a *secret*. You'd be doing the exact opposite of that. Unless...' He narrowed his eyes.

'Unless what?'

'Unless you're thinking it will help in the whole clearing your name thing. So that people see you in a kinder light. "Local village hall assisted by Hollywood actress." Is that it?'

His suggestion came out of the blue, cut her to the quick and she gasped. 'Mitch! How can you even think that? And, more's the point, *why* would you think that?'

He lifted his arms and let them fall to his sides. 'Call me cynical, but I know how much you want and *need* to clear your name.'

Her nostrils flared and she clenched her jaw. 'If that's what you think of me then why did you offer to help me? And furthermore, why did you share such personal things about your life with me? The truth about your wife, and the death of your sister aren't things you discuss with someone you don't trust, surely?'

He lowered his gaze, clearly realising he was in the wrong. 'It's nothing to do with trust. I... I didn't mean it to sound so negative. I'm sorry, Ruby.'

She was hurting. It felt like a betrayal and she snapped, 'No, never mind. Forget I suggested it. I won't bother trying to help.' She turned to walk away but stopped. 'You know, Mitch, all I want is for the truth to come out. But I don't want that by any means necessary. I would never use people like that. It's not who I am. I thought you knew that. I guess I was wrong.' Her voice broke at the end of her sentence and she walked away and up the stairs to her room and closed the door.

She sat on the bed and wondered what on earth could make Mitch think that way about her. What had happened for him to form such a negative opinion?

She decided she would visit Morag and discuss the opening of the hall directly with her. She would include Dougie too. Perhaps they could make an arrangement with the local press so that rights stayed local. Maybe they could keep it quiet? She knew that would be virtually impossible, but in spite of Mitch's opinion, she really did want to help.

Her phone rang and she picked it up to see Kitty's name on the screen.

'Hi Kitty. How are you?' she asked with a sigh.

'Is this a bad time? Are you okay? Have you already heard?'

'I'm okay. I just seem to be struggling to change certain people's opinions of me, but that's another story. What do you mean, have I heard?'

'Bloody Tyler the-wazzock-face Harrison has been at it again.'

Ruby kicked off her shoes and settled back against her pillows. 'You mean his shotgun engagement to Aurora?'

She could almost feel Kitty seething across the airwaves. 'Oh, and *then* some. Allow me to read to you from one of our delightful, trashy national newspapers.' She cleared her throat. 'Okay... *Award-winning actor Tyler Harrison has this week announced his engagement to stunning Portuguese rising star, Aurora Santos. When asked about the speed of the engagement, he is quoted as saying, "We looked at each other on the day we met and we just knew we were meant to be together. Aurora has helped me to heal my heart after the horrific realisation that I was in a relationship with a narcissistic bigot. I now know what true love is and can see a bright future ahead for both Aurora and me.* Excuse my language, Roo, but he is a class A wanker!'

Ruby smiled at Kitty's reaction. 'So, he's still making me out to be the narcissist. No surprise there. And it's nice to know they were "in love" before he and I had even considered splitting. I think you're right about the wanker bit. It stings, but I'll get over it, Kitty. I just hope for Aurora's sake that someone prettier doesn't come along.'

'I have never hated someone before, so I don't really know what it feels like, but by God this must be close. He'd do anything to boost his ego and his ratings. Anyway, enough about him, how are you doing?' Kitty asked with a huff.

'I'm... hmm... If you'd asked me that an hour ago, my reply would've been very different, but right now, I'm feeling a bit crappy to be honest.'

'Why? Who do I need to set the dogs on?'

Ruby giggled. 'You don't have dogs, you have children.'

'Oh yes, and they're much scarier! Who am I setting them on?'

'It's nothing. I'm so oversensitive just now. But... there's a village hall opening event and they've been let down by their local celeb, so I offered to step in and—'

'You didn't! Are you mad?'

Ruby rolled her eyes. 'If you'd let me finish, it's a moot point anyway. Mitch thought I was offering as some kind of publicity stunt.'

'Oh. That's awful. I thought he knew you better than that by now.'

Ruby nodded even though she was alone. 'Me too. I suppose I was wrong.'

'You're not going to do it though, are you?'

Ruby cringed, feeling as if she'd been caught with her hand in the biscuit jar. 'What do you mean?'

Kitty knew her better than she knew herself sometimes. 'Ruby Locke, you know exactly what I mean, and judging by the way you're evading the question, I'll take the unspoken answer as a yes. You're crazy, you know that, don't you?'

'Maybe?'

'Mummeeeeeeee! I think I breaked the toilet! There's water coming out of the seat!' came a voice in the background at Kitty's end.

Ruby saw an out. 'Ooh, sounds like you have an emergency, I'll let you go! Love you! Bye!' She hung up before her best friend could respond, but a text came through seconds later.

I know you, Locke! Just be bloody careful, okay?

Ruby giggled as she put her phone down and picked up her book.

26

Ruby sat at the table in Morag's kitchen drinking tea and glancing around at the homely room.

'I don't want you to feel pressured into doing it, Ruby. Mitch had a point. And to be honest, I regretted mentioning it as soon as the words fell from my mouth. I was being pressured by the co-op and that's something I never usually allow. I'm kicking myself. We can't take advantage of you like that. It's just not fair to do so, especially with everything you're going through.'

Ruby had long since been fed up of hiding out and she hadn't kept the fact a secret. She resented that she had been forced to do so, especially when the person forcing her had done nothing to help up to now. 'The thing is Morag; I don't want to be seen as guilty by locking myself away. I've said this from the beginning. I should never have agreed to it in the first place, but my agent made that decision, and I've since discovered that she's maybe not the best person to make such demands.' Morag's expression was questioning so she explained. 'She was supposed to be working to clear my name, when in actual fact all she was doing was waiting for the mess to blow over, instead of tackling the root cause. She's not tech-savvy though and I think she presumed I was making a bigger deal than necessary until the death threats came in.' She thought back to the horrible comments on the placards; the people who had turned their backs on her since this whole thing blew up.

Morag shook her head. 'Oh my, that's terrible, hen. Quite unprofessional if you ask me.'

'It is, I know. I'm still pondering firing her, but part of me knows there was no malice in it, just ignorance. And she really did look after me when I first broke into the spotlight, so I don't want to lose her from my life entirely. But this is something you can't brush under a rug. When things are put out there on the internet, people take them as fact. A small portion of society may take them with a pinch of salt, but the fact remains, once it's on the internet it can't be erased.' Sadness washed over her as she fixed her gaze on the kind-hearted older lady. 'Even when all this is over and my name is cleared, there will still be people who believe the lie, Morag. I'll still be tarred with the same brush as the people out there who are *actually* guilty of vile opinions and bigotry. So, the way I look at it is this; I need to live my life. I need to be out there and to be seen. I'm not one to shy away, never have been. And I've always wanted to use my fame to help others, but I've been stopped from doing that recently. I want to help. Please let me help.' She paused as another thought occurred to her. 'Unless you would rather I didn't? After all, there may be repercussions. The village may be swamped with angry protestors. I can totally understand if you'd rather that didn't happen.'

Morag placed her cup down and interlocked her fingers. She tilted her head and regarded Ruby with kindness in her eyes. 'I've never known a guilty person to fight so vehemently to have their name cleared. Ruby, you don't need to hide on the village's behalf. And I'm sure I can speak for everyone in saying we would be honoured to have you open our new village hall. You must let me know your fee.'

Ruby shook her head and narrowed her eyes. 'Fee? There is no fee, Morag. I'm doing this because I want to. This isn't a publicity thing like Mitch assumed. This is me doing something for people I have quickly grown to care about and a village I feel at home in.'

Morag placed her hand over her heart. 'Goodness. You really are a very special young woman. The sooner the world sees that, the better.'

* * *

Ruby tried to sneak into the house when she returned from Morag's. After all, she had left without letting anyone know where she had gone. But Mitch was sitting on the stairs when she opened the front door. 'Hi. Are you okay?'

She sighed as she removed her coat. 'I'm fine. Are you going to have a go at me for leaving the grounds at night without permission?'

She expected fireworks like the first time she left the villa in Palermo to visit 'Clark'. But it didn't happen.

Mitch walked towards her. 'No. Morag called. She told me what you'd said to her. In fact, she gave me a right old ear-chewing.' He smiled. 'It seems she thinks a lot of you. And that I owe you yet another apology. I keep hurting you.' He had the decency to look guilty about the fact. He shook his head and walked closer. 'I think it's a self-preservation thing. I guess... I guess I keep waiting for you to not actually be so nice, so genuine. I keep expecting to be wrong. I mean, let's face it, I'm not exactly the best judge of character.'

Ruby didn't know how to respond so she didn't and Mitch continued, 'Morag told me that you're doing the opening and I want to thank you. In spite of how it seemed earlier, I am grateful to you and I didn't mean to insinuate you were publicity-hungry. Far from it. It just came out wrong, like things usually do with me. This place and its people mean a lot to me. It's good to know you're starting to feel the same. Let me know if you need any help chatting to Dougie about it all. I know he was keen to escort you to the event before, but he may have something to say about how things have changed.'

He was so close now that she could smell his cologne, fresh and clean like the Highland air. Her heart rate picked up and she exhaled a shaking breath. 'Thanks. I'll bear that in mind.'

Before she knew what was happening, his arms were around her and he was holding her close, his chin resting on her head. 'I really am sorry, Ruby. I hope you can forgive me for being such an arse. And for not listening to you.'

His body was hard against hers and the feeling of him being pressed against her sent shivers to places that had lain dormant since Tyler dumped her. She lifted her arms and hesitantly wrapped them around his back. He was broad and muscular, and it felt nice to be held, even if it was just a friendly hug.

'Oh, excuse me. I didn't mean to interrupt,' came Shelby's voice from the direction of the kitchen.

Ruby and Mitch quickly stepped away from each other, both with flushed cheeks and Mitch ran his hand through his hair. 'Na. It was nothing. Just an apology. I've been a dobber, that's all.'

Ruby glanced at Shelby. A crease had formed between her brows which betrayed the smile on her face. 'Oh right, okay. Well, I was just wondering if anyone liked the idea of pizza for dinner? I thought I could maybe order in if there's somewhere that delivers.'

Mitch walked towards the kitchen. 'Already ahead of you. I made dough earlier. You can help with the toppings if you like, Shelby?'

Her face lit up. 'Wow, what is it they say about great minds?'

Mitch smiled awkwardly. 'Aye. Spooky.'

* * *

On Wednesday morning, a message came through from Philippe. Apparently, her stalker, Clark, aka Hamilton, aka Bryan, was a repeat offender. Philippe's new sports personality client knew of a female singer who had been stalked by the same man and he had now been charged in that case. There was a lot more evidence in the singer's stalking and a date had been set for trial. He was looking at a custodial sentence for sure. The message was accompanied by a photo of the kind-hearted Frenchman giving her a thumbs up. She immediately responded with a 'thank you', and asked him to hug his girls for her, as she always did. Relief flooded her at the thought that Clark/Hamilton/Bryan couldn't harass anyone again, not for a very long time, at least.

Wednesday evening, Ruby sat on Caitlin's bed in the house behind the bakery, surrounded by dresses in all the colours of the rainbow and all the fabrics she could think of. It was overwhelming. 'I really appreciate this, guys. I just didn't want to send Shelby shopping again. It doesn't feel right, making her run errands like that.' The truth was, now that she knew Shelby was here under false pretences, it felt wrong asking her to do anything and she was still contemplating telling her to go home. But she was glad to have reached out to Jules and Caitlin to ask about borrowing a dress for the village hall opening. It was fun spending time with them.

Jules held up a black wrap dress in one hand, and a flowery print summer dress in the other, her head tilted to one side as she regarded them both. 'Hey, it's our pleasure. You can't beat a girlie day. Have you figured out what you're going to say yet?'

Ruby chewed on her lip for a moment. 'I was just going to say whatever came to me on the spot. Do you think I should plan? I'm not great with speech writing.'

Caitlin entered the room with a tray of wine glasses and a bottle of something fizzy. 'What do you usually do when you're accepting awards?'

Ruby shrugged. 'To be honest, I wing it. I never expect to win so...'

Jules placed a hand on her shoulder. 'You're so bloody lovely and too modest. And I think you should say whatever you feel in your heart at the time. The locals will be blown away by the fact that you're even doing it.'

Caitlin handed the wine glasses out and topped them up. 'Has that giant of a man spoken to the local press yet?'

Ruby giggled at Caitlin's reference to Dougie. 'I think he terrified them into silence. Shelby was there to help too, I think she was worried he'd beat them up or something. The agreement is that the article should be centred on the village and the work the co-op has done to make it happen. The emphasis *has* to be on the hall, not me.'

Caitlin gasped and blurted, 'Oh my god, I've got the perfect dress! I've just remembered!'

She went dashing off and Ruby heard a clattering noise coming from the landing. She dashed out to see what was going on, closely followed by Jules.

Caitlin was pulling down a loft ladder from a hatch in the ceiling. 'Someone hold the ladder. Maybe not Jules though, eh?' She giggled and Ruby turned to Jules for an explanation.

Jules rolled her eyes and her cheeks turned pink. 'Long story.'

Caitlin disappeared into the loft and rummaged around. 'Shit! Ouch!' could be heard, and then moments later, 'Found it!'

She crawled towards the hatch and handed down a white rectangular box, which Jules and Ruby grabbed and placed on the floor.

Once Caitlin had climbed down and closed the hatch, she clapped her hands together. 'It's so good that you're the same size as me! This dress is absolutely perfect.'

Jules held up a hand. 'Hang on, Cait, if this dress is so amazing, why the heck is it in the loft?'

Caitlin huffed. 'It was an impulse buy. I absolutely fell in love with it in a fancy boutique, but I've never had the chance to wear it. I put it up in the loft because it was depressing me every time I looked at it hanging there in my wardrobe.'

Ruby reached out and gripped her hand. 'Caitlin, I can't wear your special dress. It wouldn't be right. You should be the first to wear it.'

Caitlin placed a hand over Ruby's. 'Look, it's a dress that needs to be worn. And this occasion would be perfect. Please, you'd be doing me a favour, letting it fulfil its purpose. Otherwise, it's like a Christmas tree that's never been decorated, or a bottle of delicious wine that stays on the rack. So *pleeeease* wear it.' She held up her hands. 'So long as you like it, of course. And I won't be offended if you don't! Tartan isn't everyone's cup of tea.'

Ruby's eyes widened and she reached out. 'Ooh, I *love* tartan! Gimme!'

The three friends laughed, and Caitlin carefully removed the lid and unwrapped the tissue paper. She pulled out the dress and held it aloft. Ruby and Jules gasped.

'That's gorgeous!'

'Wow, stunning!'

The dress was a fitted dark green velvet shift dress with panels of tartan on either side in lilac and green.

Jules cried out, 'I have some green velvet shoes that would go perfectly! This is definitely meant to be.'

Caitlin cringed. 'Oh god, I hope you like it on you. Come on, get it tried on!'

Ruby grabbed the dress and took it to the bathroom, where she stripped down to her underwear and stepped into it. It was even more beautiful on and fit her like a glove. It was figure-hugging and so flattering. She stared at herself in the full-length mirror on the back of the bathroom door. Of all the dresses she'd worn to the events she had attended over her years in the movie business, she couldn't remember feeling so good as she did right then.

There was a knock at the door. 'Is it okay? Do you hate it? Can we see?'

Ruby opened the door and the other women squealed. She grinned and her stomach flipped at their positive reactions.

'Oh, my goodness! It was literally made for you! It's perfect! It's such a shame that your hair colour hasn't faded much yet. Imagine it with your gorgeous red!' Caitlin enthused as Jules stood there with her hands over her mouth.

Jules interjected, 'Ooh, I've seen a hack online that shows you how to fade hair dye naturally. We have a couple of days until the opening. We could give it a try. They're all-natural ingredients that you tend to have at home, and if it doesn't work, you've not lost anything.'

Ruby's excitement ramped up. 'Would you both help me? I want to look like me again.'

Caitlin reached out and took her hand. 'Of course we will. I didn't tell you the best thing about the dress yet.'

Ruby's interest was piqued. 'Oh? Go on.'

Caitlin placed her hands over her heart. 'It's Isle of Skye tartan.'

Ruby felt a rush of emotion and her two new friends enveloped her in a hug. Ruby closed her eyes and wished that life could feel this positive and happy all the time.

Ruby pulled away. 'I'd better take this off before I get it all crumpled. I honestly can't thank you enough. Both of you. You've been amazing.'

Caitlin headed for the stairs. 'Come on, I'm off to open another bottle of fizz. We need to celebrate my lovely dress!'

27

Ruby was giggly and rather tipsy when she returned to Glentorrin House. She found everything hilarious and frustrating in equal measure. Her attempts to sneak in the front door were futile.

'Are you drunk, Miss Locke?' Mitch asked with a grin from the kitchen doorway.

She tried not to laugh as she almost fell over attempting to take off her boots. She failed miserably. 'Maybe a lil bit.' She hiccupped.

He laughed. 'I think maybe a lot. Do you need a hand there?'

She shook her head, and it caused the hallway to spin. 'I'm thanks, good. I mean... I'm...'

He nodded and there was a crinkle of amusement to the corners of his blue eyes. 'Aye, so I see. Here, let me help or you'll tie yourself in knots.' He walked over and helped her off with her coat. Then he led her to the stairs, and she sat on the bottom step while he pulled off her boots. 'What on earth have you been drinking?'

She tapped her chin. 'We started with persecco... prosecclo...' She shook her head as if it would make the right word fall out. 'Then Caitlin got out some... erm... ohh whassitcalled? Dambusters... no! Drambuie! It's Scottish, you know.' She told him with a tap to her nose.

He continued to fight back laughter, his eyes twinkling with mirth. 'Is it really? You'd think I'd know that, being Scottish, eh?' He shook his head.

'Well, you learn something new every day, eh?'

'I was being sarcastic.'

'Oh... right... well, it was tasty.' As Mitch struggled with her boot, Ruby leaned her chin on her hand, her elbow precariously on her knee. 'Why do I repulse you?' she asked, momentarily a lot more lucid.

He frowned up at her. 'Repulse me? Who said you repulse me?'

She pointed at herself. 'I said it. I'm the sayer of it. I'm a woman of the twenty-sirst fentury and I'm not afraid to ask why a man doesn't like me,' she told him sternly with a finger jab to his chest. 'Is it because I'm strong and... whass the word?' She clicked her fingers. 'Whass the word? Got it! Indipennant... Is it because I'm indipennant?' She pointed at him, narrowly missing his eye.

He pulled his lips between his teeth, almost losing the battle with laughter. 'I'm aware that you're a strong independent woman, Ruby. And I don't find you repulsive at all. Far from it. I just find you... off limits.' He shrugged.

She scrunched her face and placed her hands on her hips, even though she was sitting. It seemed like a good idea at the time. 'Why so am I off your limits then, eh? Hmm?' she slurred, trying her best to sound coherent and compos mentis.

His face softened and the laughter disappeared. 'Because you're famous. You live in a totally different world from me and soon you'll be returning to that world. And I'll be going back to my life as a property developer. I'll be a distant memory by the time you're accepting your next award.'

She could've sworn he looked sad about the fact, but in her drunken state she wasn't one hundred per cent sure. 'Oh... right... But you don't feel icky when you think about kissing me?'

A small smile returned. 'Who says I've thought about kissing you?'

Her eyes widened. 'Have you kissed about thinking me? Because I accidentively kissed about thinking you a couple times. Shhh!' She giggled.

'Okay, Ruby, I think you need to sleep this off. We'll talk in the morning. Come on.'

He pulled her to her feet and walked her up the stairs, two steps forward, a stumble and a wobble, a giggle, one step back, until they arrived in her room. He guided her over to the bed and she sat down.

She stuck out her bottom lip. 'See... you think I'm pukey.'

He gave a small laugh. 'I think you *might* be pukey tomorrow but not in the way you're suggesting. Now go to sleep. Don't bother getting undressed.'

She saluted. 'Aye, Cap'n McHotstuff.'

He nodded but laughed as he walked towards the door. 'Goodnight, Ruby.'

'Mitch!' she called as he was about to close it behind himself.

'Yeah?'

'Thank you for looking after me.' She lay down and heaved an exhausted sigh.

He walked over and pulled the throw blanket over her fully clothed form. 'No problem. Get some sleep.' He left the bedside and pulled the door almost closed behind himself, but then pushed it open a little. 'And Ruby.'

'Mhmm?' she replied without moving, her eyes drooping heavily as she succumbed to sleep.

'I've done nothing but think about kissing you since the day we met.' He closed the door as Ruby rolled over and slept.

* * *

The following morning, Ruby awoke in her crumpled clothing from the night before, with a stinking headache and a mouth that tasted like the toothbrush hadn't yet been invented. She slowly and tentatively sat up and regretted it immediately as the room tipped and swayed.

'Shit,' she said, holding her skull with both hands in case her brain fell out. 'What the hell was I thinking?'

Her phone pinged and she lifted it to see two messages. One from Caitlin and one from Jules.

Hey Ruby! I hope your head's not too sore today. I'm a bit rough to be honest. Last night was such fun though! I was thinking if you come round tonight, we could try that hack to lighten your hair if you're free. Jules x

And from Caitlin:

Oh my word! My head is trying to kill me! I feel so shitty! I hope you're okay. Maybe the Drambuie on top of Prosecco wasn't such a great idea Anyway, I think Jules is going to message you. Cait xx

She was relieved to hear the others were feeling a little worse for wear too. That meant they had all been equally as drunk, which in turn lowered the chances of her having made a total tit of herself, although she really couldn't remember much after trying on the beautiful tartan dress.

She carefully climbed from the bed and walked to the bathroom. The pasty face looking back at her from the mirror resembled some kind of zombie; the bags under her eyes had their own bags. She turned on the shower, stripped off and climbed under the soothing cascade and, as she stood letting the water wash over her face, memories of the previous night started to return. Singing, lots of loud, raucous singing, arms around each other as the three women had belted out Rachel Platten's 'Fight Song'.

'Oh my word! Ruby, this should be your anthem!' Caitlin had shouted above the music.

'Yes! Yes, it's like it was written for you!' Jules had agreed.

The lyrics had spoken to Ruby on a visceral level and she had sung along with her two friends' arms around her as they jumped around Caitlin's living room like teenagers on a sleepover. Grace had appeared at one point and had giggled before leaving the room and them to their singing.

Other memories began to return too. She had arrived back at Glentorrin House after midnight and... Mitch had been there... Had he helped her take off her coat? Yes! He had. *Oh God, how embarrassing.* And her boots!

With horror, she remembered asking why he didn't like her, but no matter how much she racked her brain, she couldn't quite remember his response.

Her heart pounded at her chest as she remembered thinking about kissing him.

Oh god, did I try to kiss him? Please no. Why can't I remember?

She rested her head on the cool tiles of the shower wall and gave up on trying to think back. Her head was pounding enough as it was.

Down in the kitchen after her shower, Ruby poured a mug of fresh black tea and sat at the table. The peace and quiet was so welcome, and she was relieved that Mitch was nowhere to be seen, considering she still couldn't recall the details of her return from Caitlin's. She punched two painkillers from the packet she had found in her handbag earlier, and swallowed them, praying they would work quickly. She rested her head in her hands and closed her eyes.

'Morning,' came Mitch's sing-song voice from behind her. 'I'm surprised you're up before lunchtime. How are you feeling?'

She lifted her head to find him smiling down at her. 'I feel like shit, thanks for asking.'

He smirked. 'No! Really? You do surprise me.' He poured himself a mug of coffee. 'I have to say though, drunken Ruby is hilarious.'

She closed her eyes again and sighed. 'I'm so sorry if I said, or did, anything embarrassing. I can assure you, I can't remember, and I don't think I want to.'

He sat opposite her. 'Well, the naked dancing was a surprise, but you've definitely still got rhythm when you're drunk.'

She opened her eyes wide, startled and filled with panic. 'Please tell me you're kidding.'

He held a serious expression and shook his head. 'I'm afraid not.'

Her stomach lurched and she covered her face with both her hands, on the verge of tears and vomiting. 'Please tell me you didn't take photos or video.'

He reached across and pulled her hands away from her face. 'I'm sorry, I actually *was* kidding. My bad. And I would never film or photograph you in that state.' He grinned and the urge to slap him was almost overpowering.

'You shithead! I was so worried!' she shouted, although, secretly, relief flooded her body.

'You did tell me you wanted to kiss me though,' he said, without looking at her.

She sneered. 'Yeah right. That sounds just like something I would say.' Her voice dripped with sarcasm; she would've rolled her eyes if they didn't hurt. She waited for him to tell her that it was just another joke. When he didn't, the blurry memory of *thinking* about kissing him returned. Once again her stomach somersaulted when she realised she had actually thought it out loud. 'Shit, I did say that, didn't I? Ugh, I'm so, *so* sorry, Mitch. I was so drunk, and I *never* get that drunk. Now you know why. Because I say stupid things that I don't mean.' She hoped he believed her, even though it was a blatant lie. She most definitely *had* thought about kissing him. More than once.

He shrugged and she thought she saw a hint of disappointment in his eyes. 'Don't worry. We've all been there.'

Silence fell and Ruby wanted the tiles on the floor to open up and pull her in.

After a few moments, Mitch spoke again. 'Look, the best thing for a hangover is some carbs, followed by a walk in the cold. I'm thinking of driving up to the Quiraing and doing the loop if you fancy it?'

She scrunched her brow. 'I don't think I would make it. I feel so ill,' she whined.

'Och, come on! I'm not kidding. It will honestly help. I'll make a flask and we can have a hot drink with us. What do you say?'

She didn't have the energy to argue. Her shoulders slumped and she simply replied, 'Okay then.'

'Great! Go away up and get your jeans on. Stick your warm coat on too, and you'll need a scarf and hat as it can get blustery up there. I'll see you down here when you're ready.'

She drank the last of her tea and left the table, walking slowly and steadily up the stairs to get dressed.

* * *

By the time they had reached the parking area for the Quiraing walks, the headache pills had kicked in and Ruby was feeling a little brighter. Dougie looked like he was about to embark upon an army expedition, and Shelby had tagged along too with her perfectly made-up face and her tightly fitting Lycra walking leggings.

As they all prepared to set off for the hike, Mitch walked over to Ruby.

'Hey, I actually meant that just the two of us should go, but Dougie was keen when I told him what we were doing, and he told Shelby. I didn't want to draw attention to the fact that you were feeling rough but...'

She smiled. 'It's fine, honestly. I suppose they both have jobs to do.' *But it would've been nice just to spend a little alone time with you, or at least without the entourage*, she thought. She would rather have borrowed Chewie for the walk, but with so many people it hadn't felt feasible.

'Hey, Ruby, are you all ready for Saturday? I can help you choose an outfit if you like. I could even go shopping for you,' Shelby said with a bright smile.

'Actually, I'm all sorted, thank you. Caitlin is lending me a dress and Jules is helping with my hair.'

The smile disappeared from Shelby's face. 'Oh, I see. Maybe I can help you with your speech?'

Ruby cringed. 'Thank you, but I think I'm just going to wing it. Say what comes to me. I think it's important it sounds natural rather than rehearsed.'

Shelby nodded and gave what appeared to be forced smile. 'Okay. Fine. Are we heading out?' She marched on ahead.

'I took the liberty to bring some hydration, snacks and foil blankets. I also have a whistle and a compass,' Dougie informed them before he too walked off, following Shelby.

Mitch turned to Ruby and mumbled, 'Welcome to boot camp. So much for a nice leisurely stroll.'

The sky overhead was cloudless, a hazy blue that merged up to a bright cerulean and the sun cast a bright haloed ring around the tops of the mountains. Before them, the path led away from the parking area and upwards towards jagged rocks that jutted out of the bracken. Behind them, it swept steeply, precariously downwards, and after around twenty minutes Ruby paused to take stock of how far they had come and to breathe in fresh air to abate the rising hangover nausea that had struck again. The view was incredible, and they weren't even at the top.

In places, loose stones underfoot made the terrain a little worrisome and Mitch placed a reassuring hand on Ruby's back to steady her. She appreciated it. She liked the physical contact.

When they reached the top, they stopped and stared out at the view.

Ruby was out of breath and stunned into silence. All around them, ragged rocks reached skywards like trees searching for daylight; they were like sculptures and Ruby decided that, in a way, they were, only they were carved by nature rather than man. Birds hovered above them, catching warm air thermals to float upon, and for a moment she watched them ducking, diving and playing. Beneath her muddy boots, the ground was every shade of green, purple and brown and appeared almost like velvet. From her vantage point, she could see way out to Staffin Bay where the water mirrored the colour of the sky; deceptively inviting even though the temperature would no doubt chill to the core, she thought.

'It was created by landslides,' Mitch told her as they stood admiring the vista before them. 'This place, I mean. Amazing what nature can do, eh? The rock formations have names. There's the needle, the table and there's even one called the prison.'

She loved to hear him talking with such passion about the area. 'Wow, it's incredible.'

'Aye. Still moving too.'

Ruby turned to face him. 'What?'

He laughed. 'Don't worry. It's very slow. The road gets repaired regularly to keep up with it. You wouldn't be allowed up here if it wasn't safe.'

'Good to know.' She turned to face the view again and took out her phone to snap some photos. 'Mitch, how about a selfie?'

He smiled and came to stand close beside her. She turned the camera lens around and snapped a photo of the two of them with the stunning view behind them. His face was so close, and he leaned his head on hers as he smiled at the screen. She took another shot, reluctant to move. He turned his face towards her and locked his gaze on hers. Once again there was a crackle of electricity between them. He glanced at her lips just like he had once before...

'Right, yous lot. We'd better head back,' Dougie said.

'Aye, I suppose so,' Mitch said as he stepped away from Ruby. He clenched his jaw and turned to face the route that would take them back down the mountain to the road.

'Be sure to hydrate,' Dougie added. 'And watch your footing. The wind's picking up.'

Ruby sighed. Had she imagined the look in Mitch's azure eyes just then? She didn't think so, although his words from the night before suddenly came back to her as a vivid and ill-timed reminder. '*You live in a totally different world from me and soon you'll be returning to that world. And I'll be going back to my life as a property developer. I'll be a distant memory by the time you're accepting your next award.*'

Sadly, she knew he was right.

28

Dougie cooked up a pot of stovies for an early dinner – another Scottish meal Ruby had never tried. It was a little bit like a stew but not as liquid, and contained potatoes, meat and vegetables. A truly hearty meal after their long chilly hike.

As they ate, they chatted about the views they had witnessed from the top of the Quiraing, and Shelby handed round her camera to show the photos she'd taken. Then Dougie regaled them with stories of his days in the army and the long treks through deserts and hostile territories; how he learned survival skills that had served him well through life. He spoke animatedly about the animal encounters he'd had and how he had narrowly avoided a wrestling match with a tiger. His stories explained a lot about his general demeanour and the way he wanted to protect others. He was a fascinating man who had dedicated the younger years of his life to guarding Queen and country, and Ruby's respect for him grew further.

After dinner, Ruby retreated to her room to get ready to go to Jules' house/home salon, but she took a moment to video-call Kitty.

Her best friend's smile greeted her as the call connected. 'Hey, gorgeous lady. How's things?'

Ruby smiled. 'Good, good. We all went on a hike today up the Quiraing.'

Kitty giggled. 'Is that a euphemism? It sounds painful.'

'No! Cheeky. And it was rather painful but only because *someone* was a bit hungover.'

Kitty narrowed her eyes and leaned closer to the camera. 'Ruby Locke, have you been a naughty girl?'

Ruby grinned and nodded. 'And boy did I regret it. I made such a tit of myself in front of Mitch.'

Kitty's eyes widened. 'I'm intrigued. Do tell.'

Ruby felt the heat of embarrassment rising from her chest to her face. 'I may have told him, in my uninhibited, drunken state, that I had thought about kissing him.' She covered her face with one hand and peeped through her fingers to gauge her friend's reaction.

'You did not!' Kitty exclaimed with a gasp of giddy excitement. 'I knew it! You go get him, lass!' When Ruby didn't reply, Kitty frowned. 'Hang on... you don't look as happy as I was expecting. What did he say?'

She sighed. 'That I was from a different world to him and that I'd be returning to that world soon and I'd forget about him.'

Kitty's expression changed to one of sadness. 'Ah. Not what I was expecting at all. Are you okay?'

Ruby shrugged. 'I'll have to be. He has a point after all. Although not about the forgetting. And he probably doesn't fancy me anyway. Just because I'm famous doesn't mean everyone finds me attractive. And if I'm logical about things, it's pointless me thinking of anyone romantically at this point. I can't make any long-term plans, seeing as I don't know what will happen.'

'I wish things were different, honey. You deserve to be happy and loved.' Kitty sighed deeply. 'Do you ever feel like jacking it all in and just being you again?'

This was a question that Ruby had pondered so much since the hacking. Even if this case was solved, there was nothing to stop it from happening again further down the line. As a well-known person, everything she did was under scrutiny already, but after this mess she worried that the spotlight on her would be even harsher, even less forgiving.

Social media could be the most wonderful, supportive place, but it could be hell too, depending on whether you were in or out. Cancel culture was on the rise and people felt they could say whatever they wanted from the safety of their home, with a computer on their lap. Keyboard warriors, that's what they were known as. The fact that real people's lives were so easily damaged at the click of a mouse didn't seem to register with some, or it did, and they didn't care.

'I'd be lying if I said I hadn't thought about it, Kitty. Life would be so much easier if I was just Ruby Locke the... I don't know... dance teacher?' The despondency she felt at admitting her feelings caused her stomach to knot. 'But, also, I don't want to give in. I don't want to let them win, whoever they are. I need to fight this before I can make any decision about my future. I may still go down, but I'll bloody go down fighting.'

'I'm so proud of you. I really am. And you'll always have me. But I think you're best not to rush into things. I just wish I could help.'

'Me too. Anyway... enough doom and gloom, how's the bump?'

* * *

Jules once again greeted Ruby with a hug. 'I've gathered all the ingredients together and I've watched the video a couple of times, so it should be fairly straightforward to get your hair closer to your natural colour again. The people who have reviewed it have had mixed results, though, so it may or may not work.' She cringed as she took Ruby's coat. 'They also say the treatment can be quite drying to the hair, so it's up to you whether we go ahead. We could just have a cuppa and a biscuit instead. I won't offer alcohol.' She grinned and gave Ruby a knowing look.

'Oh, what the heck. We'll give it a go. I can pile conditioner on it afterwards. And if necessary, I'll have it all cut off and go short for a change.'

Jules widened her eyes. 'But your hair is your signature look! I don't want to be responsible for you losing that.'

Ruby placed a hand on her friend's shoulder. 'To be honest, I don't care about my signature look any more. I just want my natural colour back. I should never have agreed to have it dyed in the first place. I have to fight this thing head-on, not hide behind disguises for the rest of my life.'

Jules smiled. 'You're braver than you realise, Ruby.'

Ruby smiled in response. 'Keep reminding me of that and I might believe you, eventually.'

They went through to the kitchen and Jules prepared the paste that was to be applied to Ruby's hair.

'So, was everything okay when you got home after our drinks last night? We were all so drunk. I can't remember the last time I was so out of it.'

'Yes, apart from me having to get Mitch to help me out of my coat and boots.'

Jules burst out laughing. 'Oh god, not you too? When we went to bed, I had to get Reid to take off my jumper. I kind of got stuck with it half over my head and panicked. He could hardly do anything for laughing. It's a good job I love him, the ratbag.'

Ruby laughed at the mental image. 'I wonder how Caitlin coped. She had Grace at home. I can't imagine what the poor kid must have thought when she saw us all rolling around like loons.'

Jules shook her head. 'Caitlin can handle her drink way better than either of us. She may have felt crappy this morning, but at least she didn't have to be rescued from a fight with her own clothing.'

* * *

A couple of hours later, Jules was blasting Ruby's hair with a hairdryer. 'Crikey, it's definitely lighter. And the intense conditioner has done the trick too. I don't think it's back to your truly natural colour, but my guess is it will fade quite quickly now.' She paused and tilted her head to one side. 'Has anyone ever told you you're the spitting image of Kate Winslet? Only with the red hair she had in *Titanic*.'

Ruby nodded. 'I've been told a fair few times. I don't see it myself. I just see me.' She shrugged. 'But my agent said that it was my similarities to Kate Winslet that drew her to me. I was very flattered. Oh, to have her talent.'

'Nonsense,' Jules said with a scowl as she handed her a mirror. 'You're every bit as talented as she is.'

Ruby smiled and examined her reflection. The dark brown had almost gone, and her hair was now a deep shade of auburn. She loved it. 'That's very kind of you. And thank you for helping with my hair. It's so much better and I definitely look and feel more like me again now. I really appreciate your help. In fact, your whole village has been amazing.' She felt a lump of emotion form in her throat. 'I don't know what I would've done without this place and its people. In the short amount of time I've been here, it's felt like the closest thing to being at home.'

Jules squeezed her arm. 'You're very highly thought of. Extremely highly by some, if you know what I mean.'

Ruby cleared her throat. 'If you're talking about Mitch, I think you may be wrong.'

Jules shook her head. 'Hey, I'm useless at spotting attraction for myself, but somehow I can see it clearly in others, and believe me, there's definitely something there.'

Ruby shrugged her shoulders and with a sad smile, said, 'Maybe in another world. In another lifetime, but not in this one, I'm afraid.' A sinking feeling inside told her how disappointed she was by the fact.

* * *

Mitch was nowhere to be seen when Ruby returned to Glentorrin House at eight, but Shelby was there in the hallway as if she was waiting for her.

She gasped when she set her eyes on Ruby as she stepped through the door. 'Oh my god! What have you done? Are you trying to draw more attention to yourself?' The look of horror in her eyes wasn't to be missed.

Defiant, Ruby stood her ground. 'I'm not hiding any more, Shelby. I'm opening the hall for the kind people of this village, and I'm doing so as me. I've done nothing wrong, so I refuse to behave like I have.'

Shelby's nostrils flared. 'Valerie will be so pissed—'

'I don't think you have any room to talk about pissing Valerie off. This whole mess should have been sorted out ages ago. But Valerie chose to take a rain check on dealing with it. So, as far as I'm concerned, I am facing things head on from now, and in my own way. Then, when the truth does come out, which it will, I will just carry on, only I'll be stronger, and I'll know I never lost belief in myself because I'm innocent.'

Shelby narrowed her eyes. 'You tried things your way before. Am I the only one who remembers how that turned out? And I think you're being unfair to Valerie. She doesn't deserve this.'

Ruby scoffed. 'Do you really want to go there?'

Shelby huffed. 'Well, for the record I think you're making a mistake, but it's your life.'

Ruby nodded. 'Yes, it is.' She turned to walk away.

'You do realise the matter is not even close to being cleared up, don't you? There are still posts going around about you. People don't believe you're innocent and may never accept that you are. Have you considered that fact?'

Ruby stopped and turned around to face her. 'I'm aware there are still things being shared, yes. I may not be on social media just now, but I have people keeping me informed of anything I need to know. And, as a matter of fact, the hacking *is* almost sorted. I've had my own people dealing with it.'

Shelby widened her eyes. 'So you've gone behind Valerie's back too?'

Ruby shook her head. 'Don't you dare insinuate that what I've done is anything like what you did.'

Shelby's colour drained. 'I wasn't saying... I didn't...'

'Good. Now I think it's best to drop it before either of us says something we might regret.'

'You're going to tell Valerie, aren't you?' Shelby asked with a curl of her lip.

Ruby didn't answer. Instead, she passed Shelby and made her way upstairs to her room.

* * *

An hour later, there was a knock on the door and initially she ignored it until Mitch said, 'Hey, Ruby, it's only me. I've been at the pub with Reid for a drink. Are you going to show me your hair?'

She reluctantly opened the door and stared blankly at him.

His smile was warm and appeared to be heartfelt. 'Oh... w-wow. I mean... you really are beautiful. I mean, your *hair* is beautiful. Much better natural, in my opinion. After giving it some thought, I think you're right. I don't see why you should change your appearance. You're not playing a part. Who you are is *yours*, no one else's, so, you should own it, just as you are doing. And I have to say, I really admire you for it.' He shoved his hands into his pockets, the way he seemed to do when he was trying to rein himself in.

Ruby was lost for words momentarily. His reaction wasn't what she expected at all. After he'd spent so much time trying to hide her away and protect her, she had expected him to react much the same as Shelby. It was a huge relief that he hadn't.

Her cheeks flushed. 'Thank you, Mitch. I can't tell you how much that means. And it feels good to look like me again.'

'I must admit, though, seeing you like this makes me a little starstruck.' His cheeks coloured pink, and his eyes crinkled at the corners.

She tucked her hair behind her ear. 'I'm still me. That hasn't changed.'

He nodded. 'Aye, don't ever change, eh?' There was another one of those moments where things were clearly left unsaid and she considered telling him once and for all how she felt, let the chips fall where they may, but as she opened her mouth to speak, he said, 'Look, I know it's nine o'clock, but there's a wee surprise for you downstairs.' And with that he turned and walked away, leaving her to wonder what, if anything, she should read between the lines.

A few moments later, she descended the stairs and could hear chattering coming from the living room. She walked through the door and burst into tears as she was enveloped in a hug.

'Mum! Dad! It's so good to see you both!'

29

The day of the village hall opening arrived and when Ruby glanced out of the window, she could see there was lots of toing and froing down at the building. She watched a PA system arrive, she saw men walking into the hall with folding tables, chairs and flower arrangements. A flutter of nerves danced inside her and she tried to figure out if they were caused by excitement or worry over what could happen if the local press didn't stick to their promise to make the day about the hall and not her.

Seeing her parents the night before had made everything feel good again, however, and she couldn't wait to see them today too. She was gobsmacked to discover that Mitch had arranged it all. He had booked train tickets and had picked them up from the railway station without her knowledge. They were staying at the B&B and were getting on famously with Morag and Kenneth. She had sat up until the early hours catching up and just hugging them. Mitch had charmed them both, obviously, and later when her parents had gone back to the B&B, she'd pulled him to one side.

'Thank you,' she'd said with so much sincerity. 'This was such a wonderful surprise and I'm so grateful.'

He'd nodded as his cheeks coloured pink. 'Aye, well, I figured you might like to see them, and I knew it would be hard for you to go to them. It's always good to have your family by you when you do something important.'

She'd hugged him. 'You couldn't have done anything more perfect.' She'd kissed his cheek, and he'd leaned a little closer, his lips hovering close to hers. Her breathing rate had increased as did her heartbeat. This was it, he was going to kiss her.

'Hi guys, just came to get a snack. Hope I'm not interrupting anything,' Shelby had said in a bright sing-song voice, regardless of the hour.

Ruby had turned to see her standing there in skimpy shorts and vest pyjamas, her hair in a messy bun.

Mitch had stepped away from Ruby and cleared his throat. He clenched his jaw. 'No, you weren't.'

Ruby had seen a hint of a smile play on Shelby's lips and knew immediately she had interrupted on purpose. *So, this is how it's going to be*, she'd thought. She'd decided in that moment that she had been too lenient. Shelby clearly still had another agenda and it needed quashing.

* * *

The event was set to begin at 5 p.m. There would be the official opening ceremony, then food, music and drinks. Ruby was definitely looking forward to the latter and could only hope, at this stage, that the former was a success. The last thing she wanted to do was to bring negative press to such a peaceful place.

Down in the kitchen, she made herself a cup of tea and a slice of toast and took it through to the conservatory, where she had a view of the pretty garden. As she ate her breakfast, she thought back to the many film sets she had been on with the same kind of nervous tension tugging at her insides. She hadn't been away from the industry for that long, but it already felt like another lifetime.

Valerie hadn't been in touch since the conversation they'd had about Tyler's engagement and Ruby had avoided the national tabloids, so was blissfully unaware of what was being said about her, if anything. She felt a little as if she had been set adrift somehow by the people she had once thought her life centred around. Yet here she was, in a place she had only just come to know, with people who were new to her, and she had felt more acceptance from them in her short stay than she ever had in the years she was involved in the movie business.

Having this time away to reflect upon her career was terrifying, however. Mostly because she hadn't missed it at all. She hadn't missed the days standing around on set waiting to be called, or the hours sitting in a chair being made up as people talked over her head. She hadn't missed the repeated takes of scenes she felt had gone particularly well, only to be told she hadn't got things quite right. She definitely hadn't missed the nights she had spent alone in hotel rooms on location, afraid to leave in case she was mobbed by fans. None of it seemed to mean anything now and she wondered how she would ever return to the type of notoriety she had put up with over the past few years of her life.

Wandering around Glentorrin with Chewie had made her crave the simplicity of normality. Of owning a little house with friendly neighbours who she could call on for coffee and a chat. Local shops she could pop into without the fear of being photographed and commented about in the media for her shopping choices, or for doing 'everyday' things. Some of the newspaper articles that had been written about her over the years really hadn't been newsworthy, in her opinion. On the rare occasions she had stepped out on her own, there had been photos of her, for example, eating takeout food accompanied with headlines like:

HOLLYWOOD ACTRESS RUBY LOCKE HITS FAST-FOOD JOINT AFTER WORKOUT.

Why did people need to know such mundane things about her? How was that in the slightest bit interesting? It baffled her. She was just a human being like every other person walking down the same street, eating a BLT, but the fact *she* did such things was apparently fascinating.

If she was materialistic, the money would have maybe been worth it. But she never had been. Any money she had earned had been donated to charity, given to her parents or invested for her future – she knew that at any moment she could be at the bottom of the pile for castings, so she was sensible enough to prepare for that.

Shelby arrived in the room and tore her from her reverie. 'Hi, Ruby. Are you excited about the big day?' she asked as if nothing untoward had happened between them.

'Hi. I'm nervous, but that's only natural.'

Shelby cocked her hip again and Ruby rolled her eyes, waiting for the barrage. 'I still think it's a bad idea, and it's not too late to change your mind,' she said with a smug smile.

Ruby sighed. 'And if it all goes royally tits up, I'll be sure to come straight to you so you can be the first to say I told you so. Okay?'

Shelby tilted and shook her head in a decidedly condescending manner. 'I'm only looking out for you, Ruby. It's my job.'

Ruby scoffed. 'Your job? I thought we'd ascertained that you don't even want your job and were only here for your audition?'

'Look, I didn't come here to argue. I came to offer my support. I can deal with the press if you prefer.'

Ruby scowled at her and the phrase 'trust issues' sprang to mind. 'No, thank you. I'm capable of dealing with press. They've already been briefed. I expect that when Tuesday's edition comes out, they will have stuck to their agreement.'

'Let's hope they do.'

Ruby's stomach clenched and churned, and she stood. 'I'm confident they will. Look, I think you should stop trying to do a job that you clearly don't want. Just enjoy the last couple of days of being here on Skye and then we can part ways.'

Shelby's cheek flushed. 'Last couple of days? What do you mean? Are you sending me back? You've told Valerie, haven't you? I knew you would.'

Ruby sighed. 'I think it's best that you should look at returning to the States. And I also think it would be a good idea for you to come clean to Valerie. I get the feeling she will find out soon enough, and it would be better if she heard it from you.'

Shelby pursed her lips and glared at Ruby for a moment before storming out of the room. Ruby was left hoping she had done the right thing; the thing she should have done when she first heard Shelby's confession.

* * *

Ruby slipped into Caitlin's beautiful Isle of Skye tartan dress and regarded herself in the full-length mirror. Her make-up was subtle, and the shoes Jules had given her were a perfect match. She had left her hair to hang in its natural curls down her back and had pinned it up with a pretty diamanté comb – supplied by Grace – at one side.

She took a deep breath and told her reflection, 'You can do this. Just smile and be natural.'

As she made her way down the stairs, she realised that her housemates, with the exception of Shelby, and her parents were waiting for her in the hallway.

'Well, look at you. You're a wee smasher,' Dougie said with a wink.

'You look beautiful, love. I couldn't be prouder,' her dad said with a glint of emotion in his eyes.

Her mum clasped her hands together and pulled her bottom lip between her teeth before saying, 'Lovely, darling. Just lovely.' Then she dabbed at her eyes with a hanky.

Mitch stood there, silently, with a small smile on his face that she thought expressed his opinion well enough. 'Shall we go?' he asked, gesturing to the door.

She nodded and inhaled a deep shaking breath as they left Glentorrin House.

Dougie walked ahead and Mitch, Ruby and her mum and dad followed. Her mum linked arms with her at one side and her dad on the other. It took a matter of a few minutes to arrive at the new hall. She could see people walking towards the building from all directions and her stomach did a little flip again.

Her mum turned to her and took hold of her hands. 'We'll get inside, lovey, you'll be wonderful. Me and your dad are so proud of you for doing this under the circumstances.'

Both parents hugged her and kissed her cheek before leaving her with Mitch.

'You're shaking, are you cold?' Mitch asked.

'Nervous,' she replied.

'I didn't say anything back at the house but... you look stunning. Every bit the movie star.'

For some reason, his mention of her status irked her a little, but nevertheless she thanked him.

They were greeted inside the hall by Morag, Kenneth and a few other members of the village co-operative. She lost count of the number of times she was thanked and told how honoured they were to have her there. A ribbon was being set up outside the building as they chatted and showed Ruby around the great new facility.

'And this is the main hall,' Morag said as they reached the final room of the tour. There were a couple of musicians setting up on the stage at the far end of the room and they smiled and waved at her. 'We're looking forward to having all sorts of events in here. I'm thinking exercise classes, ballroom dancing, tea dances, concerts. It's going to be such an asset to the village,' Morag's enthusiasm was almost palpable as she proudly showed off the building she had helped to organise.

'It's fantastic, Morag. You should all be so proud of yourselves. What an achievement.'

Morag beamed. 'Well, I hope that someday you'll return and attend one of the events. You're going to be part of the place forever now. We have a special place for a plaque and a photo.'

'Right, ladies, we're ready for you. Everyone's back outside,' Kenneth said from the doorway.

'Ooh, you're up, dearie,' Morag said with an excited clap of her hands.

Ruby was led to the entrance of the hall, where a crowd of villagers had gathered in their finery ready for an evening of fun, food and entertainment. A rumble of oohs and aahs travelled the crowd when she made her appearance outside. She located her mum and dad and smiled brightly at them; pride emanated from them in waves of joy. Beside them stood Mitch, with his parents too. She hadn't realised they would be there, but it delighted her to see them. There was no sign of Shelby.

She smiled nervously as Kenneth handed her a comedy-sized pair of giant scissors. He whispered, 'I tried to get you some of those giant Elton John specs too but they were out of stock.' He finished with a wink and Ruby burst out laughing.

'Ladies and germs... Ooh sorry, I mean gentlemen, boys and girls,' Kenneth called out to the crowd. 'It's my pleasure and the honour of the village co-operative to present to you our wonderful celebrity guest, Miss Ruby Locke!'

A raucous applause filled the air and Ruby waved her thanks, feeling rather like the Queen on tour.

She cleared her throat. 'Thank you so much, everyone. It's an honour to be here on this very special day. In my line of work, I have travelled to many different places and many different countries, and I have to say, Glentorrin, you have given me one of the warmest welcomes I have ever experienced.'

A cheer rang out, accompanied by more applause and whistles.

'You've known I've been here, who I am and what I've been through recently, yet you've treated me like any other member of the community. I've had the freedom to walk around and breathe in the fresh Skye air, and to see the wonderful scenery that surrounds this magical place. There has been no negativity and no judgement, and from the bottom of my heart I thank you. It's a true testament to the people living in and around this village. You are special, warm, wonderful people and I'm so very grateful to each and every one of you. You deserve a place to gather and share the love you have for one another. And this building is going to be that very special meeting place. And so, with no further ado, I declare the fantastic Glentorrin Village Hall... open!'

She sliced through the ribbon with the giant scissors and another huge cheer filled the air. The local press photographer clicked away, taking shot after shot of her, and the journalist accompanying him took copious notes. Relief flooded Ruby's body at the reaction from the gathered crowd and she relaxed as people shook her hand, hugged and thanked her before entering the hall for the evening's festivities.

30

Maggie, the journalist from the *Skye Chronicle*, smiled encouragingly as the photographer showed Ruby the shots he had taken of the ribbon cutting. Dougie stood close by at one side to vet the images. There was nothing gratuitous and everything seemed perfectly in order, much to Ruby's relief.

'So, Miss Locke, could I ask you a few questions for the article?' Maggie asked.

Ruby nodded. 'Of course.'

'So, Miss Locke, did you have a village hall where you grew up? And if so, what memories do you recall of the events that took place there?'

'We didn't have a village hall close by to where I lived, but we had a working men's club that was essentially the hub of our estate. I used to attend dance classes there, as well as the youth club and a biannual disco. I think facilities like these really do become the heart of a location. And I can definitely see this place as an asset for the community for generations to come.'

'And what would you say is your favourite thing about Glentorrin's new hall?' Maggie tilted her head as she listened to Ruby's reply.

'I think the size of the main room is fab. I can imagine parties and gatherings galore happening in there. The stage means it will be great for the annual talent show that usually happens in a marquee, so I'm told. This will free up the marquee for other things. More stalls perhaps. But it opens up all manner of possibilities, from afterschool clubs to afternoon teas, and even tea dances.'

'Do you dance, Miss Locke?'

Ruby felt herself light up. 'As a matter of fact, I do. I absolutely love to dance. Ballet was always my favourite, but I'm so excited about the ceilidh this evening. Although that's a type of dancing I'm not too familiar with, but I'm hoping I'll find a willing tutor.'

Maggie laughed. 'Oh, I'm sure you'll get plenty of offers. And how are you finding life in Glentorrin?'

Ruby beamed and placed a hand over her heart. 'Being completely honest, this is one of the most amazing places I have ever visited. Not only is it absolutely stunning here, but the people are every bit as wonderful.'

'Do you think it's a place you will revisit once you leave the island?'

Ruby nodded emphatically, there was no question. 'Oh, absolutely. If they'll have me. I think this village will always have a special place in my heart now.'

'That's so lovely, I'm glad to hear you're enjoying being here,' Maggie said as she scribbled onto her pad. 'Anything else you'd like to say to our readers?'

'Just that I think it's wonderful how the people of the village have pulled together to create such a brilliant facility that I know will be used for decades to come. Well done to all involved.'

'Thank you so much, Miss Locke, it's been a pleasure talking with you. I'll let you get to the festivities and I hope you enjoy the rest of your stay on the island.' Maggie shook her hand and the photographer followed suit.

Ruby shivered and rubbed her hands up and down her arms as Dougie held the door open for her. They walked inside and were greeted by Mitch, Jules, Reid, Mitch's mum and dad and Ruby's parents. She was hugged and complimented on how she good looked in the dress.

It appeared that Ruby's parents had befriended Mitch's and it warmed her heart to know they were being accepted just as she had been. They had only been in Glentorrin a matter of hours and already they had forged friendships.

A local band were performing on the stage to a group of teenagers who were watching like hawks from the front of the stage, singing along and bouncing up and down. She guessed they were a high-school band judging by their ages. The place was full; some people were enjoying the music, and some were chatting, but all were clearly happy.

'How did it go?' Mitch asked with a wide, handsome smile.

'She did great. They loved her,' Dougie replied before Ruby could even open her mouth.

Mitch grinned. 'I knew you'd be okay.'

Why does his gaze make me shiver? 'I'm relieved it's done now. I can relax and enjoy myself.'

'Aye, well, here's a drink to warm you up. It's a Skye single malt. Bloody lovely. Best whisky you'll ever taste.'

'I can attest to that, lass. It's lovely,' her dad said, raising his own glass of the amber liquid.

'You won't be having too many more, Roger,' her mum said with a nudge to his arm, and he winked.

Ruby took the glass and sniffed the contents. 'Oh, erm... I'm not really a whisky drinker.' She cringed as the fumes hit the back of her throat.

Jules told her, 'I didn't like whisky either, but this stuff is like nectar. Very smooth.' She was a little more encouraged by Jules' words.

Mitch stuck out his bottom lip. 'Just try it. Come on, live dangerously. You can't come all this way and not sample it.'

As everyone watched, Ruby sipped at the drink and felt it make a path all the way to her stomach, warming every cell as it moved. She was pleasantly surprised by the earthy heat of the flavour. 'Hmm, that's actually quite nice.'

Her friends and family cheered, and Mitch laughed. 'Praise indeed from a Yorkshire lass obsessed with tea.'

Her mum laughed. 'Oh heck, I'm afraid she gets that from me.'

Ruby scrunched her brow but smiled too. 'I wouldn't say I'm obsessed...' She tapped her chin and narrowed her eyes as she received a knowing look from her mum. 'Well, maybe a little.'

'Like my Miceli is obsessed with my baking!' Rosa said with a nudge to her son. Mitch's cheeks tinged pink and he shook his head like an errant teenager.

As Ruby laughed with her new friends, Shelby arrived by her side, eyed her glass and nudged her shoulder. 'Maybe don't drink too many of those before you've eaten. We don't want to carry you out of here. It wouldn't look good.' She smiled and giggled, but Ruby couldn't help wondering if she was being snide again.

Around the edge of the room were tables spread with mouth-watering food. She spotted haggis bon bons, Scotch eggs, exotic-looking open sandwiches and, of course, Caitlin's famous cakes. It smelled wonderful and Ruby's stomach growled in anticipation. She had been too nervous to eat lunch so was looking forward to getting stuck in.

'Come on then, let's go eat before Dougie vacuums up the lot,' Mitch said, pointing to the direction of the tables.

Sure enough, Dougie's plate was piled high, and he was still perusing the various platters. Ruby giggled and followed Mitch to the end of the line, her parents and the Adairs following closely behind.

The boy in front of them turned and did a double take. 'Miss Locke! I mean... erm Ruby. Please, go before me. You must be so hungry,' Evin said.

'That's really kind of you, Evin, but honestly I'm fine. You carry on.'

Grace stepped out from in front of him. 'Miss Locke, would you like me to show you some of the steps for the ceilidh when it gets going?' she asked with a beaming smile.

'Please, call me Ruby. And that would be great. I haven't a clue what to do.'

Mitch interjected, 'Hey, I could show you some. I'm pretty braw at the old ceilidh stuff, you know.' He did a little jig on the spot.

Ruby laughed. 'I'll need all the help I can get, I'm sure. You can all take it in turns.'

Once they had eaten the wonderful fare on offer, the blinds were lowered and the room lights dimmed, and Kenneth took to the stage. 'Right then, guys and dolls, it's the time you've all been waiting for. I'd like to welcome one of our favourite acts to the stage. He can't keep away!' He glanced to his left and whispered into the mic, 'Actually, we cannae get rid of him.' The room filled with laughter. He held up his hands. 'Just kidding, just kidding. Glentorrin, please give a warm welcome to... Greg McBradden!'

A loud applause travelled the room as a handsome man in his forties walked onto the stage carrying an electric acoustic guitar. He looked a little like a bearded Gerard Butler, and was wearing black jeans and a grey and black checked shirt that was open to expose a faded band T-shirt that Ruby couldn't quite make out. He had a bright smile and she instantly liked him.

'Evening yous lot!' he bellowed into the mic in his broad Scottish accent. 'How are yous doing?' A cheer erupted. 'Hey, it's a wee bit fancy this place, eh?' he said as he glanced around, and a rumble of agreement could be heard. 'Aye, well, I hope yous are ready for some dancing.' More cheers. 'Any Fall Out Boy fans in here tonight?'

Another cheer rang out and Ruby couldn't help squealing and clapping her hands as she jumped up and down on the spot.

Mitch threw his head back and laughed. 'I'm guessing you're a fan then, eh?' he said.

'Me and Kitty saw them live in Leeds! They were *amazing*! Patrick Stump is my hero!'

Greg continued, 'Right then, folks, this one's called "Sugar We're Going Down"! And what do I always say?'

The whole audience shouted in unison, 'Don't sing along!'

Ruby frowned at Mitch, who shrugged. She laughed at the response of the crowd and joined in the applause as Greg began to play. Sure enough, when he reached the chorus, everyone who knew the words joined in loudly and Greg shook his head but grinned and stepped away from the mic to let the crowd have their moment in the spotlight.

Ruby joined in, singing the words at the top of her lungs and, to her delight, Mitch did too. Thankfully, he was more tuneful than when singing to Italian rock in Palermo. It was good to see him let loose and have fun. He could be quite a serious man, always in charge of, or concerned about, something or other. And mostly with a crease of concentration between his eyes. Seeing him wave his arms in the air and join in was a joy to behold.

Greg played fantastic music for the next hour; classic songs by The Proclaimers, The Eagles – his rendition of 'Hotel California' had everyone linking arms and swaying along – and a whole host of other favourites, like Bon Jovi, Hozier and Ed Sheeran, to name but a few. What was the most striking was his version of Cyndi Lauper's 'True Colours'. The audience was silent, in awe as Greg's voice somehow softened and he closed his eyes, the lyrics clearly holding meaning for him. People held up mobile phones with the torches switched on – a modern take on the lighter – and couples smooched.

She glanced to her side and found Mitch watching her. When their eyes met, he turned away for a moment, then leaned in, 'Can I get you another drink?' he asked, awkwardly. 'Joren is working behind the bar and he's free just now.'

She smiled and nodded. 'That would be good, thanks.' While he was at the bar, Greg finished his set and left the stage to a raucous applause.

Kenneth returned and addressed the audience again. 'Is it me or does he get better and better?' he asked, and a cheer of agreement rang out. 'Now, I know you're all nice and warmed up, so let's make use of this incredible space, eh? It's ceilidh time!'

The cheer seemed to get louder and Ruby glanced around at the smiling faces. It warmed her heart to just be there to experience the village all coming together like that.

'Please give another warm Glentorrin welcome to the Toilichte Hens!'

More whoops and cheers ensued as two women walked on to the stage.

The brunette took to the mic. 'Evening, ladies and gentlemen! It's good to be here. Now, we're going to start with the Dashing White Sergeant! Grab your partners and let's raise the roof!'

Grace appeared by Ruby's side and took her hand. 'Come on, Miss Locke!' Inwardly Ruby chuckled at the young girl's inability to call her by her first name.

Mitch returned with her drink and she shrugged as she turned to face him.

'Get yoursel' on the dance floor, Ruby!' he said as Grace pulled her away.

Moments later, Ruby was skipping around the hall under the shouted instructions of Grace, who turned out to be quite the expert. Her heart raced and her face ached from smiling so much. It was exhilarating.

Once the first dance was done, Mitch took her hand as The Gay Gordons dance was announced. 'Ah, my speciality. I remember this one from my schooldays,' he told her.

The music began and people moved around a circle in pairs, it seemed relatively simple compared to the previous dance. Mitch looked so proud of himself as he beamed at her.

'You're really good at this,' she said as they changed direction in the circle.

He leaned closer. 'Aye, to be honest, it's one of the easier ones. Wait till it's time to strip the willow.'

'Will you dance that one with me too?' she asked with a sweet smile.

He raised his brows, evidently surprised by her request. 'Of course.'

Another sweep of the room and she spotted Dougie dancing with her mum, and her dad on the arm of Morag. Her dad was all left feet, but her mum was dainty, and Ruby couldn't help the smile that spread across her face. Having them here was so wonderful and it was all thanks to her dance partner.

The Gay Gordons finished, and everyone applauded. The Toilichte Hens announced a break in the dances but kept on playing so people could grab a drink.

Mitch took her hand and led her to the bar. He ordered two more Skye single malts from Joren and handed one to her.

'Signor Miceli Adair, are you trying to get me drunk?' she asked with a tilt of her head.

'Chi io?' he asked with an innocent smile.

'One of these says I'm going to learn Italian and surprise you,' she told him, eyes narrowed.

'Questo ti renderebbe ancora più bella,' he replied softly, and her insides turned to jelly.

She pursed her lips and narrowed her eyes. 'For all I know, you could've just told me my face looks like a smacked arse and my breath smiles like a toilet.'

He shook his head slowly and leaned closer. He opened his mouth to speak, but over the PA the Toilichte Hens announced the next dance would be Strip the Willow and before Mitch could speak, Jules and Reid appeared beside them.

'You two have got to dance this one with us!' Jules insisted, grabbing Ruby's hand. 'Come on!'

Still wondering what Mitch may have been about to say, she let herself be pulled to the dance floor once more as the music began.

Mitch took her hand again. This time she was passed down a line to different partners who spun her around in time with the music, and for a dancer she felt rather flat-footed, and the Skye single malt had gone to her head, meaning she giggled at each mistake she made – and there were several. She hadn't had as much fun in what felt like years.

Ruby didn't want to the night to end. She danced with Evin, who was light on his feet and beamed up at her the whole time, and she met a lovely old chap called Hamish whose items she had seen in the museum. Archie took her for a spin around the floor, then Dougie, then her dad, then Mitch's dad, Cullen, and finally Mitch, several more times. Every person she danced with, and every person she met, treated her like part of the community, not some movie star whom they were in awe of, and she thought her heart might burst with happiness and gratitude.

31

At the end of the night when the bands had packed away, someone put
slow tunes on the PA system and for a few moments Ruby stood at the edge
of the room, nursing her glass of whisky as she watched loved-up couples
descend on the dance floor and move together. In that moment her heart
ached a little. She wished she had someone in her life; someone genuine.
Someone who would love and like her for the real Ruby Locke, not Ruby
Locke the movie star. She knew she was a little drunk and had a tendency
to overthink at times like that.

Cullen and Rosa's taxi had arrived, and they had hugged her goodbye
with instructions to visit soon before Mitch saw them out. Then her mum
and dad walked over to her. 'Hey, love, we're going to head back to Morag's.
We're bushed,' her mum said as she removed her shoe and rubbed her foot.

'Aye, I've not laughed as much in ages. They're a great bunch of folks
this lot,' her dad said, nodding towards the crowd on the dance floor.

'Okay, I'll see you tomorrow before you set off for your train.'

Both parents hugged her tightly.

'Love you, sweetheart,' her dad told her. 'I can see why you love this
place so much.' He gave her a knowing smile.

'I wish we could stay longer but I need to get back to the shop. Night
night, love. Sleep well. I know I will,' her mum smiled and kissed her cheek.

'Night, you two. Love you both.'

Once her mum and dad had gone, she too contemplated leaving and returning to Glentorrin House and glanced around to see if she could spot Dougie. He was engrossed in conversation with a woman on the other side of the room. She didn't have the heart to break that up. Shelby was, once again, nowhere to be seen.

'I knew I'd convert you to a whisky drinker,' Mitch said as he appeared beside her.

She glanced at her glass and then at him. 'Yes, but I should've stopped a few glasses ago. I don't want to repeat the embarrassment of the last time.'

He shrugged. 'Oh, I don't know. I think I got to the see the real, unfiltered you that night. I liked it.' He smiled and she thought he seemed a little bashful.

She placed her drink on the closest table. 'Look, I think I'm going to head back. I'm worn out from all the dancing.'

He nodded. 'Okay, I'll walk you.'

Ruby waved a dismissive hand. 'No, stay and have fun. I don't want to spoil your evening.'

He shook his head. 'You're not. I'm ready for off now anyway. I don't remember you having a coat.'

She cringed. 'No, that was rather silly of me. It wasn't too chilly outside when we came down.'

He held up a finger. 'One sec.' He disappeared from view down the corridor that led to the exit, reappearing moments later with his own jacket. 'Here you go. Stick that on.'

She glanced at the jacket but said, 'No, it's fine, you'll be cold, if—'

'I insist.' He slipped the jacket around her shoulders. 'Ready?' He held open his elbow and she linked her arm through it.

They left and stepped out into the chilled mid-April air. The moon was bright in the star-filled sky above and no one else was around. The music from inside the hall could still be heard, Ed Sheeran's 'Perfect' echoed around them.

Mitch stopped and turned to face Ruby. 'Hey, I never got a slow dance with you at the end of the night.'

She crinkled her nose. 'No, that's a shame.'

He held out his hand. 'Shall we make the most of the rest of this song?' he asked, nodding towards the hall.

She laughed lightly. 'But... aren't you cold?'

He simply shook his head and smiled as he slipped his arms around her waist. She moved her hands up his arms and rested them around his neck, and they swayed to the music. Out of the blue, he took her hands from where they rested and spun her around, releasing her to the length of his arm and reeling her back in again. She giggled as she twirled. Once she was in his arms again, she smiled up at him as he gazed down at her and quietly sang the lyrics. She found herself wishing he meant them.

She could feel the alcohol in her system having the usual effect. She was feeling brave and determined, strong even. There were so many things she wanted to say to him. But, instead, she slipped her hands into his hair and slowly pulled his face towards hers until their lips were almost touching. His warm breath feathered her lips, light and slightly faster than normal. She locked her eyes on him, willing him to take the next step. He seemed reluctant and a frown graced his handsome features. She knew what he was thinking; she was leaving soon, and they could never make it work, but for this one night, she didn't want to think about that. She didn't want to be reminded of her real life. She simply wanted to be kissed in a way that stole her breath, that made her whole body hum with delight.

When he didn't move, she pushed up onto her tiptoes and gently touched her lips to his. A gentle, undemanding kiss to test the water. He closed his eyes for a moment, and when he opened them, she waited for him to push her away, ask her what the hell she was thinking. Instead, he crashed his mouth into hers, inhaling deeply, gripping her body and holding her so close she could feel every ridge and dip of his torso. He slipped one hand into her hair and one inside her coat, the expanse of his large hand almost covering her back, fingers splayed and then scrunching the fabric of her dress. It was the kind of kiss you saw in movies but never experienced in real life – well, she certainly hadn't until now.

Eventually, he pulled away and they stood there panting, out of breath, searching each other's eyes. He silently gazed down at her and she up at him, both unsure of what to say. She didn't want to break the spell and was terrified he would.

His eyes widened. 'I'm so sorry, I don't know what—'

She placed a finger on his lips. 'Please. Please don't say anything else, okay? That was probably the best kiss I've experienced in my whole life, so please don't ruin it by saying it can't happen again.' She pleaded at him with her eyes as well as her words. 'Let's just go home.'

She turned and dashed off towards the house, leaving him in her wake, tears stinging at her eyes and the cold air biting at her skin. She reached the front door and waited, out of breath, for him to catch up, unable to lift her gaze to meet his in case she saw what she expected in his expression.

'Hey, why did you go running off?'

She turned and glared at him. 'Because I knew what you were thinking.'

He frowned. 'And what might that be?' he asked as he unlocked the door.

She fought back tears as she stepped inside and removed his jacket, before hanging it on the hook and turning to face him again. 'That I'll be leaving soon, and that you can't be with me because you'd hate to be famous so you couldn't live in my world.'

He stepped closer, a look of deep sadness in his eyes. 'That's all true, Ruby. But it doesn't mean that I don't want you. I just don't want to hurt you in the long term. I can't ever see myself living how you live, everyone knowing who I am, everything I do being pored over and scrutinised.' He inhaled deeply. 'But let me tell you this, I've wanted you from the moment I set eyes on you back in Palermo. You were so incredibly sexy and feisty. And I've never known someone make me laugh like you do, whether on purpose or not. God you drove me mad, and you still do, but I'm so drawn to you. I wanted to punch Clark, because of how he treated you, but more than that, because he got to kiss you and hold you in his arms while he danced with you. I wanted that, I wanted you... I still *do*, Ruby.'

Even though she knew this was never going to be anything permanent, even though she wasn't the type to have a one-night stand, Ruby couldn't bear the thought of never kissing him again. She knew that her attraction to him had been there from the start. She'd simply fought it; good-looking men were all self-serving and extremely dangerous to her heart.

Except Mitch wasn't.

He was kind-hearted, protective and warm. His looks were just a bonus really.

Her heart ached again as she thought about the temporary nature of this whole situation, of her time in Glentorrin, of never actually being able to call Mitch hers. But in spite of all those worries and regrets dancing around in her mind, she closed the gap between them and kissed him again. His lips were firm yet yielding and the desperation he had for her was evident in his kiss. Bravely, she took his hand and led him up the stairs to her room. He followed silently but willingly, desire clear and unfaltering in his eyes.

Once inside the room and the door closed behind them, she turned for him to unzip her dress. His fingers traced the skin of her back as he lowered the fastening. He placed gentle, sensual kisses along her shoulder and up her neck until he reached the sensitive spot behind her ear, sending shivers over every inch of her skin. She closed her eyes and sighed as pleasure radiated through her veins. She let the dress fall to the ground and stepped out of it, then turned in his arms and began to unbutton his shirt.

His chest was muscular with a light smattering of dark hair. A silvery scar was visible on his shoulder from his accident, and she placed a gentle kiss on it. She traced the outline of his pectoral muscles and watched as his Adam's apple moved in his throat. His eyes closed. His racing pulse visible in his neck.

'I've never wanted anyone so much,' he whispered.

She kissed his chest as she unfastened the buckle on his belt and tugged it from the loops. Next the buttons of his jeans were unfastened, and she pushed them down until he could kick them aside.

His desire was even more evident now and he pulled her into his arms, pressing every inch of his body against her. They tumbled onto the bed, kissing and caressing each other. First hurried and passionate, then slow and measured. Their breath mingled as their limbs tangled and entwined.

Being in his arms was the most wonderful feeling; the sensation of his fingertips on her skin, divine. Knowing he wanted her made her ecstatically happy and simultaneously broke her heart. She could never really *have* him. Not wholeheartedly. He had made that clear. They were never going to be together forever, but for this one night he was hers, and she was his, and no one was going to spoil that.

* * *

Ruby awoke to the sight of a naked Mitch gathering his clothes, the shape of his body highlighted by the lamp on the nightstand. He was masculine and beautiful but without the ego to accompany it. The urge to tug him back under the covers again was almost overwhelming, but she fought her desire and glanced at the clock. It was four in the morning. She watched his body move as he pulled on his clothes, feeling her need for him rising again.

But he bent to kiss her head. 'I thought I should head back to my room. I don't want to get caught leaving here in the morning when the others are around. It wouldn't be fair to do that to you. What we've shared... It's nothing to do with anyone else in the house. I don't want to spark gossip and cause problems for you.' He rambled, but she found it endearing.

'I appreciate that. Thank you,' was what she said in reply, but what she wanted to say was, 'I don't care about them, or about what anyone else thinks, just come back to bed, please.'

He smiled but she could see melancholy in his eyes as he told her, 'Tonight was... You were...' He closed his eyes and clenched his jaw. 'I didn't want it to end.'

Sadness washed over her. 'Neither did I.'

'Look, I don't want you to think that this was... I don't want you to think I've taken advantage of you for some fling or something. It meant something to me. And... you should know that.'

She swallowed as her throat tightened. 'It meant something to me too.'

He sat on the bed beside her and pulled her up into his arms. 'I don't know how I'm going to let you go. But I have to. I hope you understand that. I'm just not cut out to be in the spotlight. And... if I'm honest, I wouldn't want to share you. I'd be so jealous every time you kissed a co-star on set, and every time you played someone's wife. I know I couldn't deal with that. But I do have feelings for you. Real feelings. Saying goodbye is going to be so damned hard.'

She clung to him and buried her face in his neck, inhaling the scent of him and committing it to memory, desperately trying to fight the tears stinging at her eyes. 'I know. I *do* understand. I wish it was different, but I get it.'

He pulled away and fixed his gaze on her. 'I spoke to Archie tonight at the ceilidh. He'll have an answer in the next few days. So, you'll be free.' He smiled briefly. 'Soon, this will all be over. But you...' He cleared his throat, emotions evidently getting the better of him. 'You will always be in here.' He pointed to his heart. And with that he kissed her forehead, hesitating a long time with his lips pressed to her skin, then stood and left the room.

Ruby lay back and let the tears she had been holding back flow freely now she was alone with only the memory of the night she and Mitch had shared.

32

Ruby awoke and stretched, the antics of the night before making themselves known in the tightness of her muscles. She relished the feeling and closed her eyes. She replayed the memories of Mitch's kisses on her skin, the heavenly weight of his body, the feel of his limbs entwined with hers. The bliss was short-lived, however, as she reminded herself that it would never happen again; that even though what they had shared had been passionate and heartfelt, he had made his feelings clear. At least he hadn't lied to her, that was one thing.

She climbed from bed and showered, and as she dried herself off, she examined her face in the mirror. Her skin was flushed, and her lips turned up in an involuntary smile. Whatever happened from now, she would always have her memories of Skye and of Mitch.

She dressed and descended the stairs quietly. It was still early, and the others were evidently still in bed, sound asleep, but that was fine; she enjoyed the peace. After Mitch's comments about her obsession with tea, she figured it would be a funny gesture to make him a cup and sneak it to him before the others awoke.

She carefully tiptoed up the stairs with his favourite mug that she'd managed to overfill and tapped lightly on his door. He didn't respond so she decided she'd open it and place the tea on his nightstand for when he woke. It'd be a nice surprise and she knew it would make him smile. She opened the door a crack and let her eyes adjust to the darkness once more. She made to step inside when there was a snuffling sound and movement coming from the bed. She waited a second to see if he sat up, but he didn't, so she stepped a little closer.

Her eyes widened and she swallowed the gasp that rose automatically from her chest, biting down hard on her lip as a scream threatened to join the stifled gasp. Beside Mitch in his bed, lay a naked Shelby, snuggled into his side, his arm a resting place for her head, a serene smile on her lips and her left breast exposed as the duvet had slipped down her arm where it lay across his stomach. Ruby's eyes stung and her stomach roiled with the feeling of betrayal. She knew they weren't forever, but she had trusted that he'd meant what he'd said about his feelings for her. Clearly, he was yet another lying man, intent on using her and moving on. But, my God, he had moved on quick. She'd thought Tyler's engagement had been a speedy manoeuvre, but at least he had waited until the bed was cold. This betrayal hurt more than any of the others. So much more.

She closed the door carefully and retreated to her room to throw the tea down the sink in her en suite. She rinsed the mug with shaking hands and tears streaming down her face. Her stomach knotted and she felt physically sick. She leaned on the sink and regarded her red-rimmed eyes and puffy face; a stark contrast from her earlier reflection. She closed her eyes, unable to look at herself any more. How could she be so damned stupid for a third time? But then another thought occurred to her; he owed her nothing. She had willingly taken him to her bed. She had instigated it; okay, he was a willing participant, but it had been she who had insisted. She only had herself to blame.

She rallied. Washed her face, applied make-up, packed up some of her belongings and went back down to the kitchen, where she collected her phone and took it to the quietest place in the house: the conservatory. There she went online and booked herself the next available flight. Her parents were leaving anyway, so she was going back to New York. It was time. The flight, which would take her from Inverness to Schiphol in Amsterdam, where she would get a connecting flight to JFK, was later that night, which gave her time to pack the rest of her things and explain to Dougie that she had been called back to America, urgently.

She wouldn't go into any details with Mitch about her speedy retreat. He didn't warrant explanations. From what he had said the night before, Archie was verging upon a breakthrough, so she would hopefully be safe to return to the USA, but perhaps to a hotel for a couple of days, until everything was sorted fully, and the truth was out there. She found a hotel situated close to her apartment, and not too far from Valerie's office, and booked a suite. She had made some big decisions about her career and needed to discuss them with Valerie as soon as possible so they could get the ball rolling.

When she had finished her calls, she headed upstairs and pushed a scribbled note under Dougie's door explaining that she was leaving and asking if he could accompany her to the airport, and letting him know about the timing of the flight from Inverness. Then she retreated once again to the conservatory. As she sat there, replaying everything that had happened in the past weeks like a terrible movie in her mind, she heard someone in the kitchen. She couldn't face anyone, so she stayed put, almost holding her breath for fear of drawing attention to herself. Sadly, her attempts to stay incognito were futile.

'Morning!' Shelby said in a sing-song voice and with a triumphant smile on her face that Ruby would've happily smacked off. She was standing in the entrance to the room, gripping a mug of coffee and wearing pyjamas that consisted of a cropped T-shirt exposing her flat midriff, with a pair of shorts that didn't leave much to the imagination.

'Oh... hi,' was Ruby's minimal, disinterested response as she returned her focus to her phone.

'Everything okay?' Shelby asked.

Ruby glanced up to see a, no doubt fake, look of concern in her eyes.

She tilted her head and eyed Ruby with pity. 'Hungover again?' She stuck out her bottom lip.

Ruby clenched her fist. She hated the way Shelby had said 'again' as if it was a regular occurrence. 'Actually, I'm perfectly fine. In fact, I'm heading home. Tonight,' she said with forced breeziness. 'So there's no need for you to stay.'

Shelby gasped and her face seemed to drain of colour. 'Oh? But... why? I mean... Valerie hasn't said things have been dealt with yet. Maybe you should reconsider?'

Ruby felt inwardly smug that she had ruined Shelby's plans for more sexy time with Mitch. She had never been a jealous person, but this situation had hit a very raw nerve.

Realising she had disappeared into her mind and not answered Shelby, she smiled. 'No, the decision is made. It's time I went back and got my life on track again. I didn't book your flight as I wasn't sure if you'd already done that after our conversation yesterday. And anyway, I don't really need you to come with me.' She was aware that she sounded snide with that last comment but didn't much care. 'I'm booked on a flight to Schiphol this evening, then on to JFK. I'm sure you understand.'

Shelby nodded. 'Right, yeah, of course. I'll speak to Valerie and maybe get a flight in the next couple days. Make the most of my remaining time here.'

Ruby smiled again, an action that held no mirth. 'Oh, I'm sure you will.'

Shelby nodded again, and Ruby thought she resembled one of the little fuzzy dogs you put on the dashboard of a car.

'Anyway, I'm heading out to see my mum and dad before they go for their train and then to see Jules and Caitlin for coffee. I think it's only fair to say goodbye to my friends after they've been so lovely.' She stood from the sofa and grabbed her phone. She'd had every intention of going to see her parents and friends but perhaps not this early, however it was a good excuse to leave Shelby's company.

Shelby chewed her lip. 'Sure. How nice for you.'

'Bye, Shelby,' Ruby said as she left the room and headed for the coat rack.

As she stood on the doorstep with the front door closed behind her, she fired a text to Jules and Caitlin in a group chat. Both replied swiftly, agreeing to meet at the museum after she had said goodbye to her mum and dad.

* * *

Morag opened the door to her when she arrived at the B&B. 'Lovely to see you, dearie. Come away in. Your mum and dad are just finishing their breakfast.'

When Ruby saw her mum and dad sitting there at their table, she burst into tears. They both stood and enveloped her in a hug.

'Whatever is it, love? What's happened?' her mum asked in a worry-laced voice.

Ruby sniffed and wiped at her eyes with a napkin from the table. 'Oh, it's nothing. I just miss you both so much. And now that you're going, I've decided to go back to New York tonight. The hacking is just about solved, apparently, so there's nothing keeping me here.'

Her dad narrowed his eyes. 'Nothing at all?'

Ruby shook her head. 'No, Dad. I need to get things sorted with Valerie. And as much as I love it here, this place isn't my home.'

Her parents sat and her dad pulled up a chair for her. She sat and her mum took her hand. 'Why don't you just come back to Yorkshire, eh? That will always be your home.'

'I know, Mum. But there are things I need to do in New York first. Hopefully once the dust settles, I can come and visit.'

'Well, we'll look forward to that, love. You know you can come home anytime. We don't care about the newspaper people hanging around. We can ignore them.'

'That's sweet, thank you. I just don't want to bring any negativity there just now. You don't need to be dragged into it. You have to live there, and people can be very unforgiving.'

Her dad shook his head. 'You're our daughter, that lot don't mean owt.'

She smiled and hugged him where he sat beside her, grateful to have the opportunity to see them but trying to forget that it was Mitch who made it happen.

They chatted for a little while about the village hall opening, and laughed about Roger's dancing and time flew by way too fast.

Morag popped her head around the door. 'Carol, Roger, I'm afraid your taxi is here.'

Ruby's dad went to their room to retrieve their bags and her mum hugged her. 'I get the feeling there's something else wrong, but I understand if you want to keep it to yourself. Just know that you can tell me anything.'

Ruby's lip trembled. 'I know. And I will tell you at some point when we have more time.'

Saying goodbye to her mum and dad was even harder than usual under the circumstances and she contemplated cancelling her flight and going to Yorkshire. But she knew she needed to talk to Valerie and that would be better done face to face.

* * *

When Ruby arrived at the Lifeboat House Museum, the closed sign was on the door, so she knocked and was greeted moments later by Jules, who hugged her.

'I can't believe you're leaving so soon. I'm so sad.'

Ruby reciprocated the hug. 'I know. But I need to get back to real life. Things are nearly dealt with and I have things I need to do back in New York.'

Jules pulled away and fixed her gaze on Ruby. 'What's really happened? I know we don't know each other that well, but... I get the feeling things aren't right.'

Ruby sighed. 'I'd rather not talk about it.'

Jules nodded. 'Okay. But please know that you can trust me and Caitlin. Whatever you say will go no further. I know you've been messed around by people in the past, but we're not like that. We consider you a friend. And we care about you.'

Caitlin walked through the door. 'Hey, gals, sorry I took so long. I was waiting on a batch of scones to come out the oven. So, you're leaving?' She frowned and pulled Ruby into a hug.

'Yes, it feels like the right time.'

Caitlin held Ruby at arm's-length. 'And what's caused this sudden decision?'

Jules eyed her too and Ruby huffed. 'Good grief, it's like being with Miss Marple and Sherlock Holmes at the same bloody time.'

'Can I be Sherlock?' Caitlin asked Jules.

Jules shrugged. 'I suppose.' They both turned their attention back on Ruby and Jules said, 'Come on, spill the beans. You know you'll feel better if you do. I've made a pot of tea and I've brought chairs round.' She pointed to a makeshift picnic area.

Caitlin held up a bag. 'I've brought shortbread.'

Ruby followed the girls, and they sat around the small table Jules had placed behind one of the displays. She took a deep breath. 'Okay, but please don't say anything to anyone. Especially not Mitch.'

The two other women shared a glance.

'You have our word,' Caitlin told her.

Ruby stared at the tea in her mug. 'So... last night, Mitch and I shared a moment on the way home from the ceilidh. We... we kissed.'

Jules grinned and said, 'I knew it.'

'Yes, but it didn't end there,' Ruby informed them with a deep sigh.

'Come on, woman, let us live vicariously. He's bloody gorgeous,' Caitlin chuckled.

'I used to think so,' Ruby whispered. 'But... to cut a long story short, we ended up in bed together.' She lifted her chin and found her two friends grinning at her. 'Don't expect a happy ending to this story. You'll be sorely disappointed.'

Jules frowned. 'But he clearly adores you. What can possibly be wrong?'

'For starters, he'd already told me he didn't see a future for us because of my career. He wants no part of being famous and fears that a life with me would shove him into unwanted notoriety. And, don't get me wrong, I knew that before we...'

Caitlin scoffed. 'That's bollocks! If he cares for you, then he'll make it bloody work. What a cop-out.' She crossed her arms over her chest.

Ruby shook her head. 'No, he was totally sincere about it. And I could never ask anyone to sacrifice a peaceful life for one like mine. You only have to remember what's happened to me to know that being famous is hard, but being famous and hated worldwide on the internet is definitely no way to live. I did understand. He was so... caring and sweet.' Her chin trembled. 'He said he had real feelings for me, and I believed him. I said the same. I've been attracted to him physically since I first saw him, but the more I've got to know him, I think... I think I was falling for him.'

Jules leaned over and squeezed her hand. 'Hey, he'll come around. I'm sure he will.'

Ruby snapped her gaze up to Jules. 'No. I don't want him to. Not now.' She angrily swiped at the tears trickling down her face.

Caitlin narrowed her eyes. 'Shit, what did he do?'

Ruby closed her eyes and in her mind's eye she could see the images again. 'I took him a drink this morning and... he was...' She sobbed. 'He was in bed with Shelby, naked.'

'Bloody hell!' 'Shit!' her two friends cried in unison.

'What a rat!' Jules said, her eyes wide and filled with anger.

'Total shithead,' was Caitlin's comment.

Ruby nodded. 'I feel like such an idiot. I'm sick of trusting people and finding out they've lied to me... or betrayed me. It's happening way too often. But I thought, and believed, Mitch was different.'

'How the hell did he explain himself?' Jules asked.

'He didn't. I didn't give him the chance. I closed the door and left before either of them woke. They have no idea I saw them.'

'But you *are* going to confront them before you go, aren't you? You can't leave it like this. He needs to know that you know he's a bawbag!' Caitlin exclaimed.

Ruby had played that scenario over and over in head. She'd thought about his answers and each was too painful to actually hear him say. 'No. I can't. I just want to leave and let it be over. Please, you have to promise me, both of you. You can't say a word. Promise me.'

The other two friends shared a look and then turned their attention back to Ruby and nodded simultaneously. 'Of course. We won't say a thing. But I wish you'd change your mind. About saying something and about leaving.'

Ruby smiled. 'Thank you. But I can't. I need to move on. I mean... I knew he wasn't offering a relationship.' She shrugged.

'Yes, but to jump into bed with another woman right after being with you. That's just plain disgusting. He needs to keep his dobber in his bloody pants.' Caitlin huffed indignantly.

'That's as maybe. But one of these days I will learn. Some men just can't be trusted,' Ruby said with a heavy heart. 'I will have the beautiful dress dry-cleaned and sent back to you, Caitlin, and, Jules, I will drop your shoes off before I go.'

The two friends shared a glance. 'We've decided you should keep them. As a reminder of the two wee dafties you met here in Glentorrin.'

Ruby's chin trembled. 'You two are just wonderful. I hope you know that. I'm going to miss you so very much.'

The women stood and shared a final hug and Jules told her, 'Not as much as we're going to miss you.'

33

Ruby decided to take a slow and steady walk back to Glentorrin House, thinking about the short but wonderful time she'd had in the beautiful little island village. She waved to Morag, who was stacking shelves just inside the shop, and she stood at the barrier around the inlet watching the ripples on the water. Spring was in the air now; the temperature was higher than it had been, and flowers had begun to bud. Easter was fast approaching and many of the windows had displays of chicks and bunnies. And there was a poster in the window of the shop advertising a village egg hunt. Ruby envied the residents of the village who would be here to witness Glentorrin in its full summer bloom. There would be the Highland games and the talent show she had heard about, plus more ceilidh dancing. She would miss it all.

With one final deep inhalation of the salty, fresh air, she turned and reluctantly made her way back to the house. Shelby was nowhere to be seen, but Dougie was waiting in the kitchen.

'Hi, hen, I've ordered us a taxi. Mitch left a note to say he'd been called away, so I haven't had time to say anything about us leaving. Are you going to leave him a note?'

She thought about it for a moment. What could she say? *Sorry but you betrayed me so I'm running away? Have a nice life and enjoy shagging my so-called assistant for the last few days she's here?*

She shook her head. 'Would you mind scribbling something down for me while I go get my bags? Just say I've been called back on urgent agency business.' She shrugged.

Dougie frowned. 'Aye, if you're sure.'

She smiled. 'I'm sure. Thanks. I won't be a minute.'

Up in her cosy, pretty room, she glanced around one last time. She stepped into the adjoining room, where she had danced, unbeknownst to her at the time, to an enraptured audience of one. She remembered the song she had chosen and closed her eyes for a moment as she realised how apt the lyrics to 'Heading West' were for her current situation. A familiar stinging needled at her eyes again, so she hurriedly turned her back and closed the door. She grabbed her cases and carried them down the stairs to the hallway.

'Ready?' Dougie asked. 'Taxi's here.'

She inhaled a shaking breath and nodded. 'Ready.'

Dougie took her cases from her hand and carried them out to the waiting Range Rover with its blacked-out windows. She was relieved that Shelby hadn't made an appearance to say goodbye; she couldn't stomach the fake concern a moment longer.

She put her keys on the hook by the door, left the house, and walked down to the car.

Dougie held the door open for her. 'I'll sit in the front, Ruby. Give you some privacy.' He gave her a sad smile. Clearly, he knew something was amiss, but she was grateful for his professionalism and the fact he didn't pry. She couldn't have coped with having to make excuses, and the truth was too hard to repeat.

They reached the airport and Dougie escorted her to the check-in desk. The clerk recognised her and asked for an autograph, so she obliged. When the same clerk asked for a photograph, Dougie stepped in and said that they weren't able to do that.

Dougie walked with Ruby to departures as far as he was allowed. 'You take care, lassie. And if you're ever in Scotland again and need my services, don't hesitate to get in touch.' Dougie handed her a card. 'Now, are you sure you'll be okay on your own? I can always get a ticket and accompany you to New York.'

She smiled, grateful for his offer. 'I'll be fine. Thank you though. I can always ask for help if things get out of hand. But I'll just keep my head down and in my book.'

Dougie nodded. 'Well, it's been a pleasure, Ruby. A real pleasure.' He held out his hand and she took it.

'Thank you, Dougie. For everything.'

He nodded again and left.

* * *

Ruby sat waiting to board and her phone buzzed, so she took it from her pocket.

Hey, why did you leave without saying goodbye? I thought what we shared meant something to you. Was I wrong? Just message me okay? I feel like I've done something wrong, but I don't know what. Mitch x

She glared at the screen and scoffed. 'You don't know what you did wrong? Are you really that stupid?' she hissed at the handset.

She texted Kitty and explained everything in as short a message as she could. She expressly told her not to ring, saying she wasn't able to speak.

Safe flight home, lovely. Fingers crossed this will all go away now. Kitty xx

She too hoped that this would be the end of the mess. Or rather messes, plural. She had managed to get into some dumb situations with no one to blame but herself. She would learn. She wouldn't let anyone even get close from now on. *No more Mr Nice Guy*, she told herself. She refused to be crapped on like a seaside pavement. She was better than that. She deserved more.

* * *

The first leg of her journey wasn't too long at an hour and a half, and she waited nervously in her seat to discover who would be sitting beside her. An elderly lady took the aisle seat and said hello, but then proceeded to read her book. It was strange to be heading in the opposite direction to New York to begin with, but this had been the fastest route to take, and Ruby wanted to get back as soon as possible.

Seeing that her neighbour was focused on her novel, Ruby relaxed and smiled as she sat back to enjoy the flight.

After a short wait at Schiphol, she boarded the transatlantic flight to New York that would take around eight or so hours. She had splashed out for business class seeing as she figured this may be her last opportunity to do so. And she had enjoyed the perks and privacy on the outward journey.

She started watching a movie on the small screen before her but soon gave up. She couldn't focus, least of all on a romance movie where two unlikely people come together and find love. Perhaps if it had been a movie about a property developer being eaten by a shark, she would've enjoyed it.

She was worried about how people would react to her back in the Big Apple. Would there be a mixed bag of those who believed she was innocent, and those too who believed she had said those vile things on the internet? She still didn't understand how people could think so negatively of her. Especially people who had met her on set, on TV shows, and the like. But she had seen some horrid comments in the press made by those who clearly believed the hype.

Perhaps music was what she needed? She stuck in her earbuds and hit random on the playlist on her phone. The opening bars of Cyndi Lauper's 'Heading West' began to play, and she closed her eyes, once more letting the poetry break her heart. Some would call her a masochist, but something about the song touched her more deeply now. The lyrics held so much more meaning. For a brief moment, she was back in the room at Mitch's house, only this time she was aware of his eyes on her; the dance was just for him. His gaze was filled with adoration as he watched, and at the end, he took her in his arms, kissed her and told her he didn't care about her job. He'd go anywhere with her. He was hers.

'Miss Locke? Miss Locke, is everything okay?'

Ruby's eyes snapped open to see the worried gaze of a flight attendant peering down at her.

'I'm sorry? What?' She reached up and touched her face to find it damp with tears. 'Oh. Gosh, yes, I'm fine. Thank you. Just watched a sad movie.' She pointed at the screen. It was blank.

The brunette frowned but nodded. 'Okay. Can I get you anything?'

Ruby shook her head. 'No, I'm good. Thanks though.'

The attendant left her alone and she gazed out of the window at the clouds highlighted by the moon before dozing off.

Eventually, she awoke when the pilot announced their descent into JFK, adding that it was raining. *Fitting*, she thought.

And, soon enough, she was out in the wet and chilly New York air again. She was home. Only it didn't feel like home. She felt like a stranger in a strange land, just like she had when she'd first arrived to begin her movie career. Only this time there was no giddy anticipation, no flutters in her stomach over who she would meet on set.

As she waited for her bags at the carousel, she fired off texts to Kitty and her parents to tell them she had landed in New York, and once her bags were off the conveyor, she exited the airport doors feeling exhausted, but the first person she saw lifted her spirits.

'Philippe!' She ran towards him and threw her arms around him, bursting into tears as she did so.

'Hey, hey, you're home now. You're safe, shhhh.' He stroked her hair and held her until her tears subsided. 'Come on. Your room is ready. My girls cannot wait to see you. All three of them.'

She wiped at her face. 'But... I booked a hotel.'

'Non! Absolument pa! My wife, she would divorce me. You are to stay with us.'

'What did Valerie say when you told her you were collecting me?' she asked as Philippe loaded her bags into the trunk.

Philippe opened the car door for her. 'I no longer work for Valerie.'

She gasped. 'Oh? How come? I hope it wasn't anything to do with me.' She climbed into the car.

He shook his head. 'Not directly.' He crouched to face her. 'I was in her office often, trying to find out what was being done to clear your name. I discovered, by chance, that she has done nothing. That she has lied. I told her she must confess this to you. Then I told her she could find another driver. I didn't wish to work for liars.'

'Oh no! Philippe, that means it *is* because of me. That's terrible.'

'Non. I will not accept this. It was my decision. And I am fine. I have another job now. Please don't worry. I just felt so strongly after how you were treated. You are like...' He glanced at the floor. 'Merde.' He shook his head and cleared his throat, his eyes glistening. 'You are like family to us. Like my petite soeur. Little sister. I will not have this treatment of you.'

Hearing him say those things lifted her heart and she once again flung her arms around him. 'Thank you so much. If I did have a big brother, I'd want him to be just like you. Now, please, can you take me home?'

He gave a single nod. 'Très rapidement.' He climbed into the driver's seat and started the engine.

* * *

Relief flooded Ruby's body as Philippe pulled the car onto the driveway of his pretty, suburban home. She felt her shoulders relax as she climbed out of the car and Jessica opened the front door. She held her arms open and Ruby willingly walked right into them.

'Hey, hi. How are you doing?' Jessica asked.

Ruby pulled away. 'Bloody awful.'

As Ruby unpacked her things for what felt like the hundredth time, in yet another location, she regaled Jessica with the goings-on of Skye.

At the end of her story, Jessica huffed out the air from her lungs through puffed cheeks. 'Wow. Honey, you really are a dumbass magnet. And I mean that in the best possible way.'

Ruby nodded. 'Yup. I think I just need to give up on men.'

'No, Ruby, don't do that. The right guy is out there. I promise you. I think you're just finding all the bad ones. So at least when you find the right one, he'll be perfect.'

Ruby scoffed. 'Yeah. I actually thought Mitch was pretty close.'

'It sounds like he was at the beginning. And yet he ended up in bed with your assistant right after being in yours. It's scary how people can be so deceiving.'

'I know. He had the audacity to message me, you know. Pretending to wonder why I had left without saying goodbye.'

'Really? Didn't you confront him?' Jessica asked, eyes wide with incredulity.

'No.' Ruby sighed. 'I felt too foolish. I just wanted to leave.'

'I can understand that. But isn't he the one who is dealing with the hacking? How will you know it's all been dealt with?'

Ruby shrugged. 'I presume I'll find out somehow.'

Jessica sighed and squeezed her arm. 'I hope it's soon. This has been going on long enough. You've been through so much.'

'I know. I'm exhausted. In fact... I've made a decision.'

'Oh? Do you want to talk about it?'

Ruby took a deep breath. 'I've decided it's time I had a change of career.'

34

Jessica and Philippe sat opposite Ruby at the table. Bayleigh and Brienne, had cleared away the breakfast plates and retreated to their rooms to get ready for school.

'I just don't want you to give up on your dreams because of all this, Ruby,' Philippe said, his stern gaze fixed on her.

Ruby shook her head. 'No, I'm not. That's the thing. I never wanted this. Not really. My dream was always to be a dancer. I fell into this business totally by accident and got swept up in it all. But it was never my dream. And after this whole hacking business and the horrid stuff that followed, I feel like I will never recover, career-wise. I think it's too late. Maybe if Valerie had done what she said to begin with, it would have settled by now. But the fact that I was stopped from defending myself didn't help, and then when I tried, everything was twisted beyond recognition. It's dragged on for too long, meaning I look guilty. It's made me just want to step away.' She gave a deep sigh. 'Being famous is too hard. I just want to be me again. On Skye, I had a small taste of freedom and I loved it. The people I met – with some exceptions, of course – were incredible. So warm and giving. I want people like that, like you guys, in my life. I'm tired of not knowing who to trust and... and of being lonely.' She paused as her own words sank in. 'Because the life I've been living has been so very lonely. I want someone to love me for me, not my fame, to have the chance at real happiness out of the spotlight.' Jessica and Philippe listened intently as she carried on. 'The film I was due to be in, *The Girl and The Rose*? They dropped me because of it all.' She scoffed. 'Val said they had "postponed", but I reckon they've just changed their minds about me. I mean, who wants a romantic lead who's bigoted and a hideous person in real life? I certainly wouldn't if I was them! It would be box-office suicide.'

'But what will you do? Where will you go?' Jessica asked with a look of concern in her eyes.

Ruby shrugged. 'I don't know. I have money in the bank. I might go back to Scotland and travel for a while. I fell in love with Skye and would love to do more exploring there. Then after that I can afford to buy somewhere off the beaten track. And maybe in a couple of years I'll go get a regular job, make some new friends. There's a world of opportunities out there. Once people forget about me and this scandal, I can live a normal life again. Do all the things I've been missing all these years. My name will have been cleared so I'll be okay.'

Jessica shook her head. 'I just think this is so sad. And such a waste of your wonderful talent. Are you sure this isn't a knee-jerk reaction? I mean, you've had a shitty time of things, especially in the last couple of days.'

Ruby smiled. 'I think if I'd made this decision as soon as I found out about the hacking it would've been knee-jerk. But I've had weeks, months even, to think about this. It feels like the right decision.' She shrugged. 'And I'm comfortable with it.'

Philippe leaned across and placed his hand over hers. 'You are welcome to stay here as long as you need. Consider this your home, please. We want to make sure you have a safe place and people who have your back.'

Ruby placed her other hand on top of his. 'Thank you. I can't tell you how much I appreciate you both. At some point, I'd like to fly home to see my mum and dad. Their visit to Skye was wonderful, but I miss them like crazy, and I want to see my best friend Kitty, and her baby when it's born, but I don't want to bring trouble to their door, so I'll only go once I know that it's safe to do so. I'll need to wait until my name has officially been cleared though. If that's okay?'

Philippe nodded. 'Absolument. Pas de question. As long as you need.'

* * *

After breakfast, Ruby returned to her bedroom. She picked up her phone and saw yet another text and several missed calls from Mitch.

Ruby, I don't know why you won't answer my calls or reply to my texts, but Archie has discovered your hacker. I need to speak to you before I go to the police. Please just call me. Mitch xx

Ruby's heart pounded. This was it. The truth. *Finally*. Her hand shook as she glanced at the clock and calculated the time difference. It was ten in the morning in New York, which meant it was three in the afternoon in Scotland. The message Mitch had sent was timed at 3 a.m. GMT, which meant he'd been up ridiculously late but may be at work now. She wasn't sure how she had missed the message.

For a moment she pondered leaving the call until later, but her nerves were jangling, palms sweating, stomach roiling.

'Sod it,' she said as she hit dial on Mitch's number.

'Ruby! Thank God. Are you okay? I've been worried sick.'

Hearing his voice made her heart squeeze. She missed him, even after what he'd done.

Idiot, she chastised herself inwardly. 'I'm fine. Please just tell me what you found out.'

He fell silent. 'Can we talk for a minute?'

She closed her eyes and imagined his worried expression. 'I have nothing to say to you. I appreciate you putting me in touch with Archie and I'm grateful for all your help, but I don't feel we have anything else to discuss other than the hacking. Please just tell me.'

There was a pause before Mitch cleared his throat. 'Right. I see. Okay. Erm... so you remember Archie discovered two fake names, characters from *The Big Bang Theory*, Howard Wolowitz and Sheldon Cooper?'

Ruby could hear the sadness in his voice and almost crumbled. But she reminded herself why she was being so harsh with him; he had slept with her under false pretences; made her think he cared when he obviously just wanted meaningless sex.

She swallowed down her emotions. 'I remember, yes. And?'

'Okay... are you sitting down? Are you alone? You maybe shouldn't be alone for this.'

'Mitch, for goodness' sake, just tell me!' she yelled and immediately regretted it. After all, this man had sacrificed a lot for her when he didn't really know her that well. 'I'm sorry. Just... just tell me, please.'

She heard him inhale deeply. 'Okay. So... The hackings have been traced back to... Shelby Copeland. Hence the use of Sheldon Cooper, I guess. I presume she used the other character name to try and send any would-be detectives off the scent.'

Ruby shook her head, confusion clouding her mind. 'Who?'

'Shelby... Valerie's assistant, Shelby.'

Ruby flopped to the bed. 'I'm sorry, *what*?' She knew she shouldn't be surprised after what she had discovered about her audition, but this news still hit her like a ton of bricks.

'Aye. Apparently, she's a bloody incredible hacker. She has links with the dark web and all sorts. She's been in trouble a few times but always managed to flutter her eyelashes and get out of it. Archie said he was worried at one point that he wasn't going to be able to trace her because her IPs were darting all over the place... but he did. He did it. She studied Data Science at MIT. She's very intelligent and very dangerous by the sound of it.'

Ruby stared at the floor, shivers of shock vibrating through her body. 'But... *why*? I don't... I don't understand. I hardly know her. Why would...'

Mitch sighed. 'Honestly, I think you'd need to ask her that.'

'Is she still with you?'

'No, after you'd gone, I mentioned that there had been a breakthrough with your hacking, before I knew the details, and by the time I got back from Archie's, she had packed up and left. Taken the hire car.'

'You must be gutted,' Ruby said snidely.

'I am. Bloody gutted that I let that woman live under ma roof.'

'Hindsight is a wonderful thing,' Ruby replied. 'Anyway, I need to go. I have to go and tell Valerie. She needs to know who she's employed.'

'Aye, well, Archie and I are going to take the evidence to the police. Finally, your name will be cleared. I'm... I'm so happy for you. You can get back to your career now.' His voice cracked and it made her chest hurt. 'You can get your star back on the rise.'

She chose not to mention her decision to quit the movie business. He didn't deserve to know. 'Thanks. And thanks for putting me up in your houses. I... In spite of everything, I do appreciate that.'

'In spite of everything? What do you mean by that? Ruby, are you angry that we slept together? Because we were both involved in that decision. I never lied to you. I told you how I felt, and you accepted that. We're adults for goodness' sake.'

She scoffed. 'My God, Mitch, I'm not going to sit here and spell it out for you. If you don't get why I'm so pissed off... Look, I have to go. Thank you for all your help. Sincerely. Have a nice life. Bye.' She hit the end call button and threw the phone on to the bed with a frustrated growl.

There was a knock at the room door. 'Ruby? Is everything okay, ma chère?' Philippe asked through the wooden barrier.

She jumped up and pulled open the door. 'Shelby! Valerie's bloody assistant, Shelby, is the one who hacked me!'

* * *

Philippe pulled the car into the underground car park beneath the building where Ruby's agents were located. Her heart was pounding so hard at her chest, she half expected her ribs to be bruised.

'Do you want me to come with you?' Philippe asked as he stopped the car and turned off the engine.

She shook her head and gave a small smile. 'No, thank you. This is something I need to do for myself. I won't be long.'

He shook his head. 'Cette fille stupide. A quoi pensait-elle? What was she thinking, Ruby? Mon dieu.'

Knowing his question was rhetorical, Ruby climbed out of the car and headed for the stairs to the elevator block. She breathed in and out slowly, trying to calm her temper. After all, Valerie didn't *knowingly* employ a hacker as her assistant. That was just unfortunate, but she had her own mistakes to answer for.

Once she arrived on the tenth floor, Ruby exited the elevator and stood outside the office, trying again to compose herself. She opened the door and stomped through, each step more determined and assured. There was an empty desk where Shelby usually sat, so there was no barrier to her barging into Valerie's office.

Valerie jumped and stood. 'Ruby! You're back. How lovely to—'

'We discovered the hacker. I think you should know that you'll need to hire a new assistant.'

Valerie scowled. 'I'm sorry? What are you talking about?'

Ruby crossed her arms over her chest. 'Shelby hacked my accounts and put a load of vile stuff on the internet pretending to be me. Not only that, but she hacked your emails and arranged an audition for herself that was meant for me by impersonating you too. Your assistant is responsible for ruining my career and could've ruined your business.'

Valerie shook her head and lowered herself back to her chair. 'I see.'

Incensed, Ruby stepped forward. '*I see*? Is that all you have to say?'

Valerie suddenly looked small and frail. 'I think you need to sit down, Ruby.'

'Oh no, I'm fine standing, thank you. I just came to tell you that. And that the police are looking for her.'

Valerie covered her face with her hands. 'No, no, no.' It sounded like she was crying, and Ruby's stomach knotted. She wasn't a cruel person and seeing her agent react this way made her want to take the pain away.

She softened her voice. 'Look, Val, I'm sorry for being so harsh. I'm just angry and I don't understand any of it. I only came to tell you because I felt you should know, face to face, rather than over the phone. I'm guessing you don't want to be associated with her, so I'm giving you a chance to get your things in order for when the police come, because they will no doubt want to interview you. But you'll find another assistant. I'm sure you will.'

Valerie lifted her chin; her eyes were red, and the colour had drained from her cheeks. 'Please, sit down. I need to tell you something.' Her voice trembled.

Ruby frowned, wondering what on earth Valerie could possibly have to say that was more serious than the news she had imparted. 'Okay. But I won't be staying long. Philippe is waiting for me.'

Valerie stood and walked to the mahogany drinks cabinet in the corner of her grand office. 'Can I get you one?' she asked, gesturing to the bottle of amber liquid.

Ruby shook her head. 'No, can you just say what you need to say?'

Valerie poured a large measure of the alcohol into a glass and gulped it down, then poured another and returned to her seat. 'I really hoped this would... blow over.' She said with a shake of her head.

'So you said. But clearly it didn't.'

Valerie closed her eyes briefly. 'I had good reason for hoping it would.'

Ruby's heart rate picked up as she became increasingly frustrated, a little worried even. 'What are you talking about?'

Valerie lifted her head and fixed her gaze on Ruby. 'I lost my daughter, you know. I mean... she's still alive, but we don't talk. Long story. But she won't speak to me.' She took another gulp of her drink. 'She felt I abandoned her for the agency. That *it* was more important to me than she was.'

Ruby scrunched her brow. 'I'm sorry to hear that, Val. But how is this connected?'

'Shelby was the one who convinced me things would blow over. She was the one who put me in touch with people who could "handle things". But... she left one day and forgot to close down her computer. I went to shut it down and I saw the comments. This was after you'd gone to Palermo. I thought it was her, but I couldn't let myself believe it.'

Ruby's eyes widened, she felt her colour drain and her heart thudded once again. 'What!'

Valerie stared at her desk. After a moment she said, 'I guessed what she might have done, but I still figured I didn't know enough, so maybe she was just checking in to see if the comments were still there. I don't know.' She shrugged. 'I wanted to confront her, but she was still saying things that made me think I was wrong. Asking about you, if you were okay. I didn't know why she would do such a thing, still don't. But I couldn't turn her in, Ruby.'

Anger and the sadness of yet another betrayal vied for dominance in Ruby's mind. 'Why the hell not? For goodness' sake Valerie, I'm your client and your friend, or so I thought! I was here long before she was! Where the hell is your loyalty?'

'She's my granddaughter!' Valerie blurted.

Ruby gasped but couldn't speak. She flopped onto the nearest chair as dizziness washed over her.

Valerie continued through a veil of tears. 'She got in contact with me after she finished college. She said she'd graduated in Literary Studies at Columbia. Showed me a certificate... I had no reason to doubt her. She needed a job. Said she had fought with her mom because of her life choices, things she'd done. People she'd mixed with. Her mom had asked her to leave.' She shrugged. 'She wanted a fresh start. I couldn't abandon her like my daughter thought I had her, and I saw a chance to help, and maybe even someday to reconnect with my daughter through Shelby. So, I gave her a job. I didn't tell anyone who she was because... well, nepotism is generally frowned upon, and she wasn't exactly qualified... well, not in PR. And I didn't want people treating her differently. I... I just wanted to give her a chance. I wasn't aware of the audition she had arranged. But I found out after she'd been working here for a month that she wanted to be an actress. I think that's the main reason she contacted me if I'm honest. I got the feeling she hoped that working for me would help. But... in all honesty, I watched her tape... she's not good enough to make it. Under normal circumstances, I would've just told her straight that I couldn't in all good conscience put her forward to have her hopes dashed. But I didn't have the heart to do that to her. But then I saw what she'd apparently done.' She closed her eyes and shook her head. 'You've no idea how disappointed I was. How angry at the fact she had potentially put all our careers at risk. But I wasn't one hundred per cent sure and I had no one to ask that wasn't connected to her. But even with all that said, I couldn't bear to confront her and risk losing her all over again.'

Ruby was flabbergasted. Regardless of Shelby's relationship to Valerie, this was her business, her reputation. If word got out, Valerie would be ruined too. 'You do realise she committed a criminal offence, don't you? She deliberately ruined my career. I don't care who she is, how could you stand by and watch that happen?'

Valerie shook her head. 'Because she was family. And I just thought it would fizzle out like she had assured me it would. I didn't realise how much trouble it would cause. I promise you I had no idea.' She pleaded with her eyes.

Ruby struggled to find compassion. Any sympathy she had felt had suddenly evaporated. 'And you sent her to Scotland with me. Knowing she had some vendetta against me. Why the hell did you *do* that?'

Valerie held up her hands. 'Like I said, I had no idea about the audition. She begged me to let her go, and she seemed to want to get to know you and to be there for you.' Valerie was clearly under Shelby's spell. 'This is why things didn't correlate. She seemed genuinely concerned about you and I hoped that either I had been sorely mistaken or that she was trying to make amends. I hoped that, if I was right about what she'd done, she had realised the error of her ways and I thought if the two of you became friends, things would work out okay. I thought she would realise you didn't deserve to be treated that way and she'd maybe undo the damage some-how. And knowing how lovely you are, I figured that you'd forgive her if you were friends.'

Ruby stood and paced the room. 'I cannot believe you were so naïve! I cannot believe you let her come to Skye to *help* me with the situation *she* bloody created! And that she only wanted to come to attend an audition. Seriously! Are you out of your mind?'

'She's a nice girl. She's just… she's troubled.'

Ruby scoffed. 'Troubled? She's a criminal! Don't get me wrong, Val, I understand family loyalty. But I wouldn't stand by and let one of them ruin an innocent person's life with lies and unfounded vindictiveness! I don't care how much I love them.' She stopped and glared at her agent. 'She didn't know me, Val, I had done nothing to deserve it. I hadn't wronged her in any way, but she set out to hurt me regardless.' She jabbed her index finger in her agent's direction. 'And you knew! You knew about this from the start and you said nothing. You let my life fall apart, let people revile and threaten me. I hid away like some fugitive and I was terrified. I feared for my safety and that of my family. I didn't deserve any of that, Val.'

Valerie's eyes gave up more tears. 'I know. And I'm so sorry. I really am.'

Ruby shook her head. 'So am I. I'm sorry I trusted you.' She swiped escaped tears of anger from her cheeks. 'I cared for you. You were one of my dearest friends. And you were of the few people I thought I could trust.'

'Please forgive me, Ruby. I'll get her to apologise to you. I'll get her to admit it on TV. You're one of my best clients. Probably my only client when word gets out. I can't afford to lose you.'

Ruby narrowed her eyes. 'What did you just say? After everything you and your granddaughter have put me through, you're worried about your client base? This all comes down to money for you?'

Valerie stood and walked around the desk towards her, palms together. 'The agency will be ruined if you leave. Let me make it up to you.'

Stunned, Ruby shook her head. 'No. I'm sorry, I can't do that. I won't do that. Not after this. I don't believe for a minute that you were unsure about what she'd done. You're an intelligent woman, Valerie. You chose not to believe, and you chose not to take action. And as far as I'm concerned, that's it. I had made the decision to leave the business whilst I was away, and any wobbles I may have been having are completely gone now. I'm more certain about this than I have ever been about anything. After the vitriol I've experienced over the past few months, all at your granddaughter's hands I now discover, I've had enough. Valerie... You're fired.'

35

Ruby sobbed as she sat on Philippe's couch with him on one side and Jessica on the other. After everything that had happened, this had been the ultimate betrayal. She couldn't begin to imagine why that young woman, fresh out of college, had taken it upon herself to bring her to her knees; take away her friends, cause her to have to go into hiding and come to hate the career she had worked hard for. On top of that, she had no doubt ruined her grandmother's business. All for what? She was determined to find out why. But with all that said, Ruby couldn't let go of the thought that Valerie, the woman who had been by her side for the last nine years, who had cared for and protected her, had been the one to betray her.

Brienne came into the room, followed by her sister, and handed Ruby a glass of what smelled like brandy.

'Is she going to be okay?' Bayleigh asked, her voice tinged with concern.

'She is, honey. This is just such an awful situation that has been made so much worse. It's a lot for anyone to handle,' Jessica replied.

Ruby had contacted Kitty and her parents on the way home from Montez and Spark before the weight of everything had really hit. And although they insisted she should come home, she knew that doing so would cause too much publicity for them, or worse still, if Shelby was still out to get her, she didn't want to be tracked back to her hometown. She would need to wait until Shelby was apprehended and the world finally knew the truth.

Ruby was once again feeling adrift. Like a nomad with no real tangible place to rest. One thing she was sure of, however, was that she no longer wanted to be in New York. Apart from the Brodeur family, the place held nothing for her now. The shine and glitter that had once surrounded the exciting, vibrant city was tarnished with betrayal. It wasn't the city's fault, of course, but she wanted to get away. This time, she wanted to escape on her own terms. She had decisions to make about her life, but New York was somewhere she could no longer compile her thoughts into anything like coherent. And she had to get used to the new life she had chosen for herself. A life where people may still recognise her, only now it would be as Ruby Locke *that actress who used to be famous*. It was a relief though.

And there was no time like the present to begin her future.

Ruby wiped her eyes and sipped at the alcohol. Feeling calmer, she took a deep, shaking breath. 'I think I'll go lie down, if that's okay?'

'Absolument. Please shout if you need anything, oui?' Philippe said with a squeeze of her hand.

She nodded before standing to face them where they sat. 'You are the most amazing friends. I have no clue how I will ever thank you properly. But please know that I love you all. And I will forever be grateful.'

* * *

Ruby lay on her bed trying not to think about everything but, of course, her mind whirred regardless. Her phone pinged and, at first, she didn't pick it up. But after a few moments, she reached to her nightstand and lifted it so she could see the screen. It was a text from Caitlin.

Hey lovely. How are you doing? Any news? Mitch returned to Edinburgh yesterday with his tail between his legs. Nothing keeping him here, I suppose. Anyway, if you wanted to return to the island at any time, you'd be more than welcome to stay with me. Love Cait xx

She reread the message and her stomach flipped. The pull to Glentorrin was still there. She would love to return, but she wondered if there were too many difficult memories now. Was the place tainted like Palermo and New York had become? She hit reply.

Hi Cait. Great to hear from you. I'm not doing so well, to be honest. Long story. I would love to come back as I really don't want to be in New York. But I'm not sure what to do. I've told my agent I'm quitting acting. I need to escape (again) but not sure Skye is the best place. Ruby xx

Moments later a text came through from Jules.

Am with Cait. Please come back! We miss you! Mitch has gone. Nothing to worry about. Chewie misses you too. ☹ Jules xx

The mention of her canine bestie clinched the deal and she smiled. Now that Mitch was gone, and Shelby was on the run, there was nothing to stop her returning. After all, she had more good memories than bad and, in addition, she'd begun to forge some strong friendships there too; genuine, real friendships. It would mean she was closer to her parents when she was able to visit, and it would give her time to think, away from the place that sparked all the misery in the first place.

She resolved to book a flight and tell Philippe, Jessica and the girls at dinner. Coming back to New York had been a mistake; but nevertheless, a necessary one.

* * *

The following couple of weeks were spent enjoying the company of Philippe and his wonderful family. The girls took great delight in doing her hair and make-up and asking myriad questions about the actors she'd kissed on screen. It was good to look back on the fond memories she'd collected.

Philippe had accompanied her to her apartment to collect her belongings and Cuthbert the doorman had hugged her, which made her cry. He told her that he had defended her wholeheartedly during the protests, and she thanked him through a flood of tears. She knew she would miss the friendly old guy and the mutual affection and respect they shared. She packed up her belongings and put into storage the things she couldn't easily take on her travels, then said a goodbye filled with mixed emotions to the place she had called home for years.

The end of April had arrived and the flight back to Scotland took a different route this time. She wasn't on a chartered jet that could land anywhere it required. Instead, she left JFK, stopping off at Schiphol to meet with the connecting flight that would take her to Glasgow. She had no security to accompany her, and people recognised her, asked for selfies and autographs. Although, thanks to the story breaking, via Veronica's newspaper, about her innocence and departure from acting, the reception was much friendlier. This time she was greeted with comments like, 'We knew it wasn't you all along,' and, 'We're so glad the truth came out for you, Miss Locke, we believed in you.'

It was nerve-wracking but exhilarating at the same time. She did it. She survived the first major journey as her new self. She was relieved, however, that Jules and Caitlin had arranged to pick her up from the airport; she couldn't wait to see them.

The airport staff had been kind, giving her the privacy she needed. People took photos of her as she exited the airport arrivals, but she did so with a smile on her face and her head held high. She wasn't hiding her identity any more. Her hair was back to its titian origins and she felt like herself again.

Jules and Caitlin grappled her into a group hug and the three jumped up and down like teenagers at a reunion. Her friends slipped back into chatting and giggling as soon as Ruby was strapped into her seat. Ruby loved the fact that Glasgow was amidst a spring shower and that as they drove on the outskirts of the city, people dashed around with colourful umbrellas, and the rain soaked the pretty flowers in the hedgerows that lined the roads. It all felt normal and natural and she smiled and laughed along with them all five hours of the journey back to Skye.

It was early evening when they crossed the Skye bridge and even though she had only been away a matter of weeks, being back in Glentorrin felt like the closest thing to home. It was a pleasant feeling, if a little unexpected. Ruby knew she liked the place, but the sense of belonging she felt with her two friends and the way they included her, treating her like one of the girls, filled her with the type of warmth that only true friendship could; something she now realised that, aside from Kitty of course, she had been missing since entering the competitive world of movies.

Daffodils and snowdrops were blooming outside the churchyard and most houses had hanging baskets on wall brackets, filled with bright, cheery, spring flowers that were attracting bees and butterflies. She opened her window just a crack and inhaled the familiar scent of the sea air.

Home, she thought again.

'You must pop in and see Chewie. He'll be so excited to see you. Every time we've walked him since you left, he's pulled us towards Glentorrin House as if he's looking for you. Bless his paws,' Jules said as Caitlin parked up outside the bakery.

Ruby placed her hand over her heart. 'Really? The feeling is mutual, I can't wait to see him.'

Caitlin fell silent for a moment, reading something on her phone. She lifted her chin, gesturing to her handset. 'Just had a message from Archie. He's saying they've had a lead on Shelby. Apparently, she's been spotted in Edinburgh.'

Ruby huffed. 'Hmm, probably hunting for her lover, Mitch.'

Jules shrugged. 'Maybe. Although I doubt he'll be interested in her now he knows what she's done and what horrors she's capable of.'

Ruby could imagine them, Shelby and Mitch, holed up in his posh Edinburgh bachelor pad, avoiding capture, snuggled up naked in bed. She shivered at the thought. She knew it was a ridiculous notion, but her imagination was in overdrive. 'Well, they're welcome to each other. Now, let's get in and get the wine open.'

Once inside, Ruby was shown to the pretty mustard and grey guest room of Caitlin's house and she unpacked the clothes she had brought. She'd allowed herself a few lighter items seeing as it was May and signs of spring were everywhere.

When she returned to the kitchen, she found Jules and Caitlin sitting at the table, a bottle of red wine open and three half-filled glasses.

Jules and Caitlin shared a look and Jules cleared her throat. 'Erm... Ruby, I've just had a message from Reid.'

'Oh!' she said brightly. 'Say hi from me.' She nonchalantly took a sip of the deep red liquid. 'Yum!'

Jules made a nervous sideways glance at Caitlin. 'I will. I will, but... I'm afraid I have news.'

Ruby frowned as she placed down her glass. 'Oh? What's up? Has something happened?' Worry niggled at her mind.

Jules cringed. 'I'm so sorry... Apparently, Mitch is back.'

Ruby gasped. 'Oh great.' She put down her glass, dropped her chin and rested her head in her hands as her heart skipped. He'd only just gone. What was the point in returning so soon? Then again, she'd done the same.

She huffed. 'Did you two know he was coming back?' She narrowed her eyes at her friends and pointed at them in turn. 'Is this a set-up?'

Jules held up both hands, her eyes wide and her head shaking emphatically. 'God no! Absolutely not! We would never do that to you, Ruby. Not after what he did. Slimeball. He has no idea you're here. Reid hasn't told him, and we'll make sure to keep him away from you. I just wanted you to know in case you bump into him in the village.' Sincerity shone through in Jules' words and her reaction.

Ruby shook her head. 'Okay. Well, I'm not going to let him spoil things for me. I'm happy to be back. I'll stay out of his way and hopefully he'll stay out of mine. It's as simple as that. And if, ultimately, things don't go according to plan, I'll have to don a disguise again and sneak home to Yorkshire.' She took another large swig of her drink.

Caitlin leaned forward. 'You know you can trust us, don't you? We would never have suggested you come back here if we'd known he was returning. We presumed he'd gone back for good.'

Again, Ruby could see the sincerity in her eyes. She nodded. 'I know. And let's face it, this is his home. I can't expect him to stay away forever. So, I need to forget about what happened with him and move on.'

Jules exhaled through puffed cheeks. 'That's great. The last thing I wanted was for you to think we'd brought you here under false pretences. We would never do that.'

Ruby reached out and squeezed a hand of each of her friends. 'I know. I do trust you both.'

Caitlin raised her glass. 'To shitty timing and good intentions!'

Jules and Ruby raised their glasses and in unison said, 'Shitty timing and good intentions!'

* * *

Ruby felt great. Two days back and she hadn't once seen Mitch and she had settled back into island life like she had never been away. Kitty had kept a regular check on her and regaled her about two trips to the hospital with what turned out to be Braxton Hicks contractions.

'You watch, I'll be the girl who cries wolf and the time I'm really in labour I won't believe it. The baby will end up being born on the kitchen floor or something! You must visit when it comes though.'

Ruby had laughed. 'Try and keep me away!'

Her mum had informed her of their plans to visit. 'We were already planning on coming up to stay with Morag and Kenneth, but now you're there we have an even better excuse!'

Philippe video-called her to inform her of Veronica Lucas' latest scoop. He held up the paper so she could see the New York Star headline:

AURORA SANTOS SPLITS FROM FIANCÉ TYLER HARRISON AFTER HARRISON CAUGHT CHEATING!

Philippe grinned. 'Voir? Sac à merde!'

Ruby gasped. 'Why am I not surprised?'

Philippe nodded, shrugged and simply said, 'Le karma.' Then he went on to tell her that he had heard Valerie had taken the decision to close her agency. It was a case of jumping before being pushed. She announced her retirement and wished her clients, past and present, a wonderful future with the big Hollywood company who had taken on her client base. Ruby was a little saddened to hear the news, but it also gave her a sense of closure. She could only hope Valerie was okay and decided that one day, when she was stronger, she would contact her.

* * *

She'd taken flowers to, and chatted for hours with, Morag and Kenneth and even been to see Archie to thank him for all his help. She had taken him a huge hamper filled with whisky and chocolate and a whole raft of other goodies that she had ordered online and hoped he would love. She'd collected Chewie – who had almost drowned her in slobber – and they were out walking. Chewie had almost tripped her up several times when he stopped abruptly, intent on a cuddle. It was as if he needed to keep checking she was really there. He had waited patiently outside Morag's shop as she bought an ice cream, her first of the year, and she sat on the bench in front of the inlet, watching the seagulls playing overhead with Chewie drooling on her sandalled feet as she ate it.

She bent to wipe her shoe with her paper napkin and to hand Chewie his promised share of the ice cream, and when she sat upright, she almost jumped out of her skin.

'Hi,' Mitch said with a sad smile. 'It's good to see you. I heard you were back.'

'Hello, Mitch,' she replied coldly.

'May I sit beside you a minute?' he asked, gesturing to the bench.

She shrugged. 'It's a free country.'

He sighed and sat. 'I know why you're angry.'

She turned to face him and scoffed. 'No kidding.'

He clenched his jaw. 'Can I play something for you?'

'If it's Cyndi Lauper, the answer's no,' she said and turned to face the water again, contemplating her next move.

'It's not. Although I have to say, I have a deeper appreciation for her music these days,' he said with a light laugh.

She huffed. 'What do you want, Mitch?'

He fumbled in his pocket. 'Me and Archie have been helping the police with their enquiries into the Shelby situation. She called me from Edinburgh asking for my address in the city. As if I'd have given it to her.' He scoffed. 'Anyway, the police were there, and they recorded everything. And I think you should listen to the conversation. You should probably listen to all of it because you might get some answers. But, selfishly, I want you to listen to a particular section.'

Ruby closed her eyes briefly and sighed. 'Mitch, I have no interest in listening to either of you. You both hurt me.'

He held up a finger. 'Ah, she did. But not me. Not knowingly. Please, just listen?'

She was intrigued, in some macabre way, as to how he was going to weasel his way out of his bedhopping antics. 'Whatever.'

'Look, why don't you come back to the house? It's quieter there. You'll be able to hear better.'

She laughed loud and without humour. 'You've got to be kidding me?'

He held up his hand. 'Okay, okay. Just listen then.' He held up his phone and tapped the screen.

'And I bet you still don't know why she bolted,' Shelby said with a snide laugh. *'It's so funny. I played you both.'*

'What do you mean you played us both? What did you do, Shelby?'

She giggled. *'I got rid of her. It was so easy.'* Her voice took on a more serious tone. *'You should've paid more attention to me. I was better for you. I'm younger, sexier, but you were blinded by her, just like everyone else. It's pathetic.'*

'Shelby, tell me what the hell you did.'

'Oh, I had fun. I watched you leave her room that night, after the ceilidh. I knew you'd slept together. It made me so angry. But I knew she couldn't keep away. So, I waited for you to fall asleep, then I climbed in bed next to you. We snuggled. It was so sweet.'

'What?' Mitch's anger was audible.

'You smelled of her though. It almost made me sick. But I knew she'd come for more. And she didn't disappoint.' She giggled again. *'I heard her walking towards your room, so I slipped off my PJ top to make sure I looked naked. The door opened and there we were, you and I, in bed together only hours after you'd slept with her. I heard her gasp, and it was sooo hard not to laugh. But I kept it together. The next day she skedaddled, right on cue. Mission accomplished. And the best part? You had no idea! You were totally oblivious. I headed back to my room once she'd gone, and before you even realised I'd been there. I'm a genius. Or so people keep telling me.'*

'*You bitch! Why the hell did you do that? That's tantamount to sexual assault.*'

'*Nuh-uh. I didn't touch you, not in a sexual way. I just snuggled and it was so cosy,*' Shelby said in a childish voice. '*But obviously I would, you know, if you were up for it.*'

'*No fucking wonder Ruby thinks I'm a bastard! Shit! I can't believe... I just...*'

'*Ooh, I have to go. My transport is here.*'

'*What transport? Where the hell are you, Shelby?*' Mitch growled.

Shelby chuckled. '*As if I'm going to tell you and your little friends in blue. Bye Mitchy. Have a wonderful life.*' The line went dead.

Ruby turned to face him. Her cheeks warm and her heart pounding. 'You didn't sleep together?'

He shrugged. 'Well, technically, *I* slept. I was so chilled after you and I... that I slept the sleep of the dead. I didn't even feel her get in with me. She delighted in sending me photographic proof. The police have that now. I certainly didn't want it.' He shivered. 'But no, Ruby, I didn't have sex with her. I wouldn't. I only wanted you.' His voice broke. 'I know it's probably too late now, and you maybe still don't believe me, but it's true.' He sighed and laughed, but his expression didn't match the sound. 'In fact, I only came back here to find out where you'd gone. I was planning on following you. I had to make sure you knew that I did nothing to hurt you. But then I realised that I'd said all that stuff to you about your career and...'

'And?' Ruby whispered.

He shrugged. 'It wouldn't have made any difference. I'd already ruined things. But I had all these things planned that I'd say to you.'

'What things?'

He gazed into her eyes. 'That I'd made a mistake. That your career didn't matter. That I'd follow you to the ends of the earth because... because I love you. I think I have since you left me those cookies and that note about whore's moans and dolphin hens.' He laughed. 'That I'd put up with being famous. And I'd get used to the cameras and the newspaper articles... if... if it meant I'd be with you.'

Ruby sniffed and laughed. 'You were going to say all that?'

He smiled and her heart melted. 'I was.'

She was desperate to reach out and touch him, to hold him, to tell him how sorry she was for making such a huge mistake in not talking to him. 'And now?' she asked, twisting the end of Chewie's lead in her hands as the dog rested his chin on her lap.

He shrugged. 'And... Now you're here, and I still feel all those things. But... I don't know if you will forgive me... Please forgive me?' His eyes glistened and his lip trembled.

She flung her arms around him. 'Oh Mitch, there's really nothing to forgive. I'm the one who's sorry. I'm the idiot and I love you so much.' She clung to him for a moment before he pulled away.

'Wait, hang on... Just so I get this clear, in my own head... Are we... are we giving us another try?'

The hope in his eyes almost broke her, and she chose to show him rather than tell him. She crushed her lips into his, her hand in his hair as he pulled her into his lap, returning the kiss with a desperate fervour like that of a man finding oxygen after being starved.

Eventually she pulled away. 'I have something to tell you.'

He cupped her face in his hands. 'What?'

'I've given up acting. I told Valerie I quit. It wasn't all to do with the hacking and her granddaughter being the cause. I decided, after being here in Glentorrin actually, that I don't want to be that person any more. So, I'm... I'm just me now. No cameras, no newspaper articles. Just Ruby Locke, unemployed former actor.'

His eyes widened and once again he pulled her into his arms. 'But you're my unemployed former actor,' he said, before he kissed her again.

EPILOGUE
ONE YEAR LATER

Mitch had asked Ruby to move in with him on the afternoon after they had talked on the bench. They'd lived together before, so it felt like the obvious step. She had her belongings shipped over from New York, thanks to the help of Philippe and Jessica. Her parents visited not long after the move and the villagers accepted her as one of their own. She almost forgot that she used to be world-famous.

In the twelve months that passed since Ruby's name had been cleared once and for all, so much had happened. Most of it amazing.

Kitty gave birth to a little girl, who she named Eliza Ruby. Of course, Mitch and Ruby visited soon after the birth and both immediately fell in love with the little bundle and her mop of downy blonde curls, whilst Kitty – rather gawkily, and much to her husband Gerry's amusement – fell in love with Mitch.

Shelby was eventually caught in the Highlands and extradited to the USA, where she had been sentenced to five years in prison. Apparently, she had been caught doing something similar before – hence the issues that caused her mother to ask her to leave – so her sentence was harsher with it not being her first dip into crime.

After listening to the entirety of the recorded phone conversation, Ruby had discovered that it was vengeance Shelby was seeking. She felt that if she ruined her grandmother's business, she could win back her mother's approval. It was twisted logic but seemed to make perfect sense to Shelby. She thought she could kill two birds with one stone; wheedle her way into the movie business via her grandmother's connections and then take Valerie down. She had got the timings wrong, evidently, and didn't actually have any acting talent. But she had become fixated on Ruby on seeing the relationship she had with Valerie and viewed her as competition. Ruby was therefore in the way and became collateral damage. Shelby ultimately wanted Ruby's life. A life that Ruby had, ironically, decided she didn't want. Shelby was clearly a troubled girl.

Following the press release about the truth of the hacking, Ruby had been hounded by magazines and TV shows begging for her story. She had rejected every single proposal but one. She agreed to one TV interview but insisted she would only talk to Veronica Lucas. It was highly unusual as Veronica, as a newspaper journalist, hadn't worked in a TV studio before, but, of course, she jumped at the chance and was excellent, as it turned out.

During the interview, Veronica asked Ruby if she had anything to say to would-be hackers, or those thinking of trolling someone on the internet. Ruby didn't have to think about her answer for too long. She looked directly into the camera. 'After the pain of what I went through, it's easy to see how these situations can escalate. How people can become unwell, or much worse, as a result of cyberbullying and hacking. I'm fortunate that I had a group of people around me who held me up when I was at my lowest. Not everyone is so fortunate. So please, before you make that derogatory comment on someone's post, before you express your opinion online, before you turn your back on someone for something you heard they supposedly did or said, stop. Think. How will this affect that person going forward? Do you really need to add fuel to that fire? Is that person truly deserving of your wrath? And if so, do you really need to fight it out in such a public forum? Do you know all the facts? Because, as an innocent person who was on the receiving end of this, I can honestly say I wouldn't wish it on my worst enemy. I don't care how hurt I am, or how angry, I will never, *ever* resort to that kind of cowardice. Kindness costs nothing. But one online incident can ruin a person's life.'

She had received a standing ovation.

In the few months following the interview, she did a little work as an ambassador in schools around the UK, talking to the pupils about the issues caused by cyberbullying, which had been a great success. After that she fulfilled a lifelong dream and took time out to study to become a qualified dance teacher.

* * *

The day of her first class arrived and Ruby dashed around shoving everything she needed in a bag. Water bottle. Headband, hair ties, tap shoes, ballet shoes, jazz shoes. She was going to be late if she wasn't careful, and that wouldn't do for her first ever class. It was to be a taster session, where she would show the attendees what was going to be on offer going forward. She hadn't specified an age range as she wanted to play it by ear and see who actually came.

'I can't find my sunglasses!' she called out in frustration.

Mitch pulled her into his arms. 'Stop stressing,' he said gently. 'And they're on your head.' He kissed her tenderly and she almost melted into him.

'I really should go.' She groaned and reluctantly extracted herself from his arms.

'Ooh, don't forget your sign. Actually, I'll carry it down for you,' Mitch said as he walked over to collect the A frame that Reid had painted for her. It depicted the village in summertime and had the words *Ruby Roo's Dance With Views* emblazoned in fancy lettering across the front. The flip side listed the class days and times. She'd cried when Reid and Jules had brought the commission to the house the night before. It was such a thoughtful thing for Mitch to have arranged. She'd told them all it was so beautiful it was worthy of a frame, and at that point Jules had produced a smaller, framed version from behind her back.

'This one is from us,' she told her.

Ruby had hugged her and sobbed, then she'd hugged Reid and sobbed on him too.

Mitch and Ruby walked down to the village hall and the A frame was placed outside the door. They went inside to prepare for the very first dance class to be held in the village, *ever*.

Ten minutes before the class was due to start, and Ruby was a nervous wreck. She paced the floor and flapped her hands. 'What if no one turns up, Mitch? What if it's all been a waste? Having the mirrors fitted, doing my teaching qualifications... What if it's all been a mistake?'

Mitch was looking out of the window towards the inlet. It was such a stunning vista and had been the very thing that had sparked the idea for her dance school name. He turned to face her. 'Erm... I think you might want to be more worried about where they're all going to fit.'

'What do you mean?' she asked and jogged over as he pointed outside.

To her amazement, the queue went around the other side of the building and ranged from toddlers to Morag!

She gasped. 'Oh my word! Is this real?'

Mitch slipped his arm around her and kissed her cheek. 'Of course it's real. I never doubted you for a second, my dancing queen.'

She hugged him tightly. 'Thank you. For everything.'

He kissed her nose. 'Go show 'em what you're made of, eh? I'll see you back at home later.'

He exited the village hall and Ruby followed to greet her students. She glanced down the line and spotted Caitlin and Grace, Jules and Evin, and even the little old chap, Hamish. She held the door open as they all filtered in.

Once everyone was inside, Ruby walked up on to the stage, feeling a little overwhelmed. 'Wow! Thank you all so much for coming,' she said into her headset mic. 'This is incredible.' Her voice wobbled with emotion. 'Seeing so many smiling faces here today is wonderful. You have all made my dream come true.' Applause rang out around the packed room and Ruby fought back tears of joy. 'Without further ado, I would like to welcome you all to *Ruby Roo's Dance With Views*!' Cheers and whistles ensued as Ruby hit play on the sound system.

At the end of the lesson, Ruby stood by the door shaking hands with people as they left. She beamed and couldn't believe how well it had gone. Everyone was filled with compliments and excitement about which dance class they were going to attend. Grace was apparently going to attend them all. Evin said he hadn't quite made his mind up but fancied the street dance. Caitlin hugged her and told her how proud she was of her. Jules did the same. Stella from the Coxswain said it was the most fun she'd had in years, and Hamish said it brought back memories of when he and his wife used to go to tea dances together.

Once the place was empty, Ruby gathered up her A frame and placed it in the store cupboard. She was raring to go now. Classes would start properly the following weekend and she couldn't have been happier.

She regarded herself in the full-length wall mirrors she had funded and pirouetted. She was now living her best life. The job of her dreams, the most wonderful man in the world and all in the most spectacular location.

Back at home after the successful first dance taster class, she let herself in and was greeted by Mitch.

'So? How was it?'

She couldn't keep the smile from her face. 'It was amazing! I've got so many sign-ups I think I might need to add more classes. Everyone seemed to love it.'

He pulled her into his arms and kissed her. 'I'm so proud of you. And I have a wee surprise.'

'You do? Ooh, I love surprises.'

'Aye, I know. And I think you'll love this one especially. Come with me.' He led her into the kitchen and pulled out a chair. 'Now, have a seat and close your eyes. No peeping.'

She did as instructed, her heart skipping in excitement. She heard Mitch scuffling around and wondered what on earth was going on.

'Open your eyes,' he said.

She did and found him kneeling on the floor before her. 'Mitch? What's going on?'

He slid a large box forward, it had holes punched in it and it moved and jiggled. She eagerly opened the lid and a ball of orange fur dived into her lap.

'Oh!' The dog licked her face and wiggled in her arms. 'You're the cutest thing! You're like a smaller, wigglier version of Chewie!' Tears leaked from her eyes and the dog caught them.

'This little guy is yours. I know how much you adored Nero and how much you love walking Chewie, but I thought you'd like one of your own. Reid used his connections, and this little fella is a Hungarian Vizsla like Chewie,' Mitch told her with a laugh as the dog wriggled and climbed almost onto her shoulders. 'I think he likes you.'

'He's perfect! Thank you so much. I love him!' She leaned forward and kissed Mitch, her heart bursting with love. 'And I love you. Does he have a name?'

Mitch chuckled. 'He does, actually. I was speaking to Evin when we went to pick up the dog and...' He shook his head and grinned. 'Do you know the movie, *Every Which Way But Loose*?'

She grinned remembering her own conversation with Evin. 'Clint Eastwood, Philo Beddoe, of course. I love that movie!'

'Well, Ruby,' Mitch reached and tickled the dog under his chin. 'I'd like to introduce you to Clyde.'

ACKNOWLEDGMENTS

Once again, I have a huge list of people to thank for making this book possible. And I will apologise for my overuse of exclamation points, but I can't help it!

As always, I will start by mentioning my lovely family. Thank you, Rich and Gee, for listening to my story ideas, and bringing cups of Earl Grey to my office to keep me going. Thank you too, Mum and Dad, for just being you. Knowing I make you proud makes me so happy, and I love you both so very much.

Although they can't read, I'm going to say thank you to my two lovely fur babies, Ruby and Marley. The long walks we've taken during the pandemic have kept me sane... well almost... And snuggles with you both always make things better.

As always, I want to shout out to the wonderful friends who've listened to my ramblings during my writing process, especially Caroline. I don't know what I would do without you sometimes, Mrs S.

A huge hug to all the members of Hobman's Hub for your encouragement, shares and overall positivity. I especially love our morning giggles and I'm grateful for your continued support.

It's always nerve-wracking when authors that I admire read my books, but I am so grateful to, and a little bit in awe of: Holly Martin, Jessica

Redland, Kim Nash, Lucy Coleman, Mandy Baggot, Nancy Barone and Sarah Bennett for the wonderful comments and feedback I received. What a list! Thank you all so very much.

Thank you to Lorella and the team at LBLA. I can't find the words to fully express how much I appreciate you all, but know that I do. And thank you for your much needed assistance with the Italian translations in the story!

Last but by no means least, thank you to Team Boldwood. Once again you have helped me to achieve a dream. Listening to my own words brought to life in audiobook is one of the most exciting events of my writing career so far! And Eilidh Beaton (Isis Audio) did such an incredible job! By the way, Eilidh, you're amazing! So, thank you to Caroline, Nia, Ellie, Amanda, Jade, Rose, Meghan and Claire, and the rest of the incredible team at Boldwood Books. May we go from strength to strength!

MORE FROM LISA HOBMAN

We hope you enjoyed reading *Under A Sicilian Sky*. If you did, please leave a review.

If you'd like to gift a copy, this book is also available as an ebook, digital audio download and audiobook CD.

Sign up to Lisa Hobman's mailing list for news, competitions and updates on future books.

https://bit.ly/LisaHobmanNewsletter

Dreaming Under An Island Skye, another uplifting and feel-good read from Lisa Hobman, is available to order now.

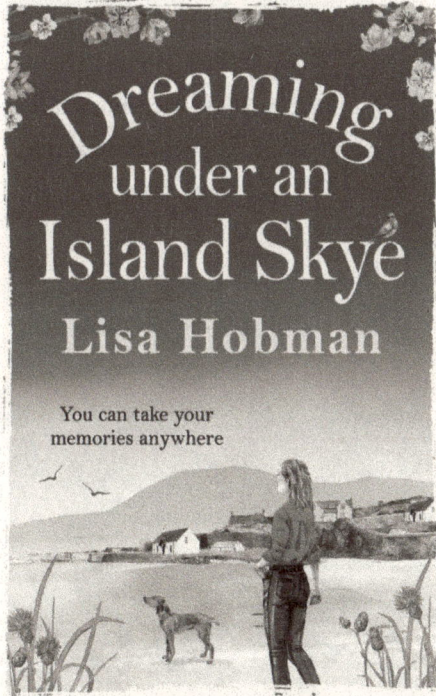

ABOUT THE AUTHOR

Lisa Hobman has written many brilliantly reviewed women's fiction titles - the first of which was shortlisted by the RNA for their debut novel award. In 2012 Lisa relocated her family from Yorkshire to a village in Scotland and this beautiful backdrop now inspires her uplifting and romantic stories.

Visit Lisa's website: http://www.lisajhobman.com

Follow Lisa on social media:

facebook.com/LisaJHobmanAuthor

twitter.com/@LisaJHobmanAuthor

instagram.com/lisahobmanauthor

ABOUT BOLDWOOD BOOKS

Boldwood Books is a fiction publishing company seeking out the best stories from around the world.

Find out more at www.boldwoodbooks.com

Sign up to the Book and Tonic newsletter for news, offers and competitions from Boldwood Books!

http://www.bit.ly/bookandtonic

We'd love to hear from you, follow us on social media:

facebook.com/BookandTonic

twitter.com/BoldwoodBooks

instagram.com/BookandTonic